arbara Taylor Bradford was born and raised in England.
he started her writing career on the *Yorkshire Evening
ost* and later worked as a journalist in London. Her first
ovel, *A Woman of Substance*, became an enduring best-
eller and was followed by twenty-two others, including the
estselling Harte series. In 2006 *The Ravenscar Dynasty*
egan an epic new family series around Ravenscar and the
ouse of Deravenel. Barbara's books have sold more than
ighty-one million copies worldwide in more than ninety
ountries and forty languages, and ten mini-series and tele-
ision movies have been made of her books. In October of
007, Barbara was appointed an OBE by the Queen for her
ervices to literature. She lives in New York City with
er husband, television producer Robert Bradford. This is
er twenty-fourth novel.

or more information and inspiration behind the Ravenscar
eries, visit www.barbarataylorbradford.co.uk

'Memorable and moving . . . a sure-fire winner'   *Express*

'Queen of the genre'   *Sunday Times*

'Few novelists are as consummate as Barbara Taylor Bradford
at keeping the reader turning the page. She is one of the best
at spinning yarns'   *Guardian*

'The storyteller of substance'   *The Times*

'A sweeping saga full of passion and intrigue'   *Hello!*

Books by Barbara Taylor Bradford

Series
THE EMMA HARTE SAGA
A Woman of Substance
Hold the Dream
To Be the Best
Emma's Secret
Unexpected Blessings
Just Rewards

Others
Voice of the Heart
Act of Will
The Woman in His Life
Remember
Angel
Everything to Gain
Dangerous to Know
Love in Another Town
Her Own Rules
A Secret Affair
Power of a Woman
A Sudden Change of Heart
Where You Belong
The Triumph of Katie Byrne
Three Weeks in Paris

Series
THE RAVENSCAR TRILOGY
The Ravenscar Dynasty
Heirs of Ravenscar

BARBARA
TAYLOR BRADFORD

Being Elizabeth

HARPER

This novel is entirely a work of fiction.
The names, characters and incidents portrayed in it are
the work of the author's imagination. Any resemblance to
actual persons, living or dead, events or localities is
entirely coincidental.

Harper
An imprint of HarperCollins*Publishers*
77–85 Fulham Palace Road,
Hammersmith, London W6 8JB

www.harpercollins.co.uk

Special overseas edition 2009
1

First published in Great Britain by
HarperCollins*Publishers* in 2008

Copyright © Barbara Taylor Bradford 2008

Barbara Taylor Bradford asserts the moral right to
be identified as the author of this work

ISBN 978-0-00-787488-0

Set in Sabon by Palimpsest Book Production Limited,
Grangemouth, Stirlingshire

Printed and bound in Great Britain by
Clays Ltd, St Ives plc

Mixed Sources
Product group from well-managed
forests and other controlled sources
www.fsc.org Cert no. SW-COC-001806
© 1996 Forest Stewardship Council

FSC is a non-profit international organisation established to promote the
responsible management of the world's forests. Products carrying the FSC
label are independently certified to assure consumers that they come
from forests that are managed to meet the social, economic and
ecological needs of present and future generations.

Find out more about HarperCollins and the environment at
www.harpercollins.co.uk/green

For Bob, with my love

Contents

PART ONE

Grasping Destiny

'I slept and dreamt that life was Joy,
I woke and found that life was Duty.
I acted, and behold,
Duty was Joy.'

Rabindranath Tagore

'I bend but do not break.'

Jean de la Fontaine

'Work is more fun than fun.'

Noël Coward

ONE

'She's dead!'

Cecil Williams made this announcement from the entrance to the dining room at Ravenscar, then, closing the door behind him, he walked across to the table in a few quick strides.

Against her will, Elizabeth Turner jumped up. '*When*?' she asked in a voice full of sudden tension, her eyes on his face.

'This morning, very early. Just before dawn, to be exact.'

There was a silence.

Elizabeth took tight control of a sudden rush of emotion; even though this news had been long expected, deep down she had not believed she would ever hear those words. She took a moment to absorb them, then said, 'There's nothing much to say, is there, Cecil? Nothing at all, actually, and anyway, what would be the point? I'm not a hypocrite, I'm not going to pretend I mourn her death.'

'Nor am I. I understand your feelings perfectly, Elizabeth.'

He put an arm around her shoulder, kissed her cheek, and looked deeply into her luminous dark eyes. They were glistening with tears, and he knew, without a shadow of a doubt, that the tears were not for the deceased woman. They were, in fact, tears of genuine relief.

'It's over, Elizabeth,' he said, very softly. '*Finally*. Your torment is at an end, and you're safe, secure. No one can tell you what to do, not ever again. You're your own woman, in control of your own destiny.'

The tense expression on her pale face instantly lifted, and she exclaimed, 'Yes, I am free. Free at last! Oh, Cecil, how wonderful that thought is! Yet, do you know, I can hardly grasp it.' A quavery smile flickered around her mouth and was immediately gone, as if she was not quite convinced of her new status.

He smiled at her. 'I believe it's going to take a few days to sink in.'

She looked at him intently, her eyes narrowing slightly. He knew her well, truly understood her, and he was correct, it would take a few days for her to truly believe that everything had changed. She took a moment to steady herself, before saying, 'I'm being rude, Cecil. Let me get you some breakfast, you must be famished. Lucas has brought in enough food to feed an army, so what do you fancy?'

'I *am* hungry, I must admit. But I'll help myself. Go and sit down, drink your coffee and relax. You have every reason to do so today of all days.'

Elizabeth did as he suggested, glad to sit down in the comfortable chair. She was shaking inside and her legs felt weak and unsteady. As she settled back, trying to relax, she experienced instead an unexpected sense of dread. The future loomed up in front of her; it was an unknown future. *Overwhelming*. A wave of nausea swept over her at the prospect of moving on, leaving her old life behind, grasping her destiny with both hands. All those years of sleepless nights, early risings, often before dawn. Constantly worrying, always fearful, numb with anxiety, forever apprehensive. About her sister. Never knowing . . . never knowing what tricks Mary would pull, what accusations the woman would level at her. She had been living on the edge . . . on the edge of danger, living on her nerves for as long as she could remember. Mary had tormented her since childhood.

A moment later, Cecil returned with a plate of food, and sat down next to her. After eating a few mouthfuls of scrambled eggs, he remarked, 'You must have been up when it was still dark outside. I was surprised when I found your door open and the bedroom empty at six-thirty this morning.'

'I couldn't sleep, so I finally got up. This past week has been quite wearing, horrendous really, and I'm afraid my feelings did get the better of me . . . it was the endless waiting and waiting, I suppose.'

He glanced at her, his steady grey eyes searching her face. He had worried about her for years, and he would always worry about her, he was well aware of that. His devotion to her was absolute, and his one thought at the moment was to protect her at all cost. But he made no comment, merely went on calmly eating his breakfast. He was a steady, careful man, and his plans were made and in place.

After finishing her cup of coffee, Elizabeth ran a hand over her mouth, and confided, 'I never worried about her being ill, you know. I didn't. What was the point? And, after all, we knew she was dying, that the cancer was eating away at her, that she was deluded about being pregnant. But last week . . . well, I couldn't help remembering things from the past. The good things. *And the bad.* From our girlhood mostly . . . the time when our father disowned us both. Well, we *were* close then, if only for a short while. And the rest of the time I spent with her –' Elizabeth broke off, shook her head. 'The rest of the time was extremely difficult. She was impossible. I was the enemy in her eyes. She was so very possessive of our father. *My* mother had usurped *hers*, and I had usurped her, my father, of course, being the great prize, that great bull of a man, to be cosied up to and adored. *Unconditionally.* She was competitive and, as everyone knows, she always believed I was plotting against her.' Elizabeth let out a long sigh. 'No matter what, I was in the wrong with Mary from the day I was born.'

'All that's over, don't dwell on it. You're starting a new life . . . this is a new beginning for you,' he said reassuringly.

'And I aim to live my new life well,' she answered, mustering a positive tone, and stood up, crossed to the sideboard, poured herself a cup of coffee. A few seconds later, between sips of coffee, she asked, 'Who knows about Mary's death? Everyone, I suppose?'

'Not quite, not yet.' Cecil looked across at the grandfather clock standing in a corner of the dining room. 'It's not yet eight. It *is* Sunday, so I've kept my phone calls to a minimum. For the moment. Nicholas Throckman was the first one to phone me, to tell me Mary was dead, and then immediately afterwards I heard from Charles Broakes, who announced the same thing.'

Staring at him, frowning, Elizabeth exclaimed, 'Your mobile! That's how everyone got in touch. No wonder I didn't hear any phones ringing.'

'I asked Nicholas and Charles to call me on the mobile. Why should the whole household be awakened at six in the morning?' He shook his head. 'Like you, I hardly slept last night, I knew she couldn't last much longer. I was on the alert.'

'I assume Nicholas is on his way here? With the black box.'

'He is. Actually, he's had possession of the box since Friday.

6

Mary's people sent it to him that afternoon, so that he could bring it to you immediately. They thought she was about to die that day, but it was a false alarm and she didn't. This morning, within half an hour of hearing the news, he set off. He's driving up here right now, and he asked me to tell you that he looks forward to joining us for Sunday lunch.'

She smiled for the first time in days. 'I'm glad to hear it.'

'Sidney Payne also phoned. He was all for rushing up here, but I told him not to, explained we would be in London later in the week, and I would be in touch then. He told me three people had called him already, so the news of Mary's death is spreading fast.' Cecil grimaced. 'Everyone loves to gossip, to speculate, so important news spreads like wildfire.'

Leaning forward, Elizabeth asked with sudden eagerness, 'Who are we inviting to our first meeting?'

'Your great-uncle Howard must be there, your cousins Frank Knowles and Henry Carray, Sidney Payne should come, plus some of the board members who have long been waiting for this day.'

She nodded. 'I know who they are, and I can't wait to see them. But what about those in the company who are against me?'

'What can *they* do?' Cecil asked, shaking his head. 'Nothing! They cannot challenge you, Elizabeth. You are the rightful heir to Deravenels through your father's will.'

'They can torpedo me, work against me, trip me up, do me in, call it what you will.' She shrugged. 'They're Mary's cronies, and they'll never like me. They never have.'

'Who cares? *Liking you* is of no import! They have to *respect* you. That's vital, the only thing that matters. And I'm going to make damn sure they do.'

Mary Turner, her sister, was dead. No, not Mary Turner, but Mary Turner Alvarez, wife of Philip Alvarez, the greatest tycoon in Madrid, a man who had used her money, weakened her resources, then abandoned her to die alone. But that's what men did, didn't they? Used women, then discarded them. Her father had taken all the prizes for doing just that. Don't think ill of him now, Elizabeth warned herself. It was *his* Last Will and Testament that had held in the end. She was his third and last heir. And now Deravenels was hers.

Towards the end, Mary had had no alternative but to follow Harry Turner's wishes. Nonetheless, earlier there had been desperate attempts on her sister's part to cheat *her* out of her rightful inheritance.

Mary had first named her unborn son as heir apparent, that non-existent child she fantasized about, the one she thought she carried in her swollen belly. It was not new life reclining there but an inoperable cancer.

After this had come her most brilliant brainstorm, as Mary had called it. Her Spanish husband Philip Alvarez must inherit. After all, wasn't he the most famous businessman in Spain, a seasoned entrepreneur, and who better than him to run the ancient company?

When this idea was promptly scuttled by those who *could* scuttle it, Mary had seized on their cousin Marie Stewart, she of Scottish-French descent and upbringing, a woman who was ninety per cent French, barely English at all. At the time, Cecil had wondered aloud what this Gallic vamp could possibly know about running an eight-hundred-year-old trading company based in London, one that was a male bastion of self-centred chauvinism. Nothing, they had both agreed, marvelling at Mary Turner's gall.

Marie Stewart had long claimed she was the rightful heir, pointing out that her right to inherit came through her English grandmother, Margaret Turner, eldest sister of Harry Turner.

But it was Harry who represented the direct male line from his father; therefore, his offspring, whether male or female, took precedence over his sister Margaret's line. It all had to do with the rule of primogeniture and the eldest son and his descendants being the true inheritors.

Once again, this idea of Mary Turner's had been swiftly killed. The board of Deravenels wanted nothing to do with Marie Stewart, whom they viewed as the enemy for a variety of reasons. And that would always be their stance.

And so at the very end her sister Mary had finally acknowledged *her*, although not actually by name. Something seemed to prevent Mary from doing that. But ten days ago she had sent a suitcase with one of her assistants. It contained Turner family jewels and a lot of keys, for bank vaults, safes, and various Turner homes.

Her wise Cecil had pointed out on that recent afternoon, 'This is her *way* of acknowledging you, Elizabeth. She *is* going to fulfil your father's Last Will and Testament in the end. You'll see. Her actions are more important than any words she might utter.'

But why couldn't her sister have said her name? Why couldn't she have said my sister, my heir Elizabeth Turner? Why had she merely muttered something about Harry Turner's rightful heir?

Because she hated you, Elizabeth now thought, and she couldn't bear the idea that you were about to take her place.

Let it go, let it go, a small voice said inside her head, and she tried to push these thoughts away. What did it matter now? Mary Turner Alvarez was dead. She, Elizabeth Deravenel Turner, was alive and well and about to become managing director of Deravenels. It was all hers now: the company, the houses, the jewels, the power and the wealth. And she wanted it. Who wouldn't want it? Also, it was hers by right. She was a Deravenel and a Turner through and through. She was Harry's girl, and she looked exactly like him. Mary hadn't resembled Harry at all. She had looked like her Spanish mother, but she had also been much smaller than Catherine – somewhat squat, and not half as pretty.

Moving across the floor of her bedroom, Elizabeth opened the cupboard door, pulled out the case Mary had sent and carried it over to the bed. She found the key for it in her desk drawer, opened the case and rummaged around, looking at some of the brown leather pouches which had engraved silver nameplates stitched on the front. One said *Waverley Court, Kent*, another *Ravenscar, Yorkshire*, a third, *the Chelsea house*, and all of them were full of keys. Then there were pouches pertaining to bank vaults at Coutts, the Westminster Bank, and Lloyds, and keys for those vaults.

Cecil had told her that these bank vaults contained Deravenel and Turner jewels, other valuables such as diamond tiaras, silver objects and tea services, canteens of silver, gold objects and ancient documents. He had pointed out that she would have to visit each bank vault when they returned to London, to check on everything as the new owner.

Placing the brown leather pouches to one side, Elizabeth smoothed her long fingers over several red leather boxes from Cartier, then opened them all. One contained a superb diamond necklace, the next a pair of extraordinary emerald-cut emerald earrings, and the last a huge sapphire-and-diamond pin. The jewellery was not only fabulous, but obviously from the 1930s, and suddenly she couldn't help wondering which member of the family had bought such gems. And for whom. She also wondered if she would ever wear any of it. Perhaps not, but she would certainly wear the South Seas pearls she had examined with Cecil the other day.

Taking the pearls out of their black-velvet case, she held

them up to the light. How lustrous they were . . . truly lovely. Yes, these she *would* wear.

After returning everything to the suitcase, she locked it and put it back in the cupboard to be dealt with later. There were more pressing things to do in the next few weeks. The bank vaults would have to wait, and so would the two houses, Waverley Court and the house in Chelsea, the house where Mary had lived for some years, and where she had died today. Later this week her sister would be buried in the family cemetery here, at Ravenscar, where all the Deravenels and Turners were buried. There was the funeral to think about and to be planned, people to be invited.

Elizabeth sat down at her desk, opened her diary and turned the pages, came to the page for today: *Sunday, November seventeenth, 1996.* At the top of the page she wrote: *My sister Mary Turner Alvarez died at dawn this morning. She was forty-two years old.*

Sitting back in the chair, staring at the wall, Elizabeth's mind raced. Going to Deravenels and taking over the running of the company terrified her. But she had no choice. How would she cope? What would she do first? How would she and Cecil implement her plans? And his, which were complex? She had no idea how she would manage. She had worked at Deravenels off and on since she was eighteen, and had grown to love the company until Mary had kicked her out last year. She was about to go back and run it. She was only twenty-five years old, and basically inexperienced. But she had to do it; she would just have to manage. Most importantly, she *must* succeed.

Elizabeth knew one thing – she had to prove to those who worked there that she was not like her sister, who had been incompetent and arrogant. It was bad enough that they were misogynists; Mary's lousy performance had simply underscored their inherent belief that women were not meant to be executives within that age-old trading company, that place of male supremacy.

I have to do it. I don't have a choice. I must be strong, tough, clever. And, if necessary, devious. I have to win. I want to win. And I want Deravenels. I want it all. It was left to me. I must make it great again.

Closing her eyes, Elizabeth put her arms on the desk and rested her head on them, her mind still racing, plans evolving in her fertile brain.

Two

Cecil Williams sat at the Georgian partners desk in the spacious study, a room which had been occupied by Deravenel and Turner men for many centuries.

Elizabeth had insisted he use it when he had come up to Ravenscar several weeks ago, since she herself preferred the smaller office which opened off the dining room. He knew she had always loved Ravenscar, the beautiful old Elizabethan house on the cliffs at the edge of the North Yorkshire moors, and over the years she had been able to make it her own. Her sister Mary had loathed the house for some reason and had never spent any time here, preferring to be in London.

More fool her, Cecil thought, glancing around the beautiful room, admiring the fine, mellow antiques, the Moroccan-leather-bound books, and portraits of Deravenel men from long ago, and Turner men of more recent years. There was even a portrait of Guy de Ravenel, founder of the dynasty, the Normandy knight from Falaise who had come to England with William the Conqueror. It was he who started the trading company which had eventually become Deravenels, now one of the most famous global conglomerates and on a grand scale.

Dropping his eyes to the desk, Cecil concentrated on his notes about the events of the day so far, also jotting down the names of everyone he had spoken to since six o'clock that morning.

Elizabeth occasionally teased him about his perpetual note-taking, but it was his way of ensuring he remembered absolutely everything pertaining to business. He made his notes religiously every day, and he had done so since his school days. He had continued this practice as a student at Cambridge, then again when he was studying law, and later, when he began to work at Deravenels, first for Edward Selmere, then for John Dunley.

He had found it hard to break the habit; long ago he had decided he shouldn't even try. It was useful, and very frequently it had given him the advantage in business. He always had his notebook and could quickly refresh his memory. Not many other people could do it quite so easily.

At thirty-eight Cecil was fully aware that he was now at the crossroads of his life, and that Elizabeth Turner was at the same point. Her sister's death at an early age meant that she was in control of this vast business enterprise; he also knew she considered him her trusted right hand and expected him to guide and advise her.

He had left Deravenels five years ago, understanding that he would never be able to work easily with Mary Turner. They were poles apart, thought differently about everything, and, when she came into her inheritance and took the power, he quietly departed, went to live in the country. But for a number of years he had helped manage some of Elizabeth's personal business affairs, and had continued to do so, along with her accountant, Thomas Parrell.

14

The sky's the limit, he decided, his spirits lifting. We *can* pull it off; we *can* revive Deravenels, bring it back to what it was when her father reigned supreme. After Harry's death things had grown a little shaky; that was everyone's opinion, not only his.

Elizabeth's brother Edward had inherited Deravenels, but he was only a schoolboy, and obviously could not run it. So his maternal uncle, Edward Selmere, had become administrator, following Harry's instructions laid out in his will.

But Selmere had eventually blotted his copy book and was given the sack by the board, and John Dunley had taken over. He was another old hand at Deravenels, as his father Edmund Dunley had been before him.

John Dunley had managed to hold the company steady for the boy Edward, and he had helped, working closely with John. But with Edward's death at sixteen and the advent of Mary Turner, so much had gone terribly wrong. She had managed to damage the company, badly but not irretrievably. He hoped.

Cecil sat back, considered Elizabeth. He believed her to be one of the most brilliant people he had ever met. Apart from having had a superb education, and having shown her true mettle when working at Deravenels, she was fortunate in that she had inherited her father's intelligence, his shrewdness and perception, especially about people. Furthermore, she also had Harry's business acumen, and his ruthlessness. The latter was a trait she was certainly going to need when she was running Deravenels, starting next week.

Elizabeth was the Turner most like her father in character, personality and looks; neither her late brother Edward, nor the newly-deceased Mary had resembled him very much.

There was a light knock on the door, and it flew open to admit Elizabeth. She hovered in the entrance, flanked by the large portraits of her father and great-grandfather which hung on either side of the door.

'Am I disturbing you?'

He shook his head, rendered mute for a split second.

The sun was streaming in through the windows, bathing her in shimmering light, and the vividness of her colouring was shown off to perfection – her glorious auburn hair shot through with gold, her perfect English complexion, so fair and milky white, and her finely-wrought features reminiscent of the Deravenels. She was the spitting image of both men; the only difference was her eyes. They were a curious grey-black, whilst Harry Turner's and Edward Deravenel's were the same sky blue.

'What is it? You're staring at me in the most peculiar way,' said Elizabeth, and walked into the study, her expression one of puzzlement.

'Three peas in a pod,' Cecil answered with a faint laugh. 'That's what I was thinking as you stood there in the doorway. The sunlight was streaming in, and the marked resemblance between you and your father and great-grandfather was . . . *uncanny*.'

'Oh.' Elizabeth turned around, her eyes moving from the portrait of her father to the one of her great-grandfather, the famous Edward Deravenel, the father of Bess, her paternal grandmother. It was *he* she admired the most, he who had been the greatest managing director of all time, in her opinion . . . the man she hoped to emulate. *He was her inspiration.*

'Well, yes, I guess we do look as if we're related,' she answered, her black eyes dancing mischievously. Taking a seat opposite Cecil, she went on, 'Just let's hope that I can accomplish what *they* did.'

'You will.'

'You mean *we* will.'

16

He inclined his head, murmured, 'We'll do our damnedest.'

Shifting slightly in the chair, Elizabeth focused her eyes on Cecil with some intensity, and said slowly, 'What are we going to do about the funeral? It *will* have to be here, won't it?'

'No other place but here.'

'Have you any ideas about who we ought to invite?'

'Certainly members of the board. But under the circumstances, I thought it was a good idea to turn the whole thing over to John Norfell. He's one of the senior executives, a long-time member of the board, and he was a friend of Mary's. Who better than him to make all the arrangements? I spoke to him a short while ago.'

Elizabeth nodded, a look of relief on her face. 'The family chapel holds about fifty, but that's it. And I suppose we'll have to feed them –' She shook her head, sighing. 'Don't you think it should be held in the late morning, so that we can serve lunch afterwards and then get them out of here around three?'

Amused, Cecil began to chuckle. 'I see you've already worked it out. And I couldn't agree more. I hinted at something of the sort to Norfell, and he seemed to acquiesce. I doubt that anyone even really wants to come up here in the dead of winter.'

She laughed with him and pointed out, 'It's so cold. I put my nose outside earlier, and decided not to take a walk. God knows how my ancestors managed without central heating.'

'Roaring fires,' he suggested, and glanced at the one burning brightly in the study. 'But to my way of thinking, fires wouldn't have been enough . . . we've got the central heating at its highest right now, and it's only comfortable.'

'That's one of the great improvements my father made, putting in the heating. And air conditioning.' Rising, Elizabeth strolled over to the fireplace, threw another log on the fire, and then turning around, she said quietly, 'What about the widower? Do we invite Philip Alvarez or not?'

'It's really up to you . . . but perhaps we should invite him. Out of courtesy, don't you think? And look here, he was always well disposed towards you,' Cecil reminded her.

Don't I know it, she thought, remembering the way her Spanish brother-in-law had eyed her somewhat lasciviously and pinched her bottom when Mary wasn't looking. Pushing these irritating thoughts to one side, she nodded. 'Yes, we'd better invite him. We don't need any more enemies. He won't come though.'

'You're right about that.'

'Cecil, how bad is it really? At Deravenels? We've touched on some of the problems these last couple of weeks, but we haven't plunged into them, talked about them in depth.'

'And we can't, not really, because I haven't seen the books. I haven't worked there for four and a half years, and you've been gone for one year. Until we're both installed, I won't know the truth,' he explained, and added, 'One thing I do know though is that she gave Philip a lot of money for his building schemes in Spain.'

'What do you mean by a lot?'

'Millions.'

'Pounds sterling or euros?'

'Euros.'

'Five? Ten million? Or more?'

'More. A great deal more, I'm afraid.'

Elizabeth came back to the desk and sat down in the chair, staring at Cecil Williams. '*A great deal more?*' she repeated in a low voice. 'Fifty million?' she whispered anxiously.

Cecil shook his head. 'Something like seventy-five million.'

'I can't believe it!' she exclaimed, a stricken look crossing her face. 'How could the board condone that investment?'

'I have no idea. I was told, in private, that there was negligence. Personally, I'd call it criminal negligence.'

'Can we prosecute someone?'

'She's dead.'

'So it *was* Mary's fault? Is that what you're saying?'

'That is what has been suggested to me, but we won't have the real facts until we're in there, and you're managing director. Only then can we start digging.'

'It won't be soon enough for me,' she muttered in a tight voice. Glancing at her watch, she went on, 'I think I had better go and change. Nicholas Throckman will be arriving here before we know it.'

Elizabeth was in a fury, a fury so monumental she wanted to rush outside and scream it into the wind until she was empty. But she knew it would be unwise to do that. It was an icy morning and there was a bone-chilling wind. Dangerous weather.

And so instead she rushed upstairs to her bedroom, slammed the door behind her, fell down on her knees and pummelled the mattress with her fists, tears of anger glistening in those intense dark eyes. She beat and beat her hands on the bed until she felt the anger easing, dissipating, and then suddenly she began to weep, sobbing as if her heart was breaking. Eventually, finally drained of all emotion, she stood up and went into the adjoining bathroom where she washed her face. Returning to the bedroom she sat down at her dressing table and carefully began to apply her make-up.

How could she do it? How could she tip all the money into Philip's greedy outstretched hands? Out of love and adoration and wanting to keep him by her side? The need to keep him with her in London? How stupid her sister had been. He was a womanizer, she knew that only too well. He chased women, he had even chased her, his wife's little sister.

And the duped and besotted Mary had poured more money into his hands for his real estate schemes in Spain. And without a second thought, led by something other than her brain. That urgent itch between her legs . . . driving sexual desire . . . how it blinded a woman.

Well, she knew all about that, didn't she? The image of that hunk of a man Tom Selmere was still there somewhere in her head even after ten years. Another man on the make, lusting after his new wife's stepdaughter, and a fifteen-year-old at that. Married to Harry's widow Catherine before Harry was barely cold in his grave. And wanting to get Harry's daughter into his bed as well. Hadn't the widow woman been enough to satisfy the randy Tom? She had often wondered about that over the years.

Philip Alvarez was cut from the same cloth.

What the hell had Philip done with all that money? Seventy-five million. Oh God, so much money lost . . . our money . . . Deravenels' money. He had seemingly never really accounted for it. Would he ever? Could he?

We will make him do so. We have to do so. Surely there was documentation? Somewhere. Mary wouldn't have been that stupid. Or would she?

My sister's management of Deravenels has been abysmal. I have long known that from my close friends inside the company, and Cecil had his own network, his own spies. He knows a lot more than he's telling me; trying to protect me, as always. I trust my Cecil, I trust him implicitly. He's devoted, and an honourable man. True Blue. So quiet and unassuming,

20

steady as a rock, and the most honest man I know. Together we'll run Deravenels. And we'll run it into the black.

Rising, Elizabeth left the dressing table, moved towards the door. As she did so her eyes fell on the photograph on the chest. It was a photograph of her and Mary on the terrace here at Ravenscar. She'd forgotten it was there. Picking it up, she gazed at it. Two decades fell away, and she was on that terrace again . . . five years old, so young, so innocent, so unsuspecting of her treacherous half-sister.

'Go on, Elizabeth, go to him. Father's been asking for you,' Mary said, pushing her forward.

Elizabeth looked up at the twenty-two-year-old, and asked, 'Are you sure he wants to see *me*?'

Mary looked down at the red-headed child who irritated her. 'Yes, he does. Go on, go on.'

Elizabeth ran forward down the terrace, 'Here I am, Father,' she called as she drew nearer to the table where he was sitting reading the morning papers.

He lifted his head swiftly, and jumped up. 'What are you doing here? Making all this noise? Disturbing me?'

Elizabeth stopped dead in her tracks, gaping at him. She began to tremble.

He took a step towards her, his anger apparent. He stared down at her, and his eyes turned to blue ice. 'You shouldn't be on this terrace, in fact you shouldn't be here at all.'

'But Mary told me to come,' she whispered, her lower lip trembling.

'To hell with Mary and what she said, and I'm not your father, do you hear? Since your mother is dead, you are . . . nobody's child. You are *nobody*.' He stepped closer, shooing her away with his big hands.

21

Elizabeth turned and ran, fleeing down the terrace.

Harry Turner strode on behind her, followed her into the Long Hall, shouting, 'Nanny! Nanny! Where are you?'

Avis Paisley appeared as if from nowhere, her face turning white when she saw the bewildered and terrified child running towards her, tears streaming down her face. Hurrying forward, Avis grabbed her tightly, held her close to her body protectively.

'Pack up and go to Kent, Nanny. Today,' Harry Turner told her in a fierce voice, glaring at her.

'To Waverley Court, Mr Turner?'

'No, to Stonehurst Farm. I shall telephone my aunt, Mrs Grace Rose Morran, and tell her you are arriving tonight.'

'Yes, sir.' Without another word Avis led Elizabeth towards the staircase, cursing Harry Turner under her breath. What a monster he was. He punished the child because of the mother. She loathed him.

Elizabeth looked at the photograph again, and then threw it into the wastepaper basket. Good riddance to bad rubbish, she thought, as she left the bedroom.

THREE

Elizabeth ran down the wide staircase and crossed the Long Hall, then she paused, listening. She could hear male voices in the nearby library, and hurried there at once. She pushed open the door and went in, and immediately came to a stop, taken by surprise.

Having expected to see Nicholas Throckman, she was startled by the sight of Robert Dunley. Her childhood friend, whom she had known since they were both eight years old, was standing with Cecil near the window. The two men were deep in conversation and oblivious to her arrival.

But as if he sensed her sudden presence, Robert unexpectedly swung around. Instantly his face lit up. 'Good morning, Elizabeth!' he said, as he strode towards her.

'Robin! I didn't expect to see *you* here!'

'You know I always turn up like the proverbial bad penny.' He grinned as he swept her into his arms and hugged her to him. He released her, kissed her cheek, and explained,

'When I spoke to Cecil earlier, I asked him not to tell you I was coming. I wanted to surprise you.'

'Well, you certainly did that,' she exclaimed, laughing with him. Tucking her arm through his, the two of them joined Cecil.

Elizabeth was glad Robin was here; he had always been her devoted friend, and she still remembered the nice things he had done for her when she was in disfavour with her sister. She never forgot that kind of gesture. Dear Robin, so special to her.

Cecil, staring at her through those clear, light-grey eyes of his, said in a quiet voice, 'Only a bit of minor deception on my part, Elizabeth.'

'I know,' she answered, smiling at him.

'Would you like a glass of champagne? Or something else perhaps?' Cecil asked, walking over to the drinks cart.

'The champagne, please.' Letting go of Robert's arm, Elizabeth stationed herself in front of the window, gazing out at the panoramic view of the North Sea and the cream-coloured cliffs that stretched endlessly for miles, all the way to Robin Hood's Bay and beyond.

What a breathtaking view it was, and most especially today. The sun was brilliant, the sky the perfect blue of a glorious summer's day, and, in turn, the sea itself looked less threatening and grim, reflecting the sky the way it did. This view had always thrilled her.

'It looks like a pretty spring day out there,' Robert murmured, coming to stand next to her. 'But it's an illusion.'

'Oh, I know that.' She eyed him knowingly. 'Like so much else in life . . .'

He made no response, and a moment later Cecil handed her the flute of champagne. She thanked him, sat down, and looking at both men, said, 'I wonder what has

24

happened to Nicholas? Shouldn't he be here by now? It's almost one.'

'I feel certain he'll arrive at any moment,' Cecil reassured her. He glanced at Robert, raised a brow and asked, 'How *was* the traffic?'

'Not too bad. But Nicholas might be a bit more cautious than I am. I'm lucky I didn't get stopped by a traffic cop. I drove like a fiend.'

'Nicholas is bringing me the black box,' Elizabeth announced, looking at Robert. But before he could respond, she changed the subject abruptly. 'If I'm not mistaken, you were rather friendly with Philip Alvarez, weren't you? Didn't you go to Spain with him a while ago?'

Robert nodded. 'Yes. But I can't say I was very friendly with him. Let's put it this way – he was always pleasant to me, and at one moment he needed advice, mostly from my brother Ambrose. Actually, we went to Spain together, to do a small job for him.'

Elizabeth opened her mouth to say something and instantly closed it when she saw the warning look on Cecil's face.

Cecil cleared his throat. 'I don't think we ought to get into a long discussion about Philip Alvarez at this particular moment. Robert, you might be able to shed some light on that resort he was building in Spain, so do let's plan to have a little talk. Later. I think Nicholas has just arrived.' Rising, Cecil walked out into the Long Hall, said over his shoulder, 'Yes, it's him.'

A second later, Nicholas Throckman was greeting Cecil, Elizabeth and Robert, a wide smile on his face. They were all old friends, and enjoyed being together. After accepting a glass of champagne, and raising his glass to them, Nicholas said, 'I'm so sorry to deliver *this* in such an unconventional fashion, Elizabeth.' He chuckled. 'In a Fortnum and Mason shopping bag, of all things. But actually, this is how it came to me. Anyway, here it is.'

'There's nothing wrong with a Fortnum and Mason shopping bag,' Elizabeth replied as she took it from him. Placing it on the floor next to her, she lifted out the black box; holding it in both hands, she stared down at it and felt a shiver run through her. The box was, in fact, more like a jewel case, and embossed across the lid in now-faded gold letters was the name she revered: *Edward Deravenel*.

Placing it on her knee, with her hands on top of it, she said slowly, in a shaky voice, 'When I was eleven, two years after my father had accepted me as his daughter again, he showed me this box. And he told me a story about it. Or rather, about what's inside. Come and sit down for a minute or two. I'd like you to hear what Harry Turner told me fourteen years ago.'

The three men did as she asked, nursing their glasses of champagne. All were curious, wanted to hear the story.

Elizabeth did not immediately begin. Instead she looked down at the box once more, smoothed her hand over it, seemed suddenly thoughtful, far away, lost in memories.

Robert Dunley, watching her intently, could not help thinking how beautiful her hands were, long and slender with tapering fingers and perfect nails. He had half-forgotten her lovely hands . . .

For his part, Nicholas was admiring her gumption and disregard for convention. Here she was, wearing a bright red sweater and matching trousers on the day her sister had died, and she didn't give a damn what any of them thought. But that was Elizabeth, honest to the core. He knew, only too well, that there had been no love lost between the sisters, and he admired Elizabeth for not pretending otherwise.

Cecil's thoughts were on Elizabeth's quick, keen mind, the way she had mentioned Philip, quizzed Robert about the trip to Spain. Dunley might well be a good source of information about the disastrous investment Mary had made . . . he would talk to him later.

Elizabeth shifted her position on the sofa, glanced up at the painting which had hung above the fireplace here in this library for seventy years or more . . . The life-size portrait of Edward Deravenel . . . what a handsome man he had been: her father had truly looked like him, and so did she.

Focusing on the three men, she said, 'This box once belonged to *him*, my father's grandfather, as you all know.' She gestured to the portrait, then, lifting the lid off the box, she took out a gold medallion on a slender chain and held it up for them to see. It glinted in the sunlight.

On one side was the Deravenel family emblem of the white rose and fetterlock, the rose enamelled white; on the other side of the medallion was the sun in splendour, commemorating the day Edward had taken the company away from the Grants of Lancashire in 1904. Around the edge of the medallion, on the side bearing the rose, was engraved the Deravenel family motto: *Fidelity unto eternity*.

'I'm aware you've all seen this medallion before, as have I. But my father first showed it to me when I was eleven years old, as I just told you. He explained that his grandfather had designed it, and had had six of them made. For himself, his two cousins, Neville and Johnny Watkins, his best friend Will Hasling, and two colleagues, Alfredo Oliveri and Amos Finnister. They were the men who had helped him take control of the company, and were devoted to him for the rest of his life. Father then went on to confide that his mother, Bess Deravenel, had actually given

27

it to him when he was twelve . . . just before she died. Apparently, her father had asked her to keep it safe for her younger brother, who would one day inherit the company. Well, you know that old story about the two Deravenel boys disappearing in mysterious circumstances. My grandmother explained to Father that she had been keeping it for his elder brother Arthur, who had unexpectedly died when he was almost sixteen. And now she wanted Harry to have it, because he would become head of the company –'

'Didn't Bess ever give the medallion to her husband, Henry Turner?' Robert asked, cutting in peremptorily.

'Obviously not,' Elizabeth answered. 'Actually, now that I think about it, my father never mentioned his father in that conversation about the medallion, he just told me how thrilled he'd been to get it, and proud. He said he treasured it because of its historical significance. He adored his mother, and I suspect it was extra special to him because it was one of her last gifts to him.'

'And now it's yours,' Nicholas said, gazing at her fondly, his eyes benign and caring. Like Cecil and Robert, he was extremely protective of her, and would always defend her and her interests.

Elizabeth went on, 'My brother Edward received it after my father's death, even though he was too young to run the company, as you all know. It was his by right. And then it went to Mary when Edward died. Whoever wears it is the head of Deravenels, but basically it is *only* a symbol. Still, it's always been tremendously important to the Turners, and it's passed on to the next heir immediately.'

Cecil said, 'It's a beautiful thing, and when your father wore it on special occasions he did so with great pride.'

She nodded. 'Yes, he did. You know, there's another bit of family lore attached to this particular medallion, which

Father told me about. Seemingly, Neville Watkins and Edward Deravenel had a terrible falling out, a genuine rift that went on for years and was devastating to everyone.' She took a sip of champagne, and continued, 'Johnny, Neville's brother, was torn between the two of them, and tried to broker a rapprochement, but couldn't. Ultimately, he had to take his brother's side, he had no choice. When he was killed in a car crash in 1914 he was wearing the medallion under his shirt. Edward's brother Richard brought Johnny's medallion to him, and Edward wore it for the rest of his life. His own he gave to his brother.'

Now picking up the medallion again, leaning forward, Elizabeth showed them the side bearing the image of the sun in splendour. 'If you look closely, you can see the initials J.W. which apparently Edward had engraved on the rim here, then he added his own initials. When my father received the medallion, he added his initials, as did Edward, and also Mary.' She passed the medallion to Cecil, who looked at it closely then gave it to Nicholas, who did the same and handed it to Robert.

After staring at the series of initials, Robert glanced at her, and announced, 'You must wear it today, Elizabeth. *Now*. Because it's yours and it signifies so much, the history of your family. Next week I'll have *your* initials added to the rim, if that's all right with you?'

'Why that's lovely of you. Thank you, Robin.'

Rising, he went over to her, opened the clasp and fastened the gold chain around her neck. 'There you are,' he said, smiling down at her. 'You're now the boss!'

Before she could say anything, Lucas appeared in the doorway of the library. 'Lunch is served, Miss Turner,' he announced.

'Thank you, Lucas, we'll be right in.'

Jumping up, Elizabeth hugged Robert, and said softly

against his ear, 'You always manage to do the right thing, ever since we were little.'

'And I can say the same thing about you,' he answered, taking her arm and leading her out of the library into the Long Hall, followed by Cecil and Nicholas.

Once they were in the dining room, Elizabeth turned to Cecil, and said, 'Come and sit next to me, and Nicholas, Robin, please sit opposite.'

They all took their seats, and Elizabeth said, 'We're having Yorkshire pudding first, then leg of lamb, roast potatoes and the usual vegetables. I hope you're going to enjoy it.'

Nicholas grinned. 'A traditional Sunday lunch is my favourite meal of the week. I've been looking forward to it all morning.'

'I bet you didn't get many of those in Paris, did you, old chap?' Cecil said. 'And by the way, I for one am glad you're back.'

'So am I,' Nicholas asserted. 'And from what I've gathered from our phone conversations, there's a lot for us to do.'

Cecil nodded. 'That's true, but before we start reorganizing the company, and getting it on a more profitable level, I think we have to do something about the board. It's top heavy.'

'It certainly is!' Elizabeth exclaimed. 'Mary added far too many additional board members, and in my opinion it should go back to the way it was in my father's time. *Eighteen*.'

'Agreed, and –' Cecil broke off as Lucas came in carrying a tray followed by a young maid.

The butler placed the tray on a side table, and then he and the maid gave everyone a plate on which there was a large, round Yorkshire pudding.

After serving the gravy, the butler asked, 'Shall I pour the wine now, Miss Turner?'

'Why not, Lucas. Thank you.'

Once they were alone again, Nicholas looked across the table at Cecil and Elizabeth, and said, 'A large board is unwieldy, don't you think? And also too many voices and lots of differing opinions create monumental problems in the long run. I'm glad you've decided to tighten it up.'

'The whole company needs tightening up,' Robert said. 'There's been a lot of waste. Not only of money, but of talent as well. The company needs new blood, new *young* blood, quite apart from anything else.'

'Robert, you took the words right out of my mouth,' said Cecil, inclining his head. 'And now, here's a toast to you, Elizabeth.' He picked up his crystal goblet of red wine, and raised it to her. 'To a new beginning at Deravenels and your great success!'

The other two men repeated her name, and lifted their glasses; Elizabeth smiled at them, her dark eyes glowing, and they all took a sip of the vintage claret.

'Thank you,' she said as she put the glass down on the table again. 'I just want to say that I'm happy the three of you are here with me today, and that we're going to face the future together at Deravenels. I don't think I could do it without you.'

'Oh, you could,' Robert said confidently. 'But it'll be better with us around, don't you think?'

She laughed, began to eat, and the men followed suit.

From time to time Robert looked across the table at her and held her gaze until she glanced down at her plate and continued to eat. She was so happy he had decided to come up, be with her on this very special day. He looked wonderful, so good-looking, so very glamorous. All of a sudden she realised she was staring at him, perhaps a little too intently, when he raised a dark brow and threw her a questioning look. Her stomach tightened and she felt herself

31

flushing. Much to her astonishment, she had become very aware of him physically in the last hour or so, extremely conscious of his presence.

FOUR

He has not changed much over the years, my friend Robin. Not in character at least. He has always been thoughtful, caring, worrying about my comfort; or second-guessing me; or showing up out of the blue, as if he could read my mind. When I was a child I was always hoping he would persuade his father to bring him to Kent to stay with us. Often I got down and prayed that he would arrive.

Sometimes he and his father would show up at Waverley Court, usually on a Friday afternoon, and John Dunley would leave Robin with us for the weekend, or often longer in the summer. Kat Ashe, my governess, had taken a great liking to Robin and welcomed him warmly. Looking back, I'm sure it was Kat and Robin's father who concocted these visits between them, knowing how isolated I was.

We first met at my father's Chelsea house, and we took an instant liking to each other. That day when he came to have lunch and play with me, I asked him how old he was, and he told me he was eight. I remember how surprised I

*was, because he was tall and looked older, and then I confided,
'I'm also eight. My birthday is on September the seventh.
When's yours?' I don't think I'll ever forget that look of
astonishment on Robin's face. 'That's my birthday too!
September the seventh. We'll have to have a joint party!' He
grinned at me and exclaimed, 'Gosh, we're actually twins,
Elizabeth!' It's often struck me how alike he and I are, in
fact.*

*I was a lonely little girl. My father had taken a terrible
dislike to me after my mother died in a car accident in France.
He shunned me, eventually disowned me, and shunted me
around to stay with any of his relatives who would have me.
I felt unwanted and unloved, and actually I was. By him,
anyway.*

*Eventually, Father sent me to Kent, to live at Stonehurst
Farm. And Kat came too. She became a surrogate mother
to me; Kat loved me very much, and loves me to this day,
but, as can only be expected, in those days I wanted my
father's love. He withheld it. In fact, he was cruel and
inhuman in his behaviour towards me.*

*My father abandoned me, showed me little or no consid-
eration, and did not bother much about my well being,
leaving everything to Kat. He was verbally abusive to me
when we did meet, calling me terrible names, telling me I
was a bastard, insisting that he was not my father, and
shouting at me, saying that my mother had been a cheating
whore. I never quite understood why he hated me so much,
and I still don't, not really. Obviously, I was terrified of him.*

*When I was little I pretended that Robin was my brother,
because I so desperately wanted a family, wanted to belong
to somebody. And needed someone to love. I loved Robin
then, and I still love him. He is my best friend. And I know,
deep inside, that I am his; certainly he's often told me so.
We were close in childhood, but we drifted apart as we grew*

older and he was sent off to boarding school. Still, if I ever needed him, he was always there for me, and in those awful days when Mary was vengeful and mean, he was kind and comforting. My loyal and devoted Robin.

I'm glad Cecil likes him. They've known each other for years because Cecil worked for Robin's father at one time, which was when they got to know each other. They are somewhat different in temperament. Cecil Williams, with his grey eyes and clever face and bright intelligence, is a man that everyone trusts and listens to. Like me, he has a degree of caution, is wary and does not make hasty decisions. He watches and waits, as I do. A lawyer by training, he scrupulously abides by the rules.

Robin is also intelligent, shrewd and clever, and has proved himself to be brilliant in business. His handsome features and dark good looks, plus an easy natural charm and a gift of the gab, add to his potent charisma. And with his height and build and flair for clothes, women tend to run after him, fall at his feet. Although he doesn't pay much attention to them, I know he likes women and their company. But he's never been a womanizer; he has a good reputation in that respect. The only thing I have ever cautioned him about is his impulsiveness. And he does appear to be more restrained these days.

I'm glad he came up to Yorkshire last Sunday. It was a lovely surprise and he, Nicholas, Cecil and I were able to talk at length about Deravenels and future plans. He and Nicholas left on Monday morning. Cecil and I stayed on, of course, working together for several days. Also, we had to remain at Ravenscar because of the funeral. Sixty people attended, and we managed to squeeze everybody into the chapel. John Norfell had arranged everything with his usual good taste and punctilliousness. The chapel was filled with flowers, Mary's favourite priest was brought from London,

*and the priest and John Norfell accompanied the coffin.
Afterwards there was a catered lunch at the house. I did my
duty and played the part, kept a solemn demeanour and said
all of the right things to everyone with a quiet dignity. At
least, Cecil told me I had been dignified and appropriate.
Once everyone left, Cecil and I loaded his car with luggage
and drove to London together.*

*And here I am on Saturday morning, back in my own
apartment in Eaton Square, waiting for my darling Kat, who's
due to arrive at any moment. I can't wait to see her . . . it's
been several months since we last met.*

'Let me look at you, darling girl,' Kat said, staring up into
Elizabeth's face. 'I must say, you look none the worse for
being all those weeks in the frozen north. I'd even go so far
as to say you seem to be in blooming health. If a little pale.'

Elizabeth began to laugh, hugging her former governess,
the woman who had brought her up. Finally releasing her,
she said, 'Kat, I'm never anything *but* pale, and you should
know that since you're the one who never let me out in the
sun or the wind.'

'That's just it, it's usually so very windy at Ravenscar.
Frankly, it crossed my mind that you might have a bit of a
windburn since you've been there for several weeks. And you
have had it in the past,' Kat reminded her.

'When I was a child.' Taking hold of her arm, leading her
across the foyer, Elizabeth continued, 'You know I listen to
everything you say, and I've been protecting my skin for
years, following *your* rules.'

Kat smiled. 'Yes, I know.'

The two women went into the living room which Kat had
helped Elizabeth decorate several years ago. Spacious and

airy, it had a high ceiling, tall windows and a fireplace where a fire burned brightly. It was cheerful and inviting with its daffodil-yellow walls, cream sofas and chairs, as well as a number of good antique pieces which had been borrowed from attics at Ravenscar.

Elizabeth said, 'I've lots to talk to you about, but first I must go and get the coffee –'

'Let me do that,' Kat cut in.

'No, no, I'll bring the tray,' Elizabeth insisted. 'Just this once, please allow me to do something for you, Kat. You've been looking after me most of my life.'

'All right, thank you.'

Elizabeth hurried out and Kat strolled over to one of the two windows, staring down at the garden in the middle of Eaton Square. The trees were bare, and there was a sense of bereftness about the garden on this cold Saturday. To her way of thinking, there was nothing quite as sad and dreary as a winter garden full of dead things. One of her joys these days was tending to her gardens; another, even greater, joy in her life was Elizabeth Turner, whom she loved and had brought up as if she were her own child.

'Here I am!' Elizabeth came back into the living room carrying a large tray which she put down on a low table in front of the fire. 'Come on, let's have coffee and catch up, Kat.'

The two women sat on the sofa in front of the fire chatting about a number of things, and then Elizabeth said, 'Please fill me in about your visit to Aunt Grace Rose, would you? How is she?'

'Quite incredible,' Kat answered, smiling, her motherly face lighting up. 'As usual, it was something of a treat to be with her. You know, it's hard to believe she's ninety-six, but she is . . . she's exactly the same age as the year. Her mind is very sharp, no sign of senility there, and she looks extraordinary, rather smart and well put together.'

'How amazing she is, still going strong at that age.'

Kat volunteered, 'Naturally she's a bit frail these days, but she told me she's out and about all the time, going to this lunch, that dinner. If I get to be that old I hope I'm just like her.'

'I know what you mean,' Elizabeth replied, and then said, 'I was relieved when you phoned me and said she had no intention of coming to Mary's funeral. I'd had visions of her insisting she must attend because of . . . well, family. You know how she puts such store in that.'

Putting down her coffee cup, and sitting back on the sofa, Kat explained, 'She confessed that she doesn't go to funerals any more. Not at her age, she said, because she'll be attending her own soon enough, without the need of previews. She also went on to say that she only accepts invitations to christenings and weddings, but really prefers christenings because modern marriages don't seem to last very long, so why bother going in the first place. She had me laughing the whole time I was there.'

Elizabeth nodded, laughing herself. 'She hasn't changed, she's apparently as forthright as she always was. Does she need anything?'

'If you mean money, no, she's extremely wealthy. However, she does need one particular thing.'

Elizabeth leaned forward eagerly. 'Tell me what it is, and hopefully I can get it for her.'

'You certainly can. She wants to see *you*. And as soon as possible. She knows how busy you're going to be, but she asked me to remind you that time is not something she has a lot of, being that she's ninety-six years old.'

'Why does she want to see me?'

'I think she *needs* to see you is perhaps a better way of putting it. *Why* she does I have no idea. She didn't explain.'

'This coming week is going to be impossible, but I'll give

38

you some dates for the following week. I'll have to see her in the evening, though,' Elizabeth answered. 'Will you come with me, Kat?'

'I'm afraid I can't, darling. Grace Rose told me she wishes to see you alone. It seems she has something to tell you, and she says it's most important.'

'I see. I'll just have to work something out.'

'What about tomorrow afternoon, Elizabeth? For tea. If she's free, of course,' Kat suggested.

'I've so much to do tomorrow, I have to sort out my clothes, prepare for the terrible week ahead.' Elizabeth shook her head, looking worried. 'I've no idea where to begin, especially at Deravenels.'

Noting her anxiousness, and detecting the genuine worry in her voice, Kat took hold of Elizabeth's hand, and squeezed it, then said firmly, 'Everything's going to be fine. You're going to run Deravenels very well –'

'Listen to me, Kat,' Elizabeth interrupted. 'I value your confidence in me, and thank you for that, but it's not going to be quite so easy. I mean it when I say I don't know where to begin. I've never run a huge company before, and I haven't worked at Deravenels for a year, because of Mary's contentiousness. I'm afraid I'm going to flounder, make a mess of everything.'

'No, you won't. I know you too well to even consider such a thing. You're very efficient. You've always had great business acumen like your father, and you have down-to-earth values and a lot of practicality. Besides, you're not running the company alone, now, are you?'

'No, that's true. I have Cecil Williams, Robin Dunley, and Nicholas Throckman, and Cecil told me yesterday that Francis Walsington has returned from Paris, now that Mary's dead.'

'All you need are a few good men,' Kat asserted. 'And you have them.'

'That's true.'

Kat looked off into the distance for a moment or two, and then turning to Elizabeth, she said, 'You're going to have far too much to cope with, without worrying about your clothes and other things like that. I have a suggestion –' She broke off, sat staring intently at the young woman she had raised, and whom she knew so well.

'What is it? Why are you looking at me like that?'

'Here's an idea, Elizabeth. Why don't you ask Blanche Parrell to get your clothes organized? She did that for you for years when you were growing up. Let her shop for you, select skirt suits, trouser suits, coats, shoes, accessories. Everything, actually. She can get things together here, and all you have to do is try them on, choose and discard. And you can do it at night.'

Elizabeth's expression brightened. 'That's a fantastic idea, Kat! And I've got another one. Would you take over the running of this apartment and Ravenscar? I've been doing that myself, as you know, but I don't think I'll have much time in the future. The demands on me at Deravenels will be huge.'

'But Ravenscar is Lucas's bailiwick, isn't it? Won't he resent interference from me?'

'No, he won't. Anyway, you'll only be supervising, visiting occasionally, making sure the estate is all right, and the exteriors of the house in good condition. You won't be intruding in any of the domestic arrangements. Lucas and his wife Marta manage the house very well, and we have a few women from the village who come in and help with the cleaning. As for this apartment, there's not much to supervise, I realize that, and certainly Angelina is a good housekeeper. But there's Waverley Court in Kent. I've been going down every few weeks to make sure that there are no problems. I won't be able to do that now, not with the workload I'm facing.'

Kat didn't have to think twice. 'Of course I'll do it! Actually, I think I'd enjoy it . . . what you're proposing is that I become a steward, as they were called a century ago, someone who administers properties, houses, estates, and the finances of those places. Am I correct?'

'Yes.' Leaning forward, Elizabeth went on, 'Then there's Stonehurst Farm to think of. Grace Rose gave it to my father years ago, and Mary always used it, just as she used the old house in Chelsea. What about those properties? Actually, what am *I* going to do with them, Kat?'

'You don't want to live in the Chelsea house?'

'No, I don't. I like this apartment.'

'That house has been in the family for years. It was passed down from Richard Deravenel to your grandmother, and Bess left it to your father. 'If I remember correctly he lived there, too, at one time.'

'But he never went to Stonehurst Farm. As you know, he preferred Waverley Court when he wanted to stay in the south of England. He loved Ravenscar the best, as I do.'

'I remember. But look here, let's go into your study and make a list of what you'll need me to attend to, Elizabeth. Personally, I think I will have to concentrate on the house in Chelsea and Stonehurst Farm first, since Mary has been living in both places for years. Someone will have to deal with all of her possessions, sort them out.'

'Oh, God, you're right. I hadn't thought about that. And there's something else, Kat.' Elizabeth jumped up, and beckoned for Kat to follow as she headed for her study. 'I've got all these bank vaults to inspect. Would you help me with those?'

'Naturally. I'll take over, don't you worry. What you have to do is concentrate on Deravenels, and the running of it.'

41

Later that day Elizabeth recalled Kat's words about concentrating on Deravenels and running it; when she had said them this morning, they had struck a chord in her mind. Now she remembered. Her father had said something similar to her when she was nine years old. But about himself, not her. That particular day had always stayed in her mind, the memory of it very clear. It had been the day her father had welcomed her back into the family . . . such a happy day. She leaned her head back in the chair and closed her eyes, remembering . . .

'Don't stand there, hanging back like that,' Harry Turner said, his blue eyes roaming over the young girl standing before him in the library.

The girl nodded, took a step closer to him, clearing her throat.

Frowning, he asked in a pleasant voice, 'Surely you're not afraid of me, Elizabeth, are you?'

Having always said she was not afraid of anyone or anything, Elizabeth denied this at once. 'No, Father, I'm not afraid of you. However, we're not very well acquainted, are we? Perhaps I'm a little shy.'

A smile tugged at his mouth, and then he said, 'Don't be shy with me, I'm your father. Now come, give me a kiss.'

Elizabeth walked forward and Harry bent down so she could kiss him on the cheek. Then he said, 'I hear that you are doing well at school, that you are an exceptional student. That pleases me, Elizabeth.'

Putting her hand in her green blazer pocket, Elizabeth pulled out an envelope and offered it to him. 'This is for you, Father. My school report.'

Nodding, he took it from her, and read it. 'Congratulations are in order, I see!' he exclaimed, a wide smile spreading across his face. 'You're the top of your class, and you have an A-plus in everything. Good Lord, do you really speak five languages?' He stared at her, obviously impressed.

'If you include English, yes.'

He laughed. 'And what are the other four?'

'Latin, French, Italian and German.'

'German's tough to master. Clever girl, clever girl, Elizabeth. Now turn around, let me look at you properly.'

She did as he asked, feeling able to smile at him, feeling more relaxed, less intimidated.

'By God, you're a true Turner!' he cried. 'My red-gold hair, my height, and my father's lean build. And a Deravenel as well. You have my mother's colouring, yes indeed. Well, I can't say I mind having a true Turner for a daughter. I'm rather chuffed about it, actually. Now let's go to the dining room and have lunch, and I shall tell you all about Deravenels, and how I run it.'

Elizabeth looked up at him, and a wide smile spread across her face. 'I'd like that, Father, and perhaps one day you will take me to Deravenels.'

'After lunch,' he promised, getting hold of her hand and leading her to the dining room in the Chelsea house.

Sitting up in the chair, Elizabeth pushed herself to her feet and went into her dressing room, stood staring at herself in the mirror. Yes, she was a true Turner all right, with a large dose of Deravenel thrown in.

The smile lingered on her face as she went into the library and sat down at the desk in the corner. How could she ever forget that day . . . ? The day she was rehabilitated and became something of a favourite of his . . . the day she had started to admire him, understanding what an extraordinary tycoon he was. And love for him had softened all that hatred, which had formed around her like a carapace. She would always have mixed feelings about her father, but loving him had become easier as the next few years had passed, and by the time he died there was little hatred left. She was glad of that.

FIVE

'Come on, Elizabeth, stop dithering and let's go,' Robert Dunley said, staring hard at her. 'We don't have to stay very long if you don't want to, but I do think it's a good idea to have a look around.'

'Oh, all right,' she answered after another moment of hesitation. Robert had invited her to have Sunday lunch at the Savoy, but when she had arrived a few minutes ago he had told her they first had to go over to Deravenels.

Nodding, looking pleased, he now took hold of her arm, propelled her through the hotel lobby and out into the forecourt. Within seconds they were crossing the Strand, heading for the humungous building that was Deravenels.

'What is it that you want me to see, actually?' she asked curiously.

'It's a surprise.' His dark brown eyes filled with laughter. 'And I can't wait to see your face.'

'But *what* is it?' she probed, impatient to know what this was.

'Can't tell you,' he answered firmly as they came to a stop in front of the huge double door of the building. Robert immediately punched a number into the keypad embedded in the stone wall to the left of the door, and stood back, waiting.

A split-second later, a disembodied voice came through the intercom system: 'Good morning. Who is it, please?'

'Good morning, Alfred, it's Robert Dunley.'

'Thank you, sir. Please enter.'

There was a loud buzzing noise; Robert pushed the heavy door and, as it sprang open, he escorted Elizabeth inside.

Standing waiting for them in the central lobby was the weekend commissionaire, Alfred Vine. His face lit up at the sight of Elizabeth and he exclaimed, 'Miss Turner! What a pleasure to see you. Welcome back.'

'It's nice to see you, too, Alfred.' Elizabeth gave him a warm smile; she had known him for years, as she had most of the service staff.

'I was sorry to hear about Mrs Turner Alvarez,' the commissionaire went on in a low tone. 'My condolences, Miss Turner.'

'Thank you, that's kind of you.'

Robert said, 'We're going up to the executive offices, Alfred, we won't be very long.'

'Take your time, sir, no problem.'

Elizabeth glanced around as the two of them walked across the gargantuan marble foyer, their footsteps clattering loudly as they made for the great double staircase that flowed up to the first floor. How impressed she had been with this foyer when she was a young girl; it had intimidated her. She smiled to herself. Perhaps it still did in a certain way. It was impressive, no two ways about that.

'It's very quiet this morning, Robin,' Elizabeth said, and instantly looked startled as her voice echoed back to her. 'Oh, goodness, I'd forgotten about the echo in here.'

'Had you now?' Robert glanced at her, grinning. 'Don't you remember the time we first discovered it? We were about ten and started "making echoes", as you called it, by screaming and shouting. There was hell to pay.'

'God, yes, I do remember! Your father and mine were absolutely furious with us, because of the noise we made. But it was Sunday, and the place was deserted, just as it is this morning. I never quite understood the fuss.'

'My father docked my spending money. What did yours do?'

Elizabeth chuckled. 'I can't recall, just shouted at me, I think.'

They went on up the staircase in silence, headed down the main corridor and stopped outside the managing director's office. Robert said, 'Close your eyes. I want this to *really* be a surprise.'

Elizabeth did as he asked; he took hold of her hand, led her into the office, switched on the overhead light and said, 'Okay, you can open your eyes.'

She did so and instantly gasped. 'Oh, my God! *Robin!* How on earth did you manage to do this?' As she spoke, her eyes swept around the room, swiftly taking everything in, and then she turned around and hugged him. 'It's Father's office once again, not *hers*! Oh, thank you!'

'Do you like it?' he asked eagerly, as always, wishing to please her.

'I love it, can't you tell?' She walked slowly around the large room which had been occupied in the last hundred years by Richard Deravenel, his son Edward Deravenel, and Edward's youngest brother Richard. Then it had been her grandfather's, and after Henry Turner died, her father Harry had occupied it for years.

Because Edward Selmere had been the administrator, running the company on behalf of her younger brother, he had used another office on the executive floor. Once Mary had become managing director it was her domain, as was proper, but she had made a mess of it, in Elizabeth's opinion.

Looking at Robert, Elizabeth asked, 'What on earth did you do with all that ghastly modern furniture Mary bought?'

'I chucked it out, with Cecil's agreement, of course,' Robert laughed, added, 'I was happy to see the last of it. And look, Elizabeth, over there on the wall behind the desk . . . it's the famous old map of the world, which Mary had sent down to storage. I rescued it and put it back where it belongs.'

Rushing over to the map, she said, 'And you had it reframed, from the look of it.'

'I did, and now you can see the map much better because I had new glass put in.'

'Robin, how lovely of you to do all this. Thank you, thank you, you've made me so happy.' She sat down at the beautiful Georgian desk that had been used by those of her ancestors who had run this company before her, smoothed her hands over the fine leather top, reverentially, momentarily lost in thought. A few seconds later, rousing herself, she took stock once more, noting the rich cream colour on the walls, the antique Chesterfield sofa with its highly polished, dark-green leather gleaming in the light from the various lamps. 'It's all here, isn't it, Robin? All of the things my father appreciated so much.'

'And his father before him, and the Deravenels,' Robert replied. 'It's even the same Persian rug. However, I want you to know I *did* have that cleaned! It all started about three weeks ago when I asked Cecil if I could have the walls repainted before you came back. I'm sure you remember that awful dreary steel-grey paint Mary had chosen. Cecil told me to do whatever I wished, and it suddenly struck us both that the furniture Mary had bought wasn't right, either for this office or for you. So . . . *voilà*! And I'm thrilled you're happy with everything.'

'I am.'

'Then let me take you to lunch to celebrate your return to Deravenels and your new job as the boss lady.'

Many heads turned as they walked through the lobby of the Savoy Hotel on their way to the restaurant. They were both good looking, and Elizabeth was almost as tall as Robert. They made a handsome, elegant couple, and Elizabeth was particularly arresting with her startlingly white skin and auburn hair. She had chosen to wear a tailored, purple wool coat and dress that showed off her slender figure to perfection, while the purple-and-green silk scarf was a dashing addition to the outfit.

Robert Dunley was well aware of the swathe they cut as they walked through the restaurant. They usually did. They both loved fashionable clothes, and he was something of a peacock. As for Elizabeth, she had always had style and a certain flair, wore unique outfits by Joseph, Versace, and Cavalli in strong colours with great aplomb. In fact, they both had enormous self-confidence and were sure of themselves when it came to their taste in clothing.

After sitting down at a window table overlooking the Thames and ordering two glasses of champagne, Robert took hold of her hand and squeezed it. 'Aren't you glad we went to the office?'

Elizabeth agreed. 'Yes, I am, you were absolutely right, but then you usually are. Nobody understands me like you do, Robin darling. I realize how much I was dreading going there tomorrow, and your little preview has made me feel more at ease. And thank you again for the work you did on Father's office. I hated what Mary had created, that abysmal steel-and-glass trap, and couldn't bear the thought of using it.'

'I shudder when I think of it, and actually I enjoyed dumping her stuff, bringing back all those lovely old pieces from the storage unit downstairs. It was not only fun but a labour of love,' Robert reassured her.

At this moment the waiter arrived with their flutes of champagne, and after toasting each other Elizabeth asked, 'What do you think I ought to do with the Chelsea house?'

'Do you want to live there?' Robert asked.

'I don't know . . . I don't think so. But now, looking out at the river flowing by, I can't help thinking how beautiful the Thames is this morning, especially in the brilliant sunshine. Don't forget, the house runs right down to the river's edge.'

'It's an important old house architecturally, and you would get rather a lot for it, I'm certain, but don't make any hasty decisions. You might well enjoy living there, but you don't have to decide right now, do you?'

'No, I don't, and anyway, I'll know what condition it's in from Kat. She's going to give it a thorough looking over. You see, she's taking charge of my properties.' Elizabeth grinned at him, and added, 'Kat accepted my offer to be my *steward*. I know it's a very old-fashioned job description, but that's *exactly* what she'll be doing – the work a steward used to do.'

'And Kat will do a marvellous job! She's one of the most efficient people I know.' He sat back, frowned, and asked, 'What were you telling me about Blanche Parrell earlier?'

'Blanche is, at this very moment, throwing all of my clothes away, at least that's what she was doing earlier, before I left this morning. On Kat's advice, she's taken control of my wardrobe, and so far the pile for Oxfam is enormous. It seems she's about to select a lot of new clothes for me. She wants me to look the part for my new job.'

'And why not?' Robert murmured, then reaching into his pocket he took out a folded piece of paper, said quietly, 'I have something for you, something you should see. It *is* a bit lethal, but I don't want you to be upset –'

'What is it?' she cut in, her brows puckering together. His words of warning and his solemn expression had telegraphed that the paper was not only problematic but also of vital importance to her.

'Read it for yourself,' Robert said, 'and we'll discuss, then we'll order lunch.' He handed her the piece of paper.

Elizabeth saw immediately that it was a bank transfer, and it was signed by Mary Turner Alvarez. Her sister, three years earlier, had transferred fifty million euros to her new husband in Madrid, Philip Alvarez. Shocked, she stared at the paper, reading it again. A furious anger swept over her, and her hand shook as she clutched the paper. She exclaimed in a low but angry tone, 'I can't believe this! She must have been insane, besotted or brainwashed by him.'

'All of those things, perhaps,' Robert replied.

A terrible thought struck Elizabeth, and she asked in a hoarse whisper, 'Do you think this was Deravenel money or her own?'

'I'm not sure. I can't really tell from the bank transfer.'

'Cecil told me she invested seventy-five million euros in Philip's real estate development schemes. Did you know that?'

'I'd heard rumours that she had been overly generous, but I didn't know the amount.'

'Please don't let Cecil know I've told you that.'

'I won't,' Robert promised.

Elizabeth asked, 'How did you get this bank transfer?'

'Never mind.'

'Surely you can tell *me*, Robin.'

'I'd rather you didn't know . . . well, let's just say this . . . I've worked at Deravenels for years, my father and grandfather also worked there. And guess what . . . people have a bad habit of not changing locks.'

51

'What you're saying is that you have a great many keys?' Elizabeth stared at him knowingly.

'You've got it.'

'This transfer is obviously a copy, isn't it?'

'Yes. The original is where it should be. You can keep it if you want, but don't take it to the office. Lock it up in your safe at home. I actually came across it quite by accident, and wanted you to have it . . . Forewarned is forearmed. God knows what you're going to find when you start digging, but I want you to be ahead of the game, Elizabeth.'

'I have to tell Cecil. I'm absolutely certain the fifty million came from her personal bank account.'

'Of course. He has to know,' Robert answered. He eyed her closely, and murmured, 'You're not as upset as I thought you would be.'

'I'm bloody furious, if you want the truth! However, Cecil's news last week forced me to recognize that the seventy-five million euros she gave to Philip might well be just the tip of the iceberg.'

Robin has done good by me yet again. Persuading me to go to Deravenels was an inspired idea on his part. I have lost my fear of the place. I had been dreading going back after a year's absence, because it holds so many memories for me, both good and bad. The bad ones are all to do with Mary and her treatment of me. Once she took over she became a tyrant in so many ways, not the least with me. She was suspicious and treacherous, and endeavoured to nullify my existence. Finally she banished me.

I really missed my job, but there was nothing I could do. She was managing director and I had been dismissed. I took myself off to Ravenscar, and although she hated that house and never came there, I remained fearful of her mood-swings and temper tantrums. Long-distance enemy she might be, but an enemy nonetheless, and I never knew when she might do something nasty to me.

The good memories are to do with my father, and when I saw his office looking exactly the way it had when he occupied it, I was happy. I had never quite understood why Mary had torn it apart, put the valuable antiques in the storage unit, and filled it with hard-edged modern furniture. Unless it was a way of obliterating our father in her mind. She had always harboured a grudge against him because he had discarded her mother; deep down, I don't think she ever forgave him for that, although she was devious enough to put up a good front.

Seeing the room looking the way it had for centuries was a thrill for me, and happy memories washed over me. Once my father had brought me back into his life, when I was nine, he often took me to the office with him in the mornings. I would sit on the Chesterfield and read books about our vineyards in France, diamond mines in India, and gold mines in Africa. He filled my head with information about our ancient trading company before taking me to lunch at the Savoy or Rules. As I grew older, he became impressed with my intelligence and knowledge, and I think that's when Mary grew more jealous than ever of me. She hated him when he praised me; she hated me because I looked like a miniature Harry Turner with his red hair and height and Turner looks. Father often told me I had the thin, wiry build of my grandfather Henry Turner, the Welshman who had married Bess Deravenel and taken over as the head of Deravenels. And it was true, I did, and I was proud of that.

My father died when I was twelve, but I'd had those wonderful few years with him and my half-brother Edward, and looking back, those years were the happiest of my *childhood. I was doing well in the classroom, my father was proud of me, and of Edward. He and I spent a great deal of time together and were close and loving. Then there was my new stepmother, Catherine Parker, a woman who embraced us, my father's children, and she was loving, kind and mothering to all of us, including Mary.*

My father had hurt my feelings when I was a little girl, but he made up for his bad behaviour when I was older. I learned a lot from him, and I suppose he became my role model in the latter part of his life. He was a brilliant man, and he ran Deravenels far better than his father had, whom he sometimes called 'the caretaker'. He once told me his father had been tight with money, and that he had never allowed his wife Bess to participate in anything to do with Deravenels. She was actually the heiress, through her father Edward, and my father thought it was wrong of his father to exclude her. He adored his mother, who brought him up with his younger sister Mary. They spent a lot of time together at Ravenscar and that's why he loved it so much, I suppose. His mother was the biggest influence on his life, and it was she who had filled his head with Deravenel family lore and legend.

Father passed that onto me, and tomorrow I shall go to Deravenels and take my rightful place as the head of the company. I am my father's heir. It is my right.

'Elizabeth, can you come and have a look at the clothes, please?' Blanche Parrell asked in her lilting Welsh voice, pushing open the door of the study, poking her head around it.

'Yes, right away,' Elizabeth answered. She was sitting in a chair near the fire, thinking about her father, but she roused herself at once and jumped to her feet.

'Purple really does suit you,' Blanche said as an aside, and hurried across the foyer.

'I think so, too.' Elizabeth followed the lovely Welshwoman, thinking how well Blanche looked today with her pink cheeks, sleek black hair pulled back in a twist, and sparkling black eyes. There was always a warm smile on her face, and she aimed to please at all times. Elizabeth had loved Blanche since she was a child, appreciated her warm and tender nature, not to mention her talent with clothes, and thought of her as one of the family.

'I know this looks a mess,' Blanche announced, sounding apologetic as they entered the bedroom. 'But actually I do know where everything goes.'

'I'd be surprised if you didn't!' Elizabeth glanced across at the set of closets lined up along one wall. To her surprise there were still a lot of clothes hanging there, and she exclaimed, 'Oh good, I guess we're keeping those!'

'Yes, we are. I hate to get rid of really good things, not to mention the haute couture pieces, and those are lovely outfits.'

Indicating several piles of clothes on the floor, Blanche continued: 'All of that stuff can go to Oxfam and other charities with thrift shops, whilst the things on the bed need altering . . . skirt lengths are wrong, some jackets might be a bit too big or too small, and those items on the chair are for the dry cleaners.'

Elizabeth nodded her understanding. 'You've done a marvellous job, Blanche. Thank you so much. I wouldn't have managed to do this myself.'

'No, you wouldn't. You're not ruthless enough about clothing, but then very few women are. They like to hang onto things in case they lose weight, or put it on, or because they might have a special occasion coming up . . . etcetera, etcetera.'

Elizabeth murmured, 'I suppose you now want me to try on some of these things?'

'It would help, don't you think?'

'Yes. And I need to pick out a suit for my first day back at Deravenels. I think I should wear something smart but low key. One of those trouser suits, perhaps?'

'Yes, with a crisp white shirt.' Blanche walked over to the closets. 'Let's go through these, and maybe we can select things for the entire week, to save your time.'

Thomas Parrell sat in Elizabeth's study watching television, except that he wasn't really watching or listening. He merely had the set turned on. Picking up the remote, he zapped it off.

The room was instantly quiet, the only noise the crackling of the fire in the grate and the faint ticking of the carriage clock on the mantelpiece. Settling back in the comfortable armchair and stretching out his legs, he glanced around.

He had always liked this handsome yet cosy room with moss-green silk fabric on the walls, a carpet of the same colour, and dark-rose brocade draperies which matched the big comfortable sofa and armchairs. The mahogany bookshelves along the back wall were filled to overflowing with every kind of book. He smiled to himself. When Elizabeth had been a young girl he had called her 'the bookworm', and she had laughed with glee, tickled by the name. Never had a more appropriate name been given to anyone. It fitted her perfectly; she never had her nose out of a book, not even today. Elizabeth had always been very learned, a favourite of all the private tutors she had ever had, and he would never forget how awed Harry Turner had been by her precociousness, her intelligence, and knowledge of so many subjects.

The thing Thomas admired most was her toughness of mind. He had come to realize that she thought with her head and not her heart. This, in fact, had been imperative; how well he knew that it was her toughness of mind and swift thinking that had kept her out of trouble – especially with her sister Mary.

Mary was dead and buried and Elizabeth was about to come into her own and he for one was not only relieved but thrilled. He had worked for Elizabeth for years, keeping her books and accounts, and serving as a kind of business manager for her. Harry Turner had appointed him, and he had always been grateful and happy in his job. His sister Blanche and he were usually depicted as members of the Welsh mafia, employees who were as Welsh as the Turners and favoured by them. Once he had told Elizabeth how they were characterized, and she had loved the idea, had burst into gales of laughter. 'How perfect! And you're all *mine*!'

He stood up at the sound of footsteps in the front hall, and when Elizabeth came in he went to greet her with affection.

'I'm sorry I've kept you waiting, Thomas. Your sister has been helping to put together my clothes for the entire week. Saves time. Would you like a drink?'

'That would be nice. Sherry, please.'

A moment later she handed him the glass, poured sparkling water for herself, and then the two of them sat down near the fire.

'I needed to see you this evening, Thomas, because next week is going to be extremely busy –'

'I'm sure it will be,' he agreed, cutting in.

'As I told you on the phone,' Elizabeth went on, 'Kat is going to look after my properties, for the time being anyway, acting as steward. I've also asked her to check out all my bank vaults, and I want to explain that situation. Those vaults at Coutts, the Westminster and Lloyds are stuffed with valuables, from silver and gold objects to extraordinary jewels, according to Cecil. Would you be willing to help her take an inventory of everything?'

'I would indeed. My pleasure, very much my pleasure, and she *will* need help by the sound of it.' He nodded, sipped his sherry, and pointed out, 'We must have a proper and true assessment made of the value of every item, and I can arrange for that as well.'

'Do it, please. I want you to move as quickly as possible on the vaults.' Elizabeth looked across at the door as Blanche suddenly appeared. 'Come in, join us, Blanche. It's about time you took a moment to relax. You haven't stopped all day.'

Blanche came over to the fire, explaining, 'I've finished selecting your clothing for the week. And tomorrow I'll start choosing for the week after.'

'You're a glutton for punishment,' Elizabeth exclaimed.

'I always have been, you know that.'

SIX

She stood outside on the Strand, staring up at the building. Her building. Centuries old, it was imposing, a landmark, and it was about to become her permanent abode as her place of work. *DERAVENELS.*

Taking a deep breath, Elizabeth Deravenel Turner pushed open the door and stepped inside. The commissionaire on duty straightened when he saw her. 'Good morning, Miss Turner.'

She nodded, flashed him her brightest smile. 'Good morning, Sam.' Moving across the gargantuan marble lobby, she took the stairs slowly, filled with a mixture of emotions: excitement, awe, anticipation, a sense of jubilation because it was now hers, but also a hint of trepidation, mixed with anxiety. That's normal, she thought, absolutely normal. I'm starting on a great adventure.

Entering her office, she hung up her coat and walked into the centre of the room, looking around, and she couldn't help thinking about those three men who had occupied this office before her... Her great-grandfather Edward Deravenel, her grandfather Henry Turner, and her father, Harry Turner, from whom she had learned so much. Men of honour, integrity and brilliance. She felt as if they were here in this room with her, felt their presence, their spirit... they were wishing her well...

Walking across the floor, she sat down at the desk. This was the beginning of a new life.

I was born for this. To be here at Deravenels on this very day. Monday, November twenty-fifth, 1996. To take over. To run it properly, to bring it through its current crisis, to bring it back to life. I must not be afraid. Not of anyone or anything. I must be determined, disciplined, dedicated, diligent, and devoted. I must think of nothing else but Deravenels. It is mine now and I must make it strong again. And I will.

I have two men on whom I know I can rely, whom I trust with my life – Cecil Williams and Robin Dunley. We will be the triumvirate that runs Deravenels and we will bring it back to its former glory, as it was in my father's day. I know that I have enemies within this company, those who were devoted to my half-sister Mary and who will want to continue with her policies. But this cannot be. She damaged the company, and her ideas have taken their toll. Those people will have to go. There will have to be a clean sweep. That is what Kat said to me last night: she called me the new broom that sweeps clean. She loves these quaint old sayings, and they're never far from her tongue. She manages to make me laugh when I'm gloomy or not feeling well, those times when no one else can get through to me. My devoted Kat, so special to me.

There was a knock on the door, and it opened immediately to admit Cecil Williams, who strode in saying, 'Good morning, Elizabeth. You're here early.'

'To catch the worms,' Elizabeth said, using one of Kat's old-fashioned sayings. 'And it's certainly a memorable day, isn't it, Cecil?'

'Indeed it is.' He sat down in one of the chairs on the other side of her desk, glancing at the old map hanging on the wall behind her. 'I'm happy to see *that* back in its proper place. Do you know, I remember it from my childhood, when my father worked for Henry Turner, your grandfather.'

'I'll never know why Mary had it removed,' Elizabeth remarked. 'But then I'll never understand some of the other things she did when *she* sat in this office. Here's the bank transfer.' She took the piece of paper out of her briefcase. 'Robin wants me to show it to you, then take it home.' She handed it to him.

'Good idea,' Cecil remarked, and looked down at the transfer, pursing his lips. He lifted his head, stared at her. 'I can't be sure until I look into it, but I think these might have been funds she transferred from her personal bank account.'

'It's still *my* money, whichever account it came from,' Elizabeth announced, her tone brisk. 'Anything and everything she had was inherited from our father and therefore it was mine as well as hers. And she had no right to give it away.' Leaning forward over the desk, her expression intent, purposeful, she asked, 'Can we get the fifty million euros back?'

'To be honest, I don't know, Elizabeth. I have to go through every single file Mary kept, and the books, and hopefully I will find the relative documents –'

'If there are any,' she interrupted peremptorily.

'Only too true. I'm afraid there might not be. After the meeting I'll start digging. And by the way, I've decided to bring in an outside firm of auditors. I'm sure you'll agree that this is absolutely necessary.'

'It certainly is. I think we should get as much information as we can, and as quickly as possible, in order to make the right moves.'

Cecil nodded. 'And which particular moves are you thinking about?'

'Sweeping clean, Cecil. I've been considering that for days, and I believe we have to let five hundred people go, globally.'

'*Five hundred*. In one fell swoop?'

'Not necessarily all at once, no, but there's a lot of dead wood at Deravenels. I knew that when I was working here and Robin has confirmed it. It's people who should be retired. Mostly.' She frowned. 'You seem surprised. Don't you like the idea?'

'I feel the same as you do, Elizabeth, but we must be careful. I don't want to create a stir in the City. There are those who might think we're in great trouble. Sacking a lot of employees all at once tends to make people nervous, and they end up thinking the worst.'

'I realize that we should do it in the best way, the nicest way. We don't want to provoke gossip. Early retirement will appeal to many.' Elizabeth paused, and there was a momentary hesitation before she added, 'We have to cull the offices around the world as well, don't you think?'

'I do,' Cecil replied without hesitation. 'We only touched on it briefly last week, but I'm well aware we're top-heavy with staff. Maybe I'll put Sidney Payne to work on that particular problem. He's such a marvellous diplomat, and it's a situation that's going to need careful handling. As I just said, Deravenels cannot look weak, at risk, in danger of going under.'

'Yes, I understand. Last Thursday, when we were driving back to town, you said Deravenels needs an infusion of money. Where do you plan to get it from, Cecil? Or haven't you thought that through yet?'

'I have. Partially, at least. I think we should attempt to get all those euros back from Philip Alvarez. And I would like to sell off certain parcels of our real estate, but we can go over those points this afternoon in more detail, if you wish.'

'I'd like that. But I just wanted to say this . . . I could give Deravenels some money.'

'*Never.*' Aghast, he gaped at her. 'I will never permit you to give Deravenels money, not ever, Elizabeth. Although there might be a moment in time when you could *lend* them money. Or buy somebody's shares. *But give?* Not on your life. That's absolutely a no-no. I would never agree to such a rash move on your part. Now, here's the list of board members, which you can look at whenever you have a moment. Don't forget, the board meeting is not for *two* weeks.'

'Any changes about this morning's meeting?' Elizabeth asked, settling back in her chair.

'No. All of those invited are coming.'

'I wasn't planning to invite any of them to lunch. Were you?' Elizabeth murmured.

'No, I'm afraid not. There's far too much work,' Cecil pointed out. 'This is my first day back in almost five years. I have a feeling I've a lot of catching up to do.'

Once she was alone, Elizabeth put the bank transfer back in her briefcase, and then picked up the list of board members

63

which Cecil had left with her. Studying it carefully, she wondered whom she could get rid of easily. Three names stood out because those board members were old, and wouldn't or couldn't put up a resistance to her. Then there were two other men whom she knew did not like her, were not of her ilk, and so they would *have* to go. 'How do I get them off the board?' she muttered to herself, and glanced at the door.

There were several hard raps; it swung open and Robert Dunley hurried inside, smiling broadly, and carrying a bowl of flowers – red roses surrounded by white roses and green leaves.

'Personal delivery, Miss Turner,' Robert said, walking across to the coffee table, where he put the vase in the centre. 'The red rose of the Turners and the white rose of the Deravenels,' he remarked, and added, 'Top o' the mornin' to you, me darlin'.'

'Robin, good morning! Thank you so much. The flowers are beautiful.' As she was speaking she stood up and walked over to him, gave him a big hug, clinging to him.

'I just popped in to wish you luck,' he said and hugged her back, holding her for a moment too long.

'I showed Cecil the bank transfer,' Elizabeth said, after they had stepped apart. Turning, walking over to her desk, she explained, 'He thinks it might have been taken from Mary's personal account.'

'Damnation!' Robert exclaimed. 'If that's the case, Philip Alvarez will say it was a wedding gift, or some such thing, and it will be harder for us to get it back. I hope it's company money.'

'Actually, it's my money,' Elizabeth pointed out in the same businesslike tone she had used with Cecil Williams. 'And I promise you I'm going to get it back from that terrible man, no matter what.'

Robert stood in the middle of the office staring at her. The set of her mouth, the tough glint in her grey-black eyes telegraphed to him her determination to get her own way, and he remembered how, over the years, he had detected a hint of ruthlessness in her. But perhaps there was more than a hint.

She asked, 'Why are you staring at me like that, Robin? Do you think I'm sounding too tough? Is that it?'

'No, not at all,' he replied, truthfully. 'I believe you *should* be tough, and, if necessary, ruthless, in this particular situation. I've been thinking about Philip Alvarez, and I'm going to find out exactly what's happening with that real estate company of his. I want to know how the development in Marbella has proceeded. I *must* find out everything I can about it.'

'That's a good idea, yes. And if necessary, you must go to Spain and be my "two eyes", Robin.'

'Let me do the research first.'

'What exactly was his company building in Marbella?' Elizabeth gave him a sharp look.

'Villas, a golf club, polo grounds. It was to be a gated community, like those in America,' he explained. 'Philip wanted me and Ambrose to go, to look over the polo grounds, the plans for the stables, and all of the things pertaining to horses, in fact.'

'I see. If he won't give the money back we'll just have to go after the development. Perhaps we could make it a viable entity, especially if we added a spa. They are big money-makers these days, and they are growing in popularity.'

'It could be up and running, and doing very well,' Robert said, 'but I think not. I remember reading something about it quite recently . . . I got the impression Alvarez had stopped building. And rather abruptly. Perhaps there *is* trouble.'

'I wasn't a bit surprised when he didn't come to the funeral,'

Elizabeth remarked. 'But it's possible he stayed away because he didn't want to answer awkward questions. About the Marbella project,' Elizabeth shook her head. 'That makes sense, don't you think, Robin?'

'It does. And I aim to find out.' He strode to the door and turned around. 'I'll see you at the meeting in an hour.'

Elizabeth nodded and went back to studying the papers on her desk. But only for a moment. Her thoughts turned to Robert. She was extremely conscious of him, of his looks, his warmth, and, if she were honest, of his sexual potency. She bent her head, sniffed her jacket: his cologne clung to it, tantalizingly. A small shiver ran through her. Why was she suddenly having such strange thoughts about Robert Dunley, her childhood friend? Dropping her eyes, she stared at the page she had been reading. She smiled to herself then, knowing full well why.

SEVEN

The three young men sitting in his office with him were the nucleus of his management team. They had each been in Cecil Williams's line of vision for years, as well as in Elizabeth's. This was because they were talented, shrewd, trustworthy and diligent, not to mention absolutely loyal to Elizabeth. And to himself.

They were sitting together at the other end of the room, chatting amongst themselves, and as Cecil studied them for a moment or two longer he smiled. Those were not the only characteristics the men had in common. All three were tall, handsome and well dressed, and they could charm, with the greatest of ease, anyone they chose to target, be it man, woman or child.

Robert Dunley was the youngest at twenty-five, also the tallest and best looking. Slightly more inclined to be a clothes horse than the other two, with his impeccably tailored Savile Row and Armani suits, and flair for dressing, he had many important qualifications. He was an old hand at Deravenels and devoted to the company, his own genuine loyalty bound up with the years of service his father and grandfather had given to the Turners, and before them the Deravenels.

He was Elizabeth's only childhood friend and without question her favourite. Robin, as she called him, was the one person who could persuade her to change her mind, make a proper decision, and he could always manage to point her in a better direction. Obviously, this was because he knew her better than anyone else, including Cecil.

They had clung together as children, especially through her terrible adversities with her father and then Mary. Robert understood her, could cope easily with her many foibles, occasional temper tantrums and bouts of chronic illness. Cecil had known him for years, and his father before him, and a lasting friendship had built up between them.

Sitting next to Robert was Francis Walsington, a year older at twenty-six. Having studied at Cambridge and Gray's Inn, Francis and he were on the same wavelength and had long been business allies. Cecil was gratified to have Francis around; he was a shrewd operator with tremendous psychological insight into people, and able to handle any situation with great aplomb and skill. He was an expert on security, intelligence, spying techniques and terrorism, and had numerous strange but useful contacts which Cecil didn't want to acknowledge but was grateful to know that he had.

During Mary's power days at Deravenels Francis had travelled throughout Europe, stayed away from London most of the time. Apart from her peculiar management style, Francis found her religious fervour somewhat sickening. Inherited from her mother, Mary's devout Roman Catholicism seemed overly zealous to him. Certainly it did not sit well with Francis's laid-back Protestant outlook on life. He had arrived in London with great alacrity a few weeks ago, fully aware that Elizabeth would soon be running the company, and Cecil had brightened considerably at the sight of him.

On the other side of Robert was Nicholas Throckman. He was the eldest of the three men. He was forty-three, and he had been a long-time employee at the old trading company. Nicholas had fled at one difficult moment during Mary's tenure, no longer able to put up with her erratic management of the company and strange behaviour in general. He was well versed in all things pertaining to Deravenels, having worked for Edward Selmere during the latter's Administration on behalf of Harry's young son. He had known Elizabeth since her teens and was, in fact, a relative of Catherine Parker, Harry's sixth wife and widow, who had been Elizabeth's step-mother and dear friend.

Of the three men, it was Nicholas who was the most gifted diplomat, in Cecil's opinion, more than likely because he had had more experience. This morning Elizabeth had said to Cecil, 'All we need are a few good men.' She was right. And fortunately, Cecil thought, three of them are sitting here now.

Rising from behind his desk, Cecil went to join his protégés, saying, as he sat down in a chair, 'Are you happy? Are you pleased with your appointments, the things Elizabeth proposed to you last Friday?'

'Absolutely!' Robert exclaimed. 'Who wouldn't be?'

'The same here,' Francis agreed.

'I'm extremely happy, Cecil,' Nicholas murmured. 'Very happy indeed.'

'I'm glad to hear it. The reason I asked is because Elizabeth's going to speak about your new positions at the meeting, and I don't want any unforeseen problems from any of you. I want this transfer of power to be as smooth as silk.'

'How have things gone so far?' Francis asked, leaning forward slightly, his attention on Cecil.

'Very well, I'm pleased to report. I saw John Norfell last Friday morning, and later in the day I met Charles Broakes. Charlie seemed profoundly relieved we'd moved in so quickly, and was extremely cooperative.'

'What about Norfell?' Nicholas probed.

'He was most reasonable. I was cautious with him. Let's not forget he was very close to Mary, and he's a powerhouse here, as well as a long-time director. I handled him with kid gloves because I don't want to make enemies for Elizabeth. I was especially mild, and I think I put him totally at ease. It didn't hurt that I'd made him responsible for planning all aspects of Mary's funeral.'

Robert's intense dark eyes settled on Cecil, and he said in a warning tone, 'But he bears watching, take my word for it.'

'Oh, I do. And I feel the same, Robert. So does Elizabeth, actually. Now, a word about the meeting. Elizabeth wants to come in once we're seated, and she will come in alone. She will run the meeting, so we have to play it by ear. Be careful what you say, don't give any of our plans away. Understood?'

The three men nodded, their expressions solemn.

Robert Dunley sat on Elizabeth's right, and as he listened to her speaking he was filled with enormous pride. She was calm, collected and confident, and spoke eloquently about Deravenels. Also, he was proud of her appearance. Elegant in her navy-blue pinstriped suit, a crisp white shirt with an open collar, and large pearl earrings, she was the epitome of style. Beautiful but businesslike, right on the mark, as far as he was concerned.

They were sitting around the large mahogany table in the

boardroom, and until she had entered a few minutes ago the men had been standing around chatting amongst themselves as they waited for her. Charles Broakes, Sidney Payne, Nicholas Throckman, Francis Walsington were grouped together at one end of the room; Elizabeth's cousins Henry Carray and Frank Knowles were engaged in deep conversation with Cecil, whilst he had been talking to John Norfell and Elizabeth's great-uncle Howard, getting on in years but still a director of the company and a viable consultant. Nine of them altogether; seven he was sure about; one had a big question mark over his head. Robert had long been wary of John Norfell because of his closeness to the late Mary Turner.

'And so I'm sure you understand that I will go beyond the call of duty to make certain Deravenels prospers and grows stronger in the next few years as we move towards the twenty-first century.' Elizabeth paused, looked around the table, smiling at the assembled men, and continued, 'I now want to announce my first appointments.' Turning to Cecil on her left, she said, 'Cecil Williams and I have long worked together because he has been looking after my personal affairs for some years. Today he will become Chief Financial Officer and Director of the Legal Department. And Robert Dunley –' She paused, turned to Robert on her right. 'I am appointing Robert Chief Operations Officer, and Director of Transport. In effect, the three of us will be running Deravenels together.'

Cecil and Robert both thanked her, and the other men acknowledged the appointments with applause.

Swiftly, Elizabeth proceeded in a brisk voice, 'I have chosen Nicholas Throckman to be Director of Public Relations and Roving Ambassador for the company, and Francis Walsington will be Director of Security Worldwide.' Again, the two men thanked her warmly, and the others nodded their approval, or clapped.

Staring down the length of the table, Elizabeth's gaze settled on Sidney Payne. She smiled at him. 'I know Cecil spoke to you yesterday, Sidney, and passed on my request that you take the job of Director of Human Resources. Let me just say that I'm delighted *you* were delighted to accept.'

Sidney, a longtime employee of the ancient trading company and devoted to Elizabeth, smiled broadly. 'Thank you, Elizabeth, and *thrilled* would be a better word, I think, to describe my feelings.'

She inclined her head, and finished, 'Those are the only appointments I'm making today, but there will be others within the next two weeks.' She focused her eyes on John Norfell and Charles Broakes. 'John, Charles, I will be offering you both new positions in a matter of days, and Henry, Frank, you'll also be included in my new arrangements.'

She smiled at her cousins Frank Knowles and Henry Carray, who nodded their understanding.

Finally, her eyes swung to her great-uncle Howard; he acknowledged her with a warm smile when she said, 'And of course you will continue as you were, Uncle, and I hope you will become one of my advisers. That would make me happy.'

'It's my pleasure to be of service,' he responded, looking extremely pleased and not a little proud.

'Well, gentlemen, that's it for today,' Elizabeth announced in her businesslike manner. 'I thank all of you for coming, for attending this meeting, and now, if you'll excuse me, I have to leave you.'

'That was the fastest disappearing act I've ever seen,' John Norfell said, adding, in a somewhat disparaging voice, 'No doubt she has better fish to fry – a lunch with girlfriends, or perhaps it's a new man?'

Cecil, appalled and angered by these critical and unnecessary comments, had a hard time concealing his furious reaction, and threw Norfell a withering look. 'Please don't speak about Elizabeth in that tone of voice. What she does is none of your business, or mine, John. She's free, white and twenty-one, and she just happens to be managing director of this company, not to mention its largest single shareholder. In other words, she's the boss.'

John Norfell, never one to apologize, nevertheless had the good grace to look uncomfortable, and suddenly regretted his comments. After a moment's reflection, he said, in a much more conciliatory voice, 'It's a disappointment, actually, Cecil. You see, I was hoping she would do us the honour of joining us for lunch but –' He threw up his hands helplessly, looking chagrined. 'She didn't give us a chance to invite her. She just left.'

'That's her way. All business. She's gone back to her office to work, if you want to know the truth,' Cecil told him in a steady, controlled manner, even though he was still seething inside. 'She never has lunch, nor will she be going to any lunches, so you might as well get used to it. You see, Elizabeth doesn't believe in them, and especially not for business. Her attitude is that one never really enjoys the food, and business never gets discussed properly.'

'I see. So, now we know, and none of us will expect any . . . *socializing*.'

'That might be the best attitude,' Cecil murmured quietly.

'What does she have in mind for me?' John Norfell blurted out anxiously.

'She hasn't discussed it.'

'That's hard to believe, Cecil. Come on, she tells you everything.'

Cecil ignored this remark, and explained swiftly, 'What I do know is that you will be getting a promotion.'

'Oh, well, thank you for informing me of this, old chap. It's nice to know I'm not going to be pushed out,' Norfell replied with a harsh laugh.

To Cecil's relief, Sidney Payne joined them, and after only a moment's casual chat, John Norfell walked across the room to speak to Charles Broakes.

Sidney said, 'I hope I did the right thing, coming over to join you, Cecil. I noticed the pained look in your eyes and decided you needed – rescuing.'

'Thanks, Sidney, I did,' Cecil replied with a chuckle. 'Norfell was never my cup of tea, nor Elizabeth's, but he's a powerhouse here, and he has to be catered to, you know.'

Sidney grinned at his old friend. 'Well, just a *little* bit, surely?'

Cecil Williams laughed, nodded, and drawing Sidney across the boardroom, aiming for the door, he confided, 'I'm glad you accepted this job. You told Elizabeth you were thrilled . . . she was happy about that, because you're not getting the easiest job, you know.'

'Removing the dead wood? Is that what you're referring to?' Sidney asked.

Cecil merely nodded.

'I'll manage,' Sidney reassured him.

EIGHT

'I've got good news and bad news,' Robert announced, looking across at Elizabeth from the doorway which linked their adjoining offices. 'Which do you want first?'

Straightening in her chair, glancing at him swiftly, Elizabeth said, 'Why do you ask? You know I like the bad news *first*.'

Robert strolled into the room, handed her the manila folder he was carrying, and sat down in the chair opposite her.

'What is this?' she asked almost warily, and did not open it. Instead, she placed it on the desk. She looked at him intently, his eyes on her, her own filled with sudden concern.

'It's a copy of the note your half-sister wrote to her ... about-to-be husband Philip Alvarez, just after she had transferred all that money to him. When I say copy, I do mean the copy *Mary* made for herself. In other words, it's the same as the original, which undoubtedly he still has. Why wouldn't he have it?'

Elizabeth opened the folder, read the note quickly,

recognizing Mary's handwriting at once. Her face settled into grim lines. The note was short, but its style was saccharine. And sickening. She closed the folder. *Fool! Fool! Mary had been the biggest fool. And she had been duped by Philip.*

Elizabeth closed her eyes for a moment, steadying herself. 'So she did give him the money as a wedding present,' she finally murmured, and shook her head. 'I won't get it back, Robin, will I?' she asked in a miserable voice.

'No, you won't, I'm afraid. I suppose in his mind it's a . . . well, like a . . . *dowry*.'

'She gave him practically everything she had, you know. Cecil told me her personal bank account is virtually empty.'

'So he explained to me, too. And you'll just have to write the money off, you've no alternative,' Robert felt bound to point out. 'But look here, since we've found the contracts for the Marbella Project there's no question in my mind, or Cecil's either, that we *can* sue Alvarez and his company.'

'In my opinion we won't get that money back either! Mary created nothing but havoc, and her ventures with Alvarez were fraught with danger. He might be called the great tycoon, but it's an empty title.'

'That's true. But I feel certain there's less of a mess than we originally thought. There are many problems, but the auditors are making good progress and Cecil's sorted out a lot. And so have I. We're stopping the downward slide. There's only one way to go, and that's up.'

She nodded, agreeing with him silently, but her face was glum.

Robert leaned over the desk and, gazing at her with his sparkling dark eyes, he said, 'Don't you want to know the good news?'

Her face instantly brightened; he could always manage to cheer her up. 'I do, yes. Tell me, Robin.'

'I've arranged for us to go away for the weekend.'

'But I can't go away! Don't be ridiculous. I've too much work, and so do you, Robin!'

'You *can* go away, and so can I. *And we're going.* We both need a break. The last two weeks have been hellish, and we've worked non-stop. It's been bloody relentless, actually. I'm tired and so are you. I know you are.'

'I've never seen you look better, Robin Dunley!' she cried, her voice rising, sounding indignant. 'Very handsome, dashing and debonair, this morning. You don't look tired one bit.'

'But *you* do, Elizabeth. Your face is whiter than ever, you have a pinched look, and there are dark circles under your eyes. For the past two weeks we've been cooped up here in these offices until all hours. It's not healthy. We should get back to exercising and riding.'

She knew Robert spoke the truth. He never spoke anything else, and he had her welfare at heart. She *was* tired, bone-tired, if the truth be known. Glancing at the calendar on her desk she saw that it was Thursday, December fifth. Sunday the eighth was circled in red . . . that was the day she had promised to have tea with Aunt Grace Rose. Monday the ninth was also circled . . . that was the day of the board meeting. The thought of this, and the board members who were coming, prompted her to ask, 'Where were you thinking of going, Robin?'

'Waverley Court.'

'Waverley Court! But it's closed!'

'No, it's not. I spoke to Toby Watson last night, and he told me you had instructed him to keep the central heating on low all through winter because of the pipes. He gushed about how warm and cosy it was, said all he had to do was put a match to the fires, which were already laid, take off the dust covers and send Myrtle shopping for groceries –'

'You called the caretaker!' Elizabeth spluttered, astonished.

'– and I told him to go ahead,' Robert finished.

'Go ahead? What do you mean?'

'I said he *should* send Myrtle shopping for groceries. We'll need food, Elizabeth, whilst we're staying there.'

For a moment she was utterly bemused, then recovered herself, and exclaimed, 'Cecil has arranged some meetings tomorrow, and I have to be present, *must be*, actually.'

'He's changed the meetings. They'll be held next week. He agreed with me you need a few days off.'

'You also spoke to Cecil!' She looked at him askance.

'I certainly did. I've taken charge for once, and I'm making damned sure I look after you for a few days. So stop arguing.'

Sitting back in the chair, Elizabeth was lost for words, but finally spoke, found herself saying, 'I will have to be back in time to have tea with Aunt Grace Rose on Sunday afternoon, Robin. She's looking forward to it . . . I wouldn't want to disappoint her.'

'Then we shan't.' He grinned, knowing he had won, then jumped up and went round to her side of the desk. He pulled her to her feet, said, 'Come with me for a moment, I want to show you something.'

Nodding, suddenly no longer resistant to him, she allowed herself to be propelled from her office into his. Holding her hand tightly, he led her to the credenza which stretched along one entire wall in his office.

'Look at this. Isn't it beautiful?' He slid his hand over the highly polished wood, and went on, 'This looks like one piece, but actually it's two credenzas sitting side by side, from the Regency period. Just look at the mahogany, the sheen on it . . . isn't it gorgeous, Elizabeth?'

'Yes, the wood *is* extraordinary, and so are these two pieces. They've been here for donkey's years . . . I remember how my father used to admire them.'

'They were bought for this room by a man called Will

Hasling. He was your great-grandfather's best friend, and this was his office.'

'How interesting. I didn't know that.' She looked at him in puzzlement. 'Why are you suddenly bringing my attention to them?'

'Do you remember how I was sorting through a lot of keys last week?'

She nodded. 'Hundreds and hundreds.'

'Ever since I took possession of this office, after Mary's assistant Neil Logan went on sick leave, I have attempted to open the cupboards in the credenzas. But I've had no success. None of my keys fit. Until last night.' He put his hand in his pocket and brought out a small old brass key, showed it to her.

'This is the one that opened the cupboard doors. It's not the correct key, it doesn't belong to the credenzas, but somehow it fits these locks. So I didn't have to have the locks removed, and so saved a lot of damage to the antiques.' As he was speaking, Robert opened the cupboard doors, and pulled out a drawer. 'The folder I gave you was in here, under a pile of magazines, newspapers, and other folders. Neil Logan more than likely has forgotten about the file, and where he put it. How is he, by the way?'

'I spoke to his wife the other day, and she told me his nervous breakdown wasn't really that at all. His doctors think he has the beginnings of dementia. I told her not to worry, that I was retiring him on a pension. She was very relieved.' Stepping closer to the credenzas, Elizabeth looked at the set of interior drawers, and glanced up at Robert, asked, 'Was there anything else in these . . . of importance?'

'No,' he answered. 'Just the note I gave you.'

'I'm glad you persevered with your keys.' Elizabeth laughed unexpectedly. 'And I'm glad you're taking me to Waverley Court. When are we going?'

'*This evening,*' he answered firmly, laughing with her, adding, 'And don't start arguing with me again.'

When you stay away from a beloved house for a while, you sometimes forget its beauty and what it means to you. And that's the way it was with me. Earlier this evening, when Robin and I arrived here in Kent, I remembered that Waverley Court has been a special place for me for as long as I can recall. Kat made it into a home for me, and over the years I learned every part of it by heart . . . all the little corners, and secret places, hidden rooms, and parts of the garden that are mine and mine alone. I love the gazebo, and the stretch of beach that faces towards the English Channel where I used to go as a child with Kat, and she would point out the lights of France, twinkling in the far distance as if they were beckoning to me. Waverley Court is at its best in spring and summer, but even in the autumn and winter the grounds are beautiful. Kat and Blanche, with the help of Toby, used to make the downstairs rooms spectacular at Christmas. There was always a big tree hung with glittering ornaments and tiny fairy lights; sprigs of holly sat atop paintings and a bunch of mistletoe was tied to the chandelier in the front hall. Christmas. It would be upon us in a couple of weeks now. Perhaps we could come down here, Robin and I, and have an old-fashioned Christmas in Kent. I shall suggest it to him. I think he might enjoy that. I know I would. I want to spend Christmas with him. Robin is the only family I have, the closest to me.

'I bet you slept well,' Robert said, staring at Elizabeth across the breakfast table on Friday morning. 'Being in a room one knew as a child is always . . . comforting, wouldn't you say?'

'I did have a good night's sleep,' Elizabeth answered. 'And naturally I love my old room, but I was just dead tired last night. I could hardly keep my eyes open over supper.'

Robert grinned. 'Aren't you glad I persuaded you to come to Waverley Court?'

'Persuaded me! What a cheek you have, Robin Dunley. *Commandeered* me would be more like it.'

'Sometimes I have to do that, just as I did in the past,' he shot back, his grin intact.

She smiled, made no comment.

Robert said, after a moment, 'Shall we go riding this morning?'

Her head came up with a start, and she seemed puzzled. 'There aren't any horses here.'

He looked at her for a long moment, and then that wicked grin she knew so well spread across his face. 'Yes, there are. *Two.* One for me and one for you, Crimson Lass and Straight Arrow. They arrived this morning. I had brother Ambrose send them. So how about it?'

Surprised and delighted, she laughed and jumped up. 'I can't wait. What a clever idea of yours . . . Come on, let's go and get changed into our riding togs.' She gave him a sly look. 'Since you must have made the arrangements with Ambrose yesterday, I know you brought yours with you.'

'I did.' He rose, followed her out of the breakfast room, and crossed the entrance hall. Together they climbed the stairs, and when they came to her room, he said, 'I'll meet you in the stables in ten minutes.'

Robert galloped on, chasing Elizabeth, hard on her heels.

She was riding hell for leather, approaching the highest fence on the property, and his heart was in his mouth. He was afraid for her, certain she wouldn't clear the fence properly, that the horse's hooves would catch against it, and that she would be thrown. And injured.

Always intrepid and fast, when they were youngsters, he realized she had become an even more fearless rider since those days, and was not against taking risks. Since they had set out, over an hour ago now, she had raced across the fields surrounding Waverley Court, following the trails they had opted for as children.

Suddenly the fence was there! Right in front of her. Robert held his breath, praying she would clear it. And she did. The young mare, Crimson Lass, sailed over lightly, took it like a dream and landed perfectly. A feeling of absolute relief swept through him, and he took the fence himself, as easily as she had. He galloped on after her, shouting, 'Elizabeth! Wait! Stop!'

She did so, finally slowing, and turned around in the saddle. 'What's wrong? Are you not all right, Robin?'

'I'm fine. Even though you almost gave me a heart attack a moment ago.'

'I did?' She looked at him oddly, and frowned. 'How did I do that?'

'I thought you were pushing Crimson Lass too hard, that she wouldn't make it, and that you would be thrown.'

She smiled a trifle smugly. 'You must trust me, Robin. You see, I've become quite a good horsewoman since we last rode out together . . . so long ago.'

'So I see.' He looked at his watch, changed the subject. 'Shall we go back to the house? It's already twelve-thirty. I'm hungry, aren't you?'

'We'd better make for home. Myrtle told me lunch would be at one o'clock prompt.'

They turned their horses and cantered side by side across the meadow in silence. It was a beautiful day, crisp and sunny, and the Kent sky was a soft cerulean blue, intersected with puffy clusters of white clouds. The red-gold leaves had not fallen yet and there was a beautiful, burnished look to the stands of trees which lined the edge of the meadows, and the woods still retained their russet and golden autumnal hues. As they rode on, Robert thought of the times he had spent here when he was a boy, how his father had driven him down to Aldington so he could keep Elizabeth company. He felt a sudden, unexpected yearning for those boyhood years gone by, when the world had been so very different, somehow nicer, better, to his way of thinking. Everything in its proper place . . . all of his siblings joyful, happy and still alive, and his parents, too. Sorrow struck at him hard, darkened his handsome face, and the pain of his losses made his heart clench.

After a moment, he straightened in the saddle, and looked ahead. He was clever, determined, ambitious, and an optimist . . . he must not look back into the past, but ahead . . . and he must keep on going . . . going forward . . .

Elizabeth interrupted his meandering thoughts when she said, 'Robin, would you come to Stonehurst Farm with me this afternoon? I want to go over there and have a look around.'

'I'll come with you, yes, of course. What did Kat have to say about it?' he asked, his interest sparked.

'That it's in perfect condition, thanks to the caretaker Briney Meadows. In fact, she went as far as to say she thinks it's worth a small fortune. The gardens have been kept up by Alison Harden over the years, and it's still something of a showplace. The gardens were spectacular, Robin, if you remember? We went there constantly to be with Aunt Grace Rose. She did love us so. You said she was a hoot, your favourite adult.'

83

'She made us laugh with her wry sense of humour, and she let us eat anything we wanted . . . fruitcake, chocolate mousse and custard tarts, and once you and I ate a whole trifle. She was aghast.'

'Don't remind me!' Elizabeth laughed. 'I was the one who was sick afterwards. Little Greedy Guts, that was me.'

Robert shook his head and scowled. 'Not you, Elizabeth, you never ate enough, and Kat was always complaining you were too thin.'

'Oh, I know, she was a bit of a fusspot, wouldn't you say? Just like you are.'

'I'm not a fusspot!' he protested, sounding not only indignant but slightly injured.

'You were just now worrying that I couldn't jump a little fence, that I'd break my neck.'

'Kat and Cecil and everyone else would have my guts for garters if anything happened to you when you were with me. And you know it,' he pointed out, still indignant.

Elizabeth merely grinned and, wanting to tease him, she spurred Crimson Lass forward, galloping ahead as fast as she could.

Elizabeth and Robert were both carried back in time as they walked around Stonehurst Farm with Briney Meadows later that afternoon. The caretaker had worked there for fifty years and had known them when they were children.

In every room the windows sparkled, the floors shone, the antiques gleamed. The carpets were fresh, looked newly cleaned, and there was not a speck of dust anywhere. Nothing was out of place; the house was perfect.

'I feel as if I were here only yesterday,' Elizabeth said,

turning a beaming face to Briney. 'It's exactly the same as it was when I was a little girl.'

'Aye, it is indeed, Miss Turner, but then Miss Grace Rose is a stickler, she always kept it up, and made sure we did. She was a perfectionist in those days, and she still is. On the phone to me all the time, issuing orders.'

'I didn't know she still took an interest in the house, Briney,' Elizabeth said, sounding surprised, looking at him swiftly.

'Oh, she does, Miss Turner! It's thanks to her supervision that the house has been very well maintained and cared for over the years. And the gardens as well. I'm sorry that Alison, the gardener, isn't here today. She'd be proud to show you around, and the sunken garden is looking lovely at the moment. You see, it's a bit of a mild winter this year, so far anyway.'

'We noticed the gardens when we drove in,' Robert remarked, 'and they're spectacular – all those lovely shrubs and bushes and the copper beeches . . . just breathtaking.'

Briney nodded, beaming, obviously pleased by this praise, and as he stood there looking at Robert he remembered the boy he had been and Briney smiled inside. Now here he was, a grown man, so tall and handsome, and before he could stop himself he blurted out, 'No frogs in your pocket today, sir, eh?'

Robert threw back his head and roared with laughter. 'What a good memory you have, Briney. I *was* rather keen on frogs when I was a schoolboy, wasn't I?'

'That's a fact, sir. You found them fascinating, and you were always fiddling around in the pond. There was many a time I thought you'd fall in.'

'You caught a tadpole for me there once and put it in a jam jar,' Elizabeth interjected. 'I bet you don't remember, though.'

''Course I do . . . it was a *gift* for you, one of my first.'
He chuckled as they stepped out onto the front steps.
'And how on earth could I forget that most glorious
tadpole?'

Elizabeth laughed, and said, 'Thanks for showing us
around.' She shook Briney's brown gnarled hand and went
outside.

'My pleasure, Miss . . . you both make me feel young
again . . . bring back memories, that you do.'

Robert grasped Briney's hand firmly and shook it. 'Yes,
it's been a bit of a trip down memory lane for all of us,
Briney. Take care now.'

Briney waved as they walked towards the flagged terrace,
and they waved back before striking out towards the sunken
garden.

At one moment Elizabeth said, 'I noticed Briney didn't
mention Mary, but then I'm not really surprised. Toby said
they didn't like each other, and he mentioned that Briney
was respectful to her but kept his distance.'

'He's a nice old chap, the salt of the earth,' Robert
responded and then looked at her, frowning. 'I wonder why
your aunt Grace Rose is so involved with the house? You
once told me she had given it to your father.'

'That was my understanding.' Elizabeth shrugged. 'Maybe
she just loves it because she grew up there, and lived there
as an adult, and after her marriage to Charles Morran.
Incidentally, Kat's right. I think the property's worth a small
fortune.'

'Do you plan to sell it?' Robert asked.

'I don't know. I can't very well live in all these houses,
now, can I? Stonehurst Farm *is* beautiful. However, I've
always loved Waverley Court the best, and it does happen
to be closer to London. I can't sell Ravenscar, you know. It's
entailed, and must pass to my heirs when I die.'

86

'Hey, no talk of dying today! You and I have a lot of living to do yet, my girl!'

'That's true, we do, Robin. Together.'

He threw her a surreptitious look, but made no comment.

NINE

Grace Rose had always had a flair for clothes, an individual unique style of dressing, and on this Sunday afternoon she looked quite wonderful, Elizabeth thought. Her marvellous abundance of luxuriant silver hair was stylishly coiffed, she was well made-up, and her outfit truly caught one's attention. She wore a loose, raglan-sleeved jacket of purple silk brocade with a purple silk camisole and matching silk trousers. Ropes of large amethyst and turquoise beads hung around her neck, and small amethyst studs were fastened to her ears.

As she sat sipping her tea and studying her, Elizabeth found it hard to believe Grace Rose was ninety-six. Her looks belied this, and so did her mental capacities. There were no signs of senility or dementia – in fact, just the opposite. Grace Rose had a keen mind, total comprehension, and her dry wit was still intact. It was true that Grace Rose was a *very* old lady, the same age as the century, but her spirit was forever young. Elizabeth was well aware her aunt kept herself constantly busy, continued to work for her favourite charities, handled many of her own business affairs and was well informed about everything going on around her.

Putting down her teacup, and leaning forward from the waist, Elizabeth said, 'I've never seen you looking better, Aunt Grace Rose. You're just beautiful.'

'Thank you, and I might say the same about you, my dear. Those russet colours really suit you, Elizabeth. I think that outfit is by Hermès. I used to favour those colours myself a long time ago.' Grace Rose paused, then asked, 'I wonder if you would do me a favour?'

'Of course.'

'Would you mind calling me *Grace Rose*? The way you did when you were a child and a young woman. In the last year or so you've been adding *aunt*, and it does make me feel rather *old*.'

Elizabeth chuckled, answered emphatically, 'Grace Rose it shall be!'

'Thank you.' Settling back against the needlepoint cushions on the sofa, Grace Rose focused on Elizabeth, studying her as she herself had just been studied. After a moment, she announced, 'Never let them see you sweat.'

Taken aback by this Elizabeth gaped at her, not quite sure how to respond.

Grace Rose, who never missed a thing, was fully aware that she had succeeded in truly startling her great-niece, as she had fully intended to do, and she smiled inwardly. Then that smile surfaced, as she explained, 'That's what my father used to say to me . . . "*Never let them see you sweat.*" And *he* never did. And you won't either, will you, Elizabeth? *Tomorrow*. At the board meeting.'

'I certainly won't,' Elizabeth managed, aware that Grace Rose knew about the board meeting because she was a shareholder.

Grace Rose continued, 'My father had another rule he lived by in business, and it was this: *Never display weakness, never show face.* He once told me that his cousin, Neville Watkins, had drilled this into him when he was starting out in business at the age of nineteen. Edward Deravenel made it his mantra, and so should you. It will serve you well.'

'You're right, it will, and as you know I've always admired my great-grandfather.'

Grace Rose gave Elizabeth a long thoughtful look, finally remarked, 'Everyone fell under his spell. Fatal charm, that's what he had. In abundance. And he was a loving, generous man, and dependable.' A small sigh escaped her, then she straightened, and continued in a brisker tone, 'We're the last, you know, you and I. *The last of the Deravenels.*'

Elizabeth nodded, afraid to say one word, afraid to remind her great-aunt that she was also a Turner, not wishing to offend her.

It was as if Grace Rose had read her mind, when she went on swiftly, 'Oh, I know, you're a Turner. But your father Harry did not resemble them. And neither do you. His genes and yours come from Bess Deravenel, my half-sister and your paternal grandmother. She and I were both redheads like you, you know.' Grace Rose patted her hair. 'It's silver now but it was once a shimmering red-gold.'

Turning slightly on the sofa, Grace Rose shuffled some folders and documents, which were sitting atop an occasional table standing next to her. She found what she was looking for . . . a silver-framed photograph. Handing it to Elizabeth, she explained, 'This is Edward with your grandmother and me . . . that's me on the left. It was taken in 1925, about a year before our father died.'

Elizabeth had not seen this photograph before, and she sat holding it in both hands, gazing at it for a moment. Her

90

grandmother Bess and Grace Rose looked very much alike, and both young women bore a strong resemblance to Edward. They were very beautiful. She said, with a wide smile, 'There's certainly no doubt who fathered the two of you! Or from whence I come, either!'

Grace Rose smiled, looking pleased, and asked, 'Could you put the photograph back, over there on the console table, please, Elizabeth. There's a space where it usually stands.'

Elizabeth nodded and rose, walked across the room to the console table between the two tall windows, and put the frame in its given place, then returned to the seating area in front of the blazing fire, settled in the armchair.

The two women were sitting in the elegant drawing room of Grace Rose's flat in Chester Street, in the heart of Belgravia. It was a spacious room, and Elizabeth had always thought it charmingly decorated, with its restful cream, pink and green colour scheme, lovely antiques and extraordinary art. Grace Rose had quite a special and unique collection, and Elizabeth had always admired the paintings on these walls and in the other rooms.

On various tables around the room, arranged in groups, were photographs of the entire Deravenel family, the Turners, and also of Grace Rose's late husband, the famous actor Charles Morran. Vases of flowers abounded, and the warm air was redolent with their fragrances mingled in with the faint scent of the potpourri Grace Rose favoured, made by nuns in Florence, which she bought at the Farmaceutica di Santa Maria Novella.

Once Elizabeth had finished her tea she placed the cup and saucer on the coffee table, and broke the silence when she ventured, 'Kat told me you *needed* to see me, Grace Rose.' She gave her aunt a questioning look.

'Yes, I do.' Grace Rose focused her faded blue eyes on Elizabeth. 'You've led an extreme life, and I suppose it will continue to be extreme, given the circumstances.' A puzzled expression struck Elizabeth's face and she responded, 'I'm not sure I know what you mean by *extreme*.'

'Exactly that. Everything about your life so far has been *extreme*. Different from most people's. Unusual. Not standard. Mine was like that, too.' Leaning forward again, touching Elizabeth's hand lovingly, she continued, 'Your mother died when you were a very small child. You barely knew her. Your father behaved in the most abominable manner, heartlessly shunting you around among us, and cutting you off. *Shunning you.* I loved Harry from the day he was born. He was the son of my favourite sister, and yes, I spoiled him, it's true. But I grew to truly dislike him over the years, especially when he became a man. And not the least because of the way he treated you. His behaviour was appalling, quite unconscionable, and I told him so. Of course he didn't want to hear that.'

Elizabeth nodded, and then asked quickly, 'He didn't own Stonehurst Farm, did he?'

'That's correct. I did offer it to him as a gift, but he didn't want it because he preferred Waverley Court. There was also another reason. Your father was reluctant to take on the burden of the upkeep . . . of the house and the grounds. So I kept it, and Charles and I continued to go there at weekends. After my husband died I felt very lonely there without him. However, I love Stonehurst. I grew up there, and so I've never sold it. Somehow I just couldn't let it go to strangers.'

'How did it come about that Mary lived at Stonehurst for the last few years? Did she also think it was hers and that Father had owned it?'

'Yes, she did, I'm afraid. I immediately explained the situation, enlightened her. But she really did want to spend weekends there and so we came to an arrangement. I agreed

to pay for the upkeep of the house and the entire property, and she said she would be responsible for paying the
wages of the staff. Unlike you, and your father before you,
Mary did not seem to care for Waverley Court, for some
reason.'

Oh, I know *all* the reasons, Elizabeth thought, but said,
'I went to Stonehurst Farm on Friday, because I truly thought
it had passed on to me, that now I owned it. I had no idea
it was still yours. But the way Briney spoke, I began to realize
that you were still very involved with the house, and I was
puzzled. I somehow felt it *must* be *yours*.' Looking apologetic, Elizabeth finished, 'I feel awful about intruding the
way I did.'

'Don't be silly, you weren't intruding, and neither was Kat
when she went over there last week. Anyway, you're family
and you can go there whenever you wish.'

'I just don't understand . . . about Father, I mean, and why
he let us believe he owned Stonehurst Farm.'

'I did offer to *give* it to him, Elizabeth, and he was
extremely flattered and pleased about my gesture. But then
he discovered how expensive it was to run, and finally he . . .
declined my offer. I think what happened is that Harry had
told everyone I was giving him Stonehurst, boasted perhaps,
but then never bothered to explain he hadn't accepted my
gift, or why. Perhaps he was embarrassed.'

Elizabeth pursed her lips. 'I believe you're right, but how
odd of Father to do such a thing.'

Grace Rose said briskly, 'I needed to see you, to talk to
you about something which troubles me, but before we get
to that, can I ask you a few things?'

'You can ask anything you want.'

'Is Deravenels going under?' Grace Rose's eyes were riveted
on Elizabeth.

'No, it isn't. *Absolutely not*. Cecil Williams and I have

been on top of things for two weeks, and we're sorting out the problems. We are positive we can solve them all.'

Grace Rose nodded. 'Are you saying Deravenels is going to be safe?'

'I am indeed. I promise you it will be safe, and that it will be even bigger and better.'

'Mary made a mess, didn't she?'

'She did.'

'She gave a lot of money to Philip Alvarez.'

'Yes,' Elizabeth said laconically, her annoyance about this suddenly apparent.

'Deravenel money?'

'Yes. She invested millions in his Marbella Project. But I can assure you we're dealing with the matter. We'll either get our full investment back, or we may take over the project. It doesn't seem to be going well for Señor Alvarez. We're currently investigating the situation.'

'I have faith in you and Cecil.' Grace Rose gave Elizabeth a shrewd look. 'Did she give him any of her own money?'

'Yes, she did. I doubt I can get that back, though.'

'It doesn't surprise me that Mary Turner had to pay to get a man to marry her. She was hardly the world's greatest beauty, nor was she very bright.'

Elizabeth couldn't help laughing. 'Oh, Grace Rose, there's no one like you . . . you're quite a card.'

Grace Rose simply smiled. 'About the board meeting tomorrow . . . I don't think you should do anything . . . *rash*.'

Surprised, Elizabeth pinned her eyes on her great-aunt, and answered, 'I'm not one for doing anything rash, and you know that. I am very cautious, and so is Cecil. What are you getting at?'

'The board *is* too big. *Unwieldy*. I know that. But what does it matter? At this precise moment, I mean? I think you should leave the board the way it is. Don't get rid of anyone, don't ask anyone to resign. Just leave it the way it is.'

'Why do you suggest this? What's the purpose?'

'Don't make any enemies, Elizabeth. Not at this moment. Get on with the business of running the company. Making changes to the board can wait . . . take your time about it . . . Make friends, not enemies.'

'You have a point, Grace Rose.'

'You are the largest single shareholder. You are managing director. You have assembled a good team. Just get on with it. Do the work, get Deravenels back on its feet. Then you'll be able to do anything you want with the board.'

Elizabeth had listened carefully and Grace Rose's words were wise, made sense to her. She nodded, asked, 'Is that why you *needed* to see me?'

'Not really. I must discuss something else with you, something which is urgent and which troubles me.' Grace Rose pushed herself to her feet. 'Come along, I want to give you something.'

Elizabeth followed her out of the drawing room, her curiosity aroused.

TEN

Elizabeth followed Grace Rose across the small entrance hall and into the red sitting room, one of her favourite spots in her aunt's flat. She loved the mélange of reds predominant in the room – the crimson silk on the walls and at the windows, the tied-back draperies, the mixture of vivid reds in the carpet, the red velvet on the sofa and armchairs arranged in front of the fireplace.

To her way of thinking, the red colour scheme was a superb backdrop for the Impressionist and Post-Impressionist paintings which Grace Rose had chosen to place in this elegant room. Yet, to Elizabeth, the elegance was balanced by a sense of welcoming warmth, even a cosiness, and the pink-silk-shaded lamps cast a lovely roseate glow, especially on this wintry afternoon.

'Sit over there by the fire,' Grace Rose instructed. As she spoke she went across to the Georgian desk in a corner, retrieved a bulging manila folder, joined Elizabeth.

'I need to speak to you about the painting,' Grace Rose

began, staring intently at her great-niece. 'That's what this is all about. And you know the painting I mean, I'm quite sure of that.'

Elizabeth nodded. 'Yes, of course I do. The painting your father bought in about 1918 because it reminded him of Bess and you.'

'Correct. And I want a promise from you, a promise that you will not sell it. Not unless you have to – in order to save Deravenels. That must be the only reason.'

'I promise I won't sell it, Grace Rose. You have my word.'

'It might be a temptation to auction it off, you know. It must be worth a small fortune today.'

'Oh, it is, I know that for a fact.'

'So you had it appraised, did you?' Grace Rose asked swiftly, giving her a keen look.

'Not exactly.' Elizabeth cleared her throat. 'I need to explain something to you, some decisions I made about the painting a year ago. I did this just after my half-sister told me I was no longer welcome at Deravenels, that I couldn't work there any more. Since I didn't know what she had in store for me, what she might do, I went to live at Ravenscar. I was sort of hiding out, if you like.'

'I remember. You spoke to me from there, wanted me to know where you were, in case I needed you. But please continue about the painting.'

'The week Mary told me to get out, I drove down to Waverley Court, and had Toby take the painting down off the library wall. We wrapped it carefully in blankets and I brought it back to London. I told him I was having it cleaned and restored. This is what I did. It is now hanging in my dressing room in the Eaton Square flat, where it is absolutely safe.'

Looking suddenly confused, Grace Rose murmured, 'But Briney Meadows saw the painting only a few weeks ago.

Toby had asked him to go over to Waverley Court, to help him fix the security system. There had been some sort of problem with the electrical wiring.'

A wide smile spread across Elizabeth's face. 'Briney saw *the copy* I'd had made, after the painting was cleaned and restored. During the period it was being copied, by the artist I'd hired, I realized that Toby and Myrtle might notice the frame was new, once the painting was back at Waverley Court. Because the *original* frame was a bit chipped, the gilt worn off in places. I told the artist to put the copy in the old frame, and the original in the new one, so they wouldn't notice the difference.'

Grace Rose chuckled. 'Very smart of you, my dear. But, out of curiosity, why did you move it in the first place?'

'I thought Mary might actually steal it. No one would deny her access to Waverley Court, and certainly I didn't trust her. Whilst she loathed the painting, she nevertheless knew it was extremely valuable, and she could easily have taken it away. No one would have stopped her. So, very simply, I didn't want to take any chances with it. She could have sold it, you know, and given the money to Philip Alvarez.'

'Good thinking, Elizabeth. However –' Grace Rose cut herself off, then said carefully, 'It was hers by right, I suppose.'

'I'm well aware of that. She inherited it from my father through our half-brother Edward. But that particular day I made a judgement call . . . I decided she didn't deserve to have it.'

Grace Rose suppressed her mirth, and after a moment she remarked, 'Elizabeth, I think I would have done exactly the same thing, if I'd been in your position.'

'Thank you for saying that.' Leaning closer, Elizabeth confided, 'It's worth an enormous amount. A dealer, who's an old friend of mine, told me that any Renoir is priceless, and especially this one, *Les deux soeurs*, because of its marvellous quality, and also because Renoir painted it in 1889, when he was in great form. When I spoke to my friend, Julian Everson, last summer, and showed him the Renoir, he was extremely impressed. He put a price on it. He said it was worth six million pounds, at least. He even added that this was a rather low estimate on his part.'

'That sounds about right. I estimated eight million pounds. Now, this folder is for you. Inside there's a great deal of documentation about the paintings which belonged to Jane Shaw, my father's great friend, his mistress, actually. Bess and I inherited her art collection after her death. It was valuable then, therefore it's *very* valuable today. I know what's hanging on my walls. In here –' She paused, patted the manila folder, and went on, '– in here are photographs of the paintings your grandmother inherited. When you have a moment, I want you to look for them in the various homes you inherited. Will you do that, Elizabeth? It's important you know where everything is.'

'I certainly will. In fact, Kat can start on it straight away. She's working for me at the moment, checking out similar things.'

'I'm delighted to hear this. Kat is extremely efficient. I think some of the paintings will be at the Chelsea house, where your father lived after he sold the old house in Berkeley Square. And there're probably others at Ravenscar and Waverley Court. Well, here's the folder. Do go through it when you have a moment. You'll probably recognize some of the paintings yourself.'

Elizabeth had taken the bulging folder over to the desk in the red sitting room, and was examining the documentation about the paintings. Grace Rose had disappeared over twenty minutes ago, to take a phone call from her great-nephew in Ireland, and she was still absent.

Entranced by the photographs of the paintings, Elizabeth knew the moment she started rifling through them that she was looking at some rare treasures. But she had never known they had been part of Jane Shaw's collection. Some of them she recognized immediately and knew exactly where they were.

She stared at a photograph of a painting by Camille Pissarro, one she had loved for as long as she could remember. It depicted a group of old houses with red roofs situated in a stand of trees which were almost leafless. This hung in the dining room at Waverley Court, and so did an eye-catching snow scene by Armand Guillaumin. She had grown up with these two paintings, and liked how well they worked together in the same room. The red rooftops of Pissarro's houses blended with the russet leaves of the trees on the snowy hillsides of Guillaumin.

A Claude Monet snow scene, a painting composed entirely of shades of black, white, cream and grey, had been one of her father's favourites, and this still hung at Ravenscar in the room where he had worked.

There were several more photographs of other paintings, and she recognized the style of Matisse, Van Gogh, Sisley and Manet. These four paintings, which seemed familiar to her, were definitely not at Ravenscar or Waverley Court. Maybe they were hanging in the Chelsea house.

At this moment Grace Rose reappeared, and exclaimed, 'I'm so sorry, my dear, Patrick doesn't usually keep me on the phone for such a long time. But he wanted to tell me all about his girlfriend . . . he's about to get engaged. He's bringing her to London later this week to meet me.'

'Oh, how nice,' Elizabeth said, looking up, smiling.

'It is, and he's thoughtful, he always likes to include me in family affairs whenever he can. Now, about the paintings, you must be familiar with some of them. They should be in one or another of the houses, in fact.'

Putting the photographs back in the folder, Elizabeth got up from behind the desk, and went to join Grace Rose near the fire. 'They are, and let me show you those which are actually in my possession. I also remember seeing some of the others, but the problem is I'm not sure where . . . more than likely those are in the Chelsea house. Unless they have been sold.'

'There's always that possibility, of course. But I don't think your father sold any art, and anyway, the paintings are by well-known artists. So I would have known if they had come onto the market. And I'm positive Mary didn't sell any, for the same reason. I would have known about it.'

Elizabeth said, 'I am going to ask Kat to go over to the Chelsea house again, to check on the paintings. She was there last week, starting to organize everything, but I never thought to tell her about the paintings in the house.'

'And what about that house, Elizabeth? Are you going to keep it? Or sell it?'

'I think I will sell it, Grace Rose. It's a lovely old place, I know, but, well, it seems rather large for a single woman on her own.'

Grace Rose threw her an appraising look, and exclaimed, 'But you're not going to be on your own forever. You'll get married, have children one day.'

Elizabeth gaped at her, a look of horror crossing her face. 'I'm never going to get married. Not ever.'

'Come, come, my dear. Don't say *never* like that. One doesn't know what might happen . . . all sorts of unexpected things occur in life.'

'No, I shall *never* get married. I'm far too independent a

woman – and besides, I don't want a man bossing me around, telling me what to do. I want to be my own . . . *boss*. I don't want to be somebody's appendage. And I don't want children, I want a career.'

Grace Rose gave her a long, reflective stare but remained silent.

'When I was eight,' Elizabeth suddenly said, 'I told Robert Dunley I would never get married, and if you ask him, he'll tell you that I'm speaking the truth.'

Grace Rose bit back a smile, then murmured in a lighter tone, 'And was that when he *first* proposed to you, Elizabeth?'

'Don't be silly, Grace Rose! He didn't propose to me then. Nor has he ever, for that matter. Nor will he in the future, I can assure you of that.'

Grace Rose swallowed the words on the tip of her tongue. She was about to tell Elizabeth that she was totally wrong. Robert Dunley had been captivated by Elizabeth Turner's allure since he had been . . . yes, an eight-year-old like her. They had spent a lot of time with her at Stonehurst Farm when they were youngsters, and she could easily recall how he had hung on her every word, been utterly entranced with her.

Unable to let the subject go, Elizabeth now announced, 'Robin's like family, like my brother. He feels exactly the same way about me.'

'Does he now?' Grace Rose murmured. 'I know he's become Director of Operations at Deravenels . . . I hope you'll bring him over to see me one day soon. He was such a darling boy.' Not waiting for an answer, moving on swiftly, Grace Rose finished, 'You must let me know what Kat finds at the Chelsea house, in regard to the paintings. I shall be anxious.'

'I'll get her on to it in the morning, so no doubt I'll be able to give you a few answers tomorrow night. Now, let me show you the paintings I have in my possession.' Opening the folder, Elizabeth took out the Pissarro first and handed it to her great-aunt.

After she had left Grace Rose and gone home, Elizabeth thought about her great-aunt's reference to Robin proposing to her. Obviously Grace Rose had forgotten about Robin marrying Amy Robson, about eight years ago now, or there-abouts. Everyone else had because she was nowhere to be seen; it was as if Amy had disappeared into oblivion.

Blanche Parrell had once told her Amy lived in Cirencester and never came up to town, because she and Robin had separated. Robin never mentioned her, and Elizabeth had not thought about her for ages until tonight. Yes, seemingly it had all gone awry, that teenage marriage. Blanche had remarked. 'Marry in haste, repent at leisure.' At the time a lot of people had thought it was a shotgun marriage, but apparently not. There were no children of that misguided union.

Robert Dunley lived like a bachelor, was relaxed and fancy-free, seemingly. He lived and worked in London, and never went to Cirencester. Elizabeth thought about Amy. How could any woman let a man like him slip through her fingers?

ELEVEN

'**D**iplomacy and dissimulation, those are your best tools. Use them with skill, Elizabeth, and everything will be fine,' Cecil Williams said.

Elizabeth, staring at him intently across her desk, and listening carefully, responded, 'I know you're right, Cecil, and Grace Rose more or less said the same thing yesterday. She said don't do anything, don't be rash, don't make enemies. Make friends.'

'She's a wise old lady. And what *is* there to do? Nothing, in my opinion. You can't start dismissing board members, or laying down the law, that sort of thing, it will only antagonize the rest of the board. Tread softly, and most definitely very, very slowly.' Cecil straightened in his chair, and took a sip of coffee. 'In any case, it's going to be a very diminished board today.'

Elizabeth looked at him alertly, surprise evident in her eyes. 'Oh, and why is that?'

'Charles Broakes came to see me on Friday afternoon,

with a list of those who will be absent.' Cecil took a small notebook from his pocket, glanced at it. 'Malcolm Allen has sent in his resignation. He's going to live in Los Angeles, to be near his daughter and grandchildren. Apparently he was recently widowed. Two members are down with the 'flu, and then there's Rodney Nethers, who had a stroke in the summer. He's resigned. And so has Peter Thwaites, who has just become a tax exile in Monaco. So that's five people less. Mary is dead, and Neil Logan is suffering from dementia and has been retired by you. That means seven people are out. Rushton Douglas dropped dead last August, making eight altogether who will not be present.'

'That's amazing!' Elizabeth exclaimed. Raising an auburn brow, she asked, 'Are some of them not coming because I've taken over, do you think?'

Cecil shook his head vehemently. 'No, not at all, I'm sure of that.'

'Well, look, how do we know that two of them are actually down with the 'flu?'

'We don't, not really. But Rodney did have a stroke, and certainly Malcolm was widowed, and I'm certain Rushton is *extremely* dead. His obituary was in *The Times*.'

Elizabeth bit back a smile. 'So there'll be ten board members and me, making eleven.'

'That's correct, and it's a much better number, not so unwieldy. I wouldn't want the board to become top heavy again.' Cecil slipped the notebook into his pocket. 'I think Charles Broakes is in agreement with that. And by the way, he's delighted you've consolidated all of the vineyards, and put him in charge of the entire division.'

'I'm glad he is, and he's always done a good job, from what I see.'

'Charles agreed Robert and I should be present at the board meeting, because we do have our reports to make.'

'Good. Anyway, he and John Norfell couldn't really protest your presence, could they?' Not waiting for his response, she hurried on, 'I'm going to nominate you and Robin, by the way. I want you both on the board. There won't be any objections, will there?'

'I doubt it. Charles and John will agree, and so will your great-uncle Howard. The other members are either for you, or neutral at least. And I'll be happy to be on the board. Thank you, Elizabeth, and –' Cecil stopped as Robert rushed in from his adjoining office, and exclaimed, 'Thank God for Francis!'

They both stared at him, and Elizabeth said, 'What is it, Robin? What's happened?'

She looked and sounded so concerned, Robert said, 'Sorry. I shouldn't have burst in like that. What's happened is this . . . Walsington has been digging around in Madrid, and has found an awful lot of dirt on Philip Alvarez. Womanizing, carousing, a lot of living it up, enjoying the high life. Bad debts. But the worst part is that the Marbella Project is at a standstill. He might go down with a crash, might *have* to declare bankruptcy.'

'Oh, my God!' Elizabeth cried, her hand coming to her mouth. 'If he goes into bankruptcy we'll never get our seventy-five million euros back. Oh, Robin, this is terrible news.'

Cecil turned pale. His eyes were fixed on Robert, who sat down heavily in the other chair. 'You'd better fly over to Madrid, Robert,' he said in a grim voice. 'As soon as possible.'

'I agree. And, in fact, I've booked a seat on the first plane out tomorrow. I'm sending my brother ahead, Ambrose will leave this afternoon, meet up with Francis at his hotel. We must move fast, and take whatever action is necessary. There's no time to waste.'

'Agreed,' Cecil said. 'Walsington's information is always accurate, you can be sure of that. I always tell him he would have made a great spy. Have you been in touch with our Madrid office?'

'I have indeed. They are onto the case.' He glanced at Elizabeth, and added, 'Don't worry . . . we're on top of this.'

'I trust you, Robin, and Ambrose and Francis. I know you'll pull us out of this Spanish mess, if anybody can. Now, we'd better go over the items we're going to discuss at the board meeting.'

Elizabeth sensed hostility the moment she entered the board-room. She had been very sensitive to people and their feelings all of her life, and quickly picked up on an atmosphere in a room. And the hostility was almost a palpable thing; she felt as if she could reach out and touch it.

Surprised though she was, she kept a neutral expression on her face, and said, 'Good morning, everyone,' as she walked towards the top of the table, accompanied by Cecil and Robert, who sat down on either side of her. They also said their good mornings, and there were responses from all of those present, genial smiles.

Once she was seated at the head of the boardroom table, Elizabeth gave them a beaming, benign smile, and began: 'I'm very pleased to see you all here today. Welcome . . . to my first board meeting.'

Her dark sparkling eyes swept around the table, and she managed to keep her neutral expression intact when her gaze fell on Mark Lott and Alexander Dawson, the two board members Cecil had told her were down with the 'flu.

They made a fast recovery, she thought, and instantly under-stood that it was from these two that the hostility sprang. *Of course*. Mark Lott had been particularly friendly with Mary, and a frequent guest at Stonehurst Farm. As for Alexander Dawson, she had never liked him when she had worked at Deravenels. He was a sneak, a cheat, and she had caught him out in numerous lies. They are my enemies, she thought, and made a mental note to keep them in her sights.

'The first order of business today is the appointment of Cecil Williams and Robert Dunley to the board. As you are aware, they are my two chief executive officers, and will be running Deravenels with me. For this reason, it is essential they sit on this board of directors, and it is my honour to nominate them. Who will second this?'

'I will,' Charles Broakes said from the other end of the table. 'I second Cecil Williams and Robert Dunley to become members of the board of Deravenels.'

'I also second their nomination,' John Norfell announced in his booming voice. 'Those in favour raise their hands. I would like a show of hands, please.'

Elizabeth glanced around the table, saw every man present brought his hand up. She smiled. Lott and Dawson wouldn't dare go against me, she thought, not with Broakes and Norfell behind me. Promoting *them*, giving *them* more power has seen me in good stead.

Charles Broakes looked around the table and said, 'With a show of hands by those present today, Cecil Williams and Robert Dunley have been *unanimously* elected to serve on the board of Deravenels. Welcome to the board, gentlemen, and very many congratulations.'

Elizabeth, in a hurry, said, 'I would now like to proceed with business . . . First with regard to the state of the company. As of today, I am unable to give you a full and accurate report, because our auditors, accountants, and analysts are still working on figures. However, I am able to tell you that although the company has suffered losses, because of earlier bad investments, Deravenels is not in serious trouble.' She kept herself steady as she said this, knowing it was a lie, albeit a white one. She did not feel it was necessary to go into the true state of the company today, nor did she want to plunge into details of the dire situation in Spain. Why alarm anyone?

'So you are saying that Deravenels is *safe*?' Alexander Dawson asked, leaning forward slightly, his eyes on Elizabeth.

'I am indeed saying that. Now perhaps I should outline some of our plans. As you all know, John Norfell and Charles Broakes have both been promoted, and have become directors of their divisions on an international basis –'

'Does that mean you have given them power over the division directors in foreign countries?' Mark Lott cut in, also fixing his steely gaze on her.

'Yes, it does. I want Deravenels of London to be run from London. In future, the division managers abroad will deal directly with their superiors in London, instead of acting on their own when it comes to making major decisions that can affect the entire company.' She glanced at Cecil.

'It's a form of control,' Cecil explained, 'a way of making sure that all divisions in foreign countries are run according to *our* plans, *our* vision of the future of the company. We are also going to reorganize most of the offices around the world, and there will have to be some . . . attrition, of course, and some people –'

'Not wholesale sackings, I hope!' Dawson exclaimed in a loud voice, interrupting Cecil. 'That will certainly telegraph to the world that we might have serious problems.'

'Some people will be let go, and some people will be retired,' Elizabeth said in a firm, businesslike tone. 'But it will be done gradually, over a number of months, and perhaps the whole of next year. We have no intention of alarming anybody, particularly since there is no need for alarm. Deravenels is perfectly safe, as I just said. But it must be run on an efficient basis.' She turned to Robert, and said, 'I would like you to outline our plans about the changes we are going to make in general, Robin.'

Unlike everyone else who had spoken, Robert stood up. He made a handsome and imposing figure as he began to explain the plans Elizabeth, he and Cecil had put in place, speaking extemporaneously, and without the assistance of notes. He was such an eloquent and precise speaker, so clear in elucidating all of their aims, everyone clapped when he had finished.

Next, Elizabeth asked Cecil to give details of their plans for closing some of the offices around the world, and the reasoning behind this. He too rose, and he addressed the board with enormous clarity, sure of himself on all the issues. He readily answered a volley of questions, and calmed any of those board members who were nervous about the closing of the offices abroad, and how this would be viewed.

John Norfell spoke about his plans and vision for the international hotel group; Charles Broakes talked at length about the vineyards, which he would now control on a world-wide basis. Both men were self-assured, knowledgeable.

Questions were asked, answers given; matters were raised that Elizabeth would have liked to avoid, but she managed to deal with everything in her usual clever and shrewd way. She had been something of an actress all her life, and brilliant at dissimulation. Certainly her talent and abilities came in useful on this cold December morning.

When the board meeting broke up at twelve-thirty, she

went around the room shaking everyone's hand and chatting for a short time. Then she quietly slipped away, leaving the board members to be entertained at lunch by Cecil and Robin in the company dining room.

TWELVE

I *miss Robin, more than I thought I could ever miss anyone. He's gone off again to Madrid, to deal with the Philip Alvarez problem, and although my days are busy, they are dull without him around. The office is quite a bleak place without his presence – his vivid smiles, his jokes and teasing, his irreverent laughter and wry sense of humour. And his wise words. It is Robin, and only Robin, who can calm me down when I become disturbed, make me see the sense in matters that are complex and complicated. He soothes me with his rationality.*

Every morning when I arrive here, I go into Robin's adjoining office and turn on all the lights, and they remain on until I leave at night. Seeing the office lit up makes me feel less lonely. It's as if he's going to arrive at any moment.

He is in Madrid, leading my team: his brother Ambrose, Nicholas Throckman and Francis Walsington. As of last night they seemed to be making progress. I hope so. I want the Alvarez problem settled to my advantage, and then I won't

112

worry any more about the seventy-five million euros which Mary gave away so blithely. Just as important to me, Robin will be able to come home.

There is no one quite like Robin. That special bond between us going back to our childhood continues to endure. Now, looking back, I understand what we missed out on in our late teens and early twenties. Our paths did not cross so much in those days. Sadly. He was away at prep school, went on to boarding school, and after that attended university. He's a Cambridge man like Cecil Williams, and some of my other friends here within the company.

When I was first working at Deravenels, Robin had a job at the New York office; after a couple of years in New York he was sent to India where he worked for the mining division at the head offices in New Delhi. In a sense, we only caught up with each other when he came back to England, to find himself somewhat in disfavour with Mary, as was I. That's when we connected once more; he was very kind to me, sympathetic and supportive when she was being a tyrant.

In the past year Robin has been around quite a lot, coming up to Ravenscar, working with me and Cecil, making plans for the future. It was a good thing we did, because we have saved so much time, have been able to put a great many things into operation immediately.

Now here we are, Robin and I, working together with such compatibility, almost joined at the hip, so to speak. But then we've been compatible since we first met, aged eight. A long friendship. We enjoy the same things and always have. Lots of exercise, walking, dancing, playing tennis, and most especially riding. He's an amazing equestrian, better than me really, although I'm a good rider. Yet I'm not quite up to his standards. There are other things we enjoy doing together: going to the movies, concerts, the opera and the theatre. I tease him sometimes about role-playing, because *there's a lot of the actor in him. And he has a most mellifluous voice, a voice that truly captivates, just as the late Richard Burton's voice entranced from the stage, held everyone in its thrall. Robin usually responds by saying that I'm the far better actor, and perhaps I am.*

Robin is highly intelligent, brilliant in many ways, and has an uncanny knack of getting to the heart of the matter, especially in business, and I learn from him every day. He is loyal and protective, just as Cecil is, and I appreciate them both. There is a new and deeper amity between Robin and Cecil, and this pleases me. Both men are the mainstay of my life, and God forbid that they might not like each other and quarrel. Fortunately, this is not the case at all.

So much is happening at Deravenels; things are moving at a rapid pace, I can hardly catch my breath. Cecil has been superb, overseeing the changes which we've been able to implement immediately. In my bones I know that everything we've planned over the years will come to fruition. But at this moment everyone in the City is focused on Deravenels. Watching, listening, waiting. We must not stumble. I've made a vow to myself that we won't.

Robin has promised to be back in time to spend Christmas with me. I hope we can go to Waverley Court. It will do us good. We've become workaholics. Robin and I...

The shrill of the telephone startled Elizabeth, and she sat up with a sudden jolt, reached for the receiver. 'Elizabeth Turner.'

'It's me.'

'*Robin!* Hello! I was just wondering when you'd phone,' she exclaimed.

'Well, here I am. And I think I might very well be the bearer of good news.'

'Don't tell me you've wrestled the money out of his hands. If you have, then you're a true genius!' she cried, her voice rising with excitement.

'I haven't, actually,' Robert said in a more sombre tone, 'but I've certainly made a lot of headway with Philip. Actually, I should say *we* have, it's been a team effort. And you were very much part of the team.'

'What do you mean?'

'He's always liked you, Elizabeth, and seemingly he has quite a soft spot for you. He perfectly understands how you must feel about the seventy-five million euros Mary invested, and he wants to play fair with you,' Robert explained. 'He's got about the same amount tied up in the Marbella Project, so, in one sense, you and he are equal partners. Well, I should say Deravenels and he are partners. Anyway, the project has not gone the way he expected, and he wants us to take over.'

'To run it?' she asked, sounding incredulous.

'That's right. He doesn't have any experience of managing this kind of resort, which is what it really is, and if we don't help him by taking total control he'll go down. And we'll lose our seventy-five million, no two ways about that.'

'Are you saying Philip will go bankrupt?'

'He won't personally, no. And most of his other companies are safe. But the Marbella Project will go bust, and then Deravenels will definitely be out of pocket.'

'Will he still be a partner?' Elizabeth clutched the phone tighter.

'Yes. But I think I can negotiate a deal very favourable to us. In other words, we'll be in charge, totally responsible for running it –'

'Lock, stock and barrel?' she cut in swiftly.

'Lock, stock and barrel, and all the horses,' Robert answered, a hint of laughter in his voice.

'Does Cecil know all this?'

'Not yet. I'm going to phone him now. But what do *you* think? About Deravenels running the show?'

'I know we could do it. We have the right personnel.' She sounded suddenly glum. 'Anyway, I can't write off that bloody seventy-five mill, just like that.'

'I know. We don't have a choice. And look, there's an enormous amount of things to go over with him. But I just wanted to get your reaction to the idea in general, and Cecil's, so that I can finish up with Philip tomorrow. Naturally, all of the contracts and documents will have to wait until after Christmas. However, if we can come to a genuine understanding with him, the team can leave Madrid almost immediately.'

'What do *you* think we should do, Robin?'

'My gut instinct tells me we should go along with Philip . . . at least at this stage of the negotiation. If I can work out the right deal, a good deal for us, then *we* might turn out to be the winners after all.'

'All right then. Please phone Cecil direct, will you? I'm going to his office right now. And thank you, Robin.'

'My pleasure, Elizabeth. I'll be back tomorrow night, all being well.'

'I'm glad to hear it. I've missed you.'

'Me, too, you.'

The phone went dead, and she hung up the receiver, hurried out of her office and across the hall. After a cursory knock on the door, she walked into Cecil's office, just as the phone began to ring. 'It's Robin,' she announced sombrely, walking over to Cecil's desk and sitting down in a chair.

Cecil, his cool grey eyes steady, his demeanour calm, nodded his understanding. He picked up the receiver. 'Williams here.' He was silent, listening, and then he said, 'Yes, she just this moment came in, Robert. So let's have it. How well did it go?'

Cecil sat back, nodding, looking across at Elizabeth several times, catching her eye. Finally, he said, 'I agree with you and Elizabeth. I don't think we have much of an alternative. We might as well go along with Philip Alvarez, at least at this time, this talking stage. You will have to make a very advantageous deal for *us* with him, you know, Robert.'

Elizabeth sat back, only half listening to Cecil, and finally when he hung up she leaned closer to his desk and asked, 'So, what do you think?' Her dark eyes were fixed on his.

'I'm in agreement with you and Robert. We don't have anything to lose. At this moment. We are only *talking*, after all.'

Elizabeth stood up. 'I'll tell you one thing, Cecil. If John Norfell gets his hands on the Marbella Project, he'll make a stunning success of that resort. It's just up his alley. If he were running it, *should* we take over, I'd rest easy.'

'And so would I,' Cecil answered.

Elizabeth glanced at her watch. 'I've got to go. I'm meeting Thomas and Kat at the Chelsea house. They sounded very mysterious when I spoke to them yesterday.'

'Let's hope they have good news, too,' Cecil responded, giving her one of his rare smiles.

THIRTEEN

The house was of the Regency period. Perfectly proportioned, it had many windows, tall chimneys and undeniable elegance. This architectural gem was hidden behind tall brick walls and stood in a lovely garden on the banks of the River Thames.

Originally purchased by Neville Watkins for his wife Nan, it had later been bought from Nan by Edward Deravenel, who had then gifted it outright to his brother Richard. In turn, Richard had bequeathed it to his favourite niece Bess Deravenel, who soon after became a Turner. Her son Harry Turner inherited it from Bess and had lived there for a while, as had his daughter Mary. Until her death, in fact. Because all of these owners had truly cherished the house, it had been treated with loving care by them for a hundred years. Just as it had been looked after exceptionally well by those who had owned it before them. In consequence, the exteriors and interiors were in excellent condition, and the house was a valuable property.

It really is a genuine treasure, Elizabeth thought as she pushed open the wrought-iron gate set in the red-brick wall, and walked into the garden.

She stood staring up at the house, admiring it, and then, unexpectedly, sudden memories assaulted her. A variety of images danced before her eyes . . . Those days spent here with her father and her little brother, Edward . . . Those happy days in the early eighties . . . her father, so full of kindness . . . then her father and his sixth, and last, wife Catherine . . . sweet, motherly Catherine, her favourite, who had loved her. And Thomas Selmere, Catherine's new husband, who had loved her too . . . Well, he had, hadn't he?

A shadow crossed her face, and she frowned, then let thoughts of Tom – the very dangerous Tom – slide away into oblivion. Involuntarily, she shivered, felt goose flesh spread. He could have been her undoing. But she had remained steady, calm, had kept a cool head, and had adopted the face of innocence, been demure, frequently silent, looking reflective. Because of her unassailable demeanour and her agile brain, she had fortuitously escaped trouble; but not Tom. Poor, foolish Tom.

She rang the bell and the front door was promptly opened by Ann Whitehead, the housekeeper, who greeted her warmly and ushered her inside.

The entrance hall was filled with winter sunlight, and Elizabeth squinted in the brightness as she glanced around. Dust motes rose in the air in the long shafts of light, and she let out a long sigh . . . there was a lovely quietness here in this vast hall, a tranquillity she remembered well . . . it had a peacefulness, this treasured house which had been so long in the family.

Ann took her coat, and Elizabeth thanked her, turned around. Instantly a wide smile spread across her face. Coming towards her were Kat, Thomas, and Blanche . . . the beloved trio who had raised her . . . who had attended to all of her interests since childhood. She loved them.

The three of them were suddenly surrounding her, hugging her, kissing her, and she could tell from their faces that they had only good intentions. And perhaps, also, good news. For as long she had known them these three had been totally and incredibly transparent. She had always known when trouble was stalking her, or bad news was imminent, been aware when happy times were ahead, or catastrophe looming. None of them had a talent for dissimulation, so they could never hide anything from her. And so it was this afternoon.

'I can tell from your beaming face, Thomas, that you have something wonderful to tell me. Now, you do, don't you?' Elizabeth stepped away from him, eyeing him, laughter sparkling in her black eyes. 'Come on, confess.'

He chuckled. 'Good news, yes. Perhaps we might also call it wonderful. But let us go into the library and sit down, have a chat.'

'Very well. Lead the way,' Elizabeth replied, and, turning to Kat, she squeezed her shoulder affectionately. 'Thanks for everything you've been doing, Kat, and for the little suppers you've been leaving for me. And thank you, too, Blanche.' She slipped her arm through Blanche's, added, 'You've done a fabulous job with the clothes. I hope you know how happy I've been with the new things.'

'Of course, and I know you're appreciative.' Blanche, a happy soul, had been involved in Elizabeth's life since she was a little girl. Blanche, the kind-hearted Welshwoman, could never do enough for her. It was the deeply-ingrained Welshness of the Parrells that appealed to Elizabeth, who was part Welsh herself.

All of them walked down the hall together, heading towards the library. It was a room Elizabeth had gravitated to ever since she was a ten year old, a room that actually appealed to everyone. Now, as they went inside, she glanced around, thinking of the days when her father had occupied this room . . . how much he had enjoyed it.

There were hundreds of leather-bound books housed in mahogany shelves around the walls, a roaring fire in the grate as always, whether it was winter, spring, summer or autumn. Incredibly comfortable deep leather sofas and chairs, eye-catching objects of art and an array of priceless paintings gave the room its unique lustre, and a true sense of timelessness. It had not changed at all since Neville Watkins's day, except for the addition of several paintings, which Elizabeth knew came from the collection of Jane Shaw, which she had left to Bess Deravenel Turner.

Taking a seat near the fire, Elizabeth said, 'I'm on tenterhooks! Come on, Thomas, what's the great news then?'

'A discovery in the basement here – a discovery that Kat made, actually, so I shall give the floor to her.'

Kat, sitting on the edge of her chair, looking excited, eager, said, 'I found the most extraordinary collection of silver and gold objects in the vault, Elizabeth, and I was so impressed with some of the pieces, I hired an expert in antique silver to examine them for us, and to evaluate them. His name is Alex Pollard, and he was amazed by the finds, rather impressed. I'd had some of the items cleaned and polished, the ones I thought were the most valuable, and I was proven right. Alex agreed. They are by master craftsmen. Have you heard of Paul Storr, William Denny or Paul de Lamerie?'

Elizabeth shook her head, then exclaimed, 'Oh, wait a minute! I think my father mentioned Paul de Lamerie on several occasions. He told me de Lamerie was the best-known English goldsmith of his generation. I believe he was appointed goldsmith to George the First.' Elizabeth frowned, trying to remember. 'I'm sure my father admired his work, and possibly owned some things made by him.'

121

'That's correct. I found a treasure trove of objects by de Lamerie in the cellar.' Kat stood up, and went on, 'I'd like you to see the collection . . . I have everything on display in the dining room.'

The dining room was handsomely furnished and appointed, and although it was of large dimensions it nevertheless had a feeling of intimacy and warmth because of its colour scheme. Red silk brocade covered the walls, red taffeta made wonderful draperies at the windows, and a red-and-black antique French rug covered the polished parquet floor.

Following Kat into the room, Elizabeth at once noticed that the mahogany dining table was fully extended; all of the extra leaves had been added. Immediately she understood why when she came to a standstill next to it. The entire surface was covered with gold and silver objects, items which were obviously of great value. Candlesticks, trays, service plates, bowls, tureens, dessert stands, fruit stands and goblets had been carefully arranged on its top.

'How spectacular *these* are,' Elizabeth exclaimed, picking up one of the goblets, examining it. Turning to Kat, she said, 'It's just lovely. And what craftsmanship went into it – I see it's designed like a tulip.'

'It's by Paul de Lamerie, as is everything on this table,' Kat explained. 'Alex Pollard put the value at approximately ten thousand pounds, just for one of the goblets. There are thirty of them altogether.'

Staring at her, Elizabeth said slowly, 'So the thirty goblets are worth three hundred thousand pounds, that *is* what you're saying, isn't it?' She sounded surprised.

Kat replied, 'And that's a low estimate, according to Pollard. At auction they could bring much more. You see,

Paul de Lamerie was one of the best-known silversmiths of his time, and you were right about him being appointed gold-smith to King George I. That was in 1716, just after he had opened his London shop in 1712. He was quite celebrated.'

Elizabeth put the goblet back on the table, frowning. She asked, 'But how could he produce so much? After all, the work is rather ornate, and truly exquisite, as you just pointed out.'

Kat looked at Thomas, who hurried over to join them at the table. 'A good question, Elizabeth. I wondered exactly the same thing myself. So last week I did a bit of research. Seemingly, Paul de Lamerie tried to ensure his financial success by opening a large workshop, with about twelve or thirteen employees. You see, he was smart, in my opinion, and worked on commissions, but also produced other pieces to be sold later. By having a workshop and using other talented craftsmen, he could meet the growing demand for his work. He was the most highly respected silversmith of his day in the first part of the 1700s and he was particularly famous for making ornamental plate. He was one of the first who worked in the Rococo style.' Thomas glanced at the table, waved his hand at the many objects.

Kat, looking at Elizabeth, explained carefully, 'Everything bears the stamp of Paul de Lamerie, as well as the English mark which indicates the year of assay and guarantees the quality of the metal.'

'Thanks for explaining, Kat. There's something that puzzles me, though. He has a French name, so why is he known as one of the greatest *English* silversmiths?'

Thomas answered her. 'His parents were French Huguenots, who left France for religious reasons, went to the Netherlands where Paul was born, and later settled in London around 1691. Paul de Lamerie grew up in London and learned his craft here.'

'I see.' Walking slowly, Elizabeth circled the table, staring down at the many beautiful gold and silver items. At one moment, she said to Kat, 'If thirty golden goblets are worth three hundred thousand pounds, what about the rest of the Paul de Lamerie items? They certainly look like works of art to me, although I'm not an expert. Still, they are obviously extremely valuable.'

'Alex is working on the inventory and making his estimates as we speak, and he will have a full report for me after Christmas. But yes, you're quite right, Elizabeth. You are, in fact, looking at a small fortune here. And also over there.' She indicated the trestle tables set up near the windows, which were holding yet another vast amount of silver objects.

Together, Thomas and Elizabeth crossed the dining room, Kat and Blanche in their wake. 'A great deal of these pieces were made by Paul Storr and William Denny, two more of England's great silversmiths,' Thomas told her. 'But Kat knows more about them, since she did the research.'

'Just look at these magnificent dessert stands!' Kat came forward, touched one of the stands, turned to Elizabeth. 'These were made by Paul Storr in 1815, the English Regency period. The silver has the most wonderful patina, don't you think?'

Bending forward, Elizabeth examined one of the stands, nodding. 'Yes, it does, Kat, and how beautiful this pair is. Just . . . extraordinary.' Her eyes rested on the dessert stands for a while longer. Each stand was an intricate design, composed of two putti on a raised base, one on each side of a leopard. Their arms were stretched up, supported a silver bowl with a crystal liner. Shifting her glance, Elizabeth stared at a pair of elegant candlesticks, and asked, 'Are these by Paul Storr as well?'

Kat inclined her head. 'Yes, they're George III candlesticks, also dated 1815. That large silver bowl is a crenellated Queen

Anne montieth, dated 1720, and that was made by another renowned English silversmith, William Denny. As for Paul Storr, he was a goldsmith particularly noted for his exquisite craftsmanship, and he made quite a lot of presentation silver, as well. Actually, the cup he made for Lord Nelson, to celebrate the admiral's victory at the Battle of the Nile in 1798, is on display at the National Maritime Museum in Greenwich.'

Elizabeth, who had listened with interest, now said, 'So what about the rest of this silver?' Her eyes swept across the two trestle tables. 'There's so much of it here. Coffee services, tea services, bowls, tureens, jugs, cups, hunting cups, rose bowls, service plates, egg cups.' She began to laugh. 'My God, who bought all of this? Who collected it?'

'You'll be happy to know that I did find some inventories in the silver vaults downstairs. Actually, they're large rooms fitted with shelves, hidden behind heavy metal doors. Anyway, not to digress. The Paul de Lamerie gold goblets were purchased at auction in the early 1920s by your great-grandfather, Edward Deravenel. It was he who also bought the dessert stands by Paul Storr. They must have been brought over here when your father sold the Berkeley Square house and moved in here.'

'I see. Is everything inventoried?' Elizabeth wondered.

'Unfortunately it isn't. However, there is one amazing collection of Georgian silver which belonged to Edward's mother, Cecily Deravenel.' Kat smiled. 'Some of your antecedents were more thorough in their documentation than others, especially your great-great-grandmother. Everything of hers is listed.'

'Don't you think Elizabeth will be bored by now?' Blanche remarked, staring hard at her brother, who sat opposite. 'I mean, she really must be fed up, viewing all this stuff. Elizabeth's not into *stuff*.' She sighed. 'Elizabeth's into being a tycoon.'

Thomas chortled, as usual amused by his sister's blunt comments. 'No, she isn't into stuff, that's absolutely true. But she's certainly into money, and that's what the *stuff*, as you call it, represents to her. Even as a child she was enamoured of money and concerned about not having enough. Remember how upset she got when there wasn't enough for new clothes? Her father was cheap at times.'

'*Very cheap*. But also greedy. All the Turners were avaricious. And in some ways his attitude traumatized her –'

'Let's not psychoanalyse her now, Blanche.' Thomas gave Blanche a long stare, and asked, 'Do you want to go down to the cellars and tell Kat to . . . cease and desist, so to speak?'

'Perhaps we should give it a few more minutes. There is a lot of valuable china in the storage rooms. Most of it has never been used, and all of it's in perfect condition. Sèvres, Limoges, Royal Doulton, Worcester, Meissen, Dresden, you name it. And there's a mountain of antique blue-and-white Wedgwood. That must be worth hundreds of thousands.'

'Cecily Deravenel's, I bet?' Thomas remarked.

'Yes.' Blanche shifted in her chair, drew closer to her brother, said in a low voice, 'You should tell Elizabeth about Alex Pollard's idea, Thomas. Now would be a good time.'

'You're right, I'll tell her over tea.'

At this moment the library door opened, and Elizabeth hurried in, accompanied by Kat. They joined Thomas and Blanche at the fireside, and, shivering, Kat said, 'It's cold down there.' She put her hands out to the fire, as did Elizabeth, who was whiter than ever from the cold.

'I shall go and ask Ann to bring the tea now,' Blanche announced, and purposefully jumped up, went off to organize the housekeeper.

Thomas caught Elizabeth's attention. 'I'm sure Kat told you how valuable the china is, and apparently it's in perfect condition.'

Turning away from the fire, Elizabeth sat down next to him on the sofa. 'I'm staggered by the amount of things I've seen this afternoon, Thomas, and this is just the beginning. There are the vaults in other houses, which I've never been into. Ravenscar and Waverley Court, not to mention the bank vaults. I know you've viewed these with Kat.'

Kat interjected, 'I was just telling Elizabeth about the twenty-two diamond tiaras in the vault at Coutts Bank.'

Before Thomas could respond, Elizabeth shook her head, laughing. 'Can you believe that, Thomas? *Twenty-two diamond tiaras*. Of all shapes and sizes, all of which belonged to the women in the family who went before me. Amazing.'

'They are *magnificent*,' Thomas answered. 'I'm sure Kat told you that many of them can be taken apart, to become necklaces . . . seemingly those are the ones which are the most valuable.'

'Because, for the most part, tiaras are out of fashion today,' Elizabeth said, laughing. 'But I bet we'll be able to sell them.'

Thomas agreed with her, and said so, then, deeming this an appropriate moment, he continued, 'There's something I would like to present to you, Elizabeth, an idea that comes from Alex Pollard. He believes it would be to your advantage to have a public auction, at either Sotheby's or Christie's, whichever auction house you prefer, in order to sell off the gold and silver items, the china, perhaps some of the art – any paintings you don't want to keep – and possibly some of the antique furniture. Especially if you intend to sell this house.'

Sitting back in the chair, Elizabeth looked thoughtful for a moment or two, mulling over his words. Finally she sat up straighter, and explained, 'I don't know what to do about the house. I'm ambivalent about selling it, but I certainly like the idea of the auction. How else would we get rid of all these possessions? Possessions I don't want.'

'There's also the jewellery,' Kat pointed out. 'You told me you didn't intend to keep many of the things which Mary sent over to you in the suitcase. They could go on auction, too.'

'Not the South Sea pearls!' Elizabeth exclaimed swiftly. 'I intend to keep those, and the earrings. I will have to look at everything else again, to make a final decision, I suppose.'

'I'm glad you approve of the idea of the Turner Auction,' Thomas said, smiling. 'Alex Pollard suggests we call it that, to give it a sense of . . . importance.'

Fast on the draw, as usual, Elizabeth announced, 'I would prefer to call it The Deravenel–Turner Collections. Then categorized underneath could be Antique Silver and Gold Plate by Eighteenth- and Nineteenth-Century Master Craftsmen. Antique China from Famous English and Continental Manufacturers, Fine Art by Renowned Eighteenth - and Nineteenth-Century Painters, Antique English Furniture and Rugs . . . and so on. And then at the end we can add something about Magnificent Jewels by World-Famous Jewellers. Something like that anyway. What do you think?'

Although Thomas knew better than to be amazed by anything Elizabeth said or did, he was nonetheless taken aback. And impressed. '*Brilliant*. And I do prefer the use of both names, which makes the auction sound more important. Well done indeed, Elizabeth.'

'I agree with Thomas,' Kat volunteered, beaming at her. 'And I think another category could be called *Tiaras*. After all, they're unique, and wait until you actually see them, Elizabeth. They are truly impressive.'

'That's a great idea, Kat. I think I would use Sotheby's for the auction. Oh, and by the way, when am I going to meet Mr Pollard?'

'Any time you want. His wife works in the real estate division of Sotheby's. You could use them if you decide to sell this house.'

'Couldn't be better.' Elizabeth smiled at her. 'Did he *say* anything about the house?'

'He remarked on its beauty and outstanding condition, said how well-cared-for it looked. He actually told me you could easily get thirty million pounds for it.'

'Oh, yes, I know I could. But I would never take *that*. In fact, I won't take anything less than seventy million pounds.'

Kat gaped at her, and so did Thomas, but before they could make any comments, Blanche returned, followed by Ann, who was pushing a tea cart.

'You're both a welcome sight!' Elizabeth exclaimed, standing up, walking across the floor to join them. 'That's just what I need to warm me up. A nice cup of tea.'

FOURTEEN

S he had forgotten how beautiful the upper floors of the Chelsea house were, with their spacious bedrooms, wide corridors and generous landings. There were windows along the main corridor, and it was light-filled as she made her way to the master bedroom.

Pushing open the door, Elizabeth went in and glanced around, remembering the last time she had been in this room. She had come to visit Mary, who had not wanted her to come, and had done so out of a sense of family duty. But her half-sister had been cold, had shown no interest in her, and had made it abundantly clear she could not wait for her to leave.

Elizabeth recalled how she had gritted her teeth and stayed, sitting in the chair which had been placed near the bed for visitors. Mary, convinced she was carrying Philip's child, had looked smug, even self-satisfied at certain moments, but also extremely ill. Elizabeth was fully aware that her half-sister's swollen belly was due to a terrible sickness, and nothing else.

This had proved to be true when Mary had later been diagnosed with cancer of the stomach.

But that day, over a year ago now, her half-sister had been unbending in her attitude. She had snarled at her, told her she could not work at Deravenels any longer, and that she was disowning her once and for all.

'Get out! Get out of my sight!' she had screamed at one moment, her dark eyes bulging in her sweating face. 'You've always been a thorn in my side, you little bitch. You took my father away from me. Some good it did you. I'm the one with the power now. Not you. You'll never have the power –'

Mary had started to cough, falling back against the pillows, and Elizabeth had risen in alarm, leaned over her, only to be fiercely pushed away.

And so she had sat down in the chair, waiting for Mary to recover. When her half-sister was finally breathing more normally, she had asked her if she could do anything to help her.

Mary's response had been swift and angry. 'Get out! *That* will certainly help. Go away and never come back here.'

And so she had done exactly that.

Elizabeth sighed under her breath, and walked across the room, glanced down at the garden. The winter landscape was devoid of colour and beyond the River Thames was the colour of lead. Dismal today. When she turned around, she stared at the huge four-poster bed, with its fresh white linen and collection of lace-trimmed Victorian pillows on display. And she thought of all those others who had occupied this room . . . other members of the family.

Her great-uncle, Richard Deravenel, and his wife Anne Watkins Deravenel . . . Richard, the uncle her grandmother Bess had seemingly adored. Her father had once told her all about him, how he had loved his elder brother Edward

131

Deravenel so devotedly, and adored his nieces and nephews, especially Harry's mother, Bess, eldest child of Edward. *The nephews* . . . her mind focused on them for a moment . . . those two little boys who had disappeared from the beach at Ravenscar . . . never to be found. A great and puzzling mystery when it happened. But not so puzzling today, when children constantly vanished, either abducted by an angry parent or by strangers with criminal intent. *Every five minutes.* Statistics showed that every five minutes a child disappeared . . . somewhere in the world, and was as often as not never found.

Harry Turner had lived here with his third wife Jane Selmere, mother of her father's first and only male heir, sister of the Selmere brothers . . . Edward and Thomas, two handsome, dangerous men.

Turning around, Elizabeth left the master bedroom and hurried along the corridor to the bedroom that had once been hers. It was shadow-filled in the late afternoon light, twilight actually, but Elizabeth could see that it was exactly the same, remained just as she had left it. Closing the door, she leaned against it, her eyes roaming around.

Unexpectedly everything changed.

The years fell away. The past ensnared her.

He is standing in the corner, near the window.

Tall, slender, dark-haired, and so very handsome. Even though the light is dim I can see the laughter in his hazel eyes . . . those eyes which are so often filled with passion and desire. For me. I closed the bathroom door, but did not move.

'Sweetheart, come here,' he said in a low voice. 'Quickly, come, let me hold you. Please, Elizabeth, I've been waiting for you.'

Still, I did not move, turned to a pillar of salt, I've no doubt. And there was no doubt in my mind what he wanted. I shivered, filled with fear. And anticipation. He had done that to me, my sailor man, taught me to want his hands on me, his mouth on mine. It was wrong, I know that. But he was . . . irresistible. Against my own volition I went to him. He pulled me into his arms and held me close. He was so tall and strong, and I could feel his heart thundering under his thin cotton shirt. He bent down and kissed me, his mouth hard on mine, and then his tongue was seeking mine. And I sought his, responded. I thought my legs would give way, and I clung to him. He pulled me closer, pressed me into him, and I felt his hardness, shivered.

'Touch me, feel me, Elizabeth,' he whispered against my hair. 'See what you do to me, my little sweetheart. This is yours, it's for you.'

I twisted, tried to pull away, suddenly afraid that we would be caught. But he was the stronger, and he bent me back against the bed, pulled up my nightgown, looked at me for a long moment, sighing. 'Elizabeth, Elizabeth, I want you so much. All of you, my little sweetheart.'

'Tom, no, we can't,' I whispered, struggling to sit up, but he pushed me back, leaned over me. He kissed me again, and then his hand was between my legs, touching me lovingly, in that clever, expert way of his. 'Oh, you lovely, moist little flower,' he murmured, touching me lightly, very lightly, pushing his fingers into me as I began to moan. 'Yes, Elizabeth, yes. You love this, don't you? And you love me, don't you?'

Sudden fear rendered me speechless, and I struggled up, pushed him away with all of my strength. My instinct for survival kicked in as my head began to clear. 'Tom, we can't do this. Not here. It's too dangerous,' I whispered and reached for my dressing gown, pulled it on. 'Please, Tom, you must go. Please. For your own sake. Please. What if someone comes in?'

He grinned. 'Nobody's going to come in, Elizabeth. It's only seven in the morning,' he murmured softly. 'But I can see you are frightened. Promise me you'll meet me later. At the Ritz Hotel.' He reached into his trouser pocket, showed me a key, and crossing to the dressing table he put the key in the drawer. 'Two o'clock. Let's finally make love to each other properly. Come to the sixth floor, the room number's on the key. All right?'

The thought of being in his arms, alone together in a bed, not stealing moments like this, sent a thrill rushing through me. Yet I was also afraid of taking that step. It could mean catastrophe. As I was hovering uncertainly on the brink. I was saved the problem of answering. The door burst open and Kat Ashe was standing there.

'What on earth's going on?' she cried aghast, looking alarmed, staring at me and then at Tom. 'Admiral Selmere, why are you in Elizabeth's room at this hour of the morning?' she demanded, staring even harder at him, her eyes appraising.

'Just came to ask Elizabeth if she had some aspirins,' he said calmly, his face devoid of all expression. As he spoke, he put his hand in his trouser pocket and brought out a bottle of the pills, showed them to her. Then he gave her a dazzling smile. To me he said, 'Thank you, Elizabeth,' and strode out.

Kat came across to me and peered intently into my face. 'I don't like this, Elizabeth. He shouldn't be in your bedroom, especially when you're undressed. It's wrong. He's married to your stepmother.'

Thankful that I was wearing my dressing gown, I pulled it tighter around me. 'I know, but he only wanted the pills.'

'I understand. But it didn't look right when I came in, and his presence in your bedroom could easily be miscon-

134

strued by one of the staff. We don't want any nasty gossip, now, do we? And lock your door in future.'

'There's no lock,' I pointed out.

'Well, there will be later.' Kat announced and went out, *forgetting to tell me why she had come to my room in the first place.*

Once I was alone again I lay down on my bed and thought about my sailor . . . Gorgeous but dangerous. Should I meet him in the room he had taken at the Ritz? I didn't know what to do.

When Elizabeth returned to the library, Thomas Parrell was standing in front of the fireplace, warming himself. 'So, did you refresh your memory about the upstairs bedrooms?' he asked, smiling at her.

'I did indeed, and I must reinforce what I said earlier, Thomas. The house is a jewel, and I want to get as much as I can for it.'

'Have you decided to sell it?' Kat asked, a brow lifting.

Elizabeth nodded, unable to speak to her, still full of the long-ago memory of that morning in her bedroom when she had been a teenager.

'I think you're wise,' Kat now said, and Blanche agreed. Then Kat asked, 'Do you want me to talk to Alex Pollard about it? Maybe he can arrange a meeting for you with his wife.'

'I'd like to meet him to talk about the auction, but I'd prefer not to discuss the house yet,' Elizabeth answered, suddenly herself again. She sat down near the fire, and continued: 'Tell me a little more about the auction, and when you think it can be held.'

She was unable to sleep.

Too many thoughts were running around in her head . . . the extraordinary possessions at the Chelsea house, staggering in their beauty and worth . . . doing rapid mental arithmetic . . . the value of the other things which now belonged to her . . . the jewels, the tiaras, the silver and gold objects, the paintings and antiques at Waverley Court and Ravenscar. Everything spelled money. That was the bottom line.

Money. The bane of her life when she was a child; there had never been enough of it to provide for her needs, according to Kat and Blanche. And it was still a problem today. Because of Mary. Instinctively, Elizabeth knew that the Spanish deal would not be quite as simple as Robin had made it sound. It had gone too well too quickly. There was bound to be a catch. And the catch would be money, she felt it in her bones.

Cecil had said he would never permit her to give money to Deravenels. But in a tight squeeze, if ever there was one, she could *lend* them money, couldn't she?

Her great-grandfather Edward Deravenel had done that when he had used his own money to finance Deravco Oil in Persia. His partners had been two American wildcatters, Jarvis Merson and Herb Lipson, men he trusted and had faith in. Once they had struck their first gigantic gusher and many more, and the company had become a success, Edward had sold Deravco Oil to Deravenels. The oil company had been a boon, a marvellous addition to the trading conglomerate, and Edward had made a huge personal fortune.

Edward Deravenel had begat Bess Deravenel; Bess had begat Harry Turner, her father. And there was no question that *she* was *his* child. She looked like him, and he looked like Edward, and it was perfectly obvious that she herself was a true Deravenel through and through. She carried their genes, Turner genes as well, and so she was a mixture of both ... Funny though, how she gravitated to the Deravenel side of the family, was drawn to them ...

Now her thoughts turned to the Chelsea house, and she dwelt on it for a long time. She had surprised herself when she had said she wanted seventy million pounds for it. But the more she thought about it, the more she realized the price was not out of the realm of possibility. In fact, she might even get more. The house *was* beautiful, and she had even been tempted at one moment to keep it, but this afternoon she had truly understood that it held too many hard memories for her ... bad memories of Mary's rejection of her a year ago ... of her stepmother Catherine's rejection of her when she had sent her away ... after she had caught her in Tom's arms ... memories of him, at times too painful to bear.

How foolish she had been, flirting with him the way she had, allowing him to pet her, touch her. Thank God she had never slept with him. Still, her silly behaviour had indirectly led to his fall from grace. Reckless, charming, witty Tom, with his devastating looks and potent sexuality. And total lack of common sense. He had been his own worst enemy.

After leaving the Royal Navy as a rear admiral, the youngest in centuries, he had joined Deravenels as an adviser to the Shipping and Cruise Line Division. But he had fallen foul of his brother when Edward Selmere was the administrator; he had had no compunction in giving his younger brother the sack. Disgraced, and with Catherine dead, Tom Selmere had moved to France, where he had subsequently been killed in a car crash.

Car crash, she thought cynically. To her it had been a fishy story right from the start, and she had often wondered if Tom had been murdered. And she still did.

She would sell the Chelsea house . . . and in so doing would expunge some of the bad memories in her head. The decision was made. No going back.

FIFTEEN

Robert Dunley stood in front of the mirror in his dressing room, a distracted expression on his handsome face. His mind was on business, the business of Deravenels, and he was anxious to get to the office.

Turning away from the mirror, he reached for his suit jacket hanging on the back of a chair, slipped it on and hurried into his bedroom. Sitting down at the desk, he went through the folder of papers he had studied on the flight from Madrid last night, made a few more notes and then put them in his briefcase.

Five minutes later he was out in the street, hailing a cab. Since it was only six-thirty in the morning, he had no problems. One was drawing up immediately and within seconds he was heading through Belgravia and soon entering the Mall, on his way to the Strand and Deravenels.

As he hunched into his overcoat and settled back in the seat, his mind focused on Elizabeth and Cecil, and the business at hand. He hoped they would approve of the tentative deal he had proposed to Philip Alvarez. He and his team had spent endless hours hammering it out in his hotel suite in Madrid, and he was positive they had covered every possible angle. He began to mull everything over in his mind, looking for any problems, any objections they might have, but he couldn't find any that were serious.

The cabbie was suddenly saying, ''Ere we are, guv,' and coming to a standstill. Robert had made it in record time; he jumped out of the cab, paid, and went into Deravenels, greeting the commissionaire on duty. Then he took the grand staircase two steps at a time, anxious to get started.

The lights were turned on in his office and he could hear Elizabeth talking to Cecil through the door which opened on to hers. He dropped his briefcase on a chair, hung up his overcoat and went in, exclaiming, 'Don't tell me I'm late. Good morning, the two of you.'

'Good morning, Robert,' Cecil said, cheerful as always. 'Welcome back.'

Elizabeth leapt to her feet and came to give him a quick kiss on the cheek. 'No, you're not late,' she told him. 'We've only been here a couple of minutes ourselves.'

Robert followed her to the seating area at one end of her office, and took a chair next to Cecil. 'Ambrose and Nicholas went down to Marbella late yesterday afternoon. They wanted to take more photographs and have another look at various things at the resort. They'll be back tomorrow.'

'I know you're anxious to tell us about the meetings with Philip Alvarez, but before you do, I have a question.' Elizabeth sat back on the sofa, and gave Robert a searching look. 'Everything seems to have gone so smoothly I can't help thinking there's a catch somewhere . . . and that the catch is *money*.'

'You're absolutely right, it is,' Robert answered at once. 'Before we can take over and run the Marbella resort we do have to *finish* the resort, and that will indeed cost us money.'

'How much?' Cecil asked, leaning forward slightly in the chair, looking at Robert alertly.

'About seventy million euros.'

'Seventy million!' Elizabeth exclaimed. 'That's throwing good money after bad!'

'It's not, actually. Because we can have the resort finished, up and running by the end of 1997, and I believe it will be a huge success. Also, I see it as a short-term investment. *If* we decide to go into the project, I think we should understand at the outset that we're going to sell it within five years. We'll get our total investment out, and make a big profit. I foresee an even bigger boom in the leisure industry, and especially with resorts like this one in Marbella.'

Cecil, listening carefully, and as usual making notes, nodded. 'Tell us more abut the resort, Robert. What's so special about it? And what makes you think it will be such a resounding success?'

'First, it's on a large tract of valuable land, and it's beautiful, located right on the edge of the sea and the beach. The golf course is finished and the clubhouse is built. The polo grounds are also ready, but the polo clubhouse is not built yet. However, the small hotel is up, but, like the golf clubhouse, it needs decorating. And the villas have to be built.'

'*Villas*?' Cecil frowned, raised a brow. 'You never mentioned villas. Aren't those going to cost a lot?'

'No, because they're not really villas. To be honest, Cecil, they're bungalows, rather like those at the Beverly Hills Hotel. It's Philip who likes to give them the far grander name. Each one has a sitting room, either one or two bedrooms, plus bathrooms. The architectural design is extremely simple, and they can be built relatively quickly, in our opinion.'

'I see. And how many are planned?' Cecil asked.

'Six. But there's plenty of land available, so more of them could be built if they're needed.'

'What about a spa?' Elizabeth ventured. 'A resort always needs a spa, and they're so popular these days. Almost a necessity, in fact.'

'I agree, and the plans for one do exist, but I wasn't particularly impressed. It should be much, much larger, more deluxe. Also, a swimming pool and tennis courts ought to be included to make it an all-around sports and leisure resort of the kind I visualize.' Robert stood up, adding, 'I've got some of the photographs in my briefcase. Let me get them.'

A moment later he was back, and sat down next to Elizabeth on the sofa, showed her colour photographs of the resort, which she passed on to Cecil.

'Well, you're certainly correct about it being a lovely spot, Robin,' she said. 'The place looks fabulous. So, tell me, what went wrong? Why couldn't Philip Alvarez finish the resort?'

'To be honest, I'm not exactly sure. I think he got distracted by his other businesses, probably lost interest in the Marbella Project. Now he's in real trouble, and if he's not rescued he'll go belly up. The banks are breathing down his neck. Seriously so.'

Cecil, who had been studying the photographs, put them down on the coffee table. 'It's obviously a lovely place. But let's cut to the chase. If we do decide to go into the project, we have to put up seventy million euros to finish building it, and to get it up and running. And we also have to finance the running of it, the day-to-day operations. Correct?'

Robert nodded.

Cecil looked thoughtful.

'What have you actually proposed to Alvarez, Robin?' Elizabeth turned to Robert as she spoke. 'And where does *he* stand in the scheme of things?'

'I made the following proposal to him,' Robert answered.

'Firstly, that his investment of seventy-two million euros stays in the project, as does Deravenels seventy-five million euros, which Mary invested with him. Secondly, that he can be a member of the board of the new management company which we'll create, but that he cannot be involved in the day-to-day running of the resort, and has no say about that. He's got to leave that to us. Thirdly, that he will not see a return on his investment until we sell the resort in five years' time. *If* we decide to do that. He was in agreement with everything.'

'He has no choice,' Elizabeth announced.

Robert smiled at her pithiness. 'Never a truer word spoken.' He leaned closer to her. 'He will agree to anything we propose, more or less, because he desperately needs us, he has nowhere else to go. Also, he wants to protect his other business interests.'

Cecil said, 'When you and I spoke on the phone yesterday, you said he'd agreed to wait for our final decision until after Christmas. But let's assume we do decide to take over, when do you envision that happening, Robert?'

'We would have to go in there in the middle of January.'

'But what about those banks you indicated are breathing down his neck?' Cecil's brows drew together in a frown.

'I said we would give him a letter of intent, which he could show them. In the letter we would lay out our proposal, providing his documentation has held up to our scrutiny, *and* if the board of Deravenels agreed that we could go ahead.'

'I suppose we *do* have to go to the board?' Elizabeth threw Cecil a questioning look.

'Yes, we do, absolutely, but I don't think there will be a problem,' Cecil answered. 'On the surface, this seems like an excellent deal, and let's face it, Deravenels already has seventy-five million euros at stake. I believe the board will agree with us that we *should* be protecting our Spanish investment. Somehow.'

'But where are we going to get the seventy million euros to finish the resort?' Elizabeth asked, looking from Cecil to Robert and back to Cecil.

'We can pull some money from our hotel division, and the wine division,' Cecil told her. 'I'll talk to Broakes and Norfell about that possibility, and I'm quite certain we can borrow the rest. Our banks will go along with us on this.'

'Don't you think John Norfell ought to go to Marbella to look things over?' Elizabeth suggested.

'I do, and I was going to suggest it. It will have to be after Christmas, of course,' Robert replied.

'Is there any deadline as far as Alvarez is concerned, with the letter of intent?' Cecil gave Robert a hard stare. 'In other words, how long do we have in order to study all the documentation before issuing that letter?'

'He indicated he could hold things steady until the beginning of January. Ambrose and Nicholas will be bringing more information with them tomorrow, as well as all of the architectural plans, sketches and some more photographs.'

'Very good.' Cecil glanced at his notebook, closed it, and continued swiftly, 'I'll talk to a few of the board members privately, but frankly I don't foresee any problems, or objections, not under the circumstances. Although we would be spending a chunk of money to save the original investment, I agree that this is a short-term investment. And we ought to come out of it with excellent profits, along with the return of Mary's original investment.'

'Are you sure Philip Alvarez won't interfere, once we take over?' Elizabeth sounded worried.

'I am,' Robert assured her. 'Because he won't be able to, we'll make sure of that in the contract we draw up with

144

him. Please don't worry about *him*. I have a feeling our Spanish friend just wants to save his skin. If we relieve him of the burdens of the resort, particularly of finishing it, he will be eternally grateful.'

Elizabeth threw him a sceptical look but made no further comment.

Cecil stood up. 'Let's have another meeting at nine tomorrow morning, so that we can consult with Ambrose and Nicholas. And thanks, Robert, you've done a great job.'

'It was a team effort, Cecil.'

Left alone together, Elizabeth turned to Robert. 'I agree with Cecil, you've done a fantastic job. But I want to ask you about something else . . . about Christmas. It's almost upon us, and I was wondering if you're still coming to Waverley Court?'

'No, I'm not.'

'Oh.' Taken aback, her face changed, and she looked crestfallen, stood staring at him.

'And you can't go there either. Because we have quite a lot of work to do, to be able to bring this deal to a conclusion. You and Cecil will have to work with me for at least part of the time.'

'That's fine. But what about Christmas Day?'

'I'm going to spend it with you. In London, not the country.'

'I understand.' Her smile was one of relief.

'Shall we have lunch together later?'

Elizabeth shook her head. 'I'm afraid I can't, Robin. I promised Grace Rose I would have lunch with her and I don't want to disappoint her. But I'm free this evening.'

'Then let's have supper. I'll take you to the Caprice and you can have your favourite fishcakes and chips.'

She began to laugh. 'It's a date.'

Robert picked up the photographs, moved towards the

door. 'I've a lot of work to do, but come in if you need me for anything.'

Elizabeth nodded, then sat down at her desk. She was glad he was back, and she smiled to herself as she picked up her pen.

'Well, don't you look beautiful today,' Grace Rose said, taking hold of Elizabeth's hand, beaming at her.

'Thank you, and so do you, Grace Rose.' Elizabeth leaned closer, kissed her cheek, filled with affection for her aunt.

'Come and sit with me in the drawing room for a few minutes. Would you like a glass of sherry?'

Remembering that she had only eaten a banana for dinner last night, and had a cup of coffee for breakfast, Elizabeth quickly declined. 'I'm not a very good drinker, and certainly not at lunchtime, especially since I have to go back to work.'

'I understand.' Still holding her hand, Grace Rose led her into the drawing room and across to the fireplace. 'Let's sit here, where it's warm, and perhaps you'd be kind enough to bring *me* a glass of sherry. The decanter is over there, on the drinks table.'

'Of course.' Elizabeth walked over to the table near the window and poured a glass of the pale Amontillado she knew Grace Rose preferred, then decided to pour one for herself. A small glass of sherry was hardly going to make her drunk.

Carrying them back to fireside, she said, 'I'm having one, too, Grace Rose. I might as well be a grown-up today.'

Grace Rose laughed, and took the small glass. 'It's not much more than a thimbleful, you know. Happy Christmas, my dear.'

'Happy Christmas.'

'I was so relieved when you told me none of Jane Shaw's

paintings had gone missing. But where are they exactly?'

'Just as I thought, there are a number at the Chelsea house and some at Waverley Court. However, most of them are at Ravenscar. Kat has visited all three houses again, and every single painting is accounted for. She also made a detailed list. Here's a copy for you.' Placing the sherry glass on the side table, Elizabeth reached into her large red Hermès Birkin, took out an envelope, and gave it to Grace Rose.

'There's a wonderful Sisley hanging in the red dining room at the Chelsea house,' Elizabeth said. 'And it struck me when I was there yesterday that you'd probably decorated the room. It's *full* of your signature red.'

Grace Rose nodded. 'I did decorate it, but quite a while ago now, you know.'

'It's held up well and still looks beautiful.'

'If I'm not mistaken, the Alfred Sisley in the dining room is called *The Bridge at Moret*, isn't it?'

'It is, yes, and there are a couple of other Sisleys at Ravenscar. Also a Rouault, two by Matisse, and two Monets. Both of those paintings are of small boats on rivers.'

'Jane Shaw had a wonderful eye. It's a very valuable collection, Elizabeth.'

'I realize that.' Elizabeth took a deep breath, plunged. 'I'm thinking of selling some of the paintings. You don't object, do you?'

If she was surprised by this question, Grace Rose did not show it. 'They are yours now, you can do what you want with them. I was only concerned that . . . well, that none had been stolen. Out of curiosity, why do you want to sell some of them? Do you need money?'

'Not desperately, no, but I certainly don't want this large art collection, or the responsibility of owning it. And I'm planning to auction off a lot of other things, so I decided it would be a good idea to include some of the paintings.'

'Not the Renoir?' Grace Rose stared at her intently.

'*Not the Renoir*. That will never be sold. However, Kat has discovered a treasure trove in the cellar vaults at the Chelsea house. It's stuff I don't need, or want, so we dreamed up the idea of having an auction. I want to call it *The Deravenel–Turner Collections*, and it would be held next year, hopefully handled by Sotheby's.'

'But what did Kat find in the vaults?' Grace Rose sounded mystified.

Elizabeth told her, 'And there is a selection of other price-less things from Cartier jewels and twenty-two diamond tiaras, to eighteenth- and ninteenth-century silver and gold plate by master craftsmen.'

Grace Rose seemed astonished, looked off into the distance for a moment. 'I think some of those things were collected by my father,' she finally said. 'But a lot of it must have been passed down from Neville and Nan Watkins to Richard and Anne Deravenel, and then to your grandmother. You know, as I think about those things, they must date back even further, several hundred years, in fact. Because Neville's father Rick was England's greatest magnate in his day, and was renowned as a collector of valuable silver, artifacts, all kinds of objects, and art.'

At this moment, the housekeeper Louisa came in and told Grace Rose that lunch was ready to be served.

Sixteen

My God, she's fantastic, Elizabeth thought, as she followed Grace Rose across the foyer. I hope I'm like her when I'm an old lady. No sign of osteoporosis or a widow's hump here. Her aunt was tall, erect, and well dressed. She's also got all *her* marbles, and all her ducks in a row, Elizabeth decided, filled with admiration for the ninety-six-year old.

Once they were seated at the table in a handsomely furnished dining room, decorated in a mélange of fir-green and white, Grace Rose picked up their interrupted conversation.

'I'm delighted you're having this auction, Elizabeth. It's very enterprising of you indeed. It's rather silly to hoard unwanted things, useless really, in my opinion. Everything should fetch a good price, and most especially the art.'

At this moment Louisa appeared, served them plates of smoked salmon with thin slices of brown bread and butter, and lemon wedges. To Grace Rose, Louisa said, 'Shall I serve white wine, Mrs Morran?'

'I don't think so, Louisa,' Grace Rose responded, glanced at Elizabeth, raised a brow questioningly.

'Not for me, thank you,' Elizabeth answered, smiling at the housekeeper.

They ate in silence for a moment or two, and then Grace Rose put her knife and fork down, said in a low, confidential voice, 'I hate to pry, and I'm only doing it now because I'm concerned about you. Are your finances in order? Adequate?'

'I'm fine, thank you, Grace Rose. Honestly. As you know, I have a trust from my father and my salary from Deravenels, and I manage quite well. I must say, though, I'm glad *your father* had such a clear vision of the future.'

'What do you mean?' Grace Rose sounded puzzled.

'Edward Deravenel was extremely smart when he created the Ravenscar Trust Fund many years ago. It's for the running of Ravenscar. The money has been well invested over the years and the interest pays for the upkeep of the house, grounds, any repairs, and also the staff wages. I don't know what I'd do if he hadn't had the foresight to create that fund. I would have to close most of the house and live in three rooms, or rent it out, because I can't afford to run it. And I certainly can't sell it.'

'I know, it's entailed.' Grace Rose sighed. 'Naturally, Mary's responsible for your finances being tight, isn't she?'

Elizabeth pursed her lips and nodded, took a sip of water, and wanting to reassure her, said, 'I'm all right financially, I promise.'

Noticing that Elizabeth looked somewhat uncomfortable, Grace Rose changed the subject. 'You spoke of Cartier jewellery earlier. Was that all from the vault at the Chelsea house?'

'A lot of it was, yes. But I also received some fabulous pieces from Mary before she died.'

'Was there a set of aquamarine-and-diamond pieces? A ring, a bracelet, and a pair of earrings? If so, they belonged to your grandmother, her uncle gave them to her.'

Elizabeth's face lit up. 'There is a set exactly like that. Oh, I shan't sell those.'

'I don't think you should. Bess loved that set and always wore it on special occasions.'

'She was very close to her uncle, wasn't she?'

'Very, and she always defended him, but then I did, too. We never thought he had anything to do with the disappearance of the boys.'

Startled by this unexpected statement, Elizabeth stared at her aunt. 'Did some people think that he did?'

Grace Rose simply nodded, her mouth tightening almost imperceptibly.

'How awful.' Elizabeth fell silent as Louisa returned and removed the plates. Once they were alone again, she leaned closer to Grace Rose. 'But what *could* have happened to your little brothers? The story I heard from my father was so strange, the way they disappeared from the beach at Ravenscar, never to be found again.'

'It was indeed, and we were all baffled, the police included. Bess and I had our own theories, of course.'

'And what were they?' Elizabeth asked eagerly.

Grace Rose was silent, looking reflective, lost in her thoughts. She said at last, 'We began to think that they had been taken away so that they couldn't inherit Deravenels. Bess and I toyed with the idea that someone wanted the company for themselves. By removing the boys there were no longer any male heirs to inherit.'

'My grandmother was the heiress, though!'

'Yes, she was, and neither of us was stupid, you know. We both understood that whoever married her would be all set to run the company. Because she would have never been accepted at Deravenels as managing director, even though our father had had the rules changed to allow Deravenel women to inherit the top job. It's always been a male chauvinistic place, as you're well aware.'

'So some people tried to put the blame on Richard?'

'Yes. But why would he do it? He loved those boys, and was running the company anyway. He had all the power, money and privilege, and would run it for a good ten to fifteen years, until the boys grew up. That theory didn't make sense to us at all.'

'Did you think that Henry Turner was responsible?' Elizabeth ventured cautiously, her eyes on her aunt.

'No, we didn't, and especially when we got to know him better. Anyway, Bess would never have married him if she had thought he was responsible for her brothers' disappearance. However, we both thought that someone working behind the scenes, someone with their own interests at stake, a hidden agenda perhaps, would be well served if the sons of Edward Deravenel vanished.'

'But who?' Elizabeth probed.

'We were never really sure who it could be. It *was* a mystery. Then Bess and I began to focus on a man called Jack Buckley. He was a Deravenel cousin, but with strong ties to the Grant side of the family, and, actually, he sort of straddled the fence, since he was married to Bess's aunt Katharine, her mother's sister. We thought he had a foot in all camps, and he was certainly a bit power-hungry, to say the least.'

'Did he benefit when Henry Turner took over Deravenels?'

'Not a lot, no. He died rather suddenly a year later of a heart attack,' Grace Rose told her.

'What about Richard's murder? Could this man Jack Buckley have killed him?'

'To be truthful, Elizabeth, that's another possibility your grandmother and I discussed. Still, there was nothing *we* could do. We didn't have a shred of evidence about anything, and remember, we were just a couple of young women of no importance . . . we knew no one would listen to *us*. And anyway, there was no one we felt we could talk to, you know. No one we really trusted.'

Grace Rose glanced at the door when it opened. Louisa came in pushing a trolley, and from it she served small lamb chops with mixed vegetables and then offered gravy and mint sauce.

'Thank you, Louisa, this looks delicious,' Grace Rose murmured. 'And please leave the mint sauce, will you? You know how I love to slather it on everything.'

'Oh, so do I!' Elizabeth exclaimed, smiling at her aunt, and picked up her knife and fork. She had enjoyed the smoked salmon, and now cut into the lamb chop, realizing how ravenously hungry she had been when she arrived here. A banana and a glass of milk wasn't much of a dinner every night, she decided, vowing to change her bad eating habits.

'You don't mind talking about the past, do you, Grace Rose?' Elizabeth looked at her aunt quizzically, her expression affectionate. She was truly fond of her, and did not wish to cause her discomfort.

Grace Rose smiled. 'No, of course I don't. Actually, the past seems much clearer to me than the present, if you want the truth. I can easily recall things that happened over forty years ago but not yesterday.' She chuckled. 'Perhaps that's because the past is more important to me, more interesting than my life is today. Mind you, I'm happy to be alive and kicking, Elizabeth. I don't want to go yet, you know. I've still too much damage to do.'

Elizabeth joined in her laughter, then said, 'So I don't suppose you'd mind talking about your sisters. I've often wondered what happened to the younger Deravenel daughters.'

'Didn't Harry ever speak about his aunts?'

'No, and when I asked him he just pushed my questions aside.'

'I don't think your father was particularly interested in them. Well, let me see . . . Bridget, the youngest, became a nun, and she was very contented in her vocation. Cecily married an older man, and wasn't happy at all. She remarried after his death.' Grace Rose's faded blue eyes twinkled as she added, 'He was good looking, charming, a toy boy, as they say today. She moved away, and I suppose lived happy ever after. Anne and Katherine also married nice ordinary men, and went to live in the country. We kept in touch with Christmas cards, but lived entirely different lives, and eventually we began to drift away, especially after Bess' death. She was the one who had tried to hold us all together.'

'Was *she* happy, do you think? My grandmother?'

'*Happy*? Such a complex word. Was Bess happy? Hard question to answer. Let me put it this way, she wasn't unhappy.' Once again Grace Rose stared off into the distance, as if staring back into the past, seeing things, seeing people she loved who were long gone.

Watching her closely, Elizabeth realized she looked suddenly sad, bereft, and a shadow touched her aunt's face. Reaching out, putting a hand on her aunt's arm, she asked in concern, 'Are you all right?'

Grace Rose nodded. 'Oh, yes, I'm fine, my dear. Now, to answer you. I don't think your grandmother had an ecstatic marriage. You see, Henry Turner was a little dull; plodding, I suppose is the best way to describe him. What I do know is that he did love Bess, he treated her kindly, was absolutely faithful. I always felt she was disappointed that he did not allow her to become involved with Deravenels in any way. She loved the company, and it was hers, and she was so bright, such a smart woman, she could have been a great help to him. To be truthful, there were other disappointments, too. She had seven children but only four lived, and then Arthur, the eldest, died when he was about fifteen. Such a shock. She was grief-stricken, everyone was. That's when she focused all of her attention on your father, spoiled him. Mind you, Harry had always been very close to her. I believe she saw Edward Deravenel in him.'

'Yes, I know, she often compared him to his grandfather. He told me that when his mother died he felt so lost without her. I'm not sure that he really *liked* his father.'

'I'm not either. However, they got on all right. Poor Bess, she was too young to die, far too young at thirty-seven. I was devastated when I lost her, she had been my best friend for most of my life.'

Elizabeth's eyes had not left Grace Rose's lined, old face, and whilst her voice had been steady, even strong, her rheumy eyes had suddenly filled with tears. Again reaching out, touching her arm, Elizabeth apologized. 'I'm sorry. Don't cry. I didn't mean to upset you, asking you about the past. Sorry, so very sorry, Grace Rose.'

Forcing a smile, the old woman exclaimed, 'I'm all right, really! I love my memories . . . what would an old lady do without her memories of the past? But come, Elizabeth, let's talk about the present. What's been happening at Deravenels?'

'Well, I think we've solved the problem about Mary's rash investment with Philip Alvarez.'

'Oh, do tell me everything.'

And Elizabeth did.

That evening Elizabeth had the sudden urge to look at some of the old photograph albums her father had given her. 'You'll be more interested in these than either Edward or Mary,' he had said, offering her one of his sly grins. 'Mary's not interested in my English past, only her mother's Spanish ancestors. As for Edward, he's mostly concerned with his studies. Mind you, that's most commendable.'

And so the stack of albums had become hers. Turning the pages of one of them, she concentrated on a series of snaps taken at Ravenscar in the 1920s. My God, there was Grace Rose, with whom she'd lunched that day. Grace Rose, a young woman, and with her was Bess Deravenel, her grandmother. But who was the man standing between them? Peering at the spidery writing on the picture she realized it was the famous – infamous? – Richard Deravenel. She studied it for a moment, then put the album down, settled herself more comfortably on the sofa.

Richard Deravenel. Good man maligned? Or kidnapper and murderer? Which had he been? She could not judge the man; still, Grace Rose had told her today that she and her grandmother had believed in his innocence. 'But you see, he had his enemies,' Grace Rose had said. 'And he was murdered by them.'

But the entire family had enemies, Elizabeth now thought, Deravenels and Turners alike. Did their fame and wealth and prestige engender such jealousy and hatred in some? She knew the answer to that question.

Do I have *my* enemies? More than likely. And who are they? She shivered and pulled her sweater around her shoulders. As yet I don't know, but I'll soon find out. They'll give themselves away. Elizabeth shivered again. She must be on her guard.

PART TWO

Love Won't Wait

'My true love hath my heart and I have his,
By just exchange one for the other given.
I hold his dear, and mine he cannot miss,
There never was a better bargain driven.'
Sir Philip Sidney

'How do I love thee? Let me count the ways.
I love thee to the depth and breadth and height
My soul can reach, when feeling out of sight
For the ends of Being and ideal Grace.
I love thee to the level of every day's
Most quiet need, by sun and candlelight.'
Elizabeth Barrett Browning

SEVENTEEN

'I think these might have been dungeons once.' Robert glanced at Elizabeth, and shone the flashlight around the large cellar at the bottom of the flight of stone steps in the basement at Ravenscar.

'You could be right,' she answered, feeling for the switch on the wall, flipping it down. Instantly the enormous cellar was flooded with bright light. 'I've often thought that myself, because deeper inside the basement there are several vaults with heavy metal doors that have small windows to look inside. But my father never told me they were dungeons, and he was always giving me interesting snippets about Ravenscar.'

'I'd hate to be incarcerated down here,' Robert announced. 'It's as cold as hell, and I'm certainly glad you told me to wear a heavy sweater *and* my Barbour. It's bloody icy, actually.'

'I know, but we'll only be ten minutes or so. Come on, my lad, let's get cracking. The really big cellar, known as vault number ten, is straight ahead.'

'Ten as in the *best*?' He raised a brow, grinning.

She laughed. 'Probably. I know there's a lot of jewellery in leather boxes from Cartier, Boucheron, Mauboussin, Garrard, Asprey, Harry Winston, Tiffany, you name it. There're French Aubusson carpets and tapestries, and naturally loads of silver and gold plate. Kat was astonished and so were Blanche and Thomas Parrell who came to help her look at everything and do inventories. They all agree the stuff should go to auction, and I'm sure they're right. Kat's done a good job, actually.'

'Mrs Efficiency, that's our Kat, and I'm pleased she's taking care of this, because you certainly don't have time.'

'True. Here's the vault.' Elizabeth came to a standstill in the main corridor and handed him a big iron key. 'You open it, Robin, Kat told me the lock's a bit stiff.'

'It probably needs a spot of oil.' Taking the key from her, Robert struggled with the lock for a few moments, finally turned the key, then twisted the iron handle on the door. It creaked open as he pushed his shoulder against it.

Stepping inside, he flipped the light switch, and even though the bulb in the ceiling was dim they could see that the vault was enormous. 'Good God, this looks like the Bank of England! Do you have more keys for these other doors in here?'

'Yes.' She handed him a ring of keys, each one numbered. As they went around opening the doors, they discovered rooms lined with shelves on which were stacked every kind of valuable.

Elizabeth beckoned to Robert when she spotted the layers of jewellery boxes piled high in one of the rooms. 'I can't believe all this. My God, such indulgence!' She took half a dozen boxes off a shelf and carried them out of the room, explaining to Robert, 'Kat wants me to look at every piece of jewellery, and make decisions about its fate. I think it's a good idea to take everything to the dining room, don't you? We'll sort it out there.'

'We can't start looking at it here, that's for sure. First of all the lights are dim, and it's also far too cold. We're both going to catch pneumonia if we linger.'

'Come on then, start moving it out of the vault. We'll put it at the bottom of the stone staircase, lock up down here, and retreat to the warmth of the dining room.'

'And we'll ask Lucas to make some tea or soup.' Robert followed her into the smaller vault, filled his arms with jewellery boxes, and added, 'We're going to need a hot drink.'

Elizabeth said, 'Lucas and Marta drove into Scarborough to do some shopping, but I can make the tea.'

'Oh, don't worry about that now, let's just keep moving the boxes, and get upstairs.'

Despite their speed, it took them another half hour to take the leather boxes of every size and shape to the stone stairs.

Even Robert Dunley, who was rarely surprised at anything, was astounded at the number of jewel cases they had retrieved. Once they had moved everything out and he had locked the inner doors, and the door of vault ten, he said, 'I think the quickest way to get this stuff upstairs is to put them into large dustbin bags, and if there aren't enough we can use pillowcases.'

'Very clever, Robin! Go to the top of the class.'

Elizabeth sat on the loveseat in the library as close to the roaring fire as possible. She was shivering, felt as if the freezing cold climate in the basement had penetrated her bones, turned her into a block of ice.

After stacking the fire with plenty of extra logs and turning up the central heating, Robert had disappeared. Now, as she sat hunched over, literally trying to breathe in the heat from the flames, she heard his step, swiftly turned her head.

He came into the room carrying a shot glass in each hand. 'I know you don't like booze, but I want you to drink this.' Coming to a standstill next to her, he handed her the glass.

She stared at it and then at him. 'What is it?'

'Calvados.'

'Why do you have brandy in a shot glass?'

'Don't ask questions, just drink it down like this.' He brought the shot glass to his mouth and tossed the brandy back. He looked startled as he put the glass on the coffee table. 'God, that took my breath away! Lethal stuff it is, but it does the trick. Drink it quickly, it's the only way to go.'

She nodded and did as he said, then shuddered and reared back slightly. 'Blimey, it *is* lethal.'

'It'll warm the cockles of your heart.'

She smiled at him, shaking her head, laughter dancing in her eyes.

'What is it?' He gave her a long, penetrating stare.

'You used to say exactly that when Kat forced me to drink her vegetable soup and I balked.'

'I must've been a very wise little boy.'

'Old-fashioned in a way,' she murmured and gazed into the fire. 'And you always said it as if you believed it.'

'I did, and I do. Calvados will warm you right through to your rib cage.' He noticed then that she was still shivering and he went and sat down next to her on the loveseat. Putting his arms around her, he pulled her close to him. 'What you need is a little of my body heat.' With one hand he rubbed her arm, then drew her closer and held her even tighter, wrapping both his arms around her. 'You'll be fine in a minute or two, you'll see. Scientists have proved that one of the best cures for hypothermia in a person is someone else's body heat.'

Especially yours, Elizabeth thought, discovering how much she enjoyed being in his arms. He was tall and strong and robust, in glowing health, and she felt his vitality and energy flowing into her. She sneaked a surreptitious look at him, then closed her eyes, leaned against his broad chest . . . remembering . . . remembering her sailor man. How like him Robin was, with his dark hair and soulful eyes, although Robin's were darker in hue. But his height, his build were the same, and he had the same long legs and athletic body as Tom Selmere. But then this sort of man was her type, wasn't it? She was always attracted to men like Robert Dunley . . . her Robin, her lovely, loving Robin . . . her best friend . . . her family . . . the man she loved . . . oh, my God . . .

Elizabeth held herself very still, hardly daring to breathe. *The man she loved.* Why had she thought that, so suddenly . . . out of the blue? No, not out of the blue at all. She had loved him for a long time, she had just never admitted it to herself. Suddenly she was feeling unexpectedly breathless, excited, filled with longing for him. I want him . . . I want him to be mine . . . he *is* mine, isn't he? No, he's not . . . he will be. He must be . . . he belongs to me, doesn't he? It was then she thought of his wife . . . the wife he never spoke of . . . seemingly hardly ever saw . . . the wife *she* had long ago decided to forget . . . and she had succeeded in forgetting her . . .

Amy . . . the young girl he had married eight or nine years ago, in the first flush of his youthful masculinity . . . the wife he must surely have outgrown . . . she knew he had outgrown her . . .

'Are you all right?' Robert asked, drawing away from her, looking down, then lifting her face with his hand so that he could see her expression better.

'I'm perfect,' she answered in a small voice. 'Why?'

'You suddenly went quite still, very quiet.'

163

'I was just . . . relaxing, and feeling warmer.' Hot and bothered and sexually aroused was more like it, she thought, and
she struggled to extricate herself from him, jumped up, startling him in the process. 'Lucas left lunch for us. I'd better
go and warm it!' Her voice was unusually brisk, and she
swung away from the fireplace, almost ran out of the library.

For a moment Robert was nonplussed by her sudden and
hasty departure. He wanted to chase after her but he needed
a moment to settle himself. He had an erection, and inside
he was shaking, felt suddenly totally undone. He had wanted
her for a long time now, since he had started to visit Ravenscar
almost a year ago, plotting and planning with her and Cecil,
preparing for the future of Deravenels, waiting for Mary to
die. All these months he had managed to keep a tight control
over himself, never placed himself in a position where he
might be tempted to . . . seduce her, make love to her, take
possession of her as he had yearned to do. How long he had
loved her, almost all of his life, since he had been an adoring
little boy in short trousers.

She had looked so white a while ago, had been chilled to
the bone, and in his attempts to make her feel better he had
managed to get himself sexually aroused. You poor fool you,
he thought, mentally castigating himself.

The one thing about Harry Turner that Elizabeth had always
admired was that when he started a project he usually finished
it in record time, and to perfection.

She thought about her father as she whizzed around the
kitchen preparing lunch. When she was eleven and back in
Harry's good graces, she had told him that the kitchen here
at Ravenscar was not only old-fashioned but that it didn't
work efficiently any more.

To her delight, and that of the staff, he had agreed, and had gone to great expense to remodel it, with her help. Once the old equipment had been torn out and thrown away, a spinach-green granite floor and matching counter tops had been put in, the walls had been painted a luscious peach and the cabinets and doors a pristine white. Then had come all of the new appliances she had helped him choose, including two large modern steel-fronted refrigerators, a wine cooler, a microwave oven, and joy of joys, an Aga. Every woman loved this stored-heat stove and cooker, and Elizabeth had insisted it be included in the plan. The Aga was never off, so that the kitchen was permanently warm day and night, and there were large hotplates and generous ovens for cooking combined in the one unit.

Since Harry had consulted her on everything to do with the remodelling, Elizabeth had suggested a granite-topped island in the middle of the floor instead of the old worn deal table. She had also insisted on a seating area for meals.

She herself had picked the perfect spot, near the Aga for warmth, but not so close that it was too hot. Now she went over to the eat-in corner, put placemats, knives, forks and napkins on the table, and added glasses.

Last year, when she had been living at Ravenscar permanently, she had found herself with time on her hands, especially at weekends. And so she had taken herself off to a cooking school in Harrogate. Whilst she didn't *love* cooking, she enjoyed making certain dishes, and she would have been happy to prepare lunch today. But Lucas had insisted on making it, and had.

He had put the food in Pyrex dishes and placed these on the island counter top, and all she had to do was put the cottage pie, peas and gravy in the microwave just before she was ready to serve lunch. After taking the plates of potted shrimps over to the circular table, she poured the water, and then went to make the toast for the shrimps.

She stood at the toaster and wondered what Robert was doing, and was startled a second later when he said, 'I'm rather hungry.'

Elizabeth swung around. He was leaning against the door frame smiling at her, looking nonchalant and impossibly handsome in his cream-coloured fisherman's sweater and blue jeans. 'So what's for lunch as well as the delicious-looking potted shrimps?'

She told him, and said in a brisk voice, 'Why don't you sit down, I'll join you in a minute.'

He did, took a few sips of the water, wondering why she sounded tense. Finally, he spoke. 'I've been looking in a few of the jewellery boxes, Elizabeth, and there are some really major pieces. I came across something rather unique, very rare, I think. It must be worth a fortune because of its provenance.'

'What is it?'

'When you sit down I'll tell you. Do you need my help?'

'No, thanks, everything's in hand.' Hurrying over to the table she put the plate of toast in the middle, went to the fridge, took out the covered butter dish and sat down next to him at last.

After taking a piece of toast and buttering it, Robert said, 'Let me just taste the potted shrimps, you know they're my favourite, and then I'll describe the piece of jewellery.'

She nodded, also buttered her toast, dipped the fork into the brown pot of shrimps encased in hardened butter and tried them, announcing, 'They're delicious, Robin. Do you want some lemon?'

'No, thanks.' After a few more mouthfuls of the Morecambe Bay potted shrimps, he sat back and put down his fork. 'It's a necklace made of old diamonds, very old actually, and it's extraordinary. A truly important piece, even I knew that at once. There was an envelope in the case, and I recognized Kat's handwriting. She had written on the front *Eugénie*, and that's all. Inside a larger envelope were several important things. A longish note about the provenance, in a spidery sort of old-fashioned handwriting, a small card which said the necklace had belonged to Elizabeth Wyland Deravenel, that it had been given to her by Edward, her husband. Anyway, this is the thing, the necklace was *made* for the Empress Eugénie of France. The crown jewels of France were sold at an auction called the Diamonds of the Crown of France. This was in 1887. A lot of the diamond jewellery was bought by the renowned jeweller Boucheron, and this necklace was amongst the pieces.'

'How amazing! And also how wonderful, too.' Elizabeth sounded excited. 'It's going to bring a huge amount at my auction, don't you think?'

'I do. There's nothing else quite like this amongst the other stuff I've seen so far, but it's all really beautiful, and it could be priceless. After lunch, we'll look at it, and then take it back to the vault. I'm only making a guess, Elizabeth, but I think you've got about five or six million pounds' worth of jewellery on your dining-room table at this moment. Maybe even eight million.'

Elizabeth was stunned, and she gaped at him. 'It can't be!' she gasped.

'Yes, it can be. Furthermore, we brought up around sixty-five boxes, but we left quite a lot behind. Maybe another fifty, at least.' He laughed when he saw how flushed she had become. 'And what are you going to do with this vast amount of money you'll make at your famous auction?'

'I'm going to buy up as many Deravenel shares as I can.'

This answer took him aback, and he frowned at her, puzzled. 'Are there any Deravenel shares available? We're a private company, after all, and we're not trading on the stock exchange. Or are you secretly planning to make a public offering?'

'No, of course not! If I were, you'd be the first to know, since I tell you everything. But there are quite a few directors who own shares, some of the older men, and I want those shares. Those men will be retiring from the board soon, and if I pay enough I'll get them, you'll see.'

'You want more control of the company . . .' He let his voice trail off.

'I do. But I won't use all the money for shares. I intend to keep a lot of cash in reserve, in case Deravenels needs it at some point.'

He nodded, not trusting himself to speak. He had always known she loved Deravenels, was dedicated to it in the way Harry Turner had been. Like father like daughter, he thought. Still, he had never quite realized just how much the company actually dominated her life and her actions.

'Oh, God! I've forgotten to put the cottage pie in the microwave,' Elizabeth exclaimed, rising at once, going to the island, and placing the pie in the oven. 'The rest of lunch is coming up in a minute,' she said over her shoulder. 'I just need to heat the peas and the gravy.'

'Take your time.' Robert asked himself if he could compete with this total and absolute devotion to the company. Seemingly, it was the most important thing in her life, wasn't it? Hey, hold on, old chap, he warned himself. What makes you think she would even be interested in you? You're her childhood chum, you twerp. When she finally looks around for a man of her own, it will be in fresher, greener fields.

Robert pulled on his Barbour and went down the Long Hall heading towards the double doors that led to the garden.

Once outside he walked along the terrace, looking for Elizabeth, and instantly spotted her on the battlements of the ruined stronghold at the edge of the cliffs.

He shivered as he took the paved path through the tiered gardens, asking himself why she was outside on this bitter March day. Good Friday it might be, but it was like the depth of winter on this northern coastline. He glanced up. The late afternoon sky was changing, darkening to deep blue, and the sun was setting; he had to admit it was turning into a beautiful night. There were no clouds and later, he felt sure, there would be a full moon.

'What on earth are you doing down here?' he asked her as he joined her in the circular enclosure which had been a watch tower centuries ago. Soldiers had stood here once, guarding Ravenscar, waiting to repel invaders sailing across the North Sea, heading for this rich and fertile land.

Elizabeth swung around on hearing his voice, and grinned. 'I needed a breath of fresh air after being cooped up in the basement, putting all that bloody jewellery away, but I'm afraid it is a bit chilly.'

'I'll say it is! You'd better come in, anyway, it's suddenly getting dark.'

'The gloaming. I've always loved that name for twilight.' Turning, she gazed out across the parapet. 'It's so beautiful out here on a night like this.' But as she spoke a blast of wind hit her and she moved closer to him. Robert put an arm around her, began to steer her towards the garden; for a moment she allowed herself to be led. All of a sudden she exclaimed, 'Race you inside!' and took off, bolting like a frightened deer.

Running after her, he caught up with her on the terrace, followed her into the Long Hall. She was struggling out of her quilted coat, unwinding the woollen scarf wrapped around her neck. He followed suit, threw off his Barbour, asked, 'What was all that about?'

169

She stared at him, said nothing.

At once he saw how white she was, whiter than ever, and she was trembling. He suddenly noticed there were tears in her eyes and glistening on her lashes.

'Is something the matter?' he asked in concern.

She shook her head.

He took a step towards her; she immediately stepped back. His eyes held hers. Neither of them could look away.

Robert felt his chest tighten and his throat closed with a rush of emotion when he recognized the expression on her face. It mirrored exactly what he himself was feeling. Desire . . . total and absolute desire.

'Elizabeth.' He said her name in a voice that shook, was almost inaudible. 'Darling . . .'

'Oh, Robin, oh, Robin.'

They moved at the same time, went into each other's arms. Bending his face to hers, he found her mouth, kissed her deeply, passionately, without restraint. So lost in each other were they, so oblivious to their surroundings, they did not notice Lucas carry a basket of logs into the library.

Eventually, against her hair, he said, 'Can we go to your bedroom?'

'As fast as possible.'

EIGHTEEN

Together they went upstairs hand in hand and walked down the corridor to her bedroom. She always kept the heating on high, and when they went inside they were immediately enveloped in warmth.

Robert smiled at her. 'Thank God it's not cold.' There was a fire burning in the hearth and he went over to it, threw on several more logs, and poked them around. 'There, that should do it. There'll be a blazing fire in no time at all.'

Elizabeth locked the door, walked over to him, took his hand in hers and drew him down onto the large sofa in front of the fire.

Looking deeply into his eyes, searching his face, she said, after a moment, 'I think we both had a revelation a few minutes ago . . . I suddenly knew I couldn't hide my feelings any longer . . . couldn't hide how much I love you, Robin.'

'I felt the same, Elizabeth. I've known for the last year just how much I cared, but I've kept it from you. How stupid we human beings are at times.' He bent forward, took her face between his hands and kissed her gently on the mouth. 'I love you very much . . . I've always loved you, and I always will.'

She moved closer to him, touched his face, that face she knew so well. It was beautiful, well defined, clean cut; he had high cheekbones, a smooth broad forehead, and the most soulful eyes she had ever seen. There was no question he was the most handsome of men. She liked the length of him, his long legs, athletic body, and broad chest. She leaned against him, and his arms went around her.

'Oh, Robin, my darling, darling Robin . . . I want you so much.'

'I know. It's the same for me.' He kissed her gently, and then more deeply, and soon their kisses were passionate, without restraint, their desire for each other flaring.

Robert said, 'Let's find that bed,' and pulled her up off the sofa. He led her across the room to the fourposter, struggled out of his sweater, and then helped her off with hers. Within seconds they were naked under the covers, wrapped in each other's arms, truly close at last.

'It's lovely in the firelight,' Elizabeth whispered. 'Don't put any lights on.'

'I won't.' Robert pushed himself up on one elbow and looked down into her grey-black eyes. 'I've dreamed about being with you like this for the longest time . . . all this past year, in fact.'

'Oh, Robin, darling, if only I'd known. We've wasted time.'

He smiled against her hair. 'We've been wasting time for donkey's years. Since we were eight, actually.'

'Haven't we been silly.'

'Utterly dumb.' There was a moment's hesitation on Robert's part before he asked in a low voice. 'You do want this, don't you?'

'It's a bit late to ask, isn't it? And can't you tell?' Not waiting for an answer, she added, 'I've never wanted anything more.'

'Neither have I . . . and the only reason I asked is because there's no going back as far as I'm concerned . . . if we make love now then it's total commitment on my part . . .'

'And mine.'

They turned to face each other, staring into each other's eyes. Robert felt as though he was looking into her soul, and his heart shifted in him. At that precise moment he understood that he was wholly her creature. He belonged to her and he always would no matter what happened to him. He was Elizabeth Turner's man for life. And he knew, without her saying a word, that she was his woman. No other man would ever have her. Because she would never want another man. Only him.

They settled against each other, and he let one hand roam over her breasts and down onto her stomach until it came to rest between her legs. Robert felt her instantly stiffen, and he raised his head, his brow lifting questioningly.

'Yes,' she said. 'Oh, yes, Robin.'

As he touched her tenderly, his fingers moving expertly, he realized he was growing even more excited. He had an enormous erection, and he stopped suddenly, wanting to prolong their lovemaking, wanting to savour everything.

Startled, Elizabeth said, 'What is it? Why did you stop?'

'Because I don't want to rush this . . . our first time together. I want to enjoy every part of you, of us being together like this. I've waited too long to have it over in a few minutes.'

Shifting slightly, Elizabeth moved closer to him, felt his hardness against her leg, and an involuntary shiver ran through her, followed by a rush of heat that spread up through her stomach. She ached for him, her desire rampant now; she couldn't wait for him to make love to her. This thought had hardly entered her head when he bent over her, kissed her breasts, then slid his hand down to the throbbing core of her.

She opened her eyes and looked at him. His face was so close to hers, intent, rapt, and her heart leapt . . . oh, how much she loved him. He began to touch her again, his fingers fluttering against her. 'Oh, yes, Robin, oh yes, don't stop,' she whispered.

He was silent. Pulling the covers aside, he moved down the bed, bringing his mouth to join his fingers, wishing to give her the pleasure he knew she craved, just as he craved her mouth on him. Suddenly Elizabeth began to spasm, and he was no longer able to curb his own desire; he moved up the bed, lay on top of her. His arms went around her, his mouth fastened on hers, and he entered her quickly, was immediately enveloped in the warmth of her.

Elizabeth sighed, wrapped her long legs around his back, and took on his rhythm, moving with him. He came when she did, his face pressed against her neck, her name on his lips.

Neither of them stirred. They lay together entwined, reluctant to separate from each other.

Elizabeth had never known such contentment, such satisfaction with any man, not with Selmere or Murrey, the other one who had pursued her . . .

She let herself drift with her thoughts, enjoying the sound of Robin's steady breathing, the lovely, familiar smell of him. It was a mingling of shampoo, soap and cleanliness, mixed with the lemony tang of his cologne which also held a hint of green . . . of meadows and trees. This was bliss, the kind of bliss she had never known before.

He's gone now, back to his own room, to shower and shave and get ready for supper. He was reluctant to go, and I was reluctant to let him leave. I can't bear for him to be out of my sight. He is so good-looking, but then he always was even as a little boy, and he's so good. There's a true purity to Robin Dunley, and I won't let anyone say otherwise. And there will be talk, there's bound to be. People will envy him, envy me, envy us. And they'll have good reason to be envious. He and I have something few people ever have – total under-standing of each other, of our needs and desires. It is not only a meeting of the minds, but of our bodies as well. We are sexually perfect together.

A moment ago, just before he left, he kissed me deep and hard, and said, 'We've just sealed a bargain, you and I, and don't ever forget it. There's no going back now.' How could I forget it. I am his and he is mine. We are as one. Forever.

An hour later when Elizabeth walked into the library she stopped in the doorway, her heart missing a beat. There he was, her Robin, standing with his back to the fire, waiting for her and looking impossibly handsome. He wore a red turtleneck sweater and well-fitting blue jeans, and he was immaculate from head to toe, right down to his highly polished loafers.

Walking towards him, she exclaimed, 'I'm going to have to keep you under lock and key.'

He took hold of her hands and brought her over to the fireside. 'Why do you say that?'

'You're gorgeous. I simply can't let you out. You'll get stolen!'

He laughed, bent into her, kissed her cheek. 'It's because I'm in love,' he murmured. 'With you.'

175

'Me too, with you.'

'And you don't look so bad yourself, you know.' His eyes swept over her, taking in the ankle-length purple wool skirt, matching sweater and the pink pashmina wrapped around her neck to look like a cowl collar. 'These have always been the perfect colours for you.'

'I know, better than green for a redhead, eh? Shall we have a drink?'

'Why not? Lucas brought in a bottle of Veuve Clicquot. How does that sound?'

'Perfect.'

He poured two glasses of the pink champagne and brought them over to the fireplace.

They toasted each other, and Elizabeth took a sip of the champagne, before saying, 'Thanks for helping me with the jewellery. I couldn't have done it alone.'

'It was my pleasure. It's going to be an important feature in the auction. When will that be, by the way?'

Elizabeth seated herself on the loveseat, sat back, nursing her drink. 'I've had a meeting with the key people at Sotheby's, and they figure that it will take about another four months to finish the inventories of everything, the various categories, and create a catalogue. There's a good possibility that it could take place in the autumn or early winter.'

'Of this year?'

'Yes, I hope so, I'd like to get it over with.'

'And the Chelsea house? Are you putting it on the market?'

'I think I will, Robin.' She was about to tell him why, explain that it was full of bad memories, and then changed her mind, mainly because she didn't want to bring up the name of Tom Selmere. She moved on. 'There's still the rest of the jewellery to go through. Do you think we can get it done tomorrow or Sunday? Once I've seen it all, Kat can have it taken away, stored in one of the bank vaults.'

'We'll whiz through it tomorrow, get it out of the way. Listen, I've got to go to Madrid next week, and I had an idea when I was showering. Why don't you meet me in Marbella next weekend?'

'Oh, yes, I'd like that, Robin, it'll be nice to be with you, and we can relax, enjoy the warm weather. Anyway, I can't wait to see the resort. There's just one thing –' She cut herself off, bit her lip, appeared to be worried.

'Go on, say it. *But what*?'

'I hope I don't have to meet with Philip Alvarez, or spend any time with him.'

'No, of course not, he won't be around. But why are you looking so apprehensive?' He stared at her, frowning in puzzlement.

She laughed nervously. 'Because he was always . . . *stalking* me, I suppose that's the best word to use, and whenever he thought no one was looking he would attempt to touch me, get hold of me, pinch my bottom.'

'The randy bugger!' Robert exclaimed, and couldn't help laughing. 'But I can't say I blame him, my sweet. You're very delectable, you know, and therefore extremely *touchable*.'

Robert walked over to the sofa, sat down next to her, took hold of her hand, wanting to reassure her. 'I'm fairly positive he won't be in Marbella, but if he does happen to show up I'll protect you, I promise.'

She turned to face him, saw the mischievous laughter in his eyes, found herself smiling. 'I always knew you'd be my knight in shining armour, Robin Dunley.'

At this moment Lucas appeared in the doorway. 'Excuse me, Miss Turner. Dinner's served.'

'Thank you, Lucas, we'll be right in.'

They finished their champagne, stood up, and went to the dining room where they sat down. A moment later Lucas reappeared, served them country pâté with cornichons and

177

toast, poured the white wine. 'Do you need anything else, Miss Turner?' he asked.

'Everything's perfect, Lucas, thank you.'

He nodded and disappeared into the kitchen.

'I have a lovely feeling I'm getting really special treatment this weekend, Elizabeth, being horribly spoilt. You've chosen all my favourite things so far. Potted shrimps and cottage pie for lunch, now pâté and cornichons.'

'I'm trying to curry favour with you,' she teased, overflowing with happiness.

Robert grinned. 'Do you remember how we once ate a huge jar of cornichons at Waverley Court and got a terrible bellyache. Kat was very annoyed with us, and told us it served us right for being greedy.'

'I still love them, though.' Elizabeth munched on one, then picked up another. 'However, I do limit myself these days.'

'Dare I ask what the main course is?' Robert cut into his pâté and put a small piece on his toast.

'Another of your favourites, Robin. Haddock fried in batter with chips and mushy peas.' She threw him a warm, indulgent look.

'How fabulous! Is Lucas going to serve the fish and chips in a newspaper? I hope.'

'Afraid not, my darling. But they're just as delicious on a plate. Listen, going back to Philip Alvarez, was all that true about him? I mean the things Francis Walsington dug up last year. You know, the womanizing and carousing, and the bad debts?'

'As far as the bad debts are concerned, yes. However, he's managing to settle those, so I understand from Francis. And his womanizing and his fondness for living the high life are his own business, don't you think?'

Elizabeth inclined her head. 'I guess so. He's lucky, isn't

he, that we stepped in and saved him, by taking over the Marbella Project?'

'He is indeed.'

'There's something else I've been meaning to ask you . . .'

'Don't stop, go on, ask me.' Robert sat back, regarding her, his eyes questioning.

'How many enemies do I have at Deravenels?'

'Not as many as you think,' he answered immediately in a cool, steady voice. 'Naturally, there are those dyed-in-the-wool misogynists who simply don't like women to shatter the glass ceiling in business, and therefore all women are disliked, whoever they are. And admittedly, there are a few of those bigoted chaps at Deravenels. After all, as you know, it's been a male chauvinistic club for years. As for actual enemies, I can think of only two who don't approve of you running the company. I could categorize them as enemies – on the other hand, I don't see them as a really dangerous threat to you.'

'I suppose you're referring to Alexander Dawson and Mark Lott?'

'There, you see! You know already.'

'I just have a feeling they don't like me, because they were certainly hostile at the board meeting. But I guess you're right, Robin, they can't really hurt me. Or can they?'

'No, I don't believe so. Mark Lott was such a crony of Mary's, he's bound to take umbrage with anyone who replaces her. As for Dawson, he's a bad lad, to put it mildly.'

'I know. And he knows I know. In the past, I've caught him out in some awful lies, and he's also very sneaky in a lot of ways. I've witnessed that.'

'Yes, you told me. Let's cut to the chase. Dawson can't do anything to harm you, except perhaps fight you on some issues at board meetings, but he'd get out-voted. The board is loaded with your men. Cecil and myself aside, there's your great-uncle

Howard, Nicholas, Francis, and your cousins Henry and Frank. As for Mark Lott, Mary's dead and gone. You're *It*, and Lott is extremely self-protective. He's hardly going to make waves, or move against you. He knows he can't win.' Robert lifted his glass. 'My money's on you, Elizabeth.'

'Likewise, Robin.' She touched her glass to his. 'I've wanted to ask you another thing . . . is your sister coming to work with me or not?'

Robert was pleased, and a wide smile spread across his face. 'If you want her, yes. Merry told me she would definitely accept your offer, if you made one.'

'Then I shall.'

Lucas came in, cleared the plates, returned a few moments later to serve the main course. 'Just ring if you need me, Miss Turner,' he said, hurrying off to his own domain a few minutes later.

Elizabeth and Robert liked the same things to eat and especially the comfort food they had enjoyed as children. And so they relished the fried haddock and chips, with peas and tartare sauce, and Elizabeth surprised herself and ate almost all of her dinner.

At one moment Robert looked at her, his eyes turning thoughtful. He cleared his throat and began. 'You do have *one* genuine enemy, Elizabeth, who's hovering on the horizon at this moment, I understand.'

Taken aback, she frowned, gave him a hard stare. 'You're not going to tell me that Marie Stewart is up to her old tricks, are you?'

'Afraid so.'

'But *why*, Robin? Why is *she* breathing down my neck again? Because that's exactly what you're implying.'

'She believes she's the rightful heir, Elizabeth, and I don't think anything is going to make her change her mind. And now she's had a taste of power, she probably wants more.'

'Taste of power. *How?*' Elizabeth demanded, her voice rising an octave.

'As you well know, she married François de Burgh last April, almost a year ago now, and he's the heir to the vast conglomerate, Dauphin, which his father owns. Although it's not quite as big as Bernard Arnault's LVMH, or Pinault's conglomerate, Artemis, it's nevertheless an important company, doing business worldwide. Marie's husband François works with his father, and so does she. Being an ambitious young woman, she probably thinks she can grab Deravenels, and roll it into her father-in-law's global business. It would give her a lot of kudos with Henri de Burgh.'

'It's not feasible! My father's will is absolutely legal. *Watertight.* Anyway, she can't inherit through the female line, through her grandmother.' Elizabeth was visibly enraged.

'Tell *her* that,' Robert replied. 'Her grandmother was Margaret Turner, elder sister of your father, eldest daughter of Bess Deravenel Turner and Henry Turner. Marie inherited Scottish Heritage through her grandmother, but obviously it's not enough for her. She wants more.'

'Oh, my God! What can I do?' Always pale, Elizabeth's face was whiter than ever.

'You're going to stay cool and calm, in the way only you can. And we're going to watch and wait, and we'll put Francis Walsington to work. If anyone can come up with dirt, he can, and he's very skilled at finding brilliant solutions to really tough problems.'

Robert reached out, squeezed her arm in a reassuring way. 'As I said earlier, my money's on you, Elizabeth. I am guarding your back and so is Cecil. We're not going to allow anyone to hurt you, or attempt to take Deravenels away from you. Trust me.'

'I do,' she said, sitting back, trying to relax. Taking a deep breath, she added, 'I trust you and Cecil with my life, and together the three of us will make the company secure. And bring it to new heights.'

'You're damn right we will,' Robert Dunley agreed.

NINETEEN

Robert awakened, reached out for Elizabeth, only to find her gone. Pushing himself up against the pillows, he glanced around the room, looking for her. It was bathed in moonlight and he saw her standing near the window staring out across the North Sea.

Throwing back the covers, he swung his long legs to the floor and padded over to the window. 'Is there something wrong? Can't you sleep, Elizabeth?'

She did not respond, merely stood there, did not even look around. Her back was rigid, and he was instantly aware of her tenseness.

Baffled and concerned, he put a hand on her shoulder and gently turned her to face him; he saw at once that her eyes were brimming with tears. 'Darling, whatever is it? You're upset.' Drawing her towards him, he brought her into his arms and held her tightly. 'Tell me what's troubling you. Don't you know by now that you can tell me anything, Elizabeth?'

'I couldn't sleep, and my mind started to work, going over so many different things, and I suddenly thought of . . . *Amy*.'

He remained perfectly still, not moving a muscle, nor did he release her. He just went on standing there, pressing her head to his chest.

After a moment or two, Elizabeth leaned back slightly, gazed up into his face. 'I'm not jealous, don't think that. I just need to know what the situation is between the two of you . . . I need the facts. I know you'll tell me the truth, Robin, because you've never lied to me ever.'

Touching her cheek lightly, he kissed her forehead. 'Come on, let's go and sit in front of the fire, and I'll tell you everything you need to know.' Together they went over to the sofa and sat down. Pushing himself into a corner, adjusting the cushions behind him, Robert gave her a direct look and said, 'Amy and I are separated, Elizabeth, and we have been for a very long time.'

'How long?' she asked, her gaze on his.

'Five years, actually. It just wasn't working.'

'Why ever did you marry her in the first place, Robin?'

He shook his head, appeared perplexed. 'I can only put it down to my extreme youth. My God, what did I know at seventeen, eighteen? Nothing. Not about women, sex, the world, life. I was full of raging hormones, and she was very pretty, a voluptuous sort of girl, and I wanted her. As my brother Ambrose often says, a stiff prick has no conscience. I wanted to get her into bed, have sex with her, and the only way I knew how to do that was to marry her. So I did. And a year later I was filled with misgivings and enormous regrets. One shouldn't jump into a vat of ice cream when one only wants a few scoops.'

'And you couldn't work out your problems?'

'We didn't really have problems. She was happy enough, it was just that I had . . . absolutely sweet bugger-all to say to her. We had nothing in common. You see, she loved being in the country, loved the rural life, enjoyed lolling around, doing nothing, just waiting for me to come home and dreaming about babies. But no babies arrived, and eventually I stopped going home. I was bored, utterly and completely bored with her. We're poles apart.'

'Why haven't you divorced?'

'It didn't seem to matter to her. Or to me. At least, not until now. I'll speak to her as soon as possible. I'm sure there'll be no problem.'

'A divorce isn't important, Robin, not to me. You see, I don't plan to marry.'

Surprised, he gaped at her. 'Oh, I see. You still feel that way, do you? About marriage?' His voice was mild, slightly amused.

'I do, oh yes. I'm far too independent to get married. I must be my own woman. And the only reason I mentioned Amy was because I need to know the way things are. And you've told me now, and that's fine, I understand everything. There's absolutely no problem, none whatsoever.' She moved closer to him, took hold of his hand. 'You and I must always be truthful with each other, Robin. Truthfulness and honesty, that's all I ask of you.'

'And what about love? Don't you want that from me?'

'You know I do. Very much so. And I have it, just as you have my love, and all of me. You know that, surely?'

'I do, I do.' Reaching out for her, he took her in his arms and kissed her. 'For what it's worth, you're the only woman I've ever loved in my whole life.'

'All twenty-five years of it.'

'You're only twenty-five, too. Am I the only man you've ever loved?'

'Yes, you are.'

'What about the admiral? Didn't you love him?'

It seemed to Elizabeth that these words just hung there in the air, hung dangerously between them, and for a moment she was angry, couldn't answer him. Finally, composing herself, she said softly, 'I didn't love him, no. But I suppose I was infatuated with him. He was handsome, dashing, and I was very young, you know.'

'Yes, I do know. My father said his behaviour was scandalous in view of your age.'

'Did he now. I see. Did *you* think that?'

'No, I didn't. Was it? Scandalous, I mean?'

'I'm not quite sure.'

'Did he make love to you?'

'We didn't have intercourse, if that's what you're getting at.'

'But you did make love . . .' His voice faded away, he half shrugged.

'There was a lot of . . . touching. You know what I mean.'

'Intimate touching?' he asked, scrutinizing her intently.

She simply nodded. 'Tom Selmere was a lot like you –'

'Oh, no, I don't think so!' Robert exclaimed, sitting up straighter, his mouth suddenly stern.

'I was about to add *in his appearance*. And you're correct, he wasn't like you. Certainly not in character, not at all. He was immoral in a certain sense, and he wasn't as intelligent or as clever as you are. In fact, he was a rather foolish man. Witty but not wise.'

'So said my father.'

Elizabeth moved on the sofa, sat back, and stared into the fire blazing up the chimney. She was silent and so was Robert, both lost in their diverse thoughts.

It was he who broke the silence a short while later, when he drew closer to her, pulled her to him. 'I love you with all my heart, Elizabeth. I truly do.'

'I didn't sleep with . . . the admiral. Honestly.'

186

'I believe you, and it really doesn't matter if you did. You've always been mine in a way, since we were little, and now you *are* mine, just as I'm yours. So let's go to bed and prove it, shall we?'

She started to say something but he stopped the flow of her words with a shower of kisses, picked her up in his arms and carried her to the bed.

'Who cares about the past?' he murmured as he lay down next to her. 'It's the present that counts.'

'When you think about me, what's the first image that comes into your head?' Elizabeth asked, drawing closer to Robert, throwing an arm over his body. Though they were sated and tired by their lovemaking, somehow they were unable to sleep.

He had his back to her and his voice was muffled when he replied, 'I guess in my mind's eye I see you when you were a little girl, my tomboy. Yes, that's the image I have.'

'That's not very romantic,' she grumbled, and kissed his shoulder.

'Maybe not, but you were quite impressive in those days, when we were kids. You had such . . . *guts*. Especially when you stood up to Harry.'

'Now that's a fantasy in your head! I never stood up to my father. I was always a bit frightened of him, to tell you the truth.'

'I really don't believe that!' Robert exclaimed and, turning over, he stared at her in surprise. 'I remember you as being the most fearless person I ever knew. And I still feel that about you.'

'What a nice compliment, and thank you, Robin, but honestly he did terrify me at times.'

'Somehow, I think of him as being sort of . . . soft about you when he got older, when he'd accepted you back into the fold.'

'Nicer anyway. He didn't abuse me any more.'

'Did he really abuse you?' Robert's eyes fastened on hers, and searchingly so.

'Not sexually or physically, I don't mean that. He abused me *verbally*. And also *emotionally*. You know very well he rejected me, disowned me at one point. And even when I was a toddler he shunned me. He was horrific as a father in those days, and everyone said so,' Elizabeth confided.

'It was because of your mother, I'm certain of that.'

'What do you mean?'

'I remember my parents talking about his attitude towards her. As I recall it, he took umbrage because Anne wouldn't give up her career as an interior designer, and he grew suspicious about her, you know. He thought she was having affairs, something like that. And then she was in that awful car accident with her brother and some of his friends . . . in the south of France . . .'

'I know she died in that crash, but what are you getting at precisely, Robin?'

'I have a feeling that . . . well . . . somehow he blamed your mother for the crash. I'm just not sure any more, it's so long ago now. However, according to my father, Harry did manage to sort of . . . well, cast aspersions about your mother's . . . character.'

'So I heard. My half-sister lost no time in telling me that. At a certain point in his life my father did become a monster and behaved badly.'

'All those wives, Elizabeth! Six altogether. Good God, no wonder you don't want to get married . . . he didn't set a very good example, did he?' Robert shook his head. 'He was certainly a dyed-in-the-wool womanizer.'

'True. Still, I think he was also trying to have a male heir. My sister and I weren't enough . . . he wanted a boy. And he got a boy, who died young, so all that pain he caused everyone was in vain, wasn't it?'

'None of us know what life has in store for us,' Robert answered, and observing the pensive expression on her face, he added, 'Now it's my turn . . . What image of me do you have in *your* head?'

She smiled, almost to herself, and gave him a flirtatious glance. 'The image I have of you goes back about a year or two – when we were out of favour with the dreaded Mary Turner. You brought me some flowers, a lovely bouquet of sweet peas, and told me you would be there for me . . . and there was another time when you sent me some money. Do you remember?'

'I certainly do. I wanted to help you because I loved you.'

'But not quite the way you love me now,' she asserted.

He bit back an amused smile. 'That's true.'

Leaning closer, she whispered, 'Now I have so many *new* images of you in my head, all of them very romantic and sexy. Did you know you're a very sexy man, Robin? I bet a lot of women have told you that.'

His answer was to pull her into his arms and kiss her passionately, and within the space of a few minutes they were making love. And that was the way it was for the remainder of the weekend.

TWENTY

*A*nd that is how it began, our great love affair, on a cold, bleak weekend at Ravenscar in March. Now it is June and we are in Paris, and as usual enjoying every moment in this glorious City of Light.

I am passionately in love with Robin, and he is with me. He calls it being madly in love, and I know what he means. Because there is a certain madness about being so completely consumed by another person and living on a strange but marvellous plane together, where the rest of the world does not exist.

We both think it's odd that after knowing each other for so many years we suddenly fell in love at the age of twenty-five. Robin says it's like being hit by a truck, and he's right. One day we were best friends, the next lovers. We are never apart now, spend every waking moment together, and every sleeping moment as well, actually. Robin has moved into my flat and we are living together. He has kept his own place and goes there every other day to check on things, but he *does not spend much time there now. It is hard for us to be apart, and I know I will feel this way for the rest of my life because Robin is part of me, part of my soul. Without him my life would be desolate, and I would be filled with total misery. He is my life in so many ways. Robin and Deravenels are my existence.*

Of course, work intrudes on our private time when he has to travel. At the moment he is going back and forth to Marbella, to check on the progress of the resort. He is very pleased with its development, and I was impressed myself when I saw it in April. There is no question that it is truly a beautiful place, and I see only success in the future. Philip Alvarez did one thing right: he bought a magnificent piece of land at the edge of the sea.

It was when we got back from Marbella that the gossip started. The news of our involvement spread through Deravenels like wildfire, and there were lots of comments, snide remarks, and jibes. But we've paid no attention. We don't care what people think . . . anyway, the world is well lost to us.

We have been very open about our relationship, and have not tried to hide it. In fact, quite the contrary. We're out and about all the time. Robin is a social animal, as am I, and we love the theatre, in particular, as well as dinner parties and entertaining friends. We give to charities, and attend charity events because we believe in giving back. As a consequence, a lot is written about us in newspaper columns, and photographs of us constantly appear in magazines. All this adds fuel to the fire.

As for Amy, Robin never mentions her and neither do I. The only thing he has ever asked me is why I was crying when I brought her name up that night at Ravenscar. And I told him the truth . . . I said I didn't know. And he accepted my answer.

191

*In all honesty, it doesn't matter to me whether he gets a
divorce or not. And my darling Robin knows that, just as
he knows I don't want to get married. I've always felt that
way. He touched on one of the reasons why recently, when
he said my father had been a bad example for me. But then
there was the admiral . . . Tom Selmere wasn't exactly the
ideal husband . . . married to my father's widow and endeavouring to get me into bed. And what of my father's fifth
attempt at marriage? His lovely young wife Katherine had
taken lovers and was so silly, rash and indiscreet she got
caught and was divorced and sent away. No, marriage does
not tempt me. Quite the opposite. I'm happy as I am. He
loves me, I know he does, and with all his heart, and honestly,
that's enough for me.*

*We often come to Paris to have a bit of privacy. I like
this hotel Robin discovered several years ago, the Relais
Christine. It's not too far from the Latin Quarter, and is a
tiny auberge which was once a former abbey dating back to
the thirteenth century. It has a quaint and lovely charm about
it; our suite overlooks a cobbled flower-filled courtyard, and
has a private terrace, another of the things we enjoy about
it. This aside, it's blessed with a unique tranquillity, and
Robin and I both feel as if we are in the middle of the country
when we are actually in the heart of Saint Germain with
Notre-Dame just a stone's throw away . . .*

At the sound of the key in the door, Elizabeth went in from
the terrace, an expectant expression on her face.

Robert smiled as he closed the door behind him, put down
the shopping bags he was carrying, and took her in his arms,
gave her a big hug.

Holding her away from him he searched her face swiftly.

192

'I'm glad to see you looking so much better, darling. You seemed awfully drained earlier.'

'I was a bit tired, but I'm fine now.' She glanced across at the shopping bags and said, 'What did you buy? You look as if you've been on a shopping spree.'

'Sit down and I'll show you.' He brought the four shopping bags over to the seating area near the French windows opening onto the terrace, handed her one. 'This is for you.'

'Chanel! How wonderful. Thank you. What is it?'

'You'll see when you open it.'

'It's the one handbag I wanted!' she cried after opening the package. 'Oh, thank you, Robin. I asked Blanche to pick it up, but Chanel in London had none left.'

'Well, there it is, and it comes with much love.'

Jumping up, she went over and kissed him, then asked, 'And what are the rest?'

'A Chanel handbag for Merry, not the same as yours, but one she had set her heart on. A wallet for Ambrose, and a couple of ties for Cecil Williams, the latter from the two of us.'

'It's so nice of you, Robin, and I know they'll like their gifts.' Settling back in the chair, she changed the subject. 'How are things at Deravenels?'

'The same. The Paris office operates very well, and I like Jacques Bettancourt a lot. He's a really good chap, runs a tight ship, but with a great deal of charm, and not a little flair. I wish the other foreign managers were like him. Some of them have been hard to deal with.'

'Naturally. We've been cutting staff to lower the cost of overheads, and why would they *like* that? But you've done well.'

'I can't take any bows, Elizabeth, it's all Nicholas. He's been brilliant the way he has retired people with pensions, let others go with really good bonuses, so there are no hard feelings. It's cost us a lot, but we'll be saving a fortune in salaries in the long run. Thanks to Nicholas, it's gone smoothly.'

'He's always been good at making people swallow a bitter pill, because he manages to have a sweeter one ready. Are we having dinner with him tonight?'

'We are. He's insisting on taking us to Le Grand Véfour . . . he insists, says it's your favourite.'

'It is, actually. I especially like the idea that Napoleon took Josephine there for romantic dinners, and anyway I love the décor.'

He laughed. 'That's what you usually say about restaurants. You talk about the decorations, not the food. And before you say it, I know you're *not* a foodie.'

She nodded, picked up the quilted red fabric Chanel handbag again and examined it, said almost to herself, 'I really wanted this . . .'

Watching her, Robert realized that she looked painfully thin this afternoon. Funny how he had not noticed it before; perhaps it was the black dress she was wearing. *Had* she lost more weight? He was constantly worrying about her eating habits. She had a small appetite, had been something of a picky eater since childhood. Highly strung by nature, she had had several fainting spells lately, and was often irritable these days.

'What's wrong? Why are you staring at me like that, Robin?'

'Just admiring you in that chic black linen dress, my sweet.'

She gave him a long slow smile and said, 'I'm so happy you brought Merry into the company. She's become my good right hand.'

'I'm glad. And Ambrose is mine, as far as the Marbella Project is concerned. He's taken a lot of the backache out of it for me, and, frankly, I'd have to be there a lot of the

194

time if it weren't for him. He's being a good stand-in.'

She nodded. 'It's nice to be surrounded by your family, Robin . . .' She reached out and touched his arm. 'Thank you for that.'

'My family, at least what's left of it, love you, Elizabeth, and they'll do anything for you . . . anything at all. They have a lot of respect for you as well as much affection.' He leaned forward and fixed his gaze on her. 'Has Cecil said anything to you about me? What I mean is, about you and me being involved?'

'No, he hasn't. Somewhat surprisingly, in my opinion. But lately I've noticed him looking at me in the most peculiar way at times. I've been trying to pinpoint the exact look in his eyes, and I think I would describe it as . . . *perplexity*.'

'I see. The gossip's risen to a bit of a crescendo at the London office, so Nicholas told me this afternoon. He says it'll die down, that we shouldn't pay too much attention, just go about our business, get on with our lives.'

'I agree, and frankly I'm not surprised. We've become a bit of an item in the press lately. Young, beautiful, successful and in Love with a capital L. That seems to be the latest headline.'

Standing up, Robert went to Elizabeth, helped her to her feet, put his arm around her and led her into the bedroom. 'I think we should have a rest before dinner, don't you?'

'A rest? *No*. But I'd like to lie down next to you, my darling, and make passionate love.'

'Then so we shall.'

Located under the ancient arches of the Palais-Royal, Le Grand Véfour dated back to before the French Revolution. It was first opened in 1784, when it was called the Café des

Chartres, and over the last few hundred years it had been the favourite watering hole of many celebrated people . . . Napoleon and Josephine, writers Victor Hugo and Colette, as well as French politicians, famous painters, great names of the theatre, and movie stars who considered themselves to be in the know.

Elizabeth had first come here with Aunt Grace Rose, who had brought her to Paris as a special birthday treat when she was nineteen. Although she had only dined here on one other occasion, she had never forgotten this beautiful, almost other-worldly restaurant. It had left an indelible impression on her.

To her, the main room appeared to float around the diners because of the old, scarred mirrors which reflected the light and were used on the ceiling and some of the walls. The mirrors were encased in pitted gold frames, and were balanced by neoclassical paintings of nymphs bedecked with flowers and vines. These paintings were covered with protective glass because of their antiquity, and overall there was a truly magical effect in the dining room. This once again entranced Elizabeth when they arrived.

Nicholas was waiting for them, and he stood up, greeting them both effusively and kissing Elizabeth on the cheek.

'Sit here, Elizabeth, and you, too, Robert.' Nicholas indicated the red velvet banquette against the wall, added, 'You'll find it comfortable.'

'If you don't mind, I'd prefer a chair,' Robert replied, and once Elizabeth was sitting down on the banquette, he lowered himself onto a black-and-gold antique chair, and Nicholas sat next to Elizabeth.

'I've ordered a bottle of Krug,' Nicholas announced, turning to Elizabeth. 'It'll be here in a minute, and we shall then toast your upcoming auction. Robert had me mesmerized this afternoon in the office, telling me all about your plans. I was gobsmacked when he said that you could make as much as fifty million pounds. Actually, I can hardly take that in.'

'It's because there's so much stuff, much of it passed down from various families, all of whom were my relatives. I can hardly believe it myself. But the experts from Sotheby's are convinced it will be *the* auction of the year. You see, there's a lot of fine art, Nicholas, really *good* paintings, mountains of Cartier jewellery, silver and gold plate, as well as furniture. And it's all very valuable.'

'Robert told me you'll be selling the Chelsea house . . . I always liked that place, it's a gem.'

'Yes, it is, and I'm hoping some Russian oligarch or a billionaire businessman will snap it up for sixty or seventy million pounds.'

'It's gone up!' Robert announced, an amused expression flitting across his face. 'Only a few days ago, it was a mere forty million.'

'Sotheby's again, Robin. Their real estate team consider it unique. You know it's Regency, it's in perfect condition, with a new kitchen and new bathrooms. Because it's on the Thames, and has a large garden, they believe I might even get more, actually.'

At this moment the waiter arrived with the bottle of chilled Krug, put it in the silver ice bucket, popped the cork, poured the pink champagne, and departed with a nod.

Lifting his flute, Nicholas said, 'Here's to the Deravenel–Turner Collections!'

'The Collections,' Elizabeth said, and they all clinked glasses.

After a couple of minutes had elapsed, Elizabeth turned to Nicholas. 'I want to ask you something . . . it's quite important to me.'

'Ask me anything.'

197

'Do you know anyone with Deravenel shares who might want to sell them to me? I'll pay a premium.'

Nicholas shook his head. 'Off hand, no, I don't. But there might be a few people, especially those shareholders who have retired recently, or widows and children of former directors who inherited shares. Knowing you as well as I do, you're thinking of Marie Stewart, but she doesn't have as many shares in Deravenels as you do. Not by a long shot.'

'That's true, but how do we know whether or not she controls shares held by straw men?'

'We don't, of course,' Robert interjected. 'But we can soon find out. We can do a discreet investigation. You know Francis is a genius at that sort of thing.'

'Is that why you're having the auction, to get money to buy more shares?' Nicholas gave her a long curious look.

'Yes. And no. Of course I need cash to buy shares, but I also want to develop a war chest, in case Deravenels suddenly needs operating money. Or if I have to fight the . . . French lady.' Elizabeth took a swallow of champagne and finished, 'But I don't want all these possessions anyway. They're a burden, a nuisance. We live in a different world today.'

'I understand.' Nicholas sat back, his eyes growing reflective. After a moment, he said quietly, 'Without a doubt, Marie Stewart is going to be troublesome at some point, because she's got a bee in her bonnet about Deravenels. However, she can't win, Elizabeth, not in the end, because of your father's will. It's absolutely legal and it will stand up in any court of law.'

'Listen to Nicholas, Elizabeth.' Robert leaned across the table, focusing on her. 'He's telling you the truth, and don't forget you're surrounded by lawyers . . . including Cecil, and Francis Walsington. You're well protected and have the best legal advice.'

'She can only get her hands on Deravenels if you die without an heir,' Nicholas pointed out.

'That's not necessarily true,' Elizabeth shot back. 'What about all the Greysons? They were particularly favoured by my brother Edward, and they are my cousins also, and in line to inherit. Furthermore, I can appoint an heir, can't I?'

'Yes, I'm sure you can, but Cecil will be able to answer that.' Nicholas frowned. 'Or you could get married and produce an heir yourself.'

'Stop worrying about that woman!' Robert took hold of Elizabeth's hand. 'She can only be a *nuisance* . . . she's truly not a threat. Now, let's order some dinner, darling. I'm absolutely starving.'

They all accepted the menus from the waiter, listened to the specialities of the evening, and finally ordered. Elizabeth selected the grilled sole, while Robert and Nicholas both elected to have pigeon stuffed with *foie gras*. Then they sat back, enjoyed the Krug and discussed other matters.

Robert Dunley was always able to distract Elizabeth, and soon had her laughing with his dry wit; she was witty in return, making her two male companions double over with mirth.

Finally relaxing, Nicholas Throckman was filled with relief that she had dropped the discussions about Marie Stewart, who had been a thorn in his side for some time. He considered her to be a dangerous troublemaker, but he had no intention of revealing this belief, and certainly not tonight. He knew it would only worry Elizabeth.

TWENTY-ONE

'Francis! What a lovely surprise!' Elizabeth cried almost two hours later when Francis Walsington appeared at the table, a wide smile on his handsome face. She glanced at Nicholas. 'Why didn't you tell me he was coming?'

'Because it wouldn't have been a surprise if I had, now, would it?'

Francis blew Elizabeth a kiss and sat down next to Robert. When the waiter came over, Francis ordered a cognac, then reaching across the table he squeezed Elizabeth's hand. 'It's good to see you, and congratulations. You're a miracle-worker, Elizabeth. In six months you've managed to reverse a great deal of the damage your half-sister did for over five years. That's quite an achievement.'

'Thank you, Francis. I couldn't have done it without the three of you, and Cecil. It's been an effective team effort.'

He nodded, went on, 'The Marbella Project has truly worked.' Turning to Robert, he added, 'You and Ambrose have done such a remarkable job on the resort, I've been wondering if we shouldn't remodel some of our other hotels along the same lines.'

Nicholas exclaimed, 'That had crossed my mind, too, but I'm not sure John Norfell would agree.'

'Why not?' Elizabeth asked, sounding puzzled. She frowned at Nicholas.

'He'll say it's too costly,' Robert interjected.

'That's right,' Nicholas agreed. 'He'll say we haven't got the money. But I know we could borrow from the bank if we had to, in order to go ahead with that kind of innovative scheme.'

'Or I could lend Deravenels the money to modernize the hotels.' Elizabeth glanced from Nicholas to Francis. 'That's one of the reasons I'm having my big auction, to fund a war chest so that I can help Deravenels if money's needed for new projects. We've got to pull the company into the twenty-first century.'

'And the only way we can do that *is* to modernize,' Robert added.

'Charles Broakes came to me with an interesting idea earlier this week.' Elizabeth paused, said to Robert, 'I told you about it, and you liked it, didn't you, Robin?'

'I did, yes.' Glancing from Francis to Nicholas, Robert explained, 'He was wondering if we could create a situation at several of our vineyards where people could come to stay, have wine tastings, lectures about different wines, and enjoy good food. I did think it was clever, because the manor houses at two of our French vineyards are not being used as homes any more, but rather as offices. We ought to cash in, I think we're missing a chance.'

'So do I,' Francis said. 'It would be quite easy to put up a small office building on each property, and then turn the manor into a guest house. That *is* what Charles had in mind, isn't it?'

'Yes.' Elizabeth began to laugh. 'I even thought we might build a spa at each one. You know how everyone loves spas these days. Also, here's another thought. Not all women are wine-aficionados, and they could enjoy spa days whilst their husbands learn about wines. If we went ahead with the idea it wouldn't make us a vast amount of money, but we would make a good profit, and I think it's a great public relations ploy because it would introduce people to our wines.'

'It's rather brilliant, in my opinion,' Nicholas volunteered. 'I suppose Charles was thinking of our vineyards in Mâcon and Provence?'

'That's right.' Elizabeth lifted her glass of white wine, took a sip. 'As we find new ways to bring Deravenels into the future perhaps we can close out some of the other divisions which are losing money, not that there are a lot of those. We're holding our own fairly well overall. But a few are redundant, I think.'

The four of them went on talking about Deravenels for a while, but when the coffee was served Francis Walsington fell silent. He appeared to be sipping his coffee and listening, but, in fact, he was lost in his own thoughts.

Like the other men at the table, he was tall, good-looking and well dressed, and although he was only twenty-seven he had a rather distinguished appearance, seemed slightly older than his years. One of the most remarkable things about him was his extraordinary self-confidence. He also had an aura of immense power. A lawyer by training, he was Director of the Security Division of Deravenels, and he enjoyed his job, was brilliant at what he did, and usually inspired in his execution of it.

He had known Elizabeth for a number of years, and it was she he had been devoted to and to whom he had given his loyalty during her sister's years at the company. He had left Deravenels when Mary Turner had inherited the top job and come to live in Paris, his favourite city after London.

Now as he sat staring at Elizabeth he could not help admiring the way she looked this evening. She was wearing a red silk dress and a string of large white pearls with matching earrings. Her red hair was longer, framed her face, and gave her somewhat angular features a softer look. She had always been striking, and unique as a woman.

He had noticed the moment he arrived that she had a glow about her, and he was well aware this was because of her relationship with Robert Dunley. They were in love, and he was pleased about this recent development. She had not had a happy life thus far, and he felt she deserved the joy she found with Robert, a man he admired and trusted. Francis knew Robert intimately; they had been friends for over ten years and got on extremely well. Francis was often amused when people dismissed Robert because he was good-looking, or because he was well dressed. Long aware of Robert's intelligence and business acumen, and his total loyalty to Elizabeth, Francis felt nothing but respect for the man. Also, he knew that it would be Elizabeth, Cecil and Robert who would always run Deravenels together, and as a very tight ship. Anyone who thought otherwise, underestimated them, and especially Robert, was not only a fool but unlikely to survive at Deravenels. They were the triumvirate with the ultimate power in their hands. And that was something which would never change.

Francis and Nicholas were old Paris hands and knew the city inside out. They had been close for years, helping each other through their difficulties and problems, protecting and shielding each other during Mary Turner's iniquitous time in the company. Neither of them had been part of her coterie; they continued to be wary about those she had chosen for her inner circle, and gave them a wide berth.

This they spoke about as they walked together under the arches of the Palais-Royal, heading for the Place Vendôme and the Ritz Hotel where they always stayed. Elizabeth and Robert had gone off alone, making for their own hotel; the two friends and colleagues were happy to have this time to chat, ponder together about the company they were committed to, and the woman who had their total devotion.

Heading towards the Louvre Museum, keeping a steady pace, they fell silent for a short time, enjoying the pleasant weather, the beauty of Paris, and the glorious night sky. Suddenly coming to a stop, Francis turned to Nicholas, and confided, 'I feel a bit sorry for those two, you know, old chap. All this silly gossip, it beggars belief, and it's got to be annoying to them.'

'I don't think they pay much attention to it to be honest, Francis, I really don't, and no matter what, I'll be on Elizabeth's side. Her father was a real bastard, and treated her like shit when she was a child, even when she was a toddler. I never understood that. There was something cold-hearted and unusually cruel about him, but then look at the way he behaved with Catherine. He was married to her for almost twenty years, and happily so, and then Anne Bowles came waltzing by and suddenly caught his eye and the rest is . . . well, history, as they say.'

'Anne led him a merry dance,' Francis murmured. 'We all know that, and it took him over six years to get her into bed. And then it went so bloody wrong it was unbelievable.'

'He blamed Anne, naturally. That was the way Harry Turner was. He was never the guilty one. One of the most selfish men I've ever come across. I met him when I was first working at Deravenels and I'll tell you this: I never liked him. He was a bit of a braggart, in my opinion, with an ego the size of the Eiffel Tower.'

'In the meantime,' Francis interjected, 'let's get back to Elizabeth and Robert. She told me a few weeks ago she is quite happy with the way things are . . . she said she doesn't want to marry him.'

'No doubt he will get a divorce though, won't he? Normalize the situation by becoming a single man?' Then Nicholas shrugged. 'I've no clue, do you?'

Francis simply let out a long sigh and took his friend's arm. They strolled on, lost in their own ruminations.

When Francis continued to remain silent, Nicholas finally asked, 'Why the long sigh, my friend? You sounded as though you have the weight of the world on your shoulders. Want to share your burdens?'

'The gossip's crossed the English Channel, Nicky. Apparently there are mutterings about Elizabeth in certain quarters . . . about her being in an illicit relationship with a colleague who's a married man. I'll give you one guess from whence those words are emanating.'

'Frenchie in a kilt?'

'Correct. She's sounding holier than thou, proclaiming to anyone who'll listen that she'll be running Deravenels one day instead of her flighty and immoral cousin.'

'She can never get her hands on the company!' Nicholas exclaimed. 'And you know that as well as I do.'

'But she can have a helluva great time making Elizabeth's life difficult, even miserable, whilst trying to buy up any shares she can find.'

'Surely there aren't many Deravenel shareholders willing to sell?'

'I doubt it. Anyway, Harry's will is watertight, Cecil has reassured us about that. Unfortunately gossip, scurrilous stories, leaks to the press, lies and inventions, all that sort of thing, can only be damaging in the long run, Nicky. We don't want Deravenels making headlines for the wrong reasons.'

'Can't you do something about the Stewart woman, shut her up?' Nicholas asked.

'I can think of a lot of things to do, but most of them are not legal.' Francis let out a chuckle.

Nicholas grunted as they turned the corner and went up a side street, heading for the Ritz Hotel. As they approached the front entrance on the semi-circular Place Vendôme, he came to an abrupt halt, grabbed Francis Walsington's arm. 'There's something I've been meaning to ask you. Why is Robert so suspicious of John Norfell?'

'Let's go to the bar and I'll give you my opinion over a Calvados,' Francis promised as they entered the hotel.

TWENTY-TWO

'So you've gone and done it again!'

At the sound of Kat Ashe's voice a happy smile spread across Elizabeth's face and she lifted her head, stared at the door. But the smile instantly faded when she saw the troubled look on Kat's face.

Immediately jumping up, she went around the desk and then stopped abruptly, filled suddenly with uncertainty, wondering what was wrong. Yet deep down she knew.

Kat, who normally rushed to greet her with great affection and warmth, was as immobile as Elizabeth; the older woman hovered on the threshold of the library, scowling, obviously ill at ease.

Frowning, Elizabeth said, 'You look a bit upset –' She cut herself off, stood scrutinizing the woman who had been the mainstay of her life since childhood, and took a deep breath. As everything fell into place, Elizabeth knew a verbal assault was imminent. She steeled herself.

'That's the understatement of the year!' Kat exclaimed accusingly. 'I'm absolutely furious with you, Elizabeth. How *could* you? How could you go off and do it again?'

'What do you mean?' Elizabeth muttered, stalling, wishing to avoid a wounding confrontation.

'You know very well what I mean. How could you get involved with another man like Selmere?'

'Robin's not like Tom!'

'He's married, isn't he?' Kat shot back angrily.

'So what? I don't want to get married, Kat. You, of all people, know my feelings about that. It doesn't matter to me what his status is.'

'But it *does* matter. You're involved in a scandal. And for the second time. This is a replay of the Selmere affair.'

'No, it's not!' Elizabeth contradicted.

'It is. You're having an illicit relationship with a married man. And you're the head of Deravenels now. Furthermore, you're sleeping with a colleague, and that's wrong, just as it was wrong for you to sleep with your stepmother's husband. Another stupid thing you did, Elizabeth.'

'I never slept with Tom Selmere,' Elizabeth cried, her voice rising, becoming unusually shrill for her. Her face was whiter than ever and she was shaking inside.

'You were very . . . *intimate* with him, and you encouraged him. That was why he came courting you after your stepmother died. Which is the reason his brother was so incensed and created problems for you, as well as for the silly, very careless Tom.'

'I never encouraged Tom Selmere, Kat. Marrying me was his idea. Actually, I didn't even know he had spoken about that to his brother . . . not until Tom was in deep trouble. I was the innocent bystander, and you're aware of that. You also know my opinion of matrimony.'

Kat was silent, and suddenly looked chastened.

Elizabeth said in a milder voice, 'For God's sake, come into the room and close the door.'

Kat did so, walked briskly into the library, making for the fireplace. She sat down in one of the chairs, and looked at Elizabeth, her expression one of expectancy.

'Whatever you might think, Robin and I have been extremely discreet at the office, and certainly we don't flaunt our relationship there. Nor have we flaunted it in public.'

'But you're always in the gossip columns, and the magazines. Whatever you say, it *is* a scandal,' Kat insisted.

'It's not our fault that the press hound us. And yes, it's true, we are seen at different functions, fashionable events in different places, and that's because we're not in hiding, nor are we planning to go into hiding. We're very open about being together. In any case, for what it's worth, Robin is separated from Amy, and has been for the last five years.'

'If that's the case then he should straighten out his marital affairs,' Kat pronounced in a firm voice, but she was now a little calmer. 'He must get a divorce at once, make himself a free man for you.'

'That's not important to me.'

'But the gossip would stop, Elizabeth,' Kat pointed out.

'Oh, what do I care about gossip! I don't give a fig for the scandal-mongers.'

Kat sighed. 'You always were stubborn, even as a child.'

Leaning forward, Elizabeth took hold of her arm affectionately. 'It doesn't matter that I'm involved with a colleague. Lots of people fall in love with their co-workers; that's where everyone spends most of their time anyway these days: at the office. Where else do we meet people? At work, of course. And there's another thing. It's 1997. Times have changed, attitudes are different, there's been a relaxation of those rigid rules of . . . long ago.'

'I know,' Kat admitted. 'It's just that I do worry about you.'

'Please try and understand that I'm *happy*. Happy for the first time in my life. I love Robin, and he loves me. I suppose we've always loved each other, actually. And you know how close we've been. I adore him. He's the love of my life. But I'm not going to marry him. You'd better get used to the idea that I'm never going to get married to anyone.'

Kat let out a long sigh, the anger in her suddenly dissipating, finally fleeing. She had never been able to remain angry with Elizabeth for very long anyway. 'I know I'm overly protective, Elizabeth. I can't help it. I've behaved like that ever since your father put you in my care. And there's another thing, I don't want you to get hurt.'

'Robin's not going to hurt me, and I know you care about me, love me, you've proved this so many times. It's just that . . . I'm free, Kat. *Free*. For the first time in my life I can do anything I want. Nobody can tell me what to do any more. Those who controlled me for so long – my father, my half-brother and my half-sister – are all dead and buried. I don't have to answer to anyone. *I am liberated*.'

Kat stood up, pulled Elizabeth to her feet and embraced her, held her tightly in her arms. After a long moment, she released her, looked into her pale face, said in a gentle voice, 'I just want the very *best* for you, that's all.'

'I'm aware of that, Kat, I truly am. And you *know* Robin Dunley. Why, you've known him since he was a little boy. He, too, wants only the best for me, and I promise you one thing, he *will* get a divorce from Amy. Will that make you happy?'

Kat nodded. 'I want him to be single so that no one can point a finger at you, Elizabeth, or call you names.'

'He'll be talking to Amy next week when he comes back from Marbella. He told me he was going to Cirencester to

see her. There won't be a problem, it's an amicable separation. Basically, he's outgrown her and did so long ago, and
she's bright enough to know that. They rarely see each other,
in fact they haven't set eyes on each other for several years.'

Immediately Kat's face brightened. 'It's such a relief to
know that. I'm afraid I've been fretting, making myself sick.'

'Stop worrying and let's get down to work. Bring out the
inventories, and we'll go over some of them. Perhaps we can
calculate how much money I'm going to make from the first
auction.'

'The Fine Art Auction is the first, and Sotheby's are
working on everything pertaining to that themselves. They're
the experts. Naturally, they'll be calculating the value of the
jewellery as well. I do have some information, and a few
thoughts, and I'd like to show you my notes.'

Elizabeth beamed at her.

For the next hour the two women went over the inventories
of the jewellery which Kat Ashe had been creating for months.
She explained how she had selected certain pieces and sets
because she believed they would be much sought after and
would fetch high prices.

'For instance, I think the diamond necklace from the
Diamonds of the Crown of France Collection, made for the
Empress Eugénie, will go sky high,' Kat said, sounding
pleased, handing her a photograph.

'How high?' Elizabeth asked, looking at the picture and
then at Kat.

'Possibly two million pounds, maybe even more. I'm
meeting with Sotheby's next week and we'll come to some
decisions then . . . about how we're going to handle everything. Then there are these Harry Winston, Cartier and

Mauboussin necklaces from the 1950s and 1960s, and we know they'll go very, very high.'

Elizabeth took the photographs, stared at them, nodding. 'I remember these pieces. When Robin and I found them in the vaults at Ravenscar we were both very impressed. The diamonds were big, some of them about twenty or thirty carats, and the workmanship was fabulous. I suppose we're talking in the millions again.'

'Absolutely. Sotheby's are very excited, and they already believe the collection will far exceed their original evaluation. You see, there's nothing comparable around these days. You've inherited something quite extraordinary, jewels that are works of art.'

'I've become aware of that, and thank you, Kat, for all the hard work you've put in, sorting the pieces, and making lists. I really appreciate your help.'

'I'm enjoying it,' Kat said, and sat back on the sofa, endeavouring to relax, glad things had returned to normal. She eyed Elizabeth. 'I'm sorry about earlier, about our little spat. It was my fault, and I apologize, Elizabeth. I made an assumption I'm afraid when I said you'd slept with Tom Selmere. It wasn't nice. Please say you forgive me.'

'Oh, Kat, come on, don't be so silly. There's nothing to forgive, for goodness' sake. And I know you only have my interests at heart. I just hope I've made *you* feel better, about Robin's situation I mean.'

'You have, and I must admit I'm tremendously relieved that he's going to speak to his wife, get all that mess sorted out.'

'He will. Just stop worrying. Everything's going to be fine. Now, I'm afraid I'm going to have to get off to the office. I told Cecil Williams I'd be there by noon for a meeting.'

'No problem. I'll finish up here and leave you some extra

notes. Blanche said she would come over a bit later with a selection of white shirts for you. We're going to have lunch together.'

'Give her my love, and we'll talk later.'

Cecil Williams looked across at Nicholas Throckman and said slowly, 'I always thought you knew that John Norfell was somewhat sympathetic towards Mary Turner.'

'Not until Francis told me in Paris. He said that's why Robert Dunley doesn't trust him, that Norfell's two-faced.'

'I think that's a very apt description, *accurate*, Nicholas. I've long been of the same opinion as Francis.'

'Why were they so close?'

'They attended the same church. And both of them were somewhat involved with church administration, that level, you know, caught up in the politics, I suspect. I'm sure Norfell still is.'

'So John Norfell's a Roman Catholic!' Nicholas sounded startled. He shook his head. 'Funny, I never knew that. On the other hand, I don't go around asking people about their religious persuasion.'

'You were in Paris most of the time during Mary Turner's tenure, and I was living in the country. We didn't realize how friendly they were.'

'And Francis was in Paris also. I certainly ran into him a lot.' Nicholas stood up, walked across Cecil's office, stood next to the window for a moment, looking out. Today the sky was a beautiful blue, without cloud, blameless. He couldn't wait to get away this afternoon, drive to Gloucestershire for the weekend: June was a lovely month to be in the country, his favourite time of year.

Cecil leaned back in his chair, watching Nicholas, and

213

after a moment he broke the silence. 'What else did Francis have to say when you saw him in Paris last weekend?'

'He confided that the gossip about Elizabeth and Robert has crossed the Channel, that was the way he put it. I don't think he was too perturbed about it, although he did say Madame de Burgh, also known as Marie Stewart, was calling Elizabeth nasty names, castigating her for her immoral behaviour, for having an affair with a married man, the usual rubbish.'

'All I can say is that I'm relieved Harry Turner was a maniac when it came to legalities, especially to do with his will. *And his successors.* Shakespeare said, "First, let's *kill* all the lawyers," but Harry Turner said "First, let's *celebrate* all the lawyers".' Cecil chuckled. 'My father was forever quoting Harry when I was growing up. Very seriously, though, Marie Stewart could be a bit of a troublemaker if she so chose.'

'For what reason?'

'Just to make trouble, create problems for us, that's all.'

'She could never attempt a takeover bid, surely? After all, we're a private company,' Nicholas said quietly.

'We are indeed, but over the years quite a few shares were given to directors as bonuses, and to certain family members, or they were allowed to buy them, and those shares have been passed down. Today they are held by other people. *They* might be tempted to sell those shares to an outsider. Nevertheless, in my opinion we *are* safe. Let me explain. A takeover bid wouldn't get very far, because of our company rules, and the way the company is structured. And there's another reason . . . Only a Deravenel, be it a man or a woman, is allowed to run the company. Also, Elizabeth does control most of the shares through her father's will.'

'The Stewart woman has *some*, according to Francis. They were seemingly passed down from her grandmother, Harry Turner's sister Margaret.'

'That's correct, yes. But she doesn't have as many as Elizabeth.'

'Why is Francis so troubled by the Stewart woman?'

'She could rock the boat, undermine current management, be a nuisance in general. We don't need dangerous rumours floating around. We have to look very strong in business, in order to counteract the impression given over the last few years, the impression that Mary Turner didn't know what she was doing as managing director. And we're doing that efficiently and very effectively.'

'Thank God!' Nicholas walked back to Cecil's desk, and sat down opposite him. 'I'm delighted *we're* in control at last.'

'Getting back to John Norfell. Robert thinks he's overly ambitious and out for himself . . . a man fervently seeking power. And that's the real reason he doesn't trust him. He says a man like that can jump anywhere at any time. He detects a treacherous streak there.'

'Francis obviously believes the same thing.'

'I'm certain he does, and I tend to go along with the theory.'

Nicholas nodded, sat back in the chair, his expression thoughtful. After a moment or two, he asked, 'Have you spoken to Elizabeth about her relationship with Robert?'

'What's the point? My words would fall on deaf ears. A woman in love hears only the words of her lover.'

TWENTY-THREE

'It's been a totally crazy morning so far,' Miranda Phillips said, coming into Elizabeth's office at Deravenels, hurrying across to the desk. 'The phone's been ringing and ringing.'

'I've just started to go through the messages,' Elizabeth answered, smiling at Robin's sister. Merry, as she was known, was her personal assistant, and one of the most breathtaking women she had ever seen, with her beautiful features, dark colouring and cornflower-blue eyes. 'I see there's one from Grace Rose. Did she say what she was calling about?'

Sitting down in the chair at the other side of Elizabeth's desk, Merry began to laugh. 'The usual. To see you, of course. "In the not-too-distant future, because I'm living on borrowed time." That was the way she put it, and with a lovely chuckle, I might add. I told her you'd get back to her today.'

'I'm not doing much this weekend. With Robin in Marbella I'm fairly free. Maybe I'll invite her to Sunday lunch at the

Dorchester. She loves that, the whole ritual of it. I'll phone her now.' Just as Elizabeth reached for the phone the door burst open and Cecil Williams rushed in, looking worried and distracted.

'What is it?' Elizabeth asked, staring at him anxiously. His normal calm demeanour had been ruffled, and there was a strained look in his steady grey-blue eyes which alerted her to trouble. 'Is there a problem, Cecil?'

'Yes,' he said crisply, coming to a standstill near her desk. He sat down and went on, 'I just hung up on Robert. Now, don't get upset, they are all right, but he and Ambrose were in a plane crash this morning.'

'Oh, my God, no!' Elizabeth gaped at him, her alarm evident, and then she looked at Merry who had stiffened in the chair and turned white. She brought her hand to her mouth.

'They're not badly hurt!' Cecil exclaimed, and added, in a reassuring tone, 'I promise you, Elizabeth. And you, too, Merry, your brothers are fine, in fact they're mostly suffering from bruises. Ambrose has dislocated a kneecap and Robert has a broken wrist. They've been damned lucky.'

'Where was the crash? Are they in hospital?' Elizabeth reached for the telephone, her hand resting on the receiver.

'First things first. They were treated at the small medical unit we built at the resort, and then taken into Marbella, to a private clinic. They've been thoroughly examined, and released. Robert will phone you shortly, Elizabeth. I asked him to wait ten minutes or so. Because I wanted to explain about the oil spill.'

Elizabeth sat back, startled. 'What oil spill?' she demanded. 'Nobody told me about any oil spill.'

'The Spanish government haven't released anything official yet, Elizabeth. I just got a few details from Robert several minutes ago. Apparently an oil tanker exploded off the coast of Spain earlier this morning and –'

'Not one of our tankers! I hope to God not!' she cried, her chest tightening. All she needed at the moment was trouble with Deravco Oil. Her heart sank at this thought.

'No, no. But it could cause us problems. If the oil slick drifts down to our shoreline we might have an ecological disaster on our hands.'

'Damn and blast!' Elizabeth snapped her eyes shut for a split second, genuine fear running through her. All that money they'd invested could be lost. Then she opened them and gave Cecil a worried look. 'That's all we need to scuttle our resort in Marbella. Oily sea, oil-covered birds and fish, ruined marine and plant life. Oh, and what about the beaches? Oh, God! *No!* This can't happen to us, Cecil. It just can't.'

'Let's *pray* the oil slick doesn't drift with the tides,' Merry said quietly, understanding only too well what was suddenly at stake for Deravenels. And Elizabeth, as head of the company.

Elizabeth took several deep breaths, steadying herself. 'What about the tanker, Cecil? In particular, what about that doomed crew? There must be a lot of men dead? No?' Her dark eyes were filled with sudden pain at the thought of lost lives.

'As I said, not all of the details are in,' Cecil replied. 'But Robert believes there are a lot of injured men. He told me they're being rescued as we speak. This is what happened earlier. As soon as he and Ambrose heard about the explosion they decided to go out in one of our small planes to view the area, gauge the situation in general. On the way back to Marbella, one of the plane's engines stalled, then died, and the pilot had to bring it down in a field about five miles away from the resort. Unfortunately, it was rocky, rough terrain, and it was a bad landing. Thankfully, only minor injuries were sustained by the pilot, co-pilot, Robert and Ambrose. As I just told you, we've been lucky. All four of them walked away from the crash.'

'What caused the explosion?' Elizabeth probed. 'Do we have any idea?'

'Robert doesn't know. He said the Spanish government are on top of it, and an announcement will be made later this morning.'

'Where was the tanker when it blew up?' Elizabeth now asked, frowning.

'In the Straits of Gibraltar –'

'Oh, no!' she cried, cutting him off. 'If the oil spill does start to drift it will contaminate our shoreline –'

The ringing phone interrupted her, and she grabbed it at once. 'Hello?'

'It's me, darling,' Robert Dunley said. 'I'm here in Marbella, totally undamaged.'

'Robin, oh, Robin! Thank God you're all right, and Ambrose, too. You could have both been killed.'

'But we weren't and we're okay, and I'm sure Cecil's with you at this moment. Hasn't he filled you in?'

'Yes, he has indeed, and Merry is here, too, so she knows everything. Look, I'm going to fly out this afternoon to be with –'

'No, no, don't come, Elizabeth! Honestly, it's not necessary. *Please.* I am all right, and so is my brother. We want to keep going here, and help in any way we can, if we can. There are rescue teams out there, picking up the injured men, and things are very much in hand. The Spanish government is being very efficient about this, and responsible. And *you* mustn't worry.'

'I can't help but worry,' she protested. 'I want to be with you.'

He laughed. 'It's just a broken wrist, sweetheart. I'll live to shower you with kisses,' he teased.

'You'd better.'

'I'll call you later. Give Merry my love, and my love to you, too.'

'When are you coming back?' Elizabeth asked, anxious now for him to return.

'Next week, as planned. I must complete what I came here to do, Elizabeth. Bye, darling, and please don't worry.'

'I'll try not to,' she said, and stared at the receiver. He had hung up.

Looking across at her assistant and raising a brow eloquently, Elizabeth said, 'He's gone! Just like that! *Typical*.' But she smiled as she spoke, an expression of relief settling on her face. 'Your brother sends you his love, Merry.' Turning to Cecil she continued swiftly, 'How *do* you clean up an oil spill? Do *you* know, Cecil?'

'I know a little bit. The key methods are to use booms, skimmers, and chemical dispersants. Or to do in-situ burning. There are many ways to make a clean-up very effective, but experts must be used. Also, methods do vary. What has to be taken into account are the type and location of the spill, and what's feasible, of course.'

'What are booms?' Elizabeth asked.

'A type of floating barrier.' Cecil then explained, 'They're placed around the oil and contain the oil so that skimmers can collect it. Skimmers are actually boats, vacuum machines, and oil-absorbing plastic ropes that skim the spilled oil from the surface of the sea. Those companies which use chemical dispersants have to be truly expert at it so as not to cause more damage. The materials break down the oil into its chemical constituents, and this does help to disperse the oil, and make it less harmful when it comes to wildlife, that sort of thing. I'm sure one of the chaps from Deravco can explain a lot better than I can. Shall I call Spencer Thomas? He could fill you in much better.'

'No, don't bother, but thanks anyway. And thanks for the information. Just what I needed to know . . . and let's hope I never need to know more than that. Do you want to talk about Charles Broakes's problems now?'

Cecil nodded. 'I'd like to get that out of the way, yes.'

Merry jumped up. 'I'll be in my office if you need me, Elizabeth,' she said, and hurried out, closing the door behind her.

'What's the *problem* with Charles Broakes? I know you said you need to discuss his plan, but I thought he was all set to go ahead. We okayed it, didn't we?'

'Yes, Elizabeth, we did. But we didn't bargain for John Norfell.'

'*Oh*. Don't tell me he's shoved a spanner in the works.'

'Afraid so. Well, sort of. He says the hotel division will not pay for the various remodelling jobs, the construction of an office and spa, and all that, because only the vineyard division benefits, and therefore that division should pay.'

'I suppose he's right, in a way, isn't he?' Elizabeth sat back, staring up at the ceiling, lost in thought. Finally she glanced at Cecil. 'On the other hand, I think the wine division doesn't have any money to spare.'

'That's it.' Cecil stretched his legs, crossed them and looked down at one of the memos in his hand, frowning to himself. 'I would like us to go ahead, you know, but I don't have a solution, I really don't.'

'The solution is money, Cecil. I'll have to pull it from somewhere. Let's have them in for a few minutes, shall we? Listen to their rantings.' She grinned at him, her good mood of earlier finally restored.

221

'The hotel division cannot, *will not*, pay for these improvements at the vineyards. And that's my last word on it,' John Norfell snapped, glaring at Charles Broakes. 'Furthermore, I want no more discussion about this. The matter is closed.'

Charles Broakes glared back at him.

The two men had been at loggerheads for days, and Charles was frustrated and angry. But he was smart enough to understand he wasn't going to win with John Norfell, so he ignored his colleague and directed his gaze at Elizabeth.

'What am I going to do?' he asked her in an even tone, striving for total composure, having long known that she detested scenes in business, was cool-hearted when it came to her wheeling and dealing. She thought with her head and not her heart, and she was ruthless.

Elizabeth gave him a sympathetic look, and sighed. Lifting her shoulders in a light shrug, she said quietly, 'I don't know, Charles, I really don't know what you *can* do under the circumstances.'

'You said the idea of turning the manor houses at the vineyards into boutique hotels was a brilliant idea on my part. Have you changed your mind?'

'No, I haven't. But the wine division doesn't seem to have any money to spare, and the hotel division obviously won't budge from their position.' She glanced at Norfell, then back at Broakes. 'They're crying poverty, Charles, don't you see?' Her mouth twitched and she swallowed a smile.

Charles Broakes was a long-time friend, and a fan, and he caught the hint of amusement in her voice, suddenly understood. She *was* going to do something to help him, but she obviously wasn't prepared to say what this was for a moment or two. She wants to play Norfell along, tweak him for a bit, Charles decided, and sat back in his chair, waiting. He was going to enjoy this.

Cecil said, 'I'd hate to think this idea might fall by the

wayside, Charles, just for the lack of a few pennies. That's all it amounts to, isn't it?'

'That's correct,' Charles answered. 'Fifty grand would do it.'

'Fifty grand, my eye!' John Norfell interjected angrily. 'You haven't included the spas. They will cost a fortune. And why should we pay for spas at the vineyards?'

'Oh, so the cost of the spas was not included,' Elizabeth murmured, pursing her lips. 'Oh, what a pity we can't do this! I mean, I love the idea of spas . . . but then didn't I come up with that idea?'

'Yes, you did,' Charles confirmed.

She turned to John Norfell, and asked, 'You're definite about not being able to fund these improvements, are you, John?'

'Yes, I am. And you can't force me to do it just because you've got a bee in your bonnet about bloody spas.'

Elizabeth was taken aback by his churlish tone, and she frowned, exclaimed, 'I've never had a bee in my bonnet, as you call it, about anything, John. And most especially *not* about business. Business has nothing to do with bees or bonnets. Perhaps honey occasionally, when the money comes pouring in. So please don't underestimate me.'

John Norfell flushed, and anger flared in him. Who was she to reprimand him in front of Broakes and Cecil Williams? And she a mere slip of a girl. What cheek she had.

As if she had read his mind, Elizabeth went on carefully, 'I know you probably think I'm just an ignorant young woman with no business experience whatsoever, and who am I to tell you what to do. Actually, I'm not going to tell you what to do, John. Why would I? After all, *you* run the hotel division, and it's your responsibility not mine. *You* rise and sink with its success . . . *you* and that division are intertwined. As for my business experience, never forget that I learned at the knee of the master, and my father Harry Turner was an undoubted genius when it came to business.'

John Norfell gaped at her, wondering if she could read minds. She had read his mind in such a way he was gob-smacked. And just a little deflated all of a sudden. She was a cool customer, one not to be taken lightly.

Taking a deep, steadying breath, he said, 'I meant no offence, Elizabeth, when I used the phrase *a bee in your bonnet*. But I apologize if you found it out of place. As far as the spas are concerned, I know what they cost. We've just revamped our spas at the hotel in La Jolla in California, and at our hotel in Los Cabos. Both remodelling jobs went sky high. If you decide to go along with spas at the vineyards you should be prepared.'

'Oh, I am, John, I am. *I'm prepared for everything.* At all times. Make no mistake about that.'

John smiled at her. She had spoken sweetly, and he had not noticed her sarcasm. But Charles Broakes and Cecil Williams had and they exchanged glances.

Elizabeth stood up, walked over to the window and looked down at the Strand. It was a busy Friday. Traffic was bumper to bumper. She saw a bit of blue sky, a shaft of sunlight, and thought: Sunny days are here again. I cannot lose this game.

'This is what I think,' she finally said, walking back to her desk. 'I'm going to start a company, and if it's successful I'll sell it to Deravenels, in much the same way my great-grandfather started Deravco Oil, and then sold it to the conglomerates once it was making money. My company's going to be one which will design and build spas.'

She sat down behind her desk and studied Charles. 'I wonder what to call it? How does Ecstasy sound? No, there's a drug called ecstasy, isn't there? Mmmmm. What about Forever Bliss . . . now that's appealing. Women will like the thought of bliss lasting forever. Would you like to hire this company to build your spas, Charles?'

He nodded, playing along with her. He said in a low tone, 'I'd hire your company in a minute, but I don't think we can afford to pay you.'

'Oh, don't worry about *that*.' She gave him a long, piercing look. 'All you have to do is sign a promissory note promising to repay the company within two years, and I'll lend you the money. How does that sound?'

Charles Broakes wanted to laugh out loud. But he didn't dare. Instead he said, 'Sounds perfectly sensible to me, Elizabeth.'

Thrusting her hand across the desk, she said, 'It's a deal! Shake on it.'

They did.

Turning to Cecil, Elizabeth gave him a conspiratorial look. 'I believe the first ten to fifteen items I am putting on sale at the auction will bring me about twenty million pounds. I'll put the jewels up for collateral at the bank, and they can give me a loan of ten million pounds. That way, I can fund my new company, Forever Bliss. We must get that done on Monday, so Charles here can start his remodelling and building in Mâcon and Provence as soon as he wants.'

The idea of the spas really took hold later that afternoon, and Elizabeth's head was teeming with ideas. By the time she arrived home at nine o'clock she had thought everything out. And she was tremendously excited.

In the past few months she had decided to open spas in all of their hotels, considering them a necessity. Spas were 'in', as were gyms, and both facilities were vitally import-ant to hotel guests. Very simply, they expected them to be available. Time and again she had said to Cecil and Robert that their hotels had to be pulled into the twenty-first century, pointing out that one way to do this was to introduce the spas and gyms. They had agreed with her and, luckily, so had the board. Her plans were already underway and building had started.

Today she had had a vision . . . a vision of the spas as an entity unto themselves. They didn't have to be confined to their hotels only. An Elizabeth Turner Spa, called Forever Bliss, could be opened anywhere, and it would be a separate business, financed by her and therefore controlled by her. The possibilities were endless. Quite aside from building the spas at the vineyards in Mâcon and Provence, Elizabeth had decided this evening that she would open spas in London, Leeds, Manchester and Edinburgh, perhaps even Paris and New York. To her the idea was inspirational, and she was certain that it would be a smash hit. There were no doubts in her mind at all, in fact. She had the will and the drive and the money to make the spas succeed.

Walking through into the kitchen, she took the plate of smoked salmon and buttered brown bread out of the refrigerator, removed the linen napkin covering it, and carried the plate back to the library.

Sitting down at her desk, she went over the notes she had made in the office a short while ago, scanning them quickly. She was pleased; she *had* thought of everything. Her perfect colour scheme was all-white with just a hint of milky pale-green underlying it: mood and atmosphere would be created by the colour scheme, as well as minimalism in the décor, barely audible music playing in the background, perfumed candles and potpourri; plus luxurious bathrobes and towels. She was fully aware that every kind of treatment must be available. Varied massages from every country in the world, facials, wraps, soaks, and reflexology. Multiple beauty services must be offered and there must also be a hair salon in each spa. The worst thing for a woman was to leave a spa with messy hair, she knew that only too well. And she would –

The jangling phone interrupted her flowing thoughts and she picked it up. 'Hello?'

'It's your favourite man here.'

'Don't you mean my damaged goods?' she shot back, laughing, happy to hear Robert's voice.

'I can assure you the most essential part of me is not at all damaged, my darling,' Robert retorted with a chuckle.

'Thank goodness for that. How are you feeling?'

'I'm well, Elizabeth. The wrist's nothing, just a tiny inconvenience. You worked late at the office, didn't you?'

'Yes, and I'm very excited about something. Let me tell you.' She quickly filled him in, her voice vibrant with enthusiasm.

'What a fabulous idea, Elizabeth! And it's going to work. I realize that by necessity you have to finance the spas yourself, but I think that will be to your advantage in the long run. Most importantly, nobody can interfere because you're sidestepping the board. And in my opinion, the spas *will* do a lot to modernize Deravenels, as will the resort, no question.'

'How are things going? Have all the tanker's crew members been rescued from the sea, Robin? And what about the clean-up?'

'Crew rescued and the clean-up is underway. As for our shoreline, I think we'll be okay. It looks as if the oil slick won't reach us . . . we're all *praying* it won't.'

'Thank God! I was worried all day that we'd be facing an ecological disaster and that we wouldn't be able to open the resort on time.'

'So was I. I'm more optimistic tonight. The reports are

good. Listen, Elizabeth, there's something I want to tell you. Francis found out from one of his contacts in the Spanish government that they suspect the explosion in the tanker was not an accident. They think it was the work of terrorists. They believe the tanker was blown up to create an eco-logical catastrophe in the Mediterranean. Francis is extremely alarmed, and he says we should really step up security at Deravco immediately, make certain that our oilfields and our tankers are exceptionally well protected. I agree.'

'So do I, Robin. Tell him to do whatever's necessary, and not to worry about cost. You see, I've actually had that worry at the back of my mind for a long time. I've felt we could be horribly susceptible to a terrorist attack. We'll talk about it in detail when you get back. Right now, could we discuss our trip to the south of France? We've not made any proper decisions and I need to know, Robin, in order to make my plans.'

'Here's what I thought . . .' he began, and talked to her for the next fifteen minutes about their summer holiday.

TWENTY-FOUR

Grace Rose was a star. There was no question in Elizabeth's mind about that. Here they were, seated at one of the very best tables in the centre of the Grill Room at the Dorchester Hotel, and it might have been the Queen of England sitting there holding court.

The staff came to pay their respects, from the maître d' to the sommelier, and everyone else who came passing by seemed to stop to say a word, whether they knew her or not. Or so it seemed to Elizabeth.

Grace Rose had something unique. Some might sum it up as charisma; Elizabeth thought of it as an aura . . . an aura of dignity, elegance, regality and, yes, *star power*. Can't get away from that word *star*, Elizabeth thought, smiling.

For an old lady of ninety-seven, Grace Rose was extremely well preserved. She didn't look her age, and she was beautiful. The silver-white hair was perfectly coiffed, and her pretty pink-and-white complexion rivalled that of a much younger woman. Well made-up, Grace Rose wore a tailored, pale-blue silk suit and a white chiffon blouse with a jabot which frothed down the front and was very feminine. Aquamarine earrings and an aquamarine-and-diamond brooch echoed the blue of her eyes, which had faded since her youth but were, nonetheless, full of sparkle today.

'Here's somebody else coming over, Grace Rose,' Elizabeth warned her.

'Probably a woman who wants to know where I bought my blouse,' Grace Rose murmured, flashed her vivid smile at Elizabeth. 'They usually ask something like that. And by the way, I think you look wonderful in white: you should wear it more often.'

'Thank you. And it's a man actually. Coming over here, I mean. I think he might know you – he's got a huge smile on his face.'

Before Grace Rose could say anything the man was standing by the side of the table, bending over to shake her hand. 'Good morning, Mrs Morran, it's Marcus Johnson. I used to do some of the press work for your husband.'

'Marcus, of course! It's lovely to see you. How are you?'

'Very well, thank you, and *you* look positively blooming, Mrs Morran.'

'I can't complain, I must admit. I would like to introduce you to Elizabeth Turner, my great-niece.'

Elizabeth smiled at him. He smiled back, and inclined his head.

Then Marcus Johnson said, 'I was just thinking of your late husband the other day. There was no one quite like Charles, he was an original. I can't find a better way to say it.'

'He was indeed, Mr Johnson, and I remember how much he enjoyed working with you.'

'Thank you, and so did I. Well, I won't disturb you any further, I can see the waiter coming with your drinks. Once again, it was such a nice surprise to see you, and looking so well.'

They said their goodbyes, and Marcus Johnson retreated. Watching him go, Grace Rose said, 'He was awfully good at his job. If ever you need a press representative, consider him, Elizabeth. He's straight as a die, very honest. Also talented. You could do worse.'

'Thank you, Grace Rose, and I *will* make a mental note about him.'

The waiter put their champagne flutes before them and disappeared. 'Cheers,' Grace Rose said, lifting her glass. 'Here's to you, Elizabeth, and your new venture. *The spas!*'

They clinked glasses, and Elizabeth thanked her. She went on, 'Friday was such a strange day... so much happened. Robin and Ambrose in a plane crash, the oil spill threatening our shoreline and the resort, solving the problems between Norfell and Broakes, and on top of it I had to deal with Kat that morning. She was hell-bent on –' Elizabeth broke off, having said more than she wished. Why even mention Kat Ashe's confrontation, her anger? That served no purpose.

But Grace Rose, who didn't miss a trick, asked swiftly, 'What about Kat Ashe? What was she hell-bent on?'

'Oh, nothing,' Elizabeth muttered, trying to brush it aside.

'Come on, tell me. You know your secrets are safe with me.'

'It's not a secret,' Elizabeth answered, and then, taking a deep breath, she explained, 'Kat decided to confront me about my relationship with Robin. She told me I was behaving scandalously, because I was having an affair with a married man.'

'You're not the first to do that, and you won't be the last, I can assure you. Illicit relationships have been going on since the beginning of time. I suppose she's been worrying about the gossip, that sort of thing?'

Elizabeth looked at Grace Rose alertly. 'You've heard the gossip also, have you?'

'Everyone's heard it, my dear. It's all over town. I haven't paid any attention to it, because I understand you, and I trust your judgement. I was a bit surprised at first, but only because I had actually forgotten Robert had married the Robson girl years ago. From the start I thought *that* match was doomed. Presumably he's in the process of disentangling himself?'

'He is. They've been separated for five years, and it's been amicable. So there won't be a problem.'

Grace Rose leaned across the table. 'Do yourself a favour, Elizabeth dear. Duck your head down behind the fence and keep it there.'

'What do you mean?'

'Here's my best advice. Beginning today, make up your mind to keep a low profile. And Robert must keep one, too. Stay out of the limelight, stop going to all these events and dos, and avoid photographers. In other words, make yourself scarce on the London scene. Within two or three weeks the gossip will die out. The press have short memories and you'll be forgotten in no time. Gossip can be hurtful, but you must forget about it now. My father used to say that when someone was gossiping about him they were leaving others alone. Remember that. Drink up, Elizabeth, and let's look at the menu. I rather fancy the roast beef – it's delicious here, you know, melts in your mouth like butter.'

After they had both ordered smoked salmon, and roast beef from the trolley, Grace Rose sat back in her chair, regarding Elizabeth for a moment, studying her intently. Finally, she said, 'On Friday evening, when we spoke on the phone, you told me you were going to borrow ten million pounds from the bank, using some of the big pieces of jewellery you're putting up for auction as collateral. I'm correct about that, am I not?'

Elizabeth nodded. 'It's the only way to go. You see, offering to finance the building of the spas at the vineyards seemed the best way to solve the impasse between Broakes and Norfell. I honestly thought Broakes's idea about turning the manor houses into small boutique hotels was a really good one, inspired, in fact. Also, I've been in favour of spas for ages, and when I heard myself saying to Broakes that I would finance his scheme, I suddenly understood how much I would enjoy owning my own company. Look, I know Deravenels is mine, and that I run it . . . with Cecil and Robert. But actually *creating* something of my own genuinely appeals to me. I can do whatever I want with it, and I don't have to answer to anyone.'

'I understand exactly what you mean, Elizabeth, but why are you borrowing ten million pounds? It seems such a lot.'

Elizabeth smiled. 'I guess you could say I'm impatient. I want instant spas, instant success, and I'm going to start work on all of them at the same time, to that end. I want to open them at the same time, one after the other, with big announcements, splashy publicity. I call it *absolute impact at once*. Elizabeth Turner Spas: Forever Bliss. I can just see it all happening in my head.'

'So can I, but it is awfully ambitious of you, my dear. On the other hand, I've believed in bold gestures all my life – big schemes, big results. So my money's on you. If anyone can pull it off, you can. And don't forget the fellow we just ran into. Marcus Johnson is more than merely talented, in my opinion, he's something of a genius, and not only with press representation. He's got a unique knack for marketing.'

'Seems like fate that we ran into him, Grace Rose, and

when I'm ready I'll get in touch with him.' Elizabeth paused, then said, 'I had another idea during the night. It occurred to me that we'll be using all kinds of beauty products in the spas and why shouldn't they be mine? I can hire laboratories to make products which bear my name. It would be yet another money-maker.'

Grace Rose burst out laughing. 'Elizabeth, you're a *true* Deravenel even if your name is Turner! You sound just like my father. He was forever coming up with the grandest of schemes, the most extraordinary plans, and let's not forget that your father *was* the king of the takeover business at one moment in time. Harry was a genius at that.'

'I know, and as I pointed out to John Norfell on Friday, I learned at the knee of the master.'

'Norfell is an enigma to me,' Grace Rose remarked, frowning. 'He was very much in your half-sister's little clique, and I would have said also in her knickers, if I didn't know better. She wouldn't have appealed to him sexually. John Norfell has always gone for the beautiful face, you know. Quite the ladies' man.'

'How extraordinary!' Elizabeth grimaced. 'What woman would be interested in Norfell? He's not all that attractive.'

'True. But he does have two things a lot of women can't resist. *Power. Money.* And as my husband always said, you don't look at the mantelpiece when you're poking the fire.'

'Oh, Grace Rose, you're priceless!' Elizabeth laughed, picked up her flute of champagne and took a sip. 'Don't you agree with me about the products, Grace Rose? I know just the kind of scents I would choose, and I think I can create a distinctive line with the assistance of some excellent chemists.'

'I do like the idea, very much, and I suppose you'll go for florals. You did love my gardens when you were small and you were keen on picking my flowers.'

'Fancy you remembering that, and yes, florals do come to

234

mind, especially night-blooming jasmine, summer roses, hyacinths, carnations, and lily-of-the-valley. But I also enjoy the green scents, you know, the smells of summer grass and spring leaves. A really clever chemist will be able to interpret what I want, what I'm seeking.'

'You've put a great deal of thought into this, my dear. I have a feeling you're looking success in the face.'

'I hope I am. Ah, here's the smoked salmon, Grace Rose, and for once in my life I'm quite hungry.'

'So tell me what the spas are going to look like,' Grace Rose ventured at one moment, as they were eating the smoked salmon.

Elizabeth did so for the next half hour, her enthusiasm high, her voice full of excitement. 'I see each spa as being a vast white space, with just the merest hint of the palest of greens . . . filmy white muslin curtains, not one object of art, because the whole space must be empty, minimalistic. I will have tall celadon green vases filled with white blossoms and white orchids. But everything else will be white. I don't want anything to distract the eye. Simplicity is my aim. I want women to come to my spas to have the best, most blissful treatments, to feel pampered and cared for . . . they must be able to leave their cares outside. I want them to relax completely, to float on their dreams.'

'I understand. And by the way, that's the sort of line Marcus Johnson would appreciate . . . *float on their dreams*.'

'You're right, it's not half bad, is it? Maybe it can be used in advertising.'

Grace Rose sat back, smiling broadly. 'Elizabeth, you're inspired. I admire this positive attitude of yours, this determination, enthusiasm and sense of adventure. I predict your spas will be a big success.'

Elizabeth and Cecil Williams sat together in Elizabeth's office at Deravenels on Monday morning. This early meeting on the first day of the week had become a ritual. Usually Robert Dunley was present, but because he was still in Marbella it was just the two of them today.

'When do you think you'll meet with the bank?' Elizabeth began, anxious to discuss the spas.

'I'll give Ed Aspley a ring after our meeting, and set it up for tomorrow, if that's possible. But you don't have to wait for the bank's approval, Elizabeth, they'll lend you the money. You can get started on the spas today if you want. I know you're itching to do so.'

'I can? Oh, how wonderful, Cecil! I do want to start meeting with architects and designers, and I must phone some of the top real estate agents. I came up with the idea of creating our own products, and I want to look at various laboratories, seek out the best chemists.'

'Talk to Melanie Onslow in the hotel division, Elizabeth. You know she's an expert on products, chemists and laboratories. We put her in charge of stocking the spas which have been completed in the two American hotels. She'll be helpful.'

'I should have thought of Melanie at once. She's done a fantastic job. I'll call her later.'

Cecil said, in a slightly lower voice, 'I know Robert spoke to you about Francis Walsington's worries regarding terrorists. I do believe Francis is right. We must make sure all of our facilities are well protected, and we may well have to bring in an outside security company. What's your feeling?'

'I agree with you, I've had a nervous wobble in the pit of my stomach for quite some time. Terrorists are not going away and they're getting more dangerous. Furthermore, we are the perfect targets. I notice the Spanish government is being somewhat guarded in their public statements, and last night Robin told me most of Francis's contacts say it *was* terrorists who blew up that tanker.'

'Francis usually gets the correct information, as you well know, and I'll always go along with him. So shall I tell him to start evaluating Deravco's security first?'

'*Absolutely*. And immediately.'

The two of them talked for another half hour. Eventually Cecil went back to his own office and Elizabeth began making phone calls to set in motion the creation of her spas.

TWENTY-FIVE

'What did you mean, Robin, when you said to me that love won't wait?' Elizabeth sat with her elbows on the kitchen table, staring at him in the candlelight.

'Just *that* . . . Love won't wait. You have to immediately grab hold of it, hang on to it, when it suddenly appears in all its glory. Yes, you really do, because it certainly has a way of disappearing on you. In fact, you could say it's ephemeral. It evaporates . . . just like that!' Robert snapped his thumb and finger together. 'Blink, and you'll find it's gone.'

'You and I certainly grabbed it, didn't we?'

'We did, thank God!' Reaching out, he took hold of her hand, kissed her fingers. 'I love you, Elizabeth, I always have. But then one day I *fell in love with you*, and love wouldn't wait. It had to be the same for the two of us, didn't it? Exactly then, at the same moment.'

'It was. And I love you, Robin, you're my whole life. I

hate it when you're away. June and July were positively awful, what with all your trips to Madrid and Marbella. I'm glad they're finished.'

'For the moment, anyway,' he reminded her, and stood up. Going around the kitchen table, Robert put his hands on her shoulders, bent over, kissed the top of her auburn head, and pulled her to her feet. He looked at her intently, his face suddenly turning serious when he said, 'Can I inveigle you to come upstairs?'

'You don't have to inveigle me, I shall come willingly.' Taking hold of his hand, she blew out the candles, and together they went up to her bedroom.

A bright August moon shone in the dark night sky, filled her bedroom with soft silvery light, so that everything looked smudged, slightly diffused. Robert threw a log on the remaining embers in the fireplace and turned around, took Elizabeth in his arms. He held her close to him, marvelling yet again how perfectly she fit into him. They were both tall and slender, similar in build, so much alike. Her arms went around his back; she rested her head against his chest for a moment, and stepped away, began to unbutton his cotton shirt. Leaning forward, Robert kissed her deeply on the mouth; as he felt himself growing harder he put his hands on her buttocks and brought her closer. He wanted her so badly he could hardly breathe.

Looking at him swiftly, observing the longing on his face, Elizabeth whispered, 'Remember, love won't wait,' and began to pull off her T-shirt; then she unzipped her skirt, stepped out of it, stood in the middle of the bedroom, staring at him.

Robert took off his shirt, undressed rapidly, and strode towards her, lifted her up and carried her to the bed. 'Love can't wait. And I *won't*,' he said against her neck.

He placed her on the bed and lay next to her. Resting on one elbow, he gazed down into her face. 'You're beautiful,

Elizabeth.' He smiled at her. 'I've never felt this way about anyone else, you know.'

She merely smiled back, made no response, simply touched his cheek with her fingertips.

Bending over her, he kissed her forehead, her cheeks, her neck, smoothed one hand across her breast. The nipple instantly hardened, and he kissed it; a moment later his hand was moving along her thigh and settling at the core of her.

'It's as if I've never had you before,' he said. 'I love it, this feeling of . . . discovery . . . it's always like this with you. As if it's the first time we're making love.'

'I know,' she murmured, and closed her eyes, let him do what he wanted. She felt herself growing warmer, the heat rising up from between her legs to flood her belly. She savoured this feeling he induced in her, of melting under his hands, growing hot and excited at the same time. Losing herself in him filled her with joy. Thinking only of him, of nothing but this: their sexual bonding was all that mattered to her at this moment.

He moved on top of her, slid into her, lifted her to him, held her tightly in his arms. Her legs and arms went around him, felt like a velvet vice, and he gasped with delight and pleasure as he moved. In a strangled voice he muttered, 'I can't wait, Elizabeth, I can't wait.'

She pulled his head closer to hers, found his mouth, and their tongues entwined as their bodies entwined and they moved together like one being. They came together, cresting on waves of intense feeling.

Sated and blissful, they remained in the same position for a long time, until Robert moved, looked into her dark eyes which were brimming with love for him. 'It *was* good, wasn't it? Good sex, yes?'

'The best sex. We're getting better at it, Robin.'

'We need to do a lot more practising though.'

240

She smiled, loving him so much. 'You won't ever stop doing this to me, will you, Robin?'

'Wild elephants couldn't stop me,' he murmured, laughter echoing in his voice.

They sat in front of the fire in her bedroom, wrapped in their robes and drinking the bottle of chilled champagne Robert had brought up from the kitchen.

Leaning back, sipping the sparkling wine. Elizabeth stared into the fire for a moment or two, before turning to Robert, asking, 'What do you think will happen with the French conglomerate? What I mean is, will François de Burgh run Dauphin? Or will the top executives remain in charge as they were under his father?'

'I don't know. He's sort of young, wouldn't you say.' Robert grinned. 'Whoops. Sorry about that! Wrong person to say it to, eh?' He shook his head. 'Everybody's in shock in the company. Well, that's what Francis Walsington says. It stands to reason, Elizabeth. Who expected Henri de Burgh to get thrown by his horse in a hunting accident in the woods at Versailles?'

'And trampled on the head by the horse, no less!'

'He was quite an exceptional equestrian apparently. Sheer bad luck.'

'You never know what life's going to toss at you, Robin. We're both aware of that, aren't we?'

'Funny, Ambrose said almost the same thing to me just the other day . . . To think that we lost all of our brothers one after the other . . . it just beggars belief. I don't suppose we'll ever really get over it . . . Ambrose and Merry feel the same way I do.'

'There's no way to make a bargain with Death,' Elizabeth said. 'When It wants you, It takes you.'

Robert said, 'I spoke to Amy the other day. About the divorce, Elizabeth.'

'Oh,' was all she could say. Coming out of the blue, his words had surprised her.

'She wants me to go down to see her in Cirencester some time next month.'

'So you're going, are you?'

'I have to. I have to disentangle myself, to quote you quoting Grace Rose.'

'I suppose you will –' Elizabeth broke off, cocked her head on one side, listening. 'I think your mobile phone is ringing. Yes, it is, Robin. But where is it?'

He jumped up, went in search of his trousers, found the mobile in his pocket, spoke into it. 'Hello?' he said, and listened. 'Oh, it's you, Ambrose. Yes, everything's fine. Why are you phoning at this hour?' He listened again, moving closer to the window, for better clarity. 'No, there won't be any problem, I'm sure of that.' He looked across at Elizabeth, asked, 'Do you mind if Ambrose comes to lunch tomorrow? He has to be in Harrogate this weekend.'

'I'd love it,' she exclaimed.

'She'd love it, Ambrose, and so would I. See you when you get here.'

The Dunleys had to be the best-looking family in England, Elizabeth decided as she walked along the beach at Ravenscar with Robert and his older brother.

Ambrose was a good-looking man, if not quite as startlingly handsome as Robin, and their sisters Miranda and Catherine were unusually beautiful, as eye-catching as movie stars, in fact. They were all dark-haired and had brown or hazel eyes, except for Merry. Hers were as vividly blue as cornflowers. Their brothers, now dead, had been of the same ilk. Gorgeous was the only word to describe them.

Funny about the Dunleys. Their grandfather Edmund had worked for her grandfather Henry Turner, and his son John, their father, had been in the employ of Harry Turner. Her father had always praised John Dunley to the hilt, but, like his father before him, John had subsequently fallen into disfavour.

It had been her half-sister Mary who had struck the final unjust blow against John Dunley and banished him from Deravenels forever. John had not deserved the treatment he received, and neither had *his* father before him. Injustices had been inflicted upon them both. Now she was making amends. She was raising up the Dunleys, bringing them back to prominence and power at Deravenels once again.

Robert shared her power at the head of the company, and his sister was her executive assistant, whilst Ambrose was now totally in charge of the Marbella Project. Once again he was fully employed by the conglomerate in a position of importance. In several weeks his wife would come to work at Deravenels, as her second assistant, and Anne would be put in charge of the Elizabeth Turner Spas, her own company.

The two brothers were in deep conversation as they walked along the beach, but Elizabeth was only half listening. She was enjoying her own thoughts, laughing to herself. She knew full well about the endless gossip within Deravenels, how certain executives were constantly ranting and raving about the return of the Dunleys. In particular, John Norfell was vociferous in his condemnation of them, and therefore, indirectly of her. Robert had always been suspicious of him, and rightly so. *She* now had him in her sights.

Elizabeth stole a surreptitious look at Robert, the man she had fallen so deeply in love with. *Her man*. He looked wonderful this morning in a black turtleneck sweater, a tan-and-burgundy tweed jacket – old, but all the nicer because of that – beige slacks, and with a burgundy cashmere scarf wrapped around his neck. Ambrose was similarly dressed in a sweater, tweed jacket and blue jeans. Although it was late August, it was still cool here at Ravenscar despite the sunshine. A wind came off the North Sea, as usual, chilling the air.

'Don't you agree?' Robert said, turning to her.

'Oh, sorry. I was miles away. I missed that,' Elizabeth answered. 'What did you say?'

'That Tony Blair has something –' He lifted his hands in one of his typical gestures. 'I suppose I would characterize it as something rather special.'

'I agree. He's got charisma, Robin. Tons of it, and I admire his style. Mind you, I always liked John Major. He's one of the greatest charmers I've ever met.'

'I second that, Elizabeth,' Ambrose remarked, glancing at her, smiling warmly. 'He was, unfortunately, grossly under-estimated. Good-looking, clever, charming, personable, but the public somehow didn't quite get it, or get him. Pity, really.'

'I suppose you click with the camera or you don't,' Elizabeth said. 'He didn't always come across on television, certainly not as well as he performed in person.' Now slipping her arm through Robert's she said, 'Have you discussed the French conglomerate with Ambrose?'

'Yes, he has,' Ambrose interjected before Robert could answer. 'I think that François de Burgh will be trained to step into his father's shoes, to run the show. He was working there anyway, as was that wife of his. Frankly, I think we'll see them totally in control and in no time at all.'

'Is François de Burgh that clever? That skilled a businessman?' Elizabeth asked. She threw Ambrose a sceptical look.

'Walsington believes he's shrewd, and much more experienced than we think. He's also got an exceptionally clever mother who's going to make sure absolute power at Dauphin rests in the hands of her eldest son and not the hired help. She's going to be in there, overseeing things. So I understand from Francis.'

'And what about my erstwhile cousin Marie Stewart de Burgh? Do you think she'll be troublesome to *us*?'

'I'm not sure. But hazarding a guess, I would say that she will be far too busy helping her husband run his company to be casting an eye on Deravenels.'

'I hope so,' Elizabeth murmured, and shivered.

Robert looked at her, put an arm around her shoulder. 'Are you cold, sweetheart?'

'It's the wind,' Elizabeth responded, but it wasn't the wind at all. The shiver had been involuntary. She felt as if someone had just walked over her grave.

'Do you want to go in?' Ambrose asked.

'Let's do that,' she answered. 'The champagne awaits.'

Elizabeth and Ambrose went into the library and Robert hurried off to the kitchen to let Lucas know they had returned from their walk.

Ambrose threw several logs on the fire, moved them around with the poker, then straightened. He sat down opposite Elizabeth, shaking his head. 'It's so much colder here at Ravenscar than it is in Harrogate. It was really mild there when I set out this morning.'

'It's the North Sea,' Elizabeth explained, 'and there's always a light breeze coming off the water even on the hottest of days.' She grinned. 'Woolly jumpers are mandatory.'

'My mother once told me that my grandfather Edmund

never liked to visit your grandfather Henry when he was up here, because of the icy weather. He called it the Arctic Circle.'

Elizabeth laughed; she liked Ambrose. He had always been one of her favourites, just as Merry was. 'I shall be forever grateful to my father because he put in central heating. It really makes life easier in winter, believe me.'

'I bet it does. These old piles are hellish to keep warm, not to mention expensive.' He settled back in the chair, stretched out his long legs.

Elizabeth leaned forward slightly, and said, 'I want to thank you, Ambrose, for all your hard work in Marbella. You've done a really sensational job, pulling everything together the way you have, and so very quickly really.'

'Thank you for saying that. It's been tough going at times, I can tell you, but the place was well worth rescuing. It will be the most extraordinary resort when it's finally finished, even though I do say so myself.'

'I'm glad you're now working at Deravenels on a permanent basis, and it's lovely to have Merry as my assistant. I don't know how I ever managed without your sister, and soon Anne will be running the spas for me. I must admit, I do enjoy being surrounded by Dunleys. It's like having my own family.'

'But we *are* your family, Elizabeth, at least we will be when Robert finally gets everything sorted out with Amy, and you two get married. Actually, Anne and I were hoping that you would let us have the reception at our flat – after all, as you just said, we're like family.'

Elizabeth could only nod. She sat frozen in the chair, not only startled but stunned by his words. She was also annoyed. Why had Robin discussed these private matters and indicated that they would marry once he was free to do so? He knew very well she had no intention of marrying anyone.

Quite unexpectedly, she felt as if he had broken her trust.

'Here we are with the Krug,' Robert announced as he came into the library with Lucas, who was bringing the bottle of champagne in a silver bucket filled with ice. Robert was carrying the three champagne flutes by their stems.

Lucas opened the bottle, filled their glasses, handed them around and mentioned that lunch would be at one o'clock. He then departed, heading in the direction of the kitchen.

They toasted each other sitting around the fire, talked about the opening of the Spanish resort the following spring, and Robert encouraged Elizabeth to tell Ambrose about her auction.

Filled with tension, her face taut, Elizabeth tried to relax. After taking a few sips of the champagne, she managed to quell her irritation with Robert by pushing the remarks Ambrose had made to the back of her mind.

She talked about the various aspects of the auction, how it had been separated into different categories, covering the art, the diamond tiaras, the jewellery, and so on. But she mostly concentrated on Ambrose, directing her conversation to him, genuinely unable to look Robert in the face.

'My God, what a fabulous auction it's going to be!' Ambrose exclaimed when she had finished. 'I'm certain it will bring in millions. I'm not going to miss it, and I bet you're not either, Robert, are you?'

'I shall be there with bells on, standing right next to Elizabeth, praying that everything goes for the highest price.'

At this moment Lucas appeared and announced that lunch was ready. Elizabeth put down her glass and stood. 'Let's go in, shall we?' she said, striding ahead, stifling her irritation.

TWENTY-SIX

'Ambrose thinks he might have offended you in some way without realizing it,' Robert said, leaning against the door jamb, looking across the room at Elizabeth, endeavouring to appraise her mood.

She sat behind the desk in her small office, papers spread out in front of her, and instantly lifted her head at the sound of his voice. She replied, after a moment, 'No, he didn't offend me.'

He knew at once that she was still put out, as she had been at lunch, obviously annoyed by something. Irritation echoed in her voice and her face was tauter than ever. 'But there *is* something wrong,' he said, walking forward, coming to a stop in front of her desk. 'I know you too well and for too long not to understand that, so don't deny it.'

For a moment she was silent, uncertain about getting involved in a difficult discussion at this moment, and then instantly changed her mind, decided to tell him the truth.

She said in a low, steady voice. 'It's *you* I'm annoyed with, not your brother. He's just the innocent bystander.'

Robert frowned, appeared puzzled. 'Why? What have I done?'

'You told Ambrose we're getting married when you're divorced from Amy. I was so taken aback I didn't know what to say to him.'

He shook his head vehemently 'Oh, no, I did not! If Ambrose mentioned the word marriage he did so of his own accord. Of course he knows I wish to straighten out the mess, and he made an assumption, I suppose. And that's all there is to it.'

Elizabeth stared at him, made no comment.

'Anyway, why didn't you bring it up earlier? When we were having drinks before lunch? Because that's obviously when he said something to you . . . when I was in the kitchen with Lucas, getting the champagne.'

'I didn't want to create a scene, make a fuss.'

'But you did create an extremely bad atmosphere during lunch, Elizabeth, made us feel uncomfortable, and you know it. You were clipped, even curt when you deigned to speak to either of us, but mostly you were silent and looked like the wrath of God. We both understood you were in a temper. *You* made sure we did.'

'I wasn't in a temper, I just felt . . . *betrayed*.'

He sighed, shaking his head. 'Ambrose made an assumption, and so did you. How can you think I would betray your trust? *Me*, of all people?'

For a moment she remained silent, and then she exclaimed, 'He said he and Anne wanted to give the wedding reception at their flat. Why would he say such a thing if you hadn't confided in him?'

'Oh, don't be so damned silly! Again, it was based on his assumption that when I was free, you and I would get married.

And it's perfectly natural for him to think that, isn't it? I'm sure most people would do the same. After all, we've created a scandal, you and I, with our very public affair, haven't we? So marriage would be the next step surely in everyone's minds.'

She shook her head. 'You know I don't want to marry you, Robin. You don't even have to get a divorce as far as I'm concerned.'

Her words unexpectedly inflamed him. 'Why don't you want to marry me?' he demanded, placing his hands on her desk, leaning forward, staring into her face intently, his eyes narrowing. 'What's wrong with me? Am I not good enough for the Turner heiress? The inheritor of Deravenels? Is that it? Or do you think I'm after your money and your power?'

He was furious, and Elizabeth sat up straighter in the chair, thunderstruck by his angry tone, harsh words, and the hard expression on his face. 'How can you say such things?' she cried heatedly. 'Of course you're good enough. More than good enough, and I know you're not involved with me because you want what I have. It's *me* you want.'

'You're damn right. And I want you to be my wife,' he cried. When he noticed how she had suddenly stiffened in the chair, turned pale, he stepped away from the desk. Adopting a gentler tone, he went on, 'Once I'm free, let's get married, Elizabeth. We can just . . . run away, if you like. *Elope*. It doesn't have to be a big fancy wedding, you know, just the two of us and two witnesses.'

As she looked at him, at a total loss for words, that mischievous, very charming smile of his flashed across his handsome face, and he said, very softly, 'We *should* get married, darling, we love and adore each other. And eventually, when you're ready, we can have a child, the heir that everyone's always on about. An heir to keep Deravenels safe. Don't you want that?'

She couldn't answer. She was mortified he had brought up this matter, and before she could stop herself she snapped, 'No, I certainly don't want that. I'm only twenty-five. I've plenty of time to think about an heir. You see, I've no intention of dying young. And anyway, you've taken offence over nothing.'

'How can you say that?' He gave her a hard stare.

'Because it's true.'

'*Nothing*? I've taken offence about nothing, you say. What about me, my feelings? Don't I matter in this relationship, Elizabeth? It takes two to tango, doesn't it? Hasn't it ever occurred to you that I would be much happier *married* to you than not married?'

'You've always known I don't want to get married. Not ever. I told you that when I was eight.'

'You're a grown woman now,' he replied in a sharp voice, his anger flaring again. 'And you're having an affair with me, a grown man, not a little boy in short trousers. We are in love, emotionally and physically involved. Surely marriage is the natural outcome, isn't it?'

An obdurate look settled on her face. 'I don't want to marry anyone, Robin. This is not against *you*, and you're taking it too personally.'

'I sure as hell am taking it personally!' he shouted and swung around, strode out of her office, slamming the door so hard behind him a painting on the wall rattled.

Elizabeth sat back in the chair, her face suddenly stark, strained. She hadn't meant to hurt his feelings, or demean him in any way, but she had done so, unintentionally. Wondering what to do, how to make amends, to soothe his wounded ego, she got up and went out onto the terrace.

She could see Robert striding down the path through the tiered gardens, making for the ruined stronghold no doubt. I'd better let him cool off, she decided. It's better I talk to him when he's calmer. I must make him understand how much I love him.

Try though she did, Elizabeth found it very hard to concentrate on her plans for the spas, and after an hour she rose, picked up her shawl and went outside. The blue sky of earlier had curdled, was a peculiar greyish-green, and she could smell rain in the cool air. Glancing up at the sky, she had the feeling there was going to be a thunderstorm, and she wrapped the cashmere shawl around her, ran down the path, calling Robin's name. There was no response.

To her surprise, he was not in the ruined stronghold; in fact, he was nowhere in sight. Where could he have gone? She had no idea. He would have had to pass the window of her office if he had come back to the house; he must be outside. Then it occurred to her he may have gone down to the beach; as she hurried out of the ruined stronghold there was a crack of thunder and large raindrops began to fall.

Half an hour later Elizabeth and Lucas found Robert on the beach, huddled under a cluster of rocks. The thunderstorm was still raging furiously, and the rain was coming down in sheets.

'I was worried to death about you,' Elizabeth cried when she spotted him, rushing towards the rocks with a raincoat and a heavy sweater. 'Why didn't you come back to the house?'

'I had just started out when there was a cloudburst,' he explained, struggling out of his soaked tweed jacket, laying it on a rock, pulling on the fisherman's sweater. 'Gosh, that's better. I was freezing. Anyway, I thought it was wiser to wait under the rocks until it eased off, but it hasn't.'

'I think it's set in for the night. Here, put this raincoat on.' Turning around, she said to Lucas, 'Bring the scarf, please, would you?'

'Here you are, Miss Turner.' Lucas handed it to her and, glancing at Robert, asked, 'Are you all right, Mr Dunley? You haven't hurt yourself, have you?'

'No, no, I'm fine. Tripped over those small rocks over there, when I started to run for shelter, but nothing damaged.'

'I saw you trip through the window, sir, and I was getting ready to come down to the beach just as Miss Turner came into the kitchen. Glad you're all right.'

'Thanks, Lucas.' Wrapping the scarf around his neck, Robert took the umbrella from Elizabeth, picked up his soaked jacket, and half smiled. 'Thanks for rescuing me.'

She smiled back, nodded, then set out, walking up the beach holding her own umbrella, followed by the two men with theirs.

Once they were back at Ravenscar, Elizabeth insisted that Robert take a hot shower, and whilst he was doing so she made a pot of tea, which Lucas carried up to her bedroom.

Ten minutes later Robert joined her in front of the fire, wrapped in a thick terry-cloth robe. 'My God, I can't believe it!' he said, walking over to the window, glancing out. 'You were right, I think it *has* set in for the night.'

As he turned around, Elizabeth said swiftly, 'Robin, I'm sorry, I'm so very sorry. I didn't mean to hurt you, my words came out all wrong. I was only trying to say that I don't want to get married. But it has nothing to do with *you*, darling, honestly. It's all to do with me. I love you, I want to be with you for the rest of my life, and you know this. I would never hurt you in any way, certainly not knowingly.'

He sat down in the other chair, poured himself a cup of tea, dropped in sweetener and a sliver of lemon. After taking a long swallow, he placed the cup on a small table. Reaching out, he took hold of her hand, brought it to his lips, kissed it.

'There's nothing to forgive, sweetheart. I admit I reacted heatedly, perhaps over-reacted would be the best way to put it. We do feel the same about each other, and I want to be with you always, but suddenly this afternoon, I realized how much I do want us to be married. However, since you don't care to make it legal, so be it. We'll live together as we are doing now.'

She let out a long sigh of relief. 'Oh, Robin, I'm so happy you've said that. I couldn't bear to lose you.'

'You won't. I'll be here no matter what.'

'Marriage has never tempted me,' she announced. Shaking her head, she continued quietly, 'It has never appealed to me. Just the opposite. I suppose because I've only seen ruinous marriages, unhappy wives, domineering husbands – *cheating* domineering husbands, I should perhaps add.'

'I know you haven't had many happy examples. Ever since you were a child you've been faced with volatile scenes which had to do with matrimony, so it's not surprising you think the way you do.'

'My father was the prime example of a domineering, angry, frustrated husband, Robin, a man who was probably verbally abusive to some if not all of his wives. He was certainly verbally abusive to me.'

'He was happy with his first wife, you know. He and his Spanish Catherine were very much in love, that I was told by my mother, who knew her quite well. The only problem in their marriage was actually the lack of an heir – otherwise they got on very well. She was inordinately clever, Elizabeth, a hard worker, efficient, energetic, and she had been extremely well educated in Spain. Your father's head got turned by . . . well, by your mother. After he met her, he became besotted with Anne. Anyway, let's not go into all of that, you've heard the story before.'

'Then he met Jane Selmere, and fell hook, line and sinker for her, and decided to marry her. He suddenly saw only faults in my mother and no doubt drove her to desperation. When Jane died after Edward was born, he married the German Anne. But she was plain.'

'Ugly is a better word to describe her,' Robert interjected.

'She was a nice person, Robin, and certainly kind to me and Edward. And Mary, too. I always thought she was dreadfully *afraid* of Harry, and I know for a fact she was happy to be quietly divorced. I always felt much more sorry for Kathy Howard Norfell, his gorgeous trophy wife, too young for him. And unfortunately she was not very bright.'

'Are you kidding? She was as thick as a plank! Infidelity was her undoing, my father confided quite a lot about that to me. He was working for your father then. But who can blame her? By the time Harry married young Kathy he had become somewhat portly, ungainly, and monstrous, to be absolutely honest. No wonder she hopped into those many different beds . . . of more handsome and virile younger men. *Her undoing*. Ghastly divorce it was. Thank God Catherine Parker outlived him.'

Elizabeth said, 'And then along came the gorgeous Rear-Admiral, full of charm and potent sexuality. And infatuated as she had long been, Catherine Parker married the irresistible Tom Selmere, who then started to flirt with me, even tried to seduce me on the side.'

Robert laughed. 'Selmere was a bit of a bounder and a poor example of husband material, wasn't he, my pet?'

'That's true, he was. But, so was Philip Alvarez. He married Mary for her money, I'm certain of that now. And then he dumped her, to be brutal about it.'

'Didn't even come to her funeral, the rotten sod,' Robert said. 'But *listen* to me,' he went on, his voice growing serious. 'Not all men are like your father, Selmere and Alvarez. I'm not. Surely you understand that after all these years.'

'I do. I do, Robin, honestly. But I want . . . to be *free*, independent, my own woman. I don't want marriage, not at any price.' She gave him a pleading look. 'Can we drop the subject now? *Please?*'

'Absolutely. We won't discuss it any further.' He took a sip of tea, and went on, 'Thanks for coming down to the beach with Lucas.'

'You didn't hurt yourself when you tripped over the pile of rocks, did you?'

'No, I just got cold and wet. I'm feeling better now. In a few minutes I'll get dressed, and we'll have a drink.'

'You have forgiven me, haven't you, Robin?'

'There's nothing to forgive,' he said for the second time.

'It's a beautiful sunny day, Robin,' Elizabeth said, as she drew back the curtains and looked out of the window on Sunday morning. 'The storm's gone farther north, I suspect. Come on, get up, lazy bones, let's go downstairs and have breakfast.'

'It's not even six o'clock,' Robert muttered, but nonetheless he was awake and he threw back the bedclothes, got out of bed. Reaching for his robe, he pulled it on, and found his slippers. 'So, what do you plan to make for breakfast, Miss Turner?'

'I'm sure there are all sorts of things in the refrigerator.

Lucas always buys kippers. Would you like some of those? Or mushrooms and kidneys? They're his standbys.'

'How about simple boiled eggs and toast?' he suggested, leading her out of the bedroom and down the stairs.

'Boiled eggs it is,' she agreed. 'I'll have the same.'

Once they were in the kitchen Elizabeth turned on the coffee pot, went to the refrigerator, took out the carton of milk and the eggs, and hurried over to the island in the middle of the room.

'Is there any orange juice?' Robin asked.

'Oh, sorry, I forgot. Yes, it's in the fridge.'

After filling two glasses, Robert carried them over to the kitchen table, picked up the remote control and turned on the television. 'I just want to see what they say about the weather –' He broke off, frowning, staring at the set, and Elizabeth swung around, followed his gaze.

'The car Princess Diana was travelling in drove into the Point D'Alma Tunnel at twenty-three minutes past midnight,' the voice of the newscaster was saying. 'The ambulance which arrived just after the crash took her to Pitié-Sâlpetrière, the hospital where she died in the early hours of the morning.'

'Oh, my God!' Elizabeth cried. 'It can't be possible. No, no, it can't be.' She turned to Robert, who was rooted to the spot near the table, and very carefully put down the carton of eggs before she dropped it. Her voice shook as she added, 'It just can't be, Robin. Not Princess Diana.'

Robert was speechless. Putting his arm around Elizabeth, he eased her down into the chair, then sat next to her, all the time staring at the television set in disbelief. Like Elizabeth, he was unable to absorb the horrific news for a few seconds.

Tears were rolling down Elizabeth's cheeks, and she pulled a tissue out of her pocket, wiped her eyes. 'Those poor little boys, her young sons,' she whispered, filled with enormous sorrow, and began to weep again.

It was Robert who eventually brought two mugs of coffee to the table, which is where they sat for the next few hours listening to the reports coming in from Paris and London. It was August thirty-first, 1997. Like the rest of Britain, and of the whole world, they were stunned and grief-stricken by the tragic death of the beautiful princess who had been cut down in the prime of her life.

TWENTY-SEVEN

Quiet as death. That is how it is here today. I've never known Deravenels to be like this. So silent, so heavy in spirit. People are working as usual but sadness casts a strange haze over their faces. They slowly move along the corridors, talk in whispers, do their jobs efficiently, but that cloud of pain is a palpable thing, hangs over them like a mist. And that is the way it is in the whole of Britain, and even in the rest of the world, at least part of it.

A vibrant and beautiful young woman no longer exists on this planet. And yet . . . she does. She is in our hearts and minds where she will live with us forever. Sudden and unexpected, her violent death has had a violent impact on us, made us feel mortal and vulnerable, somehow at risk. Grief stuns, brings us to mourning.

It is five days since she died and we remain in shock, unable to truly comprehend that she is gone. I feel it strongly . . . the sense of hurt and staggering loss, as though a shimmering dream has been smashed to smithereens. She was so vitally alive, so exuberant, so caring and full of love to give, especially to the lost, the abandoned, the helpless and the frail. The flash of that valiant smile. the sparkle in those bright blue eyes . . . it hardly seems believable that we will never see them again . . . except in our memories . . .

The death of Princess Diana has made me feel vulnerable, in so many different ways. Not about my own mortality, but about Robin and the different aspects of our relationship. Last night I could not sleep . . . I lay awake worrying about him . . . what if he was killed or suddenly died? What would I do without him? My life would be over. That is the way I feel because he is my whole existence. And yet I hurt him so badly this past weekend. My words cut to the quick, I know that. I should be more careful in the things I say . . . I should not rush in where angels fear to tread. That was one of my father's often said remarks, borrowed from one of his favourite songs. He had a good voice, my father. I can hear it now in my head, hear him singing: 'Fools rush in, where angels fear to tread.' He was a tenor and so good he could have sung in the opera.

My father loved music, and he frequently wrote it. He might well have written this song, but he didn't. I asked him once and he said he wished he could claim it as his own but that it had been written by Johnny Mercer and Rube Bloom. My father the romantic . . . the romantic fool. Robin called him a monstrosity the other day, and perhaps he did become that. But once he had been the Golden Boy. Glorious. Handsome, charming, irresistible. Women fell at his feet.

What's this? Tears on my cheeks? Am I crying for my father? Or Robin? Or Princess Diana? My feelings are muddled up today and my emotions are on the surface.

My father Harry Turner. I loved him and now I also revere him. How proud I am of his great accomplishments and what he did for Deravenels during the years he ran it . . .

Does the victim always love the tormentor? Is that the way it is with everyone? I have often wondered why my father treated me so shabbily when I was a child, why he was so violent verbally, so appallingly nasty to me. He shouted and ranted and sent me away. He was a wealthy man and yet he kept Kat Ashe on a tight budget and we were always short of money those years when I was growing up. It was people like Aunt Grace Rose and John Dunley, Robin's father, who showed me kindness and brought some happiness into my life. John because he allowed his son to come and stay at Waverley Court, and Grace Rose because she invited me to visit her at Stonehurst Farm. And when I was there, either alone or with Robin, we were dreadfully spoiled by her. She created magical times for us.

Why did my father hate me when I was a little girl? Was it because he saw my mother in me? And had he hated my mother so much that he had to take it out on me? An innocent child, who could only have been HIS, with my bright auburn hair and tall, slender build like my grandfather Henry Turner. Harry Turner never laid a hand on me in violence, but his tongue was like a lash. I was his victim and yet I loved him, and tried so hard to please him. Was that because I wanted him so desperately to love me; to bring me back into the fold? He did that when I least expected it, when I had not seen him for years. He invited me to come and visit him with Mary, my half-sister, and we all had lunch together. He liked what he saw, I think, and he was impressed by my intelligence and tickled to death that I had his colouring and bright red hair. And so I was accepted. According to Kat Ashe, my father was awed by my knowledge, and proud of my extraordinary education, at least so she informed me at that time.

Robin believes my vow never to marry springs from my fear of it. And he says I fear marriage because I've seen such terrible examples of the state of matrimony. Perhaps he's correct. I cannot fathom out why a piece of paper makes a difference in a relationship. It is, after all, just a piece of paper . . . no, not true. It's a LEGAL piece of paper that has a great deal of importance in many matters in our lives. I am not enamoured of it even though I am enamoured of Robin. I must therefore consider that piece of paper . . . most carefully. I must also do my best to make Robin feel better. I must reassure him . . .

'Come in, Merry,' Elizabeth called out, in answer to the loud knock on her office door.

Merry's beautiful face appeared around it, and she said, 'Marcus Johnson's here. Shall I show him in?'

'Yes, and will you please let Grace Rose know that I'll be there for drinks with her at six o'clock, as I promised.'

'Yes, I will.' Merry disappeared and closed the door behind her.

Elizabeth pulled the black folder towards her, opened it, and ran her eyes down the list of points which had been made on the first sheet by Marcus Johnson. Then she looked up as Merry showed him in.

Standing, she went around the desk, took his outstretched hand and shook it. 'Good morning, Marcus, I'm glad you could come today instead of tomorrow. I'm very appreciative.'

'Morning, Elizabeth, and there was no problem at all.'

'Do sit down,' she murmured, and took a seat opposite him behind her desk.

'Tragic, wasn't it, about Princess Diana? Everybody's still reeling,' Marcus remarked as he settled in the chair.

'Including me. I haven't been able to shake off the sadness

or the sense of . . . *doom*,' Elizabeth said. 'I can't help thinking it was an accident that needn't have happened.'

'I think that as well, and so do a lot of people. Not enough care was taken of her . . . it seems to me that it was a . . . well, a bit of a chaotic situation.'

'Now that you mention it, I have a feeling it probably was.' Glancing at the page in front of her, she went on, 'Well, let's get down to business, Marcus. I'm really pleased with this proposal of yours, thrilled actually.' She smiled, and added, 'I want to hire your company to do the launch of the Elizabeth Turner Spas, and also I'd like you to help with the publicity for the auction of the Deravenel–Turner Collections. Sotheby's will be doing a great deal, of course, but I have a feeling I might need some . . . well, let's just call it auxiliary publicity, shall we? How do you feel about this?'

'We can handle everything for you, and thank you for your confidence in us, Elizabeth. I'll put two different account executives on. One, with her own staff, will deal with publicity for the spas, and the other person, also with a staff, can work on the auction.' He leaned forward slightly. 'You obviously like our plan, and the way we wish to launch the spas. How do you feel about the launch party being held at a hotel though, rather than at the spa in London?'

'I love it! And you came up with the best suggestion, in my opinion, the *perfect solution*,' Elizabeth laughed. 'I was really worried about my white floors, white curtains and white furniture. And masses of people spilling drinks, dropping food and scuffing the floors.'

'I know what you mean. It's a nightmarish scenario. And that was the first thing Isabella Fort came up with. She focused on it immediately and opted for the hotel reception. She suggested the Dorchester for the launch, as you've read in our presentation. Or do you prefer another hotel?'

'The Dorchester is fine for the reception. Also, I'm keen

on the idea of giving tours to a few beauty, health and fashion editors. Showing the spa to them in groups of six, with a catered lunch at the spa afterwards is brilliant. In fact, I approve of all of your ideas, which is why I'm hiring you. When do you think you'll need to start?'

'If you still plan to open the first spa in London in April of 1998, then it would have to be now. Immediately. We do need six months to plan everything properly.'

'I'll give the contracts you prepared to Merry and she'll look them over, as will my lawyers, before I sign them. We'll get them back to you as quickly as possible. In the meantime, there are a couple of things I'd like to discuss with you.'

'Then let's do it,' Marcus said. 'I've plenty of time this morning.'

'I really believe she's going too fast, too soon,' Mark Lott said, lifting his dry martini, taking a sip. 'Too big for her breeches, this one.'

Alexander Dawson laughed gleefully. 'Got it in for her, Mark, have you? Or would you rather have it *in* her, eh?'

'Don't be bloody daft! Do you honestly think I'd even consider putting my most prized possession where bloody Dunley's been? Not on your life, mate. Anyway, she's not my type.'

'She's certainly *his*. Those two are fucking like rabbits day and night, and the whole bloody town knows it. And don't think it sits well in the City. There's a lot of talk about the lady boss of Deravenels and her right-hand man having it off. Those guys might like to have a bit of the old fornication on the side, but they're very disapproving when it comes to doing it in the office.'

'They're not doing it in the office, are they?' Mark asked shrilly, staring at his colleague askance.

'Don't be a twit! It's a matter of speech. *Colleagues* doing it together, that's what's verboten. But getting back to your first point, about her going too fast, are you referring to the spas?'

'Of course I am. They're going to cost a fortune,' Mark asserted.

Alexander motioned to the waiter, ordered two more dry martinis, then addressed Mark. 'Where are your brains today, you old duffer? The company's not paying for the spas. She is, with her own money.'

'She doesn't have any money, as you well know. Sweet little Mary saw to that, dropping all that lovely lolly into the hot greedy hands of that Spanish conniver, Alvarez. He certainly knew how to diddle her.'

'In more ways than one,' Alexander shot back with a suggestive smirk. 'Much to the horror of Norfell. I've always thought he'd have liked to slip into her knickers any time he could. They were as thick as thieves, you know. In fact, maybe he did have a go now and then.'

'Talking bloody nonsense, you are, laddie. Norfell and Mary went to the same church and that's the sum total of it. Norfell's picky when it comes to his tarts. He likes them pale-skinned and thin. And *hot* . . . hot to trot. Mary wasn't his type; too dark, heavy and . . . mournful,' Mark finished knowingly.

'I always rather liked Mary,' Alexander announced, and then absently glanced around the Grill Room of the Dorchester Hotel. 'Bloody hell, talk of the devil!' he suddenly exclaimed. 'There she is. Elizabeth. Over there. And who's the handsome guy she's with? Don't tell me she's ditched Dunley for an older man? That would be a belly laugh indeed.'

'That's Marcus Johnson, you twit, the famous PR man. I

was at Eton with him. His father's Lord Johnson of Beverley. A Yorkshire family with pots and pots of it. And as far as I know, he wouldn't be interested in her. Marcus has different interests . . . he used to have anyway.' Mark sat back and smiled at Alexander. 'He's married though. Now, getting back to the spas. As I just said, they're going to cost a lot of money, and she's borrowed ten million pounds from the bank. Now tell me this, my lad. What if the spas fail? Who pays back the money? Elizabeth or the company? My guess is the company, because she won't have the money to repay the bank loan.'

'No, no, you're wrong.' Alexander shook his head, his expression vehement. 'You're forgetting she's going to make at least fifty to seventy million pounds on the Sotheby's auction of those antiques and possessions she's inherited from the Deravenels and the Turners.'

Mark frowned, his eyes narrowing. 'Are you certain of that, Alex? It seems an awful lot of money to me. What on earth is there to sell? Do you know?'

'Yes, I do. Because it just so happens that my niece works at Sotheby's, and I was staying with her parents in Hampshire last weekend. She was there, too, and she made mention of the auction. She says it's the biggest auction Sotheby's have had in many years, and that the stuff is simply marvellous. A lot of diamond tiaras and mind-boggling jewellery, but mostly she raved about the art. Impressionist and Post-Impressionist paintings that will go for millions.'

'Get on with you!'

'It's *true*,' Alexander insisted. 'Believe me, it is, Mark. Elizabeth's fallen into a sweet pot of shit, and the art is extremely valuable. Apparently a great deal of it came from Edward Deravenel's mistress, a woman called Jane Shaw. Matisse, Manet, Monet, Van Gogh . . . big-name artists. In fact, my niece, Venetia, told me the first estimates are now considered too low, and the auction house is currently re-adjusting them.'

'So what you're telling me is that she's not vulnerable after all?' Mark's brow lifted. 'That we can't topple her?'

'I didn't say that. She's vulnerable all right. I was just pointing out that the spas will *not* be her downfall. But perhaps something else will. You never know. Come to think of it, Robert Dunley might well bring her down. There are plenty of people gunning for him in the company. And the gossip about them is still rampant.'

Drawing closer to Alexander, Mark asked, 'Who's gunning for him? Do tell.' He grinned maliciously.

'Norfell,' Alexander said sotto voce. 'And he has his own axe to grind, believe you me. He's got his feet in both camps, of course.'

Baffled, Mark frowned, and muttered, 'Who's really gunning for him?'

'If you don't know, I'm not going to tell you.' Alexander sat back as the waiter arrived with a plate of oysters, and said no more.

Once Mark had been served his plate of smoked salmon, he probed, 'What camps? Tell me, for God's sake! What's the big secret?'

'To be honest, Mark, I'm not sure of my information. I'd be guessing, and that's not fair, now, is it?'

Mark Lott, much shrewder than his colleagues, knew that Alexander Dawson was lying, and so he persisted. 'Come on, give me a clue at least. Then we can all join forces and push Elizabeth Turner over the cliff.'

Alexander threw back his head and roared with laughter. Then once he had settled himself, he said in a voice that was almost inaudible, 'I had a great-uncle, now dead, whose own uncle had been at Deravenels in the early part of the century. He was head of the mining division at one moment in time.

He died suddenly in strange circumstances, in fact his sudden death always remained something of a mystery. My great-uncle seemingly suspected that his uncle was murdered, and by someone from the Edward Deravenel clique within the company. He always tried to find out about that death, said he wanted to take his revenge.'

'And did your great-uncle work at Deravenels, Alexander?'

'Indeed he did, in the mining division, and he was actually named for his uncle who had died so oddly.'

'What was his name?'

'He was called Aubrey, after his uncle Aubrey Masters, but he was a Dawson actually. His name was Aubrey Dawson.'

'I see. And did your great-uncle Aubrey get his revenge?'

'Oh, no, it was too late by then. Years passed and everyone forgot. He remained unmarried and when he died he left me his shares in Deravenels. It was through his connection to the company that I got my job here. I love this conglomerate and I *will* protect it.'

'I got my job through my father, who worked for Harry Turner, and my grandfather was on the board when Henry Turner was running the company. But I think you knew that.'

'Yes, I did. Old company hands, that's us. And let's keep this sacred conglomerate safe, especially from meddling female hands,' Alexander responded.

'You bet we will,' Mark assured him, and marvelled at the way Alexander had changed the subject so adroitly.

Cecil Williams glanced up when there was a knock on the door of his office, and Francis Walsington walked in swiftly, closing it behind him.

'Francis, hello! I didn't expect to see you in the office today. I thought you were taking a long weekend.'

'I was, but I changed my mind and my plans. Because of this.' Leaning forward, Francis placed a folded piece of newspaper on Cecil's desk, then sat down in the chair opposite him. 'Read and digest *that*.'

Cecil stared at him, frowning in concern, noting the gravity of Francis's voice, and picked up the newspaper. It was a page from the business section of the *International New York Herald Tribune*, published in Paris. He scanned it quickly, exclaimed, 'You think that François and Marie de Burgh are referring to Deravenels, is that it?'

'Well, they certainly don't have their sights on Marks and Spencer, that's for sure. Read the second sentence again, and read between the lines, Cecil.'

Nodding, Cecil perused the newspaper story. It was an interview given by François de Burgh and his wife Marie Stewart de Burgh, and when he came to the particular paragraph Francis was referring to he read it out loud. 'My wife and I are planning to expand Dauphin, which is what my father had intended to do himself before his tragic and fatal accident. We wish to take the Dauphin conglomerate worldwide, and our first priority is to stake a claim in the UK. To that purpose we are planning to take over an existing business which has a global span and one which we can fold seamlessly into Dauphin.' Cecil sat back in his chair. 'I guess you're right, he is referring to Deravenels. But we all know they can't take us over. They don't stand a chance.'

'However, they can create a lot of noise in their attempts, point fingers at us, damage our reputation, or at least endeavour to do that.' Francis grimaced. 'It's what we've always known, actually, you and I . . . that Marie genuinely believes she has a right to Deravenels. She's deluded, of course.

269

She has no right at all. Nonetheless, she plans to attack us, in my opinion.'

'But only *verbally*!' Cecil looked across at his colleague, and added, 'She can do only that, nothing else. Elizabeth owns a hell of a lot more shares than she does, therefore she has the power.'

'That's true, and we're a private company with a number of strange rules made over the centuries that truly protect us from marauders. And few know of the existence of those rules. On the other hand, some people who don't particularly care about Deravenels do own shares, as you are aware, Cecil. And they might be tempted to sell their shares to Marie. For the right price. A very high price.'

'I agree with you. But to my knowledge no one ever sells their Deravenel shares. In other words, there's not much trading in them, if any at all. How did you come across this story? Do you subscribe to the *Herald Tribune*, Francis?'

'No, but I shall do so from now on with those two loose cannons spouting off in Paris. A friend called me from Paris this morning and read the story to me, then faxed it. But it was a poor fax, I could hardly read it, so I sent someone out to buy the paper. Shall we go along and show it to Elizabeth?'

'I think she ought to read the paper for herself, yes. There's no point in keeping it from her out of protectiveness,' Cecil answered. 'She'd have our guts for garters if we did. However, she's not here. She did something she rarely ever does, she actually went out to lunch today with the PR man she's hired, Marcus Johnson. We'll have to wait until she gets back.'

'Did Robert go with them?'

'No. He's in his office. Let me give him a buzz.'

Several seconds later Robert Dunley came into Cecil's office, a concerned expression clouding his eyes. 'What's wrong? What is it?' he asked as he strode over to Cecil's desk, put a hand on Francis's shoulder to acknowledge him, took a seat in the other chair.

Cecil handed him the page from the paper. 'Read that.'

Robert did so, looked first at Cecil and then at Francis. 'We've always known she'd make her move one day. This is sooner than I thought, but with her father-in-law dead, she and the husband are in full control of the company. Mmmmm.' He brought a hand to his chin, rubbed it, and then handed the paper back to Cecil. 'There's nothing we can do about this. Except shut her up. But quite frankly I just don't think that's possible.'

Turning to Francis, he said, 'What's your opinion?'

'The same as yours. We've been talking about her making problems for us for ages, but we never did anything.'

'There was nothing we could do,' Cecil pointed out.

'Elizabeth has to be shown this when she gets back,' Robert said. 'She has to know.'

'We agree.' Francis sat back in the chair, staring into space, a reflective look in his eyes. He finally said, 'I think we can put François de Burgh on notice that we know his intention and that he has no chance of succeeding because of our complex company rules. Let's nip this in the bud, even threaten to send in lawyers if we have to.'

'That's a good idea, Francis, and perhaps you ought to deliver the message in person. Why don't you go to Paris to see de Burgh?' Robert suggested.

'Why not?' Francis answered. 'We must talk to Elizabeth first, though.'

TWENTY-EIGHT

'I took your advice and hired Marcus Johnson,' Elizabeth announced, smiling at Grace Rose as she settled on the sofa.

Her great aunt sat up straighter and returned her smile. 'Clever girl!' she exclaimed. 'You won't regret it, I can assure you of that, my dear. He's going to handle publicity for the spas, I presume?' Turning to the small table next to her chair, Grace Rose picked up her glass of white wine and took a sip.

'The spas and also the auctions, if I need additional publicity,' Elizabeth explained. 'Sotheby's will do a fine job, I'm sure, but I want to cover every angle, leave nothing to chance. Anyway, I've met him several times, and today we sealed the deal. He took me to lunch at the Dorchester to celebrate.'

'Good Lord, that's almost a first, isn't it? You having a business lunch?'

Elizabeth couldn't help laughing. 'Just about, yes,' she admitted.

The two women were sitting in the drawing room of Grace Rose's flat in Belgravia, and as usual they were completely at ease with each other. Looking across at Elizabeth, Grace Rose saw how well she looked, and smartly dressed in a pale grey suit with a white blouse, pearl earrings, and her string of lustrous white South Sea pearls.

'I'm glad to see you wearing the pearls,' Grace Rose remarked. 'I know your half-sister sent them over with other jewellery when she was dying, but, in fact, they originally belonged to Jane Shaw. I remember when my father gave them to her.'

'Oh, how wonderful,' Elizabeth exclaimed, her hand going to her throat, touching the pearls. 'I never knew that. But then why would I? There was no explanation or papers with any of the jewellery Mary sent.'

'In her will, Jane Shaw left them to your grandmother, Bess Deravenel Turner, and of course Bess left them to your father. But I never saw any of his wives wearing them.'

'Neither did I. And I just fell in love with them when I came across them in the suitcase. I'd no idea of their history . . . they're so much more meaningful now.' Elizabeth touched the pearls again, continued, 'Come to think of it, though, I do have a vague memory of my stepmother, Catherine Parker, once wearing a string of large pearls like these at a dinner my father gave at the Ritz Hotel. It was one Christmas. Perhaps Catherine got to wear them for a while.'

'I hope so, and I hope she wore them whenever she could. Pearls *must* be worn, always remember that, Elizabeth. Don't hide them away in the safe. They need light and air, and they must be allowed to breathe. Pearls that are stored away for years can suffer damage. They can crack, even crumble. And incidentally, my father told me that those pearls he bought for Jane, which you are now wearing, are flawless. And very, very valuable.'

'I'm glad I wore them today, and that you told me all this, Grace Rose. Not only am I glad to know the history behind them, I also appreciate the information you've given me about how to look after them.'

After taking a sip of champagne, Elizabeth added, 'And Edward Deravenel certainly had good taste, didn't he?' As she spoke her hand went to the pearls again and she fingered them lovingly.

Grace Rose nodded. 'My father had a great eye, and for just about everything, including women. As did your own father, when it came to women. When you phoned you said you wanted to talk to me about Harry.' Grace Rose, her head on one side, eyed Elizabeth with curiosity. 'What about him, Elizabeth?'

'His treatment of me when I was a child. You're the only person alive who can actually give me an insight into his behaviour. Yes, Kat Ashe, and Blanche and her brother, Thomas Parrell, all knew him, but not in the way you did, nor did they see him very often. I have a *need* to know . . . I'm troubled by it, and let's face it, I *was* a tormented child.'

'Indeed you were, and I frequently said that to Harry. He verbally, psychologically and emotionally abused you, Elizabeth, and I once told him he ought to be horsewhipped for treating you the way he did. It was unconscionable on his part.'

Elizabeth felt herself letting go of the tension inside her, and she leaned back in the chair, relaxing. 'I'm glad to hear you say that, because it's what I have come to believe . . . yet sometimes I doubted myself, wondered if I was exaggerating it in my own mind. You see, I do love him and I certainly admire his achievements. But why do I *love* him, Grace Rose, when he behaved so badly? Or does the abused *always* love the abuser?'

'*You* love your father because you *forgave* him, Elizabeth.

274

When you were nine, going on ten, his whole attitude towards you changed, and therefore so did yours. Now you're suddenly re-examining those early years, and I think there must be a good reason.'

'Robin wants to marry me when he's divorced. But I don't want to get married to anyone. That's nothing to do with Robin personally. And I think I've made him understand that. But he says my reluctance to marry has to do with my father, that Harry set a terrible example and turned me off marriage.'

'I think that perhaps Robin has a point.' Grace Rose gave her a sharp look. 'I tend to agree.'

Elizabeth merely nodded.

'Let's get to the crux of this, Elizabeth, which is why did Harry treat you so badly? In my opinion it was because of his own turbulent emotions about your mother, Anne.'

'He did love her very much, didn't he?' Elizabeth leaned forward eagerly, an anxious look on her face.

'Harry was besotted with her, and waited a long time to marry her. Because Catherine, his first wife, was a Roman Catholic she didn't believe in divorce. Finally they were able to marry, and after waiting so long for a son he was shattered when Anne's child was a girl. *You.* He was bitterly disappointed, wretched, even grieving in a way, though he put a good face on it. Then Anne had one miscarriage after another. She couldn't even bring a child to full term, never mind deliver a male heir. I think he began to hate her as much as he loved her. And he resented her career, resented that she went back and forth between London and Paris, running her interior design business. I suppose he grew suspicious of her, convinced himself she had a lover – which I don't believe for one moment that she did. It was all in his imagination. He was overwrought at a certain point. I remember quite well that he was putting on weight, eating and drinking too much, and being exceedingly impossible with everyone. Charles often commented about him.'

'So, disappointment at not getting a son and heir turned to bitterness, then became anger, and finally *hatred* of my mother. Is that what you're saying, Grace Rose? And also *hatred* of me?'

'I am saying that, Elizabeth, yes. Most especially when you were a toddler. Because you had her dark eyes, certain mannerisms which he associated with her even at your tender age. Then suddenly she was dead, gone from him, and he was grief-stricken. Whatever you think you know, believe me, he was. Whenever he set eyes on you something terrible must have erupted in him.' Grace Rose shook her head. 'There was no excuse for him. He was a grown man and he was your father. But then who can explain human behaviour?'

'I think you just have, Grace Rose, and thank you for trying to explain Harry to me. I did forgive him years ago, that's true. And actually I began to hero-worship him, in a sense, even though it was your father Edward Deravenel whom I held in my head . . . as a role model . . . That's the best way of putting it. Robin believes my father traumatized me because of the way he treated his women. No, I should say his *wives*. He says Harry's horrible cruelty to them has ruined me for marriage.'

'And do you think that?' Grace Rose asked, peering at her.

'I'm not certain, to be honest. I do know that I became very independent, have tried to be a brave and strong woman, because for much of my life I've had to fend for myself. *I'm in control*. And I don't want anyone else controlling me. Nor do I wish to be someone's appendage. I like being Elizabeth. I like being me.'

'I understand that, and I tend to agree with you. We must

be true to ourselves, be who we are.' Grace Rose paused thoughtfully, then asked, 'Is Robert pestering you to marry him? Is that what this is all about?'

'Not really. He did propose. However, he does understand. Grace Rose, I hurt him, hurt his feelings last weekend. And I guess I've been dwelling on that rather a lot.'

'My advice to you is to take it one step at a time. Robert's still married, so he can't marry *you* at this moment. When he's free, think about it all again. Discuss it again. Is he prepared to live with you without the benefit of marriage? And are you?'

'Yes, we both are.'

'Then let matters rest as they are. For the moment.'

'All right, Francis, I'll tell her,' Robert Dunley said, 'and stay in touch.' He listened attentively as Francis Walsington added a few words about the stance he would take in Paris, and said goodbye, clicked off his mobile phone.

He climbed the few steps of the building in Chester Street where Grace Rose's flat was, and pressed the intercom button. He gave his name to the disembodied voice that answered and was immediately buzzed in. A few seconds later he was being shown into the drawing room where Elizabeth was sitting with Grace Rose.

'Darling, there you are!' Elizabeth cried when he walked in, and jumped up, ran to kiss him.

'Francis got the appointment with the Dauphin people,' he said against her neck. 'He's off to Paris tomorrow, and they'll meet first thing Monday.'

'I'm glad to hear it.' Taking his hand she led him to Grace Rose, who beamed with pleasure at the sight of him.

Bending over her, Robert kissed her on the cheek, then

stood away, gazing at her. 'You're a wonder! A genuine wonder, Grace Rose,' he said, meaning every word. 'I'd never guess your age. You look absolutely glorious. And I do like your dress. It suits you, and the delphinium blue echoes the colour of your eyes.'

'My, my, Robert Dunley, you're just too charming for words.' She squeezed his arm, and added, 'Help yourself to a drink, it'll be quicker if you do it. There's champagne and all the usual on the table over there.'

'Champagne it is, thank you.' He strode across the floor, asking, over his shoulder, 'Do you need topping up, Elizabeth?'

'No, but thanks anyway.'

Grace Rose said, 'Before I forget, Elizabeth, there are two gifts in my den. For your birthday and Robert's. Would you mind getting them, my dear?'

'Of course not. Back in a jiffy.' Elizabeth stood up and went out, saying to Robert as she passed him, 'I won't be a moment, Robin.'

He nodded, went and sat with Grace Rose. 'Sad business, Princess Diana's death, wasn't it?' he remarked, putting his glass down on the coffee table. 'A national tragedy.'

'Indeed it is,' Grace Rose responded. 'People are still in shock. They just can't quite comprehend it, and the extent of the grieving is most extraordinary. The English must've changed, showing their feelings in this way. The flowers outside the gates of Kensington Palace are rapidly growing into a . . . *mountain*.'

'I know. I saw the news on television this morning, and it's just amazing.'

'What is?' Elizabeth asked as she came back into the drawing room, carrying two small, gift-wrapped packages, which she placed on the coffee table.

'The mountain of floral tributes to Princess Diana being

left outside Kensington Palace,' Grace Rose explained. 'Now, to the gifts. The smaller package is for you, Robert, and it comes with much love. The other one is yours, Elizabeth dear.'

'Thank you so much,' Robert said. 'Can we open them now, or do we have to wait?' He grinned at her.

Grace Rose chuckled, throwing him a fond look. 'I think I've heard you ask that question before. Many times, in fact, when you were a small boy. And of course you can open it, and you too, Elizabeth.'

'I shall. Anyway, I think it's rather nice to open our gifts from you when we're with you,' Elizabeth murmured. 'Especially since we've cancelled the little dinner party we'd planned for Sunday. Neither of us was in the mood, under the circumstances.'

'I understand. The whole country's in mourning.'

Robert said, 'You open your present first, Elizabeth.'

'All right, I will.' Reading the card, smiling and tearing off the silver paper, she found herself holding a black leather box. It was obviously a jewellery box, old and a little worn, the leather scuffed in places. Elizabeth lifted the lid and gasped as she stared down at the diamond brooch. 'It's simply beautiful!' she cried. 'I love these flowing, old-fashioned bows. Thank you so much.' Jumping up, she went to Grace Rose and kissed her on the cheek. 'I love it, I really do.'

'I'm glad. I wanted you to have this particular brooch, because, you see, it was given to me by my father. One Christmas long ago. I know you have special feelings about Edward Deravenel, and I thought this most appropriate.'

'It is. I just wish I'd known him. And I shall treasure this always.'

Grace Rose smiled, looked across at Robert, admiring him. As usual, she was startled by his extraordinary good looks. Every time she saw him she was taken aback by his presence, his charisma. He had turned out to be the most handsome man she had ever seen, with his height, dark hair, and chiselled features. Movie-star good looks, she thought to herself, as she studied him. Many underestimated him because of those looks, but Grace Rose knew his true colours. He was brilliant, shrewd and determined.

He was carefully taking off the ribbon and the paper, and putting them on one side. After reading the card, he opened the red leather box and he, too, was surprised.

Robert was staring at a pair of gold cufflinks set with diamonds and rubies. 'Grace Rose, you spoil me! These are quite the most beautiful cufflinks I've ever set eyes on. Thank you.'

He rose, smiling at her with great affection, and went to kiss her as Elizabeth had just done.

She looked up at him and said softly, 'You're very special to me, Robert, as is Elizabeth.' She turned to her great-niece. 'I'm glad I was able to borrow the two of you when you were growing up. You gave me such a lot of pleasure.'

'And you gave *us* magical times,' Elizabeth answered.

'These cufflinks are absolutely superb,' Robert murmured, studying them. 'And I see from the box they are by Cartier. You've given me something very special.'

'They belonged to my husband, Charles. I gave them to him just after we were married, and he always wore them on his first nights, at the party after the performance. Charles considered them lucky. And I hope you will, too.'

'I will.' The mobile phone in his pocket shrilled, and he made a face, said, 'Please excuse me.' Robert walked to the end of the drawing room, stood near the window as he answered the phone.

Leaning closer to Elizabeth, Grace Rose said, 'There's one thing I meant to tell you earlier, and it is this. At the end of his life your father was not only exceedingly proud of you,

Elizabeth, proud of your academic achievements and the way you handled yourself, but he did love you. He really did. I want you to remember that.'

Elizabeth took hold of her hand, held it tightly. 'Thank you for telling me that. It means so much to me.'

It was Sunday the seventh of September, their mutual birthday, and they had opted for an evening at home in Elizabeth's flat in Eaton Square.

They had spent a lazy day together, opening their presents over a late breakfast, enjoying each other's company, doing nothing in particular. Something of a novelty for both of them. They were perpetually busy.

Robert had insisted on preparing supper, and Elizabeth had gone to change. He had made a quick, simple meal, one he knew she would enjoy, and now, as he came in from the kitchen, he went to the fireplace, put a light to the logs, opened the bottle of Krug champagne in the ice bucket, and dimmed the lights. Music, he thought suddenly, that's what's missing. Within seconds he had selected one of their favourite Frank Sinatra discs and put it on, adjusting the volume.

He was standing with his back to the fire when he heard the click of her heels in the foyer, and there she was in the doorway of the drawing room, beaming at him.

A look of genuine amazement crossed his face, and he just stood there not able to say a word for a moment.

'Well, you did tell me to dress casually!' she exclaimed when she saw the look of amazement on his face. 'So I *did*.'

He threw back his head and roared with laughter. 'Casual. You look as if you're on your way to Annabel's in that get-up! You're priceless, Elizabeth.'

She began to laugh with him; she had known as she was

dressing that he would appreciate the joke. And he had. She was wearing a pale-blue silk nightgown and peignoir and high-heeled silver Manolo Blahniks. It was the jewellery that took the outfit right over the top: her string of South Sea pearls and matching earrings, the pearl bracelet and ring he had given her that morning, and the Edwardian diamond bow pin from Grace Rose.

'*Gorgeous.* You're gorgeous,' he said, crossing the room, taking her in his arms, kissing her. Then against her hair he whispered, 'Can I have this dance, my love?' She nodded, but neither moved. They simply stood together, entwined, swaying to the music, knowing they needed nothing more than each other to be happy.

Finally Robert led her over to a chair near the fire, poured the champagne, sat down next to her, clinked his glass to hers. 'Happy Birthday!' they said in unison.

After a moment, Robert murmured, 'I know it's meant to be a joke, but the outfit is rather smashing, you know. Obviously it's the jewels that make it really work.'

Elizabeth nodded, her dark eyes mischievous. 'I wanted to get all fancied up for you, Robin, all dressed up like we used to do when we were little.' She put out a leg, showing her ankle and wiggling her foot. 'I even put my Manolos on for you. I aim to please.'

'You do, you please me very much.' He shot his cuff so that she could see the Patek Philippe watch she had given him earlier, as well as his ruby cufflinks from Grace Rose. 'I got dressed up for you, too.'

'Well, great minds think alike! We're always on the same track.'

'I hope I've been on the same track as far as supper's concerned.'

'I'm sure you have, but I'm not all that hungry.'

He nodded, said no more. He constantly worried about

her peculiar eating habits, often thought she looked far too thin. But he knew she was never on a diet: her thinness had nothing to do with vanity. It was because she seemed to have little interest in food, which was the reason he had prepared the kind of meal he had for their birthday dinner. Now he changed the subject. 'Grace Rose was very generous, giving me cufflinks that belonged to her husband. I was very touched, and I know you love your brooch. I suspect that's partially because it was bought by Edward Deravenel.'

'You're right. Although to be honest, it truly is unique, Robin, and I do admire those Victorian and Edwardian bow brooches.' Shifting in her chair, Elizabeth went on, 'I'm happy Grace Rose has lived so long, has good health and perfect mental capacities. I like having her around, she's such a big part of the past, and *our* past. When I look back now, I realize how lovely she was to us when we were little, took an interest in us. Perhaps because she never had children of her own.' Elizabeth suddenly began to laugh. 'And she certainly is a mountain of information about the Deravenels and the Turners! Why, Grace Rose is the family historian, don't you agree?'

Nodding, laughing with her, Robin said, 'Scandals, sex and secrets, that could easily have been their family motto, the Deravenels, I mean. And the Turners, too, I think. My parents told me quite a lot about the juicy stuff, when I was old enough to know.'

'Forget the juicy stuff, that's *nothing*! There's much more.' Elizabeth eyed him knowingly. 'What about murder, and murder again, and kidnapping, and all kinds of foul play? You name it, it's there. Sometimes I wish I knew more than I do, but quite truthfully, I don't like to pump her.'

'The next time we see her maybe I can wheedle a bit more out of her. *Secrets*, I mean.' Robert got up, brought the champagne over and filled their flutes, returned the bottle to the silver bucket.

Elizabeth said, 'So go on, tell me what's for supper. I'm curious.'

'It's a nursery tea.'

'You're joking.'

'No, I'm not.' Robert pulled her to her feet, guided her to the kitchen. 'Here it is!' He waved his hand at the laden trolley, then whipped off the napkins covering numerous plates. 'Your favourite meal, so you're continually telling me. A nursery tea *par excellence*, my darling.'

'Oh, Robin, how wonderful!' She threw him a loving smile and went over to the trolley, looking at everything he had made. There was every kind of narrow finger sandwich, with the crusts cut off the way Kat made them. They were her favourites . . . egg salad, sliced cucumber on cream cheese, sliced tomatoes, smoked salmon, potted meat, mashed sardines, and even small sausage rolls.

'After the sandwiches I'll be serving you warm scones with clotted Devonshire cream and strawberry jam, and finally your other favourite, jam roly-poly. That's your birthday cake.'

'And *yours*. Oh, Robin, I do love you so.'

'I love you more.'

They moved together at the same moment, were suddenly in each other's arms, kissing each other passionately. When they finally drew apart, Elizabeth stared at him intently. 'We have time to make love, if you want to, that is,' she murmured.

'I do,' he answered, without a moment's hesitation, took hold of her hand and led her to the bedroom.

TWENTY-NINE

Francis Walsington left the Plaza Athénée Hotel on the Avenue Montaigne at exactly nine o'clock on Monday morning. No longer able to stomach staying at the Ritz, after the débâcle of Princess Diana's tragic death, he had booked at the Plaza instead. It was a familiar place, an old favourite of his, where he felt comfortable and at home. He had stayed there off and on over the past few years and knew many of the staff.

His appointment at Dauphin, the French conglomerate, was not until ten, but he wanted to get a breath of fresh air and *think*, before going into the meeting. He walked down the street at a leisurely pace, heading for the Champs-Élysées.

It was a beautiful morning, the air balmy, the blue sky clear and dazzling as it could be only in Paris, at least to his way of thinking. Paris was the city he loved the most after London, and he enjoyed being in it whatever the weather. Rain or shine, it was unique and beautiful, but on a day like this he considered it to be truly spectacular. A visual treat as far as the eye could see.

He thought about Elizabeth as he walked along. She had proved to have all the qualities he admired in a top executive – self-confidence, vision and courage. She was one of the most disciplined people he had ever worked with, and her dedication and determination were commendable. Cecil had recently commented to him that she had that special kind of brilliance that separated the merely clever from the truly inspired, and he agreed. He knew she was an honourable person: her word was her bond, just as her father's had been. Harry Turner's handshake had been considered the most meaningful in the City, and was still spoken about.

Francis was pleased that Elizabeth had Robert Dunley by her side. Not only as her business adviser and one of her chief executives, but as her lover and partner. He admired and respected Robert, trusted him implicitly, had enormous confidence in his abilities. He knew he was an honest man, and dependable.

In a certain way, Robert's good looks were a detriment to him, as was his elegance. Francis was aware that all too often he was dismissed as a preening peacock by some, when nothing could be further from the truth. Jealousy and envy, how they twist some people's minds, and lives, he thought as he reached the broad avenue which was the main thoroughfare in the City of Light.

Traffic on the Champs-Élysées was already heavy, marking the beginning of the first business day of the week. Francis turned right, sauntered on, his destination a large building located at the end of the avenue, close to the Rond-Point and not far from the Place de la Concorde.

He realized he had plenty of time before his meeting at Dauphin, decided to have a cup of coffee, and chose a pavement café not far from his destination. After ordering a *café au lait* and a croissant, he sat back in the chair, watched the world go by. But after a short while his mind focused on the young couple he was soon to meet: François de Burgh and his wife, Marie Stewart de Burgh.

Some time ago he had made it his business to find out as much as he could about them, but his operatives in Paris had not turned up anything special. On the surface there appeared to be nothing bad or sinister about them. However, as far as their characters were concerned, both of them seemed to be rather spoiled, and Marie, in particular, was wilful.

François was the pampered son of Henri and Catherine de Burgh, his late father French, his mother Italian. François had several siblings, but he was the eldest and heir to the vast business empire which was one of the rivals of LVMH. According to the information Francis had received, François de Burgh was a proud young man, considered shrewd by many but also viewed as lazy and a trifle too easy-going. It was well known he was not as clever as his wife. Now that his father was dead he was head of Dauphin.

Marie Stewart de Burgh, his wife and business partner, was the heiress to Scottish Heritage, a large business enterprise based in Edinburgh. She was the titular head, if in absentia, who left the management of the company to her mother, who appeared to be doing a fine job and was well respected. Marie's mother had controlled Scottish Heritage for years, and she had held the company steady. An aristocratic Frenchwoman of considerable background and breeding, she had three rich and powerful brothers who were extremely prominent in French society, business and politics.

As a child of five, Marie Stewart had been sent to live with her renowned uncles in Paris. She grew up with these shrewd and clever aristocrats, speaking only French. Later she was given an expensive education, sent to finishing school, and consistently brainwashed into believing she was destined for great things.

The information he had received told Francis Walsington that she was a beautiful young woman who was rather proud and snobbish, overly ambitious, and had been schooled by her uncles to set her sights high. There were no scandals attached to her, nor to her young husband François de Burgh, who was considered quite a catch.

As he sat sipping his coffee, Francis contemplated Elizabeth and smiled inwardly. He was convinced that Marie Stewart was no match for the woman he worked for. Elizabeth Deravenel Turner was a genius. She had already proved herself to be a brilliant businesswoman in the short time she had been at the helm of Deravenels, and highly educated though she was, she was a graduate of what Francis called 'the school of hard knocks'. She was also the daughter of one of the greatest tycoons the world had ever known, and had learned at the knee of the master. She happened to be a consummate actress by natural inclination and was long practised in the art of dissimulation. Quick-witted and shrewd, Elizabeth could be exceedingly tough when it came to business matters; Francis knew she always thought with her head, never permitted emotions to cloud her judgement.

What he knew about Marie Stewart de Burgh told him she was no match for Elizabeth. She was the spoiled darling of her doting uncles and husband, and certainly well educated, but without any business experience. Socially prominent and wealthy, she had a degree of charm and looks. But that was it.

No contest, Francis decided, as he sipped his coffee. Besides which, she has no genuine claim to Deravenels, whatever she believes. Madame de Burgh likes the idea of being the heiress to Deravenels, revels in the thought that it's hers through her grandmother Margaret Turner Stewart, Harry's sister, but all of this is in her imagination. It's wishful thinking on her part, she's living a delusion.

Finishing his coffee, he reached into his pocket for money and motioned to the waiter that he wanted to pay.

Beautiful she was, but not quite as beautiful as some had made her out to be. So much for myths, Francis thought, as he walked across the antique Aubusson rug to meet Marie Stewart de Burgh and her husband François.

There was something of Elizabeth in her. She had the same Turner build, was tall, willowy, slender. Her oval face with its regular features was very pale like Elizabeth's, her complexion perfect, and she had lovely amber-coloured eyes. But it was her hair that was indeed her crowning glory. Red gold, it shimmered around her face, was worn shoulder length. She and Elizabeth were cousins, and it was patently obvious that they shared a few genetic characteristics.

'Good morning, Mr Walsington,' Marie Stewart said in accented English, as she took hold of his outstretched hand in a firm grip. 'It is my great pleasure to welcome you to Dauphin. I would like to introduce you to my husband, François de Burgh, President of Dauphin.'

'Good morning, Madame de Burgh,' Francis said, turned, and shook her husband's hand. 'Monsieur de Burgh, *bonjour*.'

'*Bonjour*, Monsieur Walsington,' François murmured, his voice also accented, low but pleasant. He gave Francis a friendly smile. Shorter than his wife, he was as dark as she was fair, with a somewhat plain face. They seemed an odd couple to Francis, most especially because of the disparity in their heights.

Marie Stewart led them to a small seating arrangement at the far end of the large office, and they all took their seats.

She sat on the edge of her chair, seemed eager to begin, and leaning slightly forward she focused on Francis. 'When I was informed you wished to come and speak with us, I knew at once that Elizabeth had sent you. That is true, is it not, monsieur?'

'It was the board of directors as well as Elizabeth herself who wished me to come and see you, Madame de Burgh. And our lawyers. Indeed, we all thought it was a good idea that we meet, regarding the announcement you made.' He glanced at François, and added, 'An announcement about staking a claim in the UK and taking over a global company, so well spelled out in the interview you recently gave to the *New York Herald Tribune*.'

François was quick to answer. 'Yes, that is indeed what we wish to do, Monsieur Walsington. Like everyone else these days, we wish to take Dauphin global.'

'By attempting to take over Deravenels?'

'I did not mention Deravenels, Monsieur Walsington,' the Frenchman said swiftly, sounding a little indignant.

'That's perfectly true, but Deravenels is the largest and most successful *global* company in Britain, and we are well equipped to read between the lines; as are our lawyers.'

Fixing her amber-coloured eyes on Francis, Marie Stewart said in a somewhat colder tone than before, 'That is the *second time* you have mentioned lawyers, monsieur. Are you making . . . a threat?'

'No, not at all, madame. But it is usual for us to consult our various solicitors when there's even the merest suggestion that another company might be eyeing us, considering us a possible target. And very frankly, the board thought it was vital that I talk to you, mainly to explain how complex Deravenels is as a company.'

She looked at him intently, and after a moment asked, 'What do you mean by *complex*?'

'Let me explain as concisely as I can, madame. As I'm sure you know, Deravenels is a private company; the shares are not publicly traded and they are very rarely sold. In fact, they only occasionally change hands, usually when someone holding our shares dies and leaves them to a family member, as part of an inheritance. And –'

'I have shares!' Marie Stewart exclaimed, cutting in, giving him a hard stare.

'I know that, madame. Shares which you inherited from your grandmother.'

'And it is through her that I am the heir to Deravenels.'

Ignoring this, Francis went on in a cool, steady voice, 'Quite apart from this particular and rather unusual situation with the shares of Deravenels, there are also other rules which make it virtually impossible for any kind of takeover. Certain rules were introduced within the last seventy odd years. However, most of those changes don't need discussion here. Except for one, which was made by Harry Turner. In his will he debarred Deravenels from passing to a foreigner . . . only an English person can inherit.'

'I *am* English,' Marie Stewart announced in a rather harsh voice, her face livid.

'Hardly, madame, with all due respect. Your mother is French and your late father was Scottish, therefore you are not English by any stretch of the imagination. Also, you were brought to France at the age of five and have been raised as a Frenchwoman. The claim won't fly.'

'But my grandmother was English!' Her voice rose, becoming shrill.

'That's not enough. It does not comply with Harry Turner's will. Also, you must remember *he* inherited Deravenels from his father, and in Harry's will it is very clearly written that the company must be inherited first by his son Edward, then his daughter Mary, and finally Elizabeth, if his other issue are deceased, and have left no issue of their own. Harry Turner's will aside, there are numerous other rules that simply preclude a takeover, rules which block this absolutely. Anyone attempting to grab Deravenels cannot succeed. Furthermore, Elizabeth Turner, the current managing director, is the largest single shareholder, holding fifty-five per cent of the stock. She is inviolable.'

Marie Stewart sat back in the chair, regarding Walsington. Although she was inexperienced, she was by no means stupid. But she was naive and her right to Deravenels had been inculcated in her since she was a toddler. Her French uncles and her mother had done their work well, had completely brainwashed her and she was not about to give in quite so easily.

'I do have a claim, Monsieur Walsington,' she finally said in a clear, light voice, suddenly full of confidence. 'Through my great-grandfather Henry Turner and his wife Bess Deravenel Turner, my great-grandmother. They had a daughter, Margaret, sister of Harry, and it is through her that I am the heir. But since Elizabeth, *my cousin*, is running the company, let me address myself to her situation. If she fell ill and died, or had an accident, *I would be the heir*. There is no one else.'

'But Deravenels cannot pass to a foreigner, I just told you that. Madame de Burgh, you *would* be considered a foreigner.'

'But there are no other descendants of Henry Turner,' she protested shrilly.

Francis Walsington, who knew everything there was to know about everybody involved with Deravenels, was very well aware that there were other cousins. But he decided to cut this conversation short. 'I do believe I've explained things extremely clearly, and put you on notice that you should not in any way attempt a takeover of Deravenels. It just won't happen, because it cannot happen. Please believe me, our complex rules are watertight. It would be a waste of your time, effort and money. Or anyone else's for that matter.'

Marie Stewart looked reflective, her slightly hooded eyes lowered as she stared down at her hands in her lap. Francis noticed that, like Elizabeth, she had the most beautiful hands, well shaped and with long tapering fingers. Finally she lifted her head, and gave him a direct look. 'I would like you to convey my respects and give my love to my cousin, Monsieur Walsington. *My cousin*. Do remember that. And I would deem it a great favour if you would ask her if she will name me as her heir in her will.'

For a moment Francis Walsington was gobsmacked, and he blinked. But he was a past master of dissimulation and his face remained expressionless as he answered with swiftness, 'I think that is a little premature on your part, Madame. Elizabeth Turner is only twenty-six, and she is certain to marry and —'

'Robert Dunley? He is a married man!'

'— and have children,' he continued, undeterred by her interruption.

'But will you ask her?' Marie Stewart persisted. 'And please tell her I wish to meet her.'

'I will repeat this entire conversation verbatim,' Francis answered, and stood up. 'If you will excuse me, I must leave. I have a plane to catch. Thank you for your courtesy, madame, and yours, Monsieur de Burgh.'

THIRTY

Francis, Robert, Cecil and Nicholas sat with Elizabeth in her office, the five of them grouped around the coffee table which was placed in the centre of the seating arrangement near the windows.

It was Francis Walsington who had held their attention for the last thirty minutes, filling them in about his trip to Paris, and relating his conversation verbatim, giving every detail of the meeting with Marie Stewart de Burgh and her husband François de Burgh.

None of the men looked happy, and all of them sat staring at Elizabeth, who appeared extremely thoughtful. After a moment, she said quietly, 'I don't want to meet Marie Stewart. I think doing so would be totally wrong, harmful to me in the long run.'

'It would certainly give credence to her claim that she should be your heir,' Cecil said, his eyes troubled. 'And you *cannot* name her your heir. *Ever*. In fact, at this moment in time you cannot name anyone.'

'It would put you in danger if you named Marie Stewart de Burgh,' Robert Dunley announced, his voice tense, his expression worried. 'There's been many a murder made to look like an accident.'

'You think Marie Stewart de Burgh might have me bumped off, do you, Robin?' Elizabeth threw him a look, and went on, 'Well, you and I certainly know about murder being committed over the ownership of Deravenels, don't we?'

'There have always been rumours,' Nicholas Throckman announced before Robert could answer. 'And in my opinion those rumours have been based on truths. Fishy deaths seem to have been the norm around here for eighty years or so.' He glanced at Francis, and asked, 'I'm not wrong, am I?'

'No, you're not. Aubrey Masters was head of the mining division and his death was highly suspicious. And so was Lily Overton's, Edward Deravenel's mistress. She was carrying his child at the time. Then there was the extraordinary disappearance of Edward Deravenel's young sons, as well as Richard Deravenel's death by stabbing on the beach at Ravenscar. That was most definitely a murder, it certainly wasn't suicide, he didn't stab himself. And let's not forget Will Hasling's untimely death. There are those who believed he had been in a fight with Richard Deravenel in this very office. Old reports I've read claim he struck his head hard in here when he fell . . . and that this led to his subsequent death. I would still call it murder.'

'You don't have to tell me that people commit murder for personal gain, for money and power,' Cecil remarked. 'I know that only too well. Which brings me back to my original point.' He glanced at Elizabeth. 'You must not name anyone as your heir. Or if you do, no one can know about it. Robert is correct. Naming your heir publicly could genuinely put you in danger. Let's not forget that people, whoever they are, can be quite unscrupulous.'

Nicholas turned to Elizabeth and said, 'There is a certain amount of truth in what Marie Stewart said to Francis. If you were dead she *would* actually be the heir, because she is directly descended from Henry Turner.'

'You have other cousins, don't forget that!' Robert interjected in a strong tone, staring at her. '*First cousins*, no less, which makes them closer to you than Marie Stewart. She is your first cousin *once removed*.'

'You're correct, Robin.' She threw him a curious little half smile. 'As you well know. And they are indeed first cousins.' Now focusing on Nicholas, she explained, 'You may have forgotten that my father's youngest sister Mary, his favourite, married his best friend Charles Brandt, and they had two daughters. One of them, the eldest, is Frances Brandt, my first cousin, and she is married to Harry Greyson. Three of their children survived . . . Jane, Catherine and Mary – favourite names in our family, I suppose. And of course they do figure in the "cousins" equation. Very much so.'

'But not Jane Greyson,' Robert reminded her. 'She died.'

'Yes,' she responded quietly, remembering that Jane had been married to one of Robin's brothers, and that sadly they had been killed together in a plane crash.

Cecil said, 'I think this calls for some very special security for Elizabeth, Francis. Don't you agree?'

'I don't want any bodyguards!' she cried.

Francis nodded. 'I think it would be wise if you did. A driver who's also a bodyguard, Elizabeth. Think about that. And I promise it won't be someone who gets in your way, or is heavy-handed.'

'All right,' she agreed with a small sigh, wanting to move on. 'So what's your assessment of the de Burghs? Can you sum everything up for us, please, Francis.'

'I surely can. First of all, let's talk about the de Burghs themselves for a moment. They're playing silly buggers, in my opinion. He's naive and inexperienced, especially in business. So is she, and they are both young, also extremely spoiled. Used to getting their own way, I'd say. He didn't participate at all in the meeting. She did all of the talking and I suspect she wears the trousers. She's six months older, by the way. I would characterize François de Burgh as an empty suit. As for Marie Stewart, it was very obvious to me that she is obstinate, wilful, a bit imperious and certainly obsessed about her connection to the Turners, through her late grandmother. However, the connection seems to impress *her* more than anyone else. I have it on good authority that the executives who *really* run Dauphin couldn't care less about the Turner connection. Nor are they interested in Deravenels. I learned last night that the top brass at Dauphin weren't too happy about the *Herald Tribune* interview, or about the idea of Dauphin staking a claim in the UK. Contrary to what I originally thought, I don't believe the de Burghs will have much say about what happens at the head office.' He grinned at them, and shrugged. 'We are perfectly safe.'

Nicholas and Cecil laughed, and Elizabeth asked, 'What is she like *actually*? What was your first impression of her?'

'She has a pleasant personality, but let's not confuse personality with character,' Francis said. 'Her husband is weak, so she seems the stronger of the two. I don't believe she's too swift.'

'Is she as beautiful as everyone says?' Elizabeth now asked.

'No, she's not, but she's an extremely attractive young woman,' Francis answered. 'She's got the famous Henry Turner build . . . tall and slender, and she's willowy, moves gracefully. She's inherited the Turner colouring as well. Pale complexion, red-gold hair. I would go as far as to say that she has a look of you.'

'Some good that'll do her,' Elizabeth said pithily.

'It's like this, Cecil,' Elizabeth explained later that morning. 'I want to own as many Deravenel shares as I possibly can.'

'But you are already holding more than anyone else,' he pointed out. 'Fifty-five per cent.'

'I'm well aware of that. But I would like to have at least seventy per cent of the company. It would make me feel *better*. Safer.'

'I doubt very much that anyone will sell their shares to you. Not because it's *you*, and they're holding out, but because the shares are extremely lucrative, even now, despite Mary's careless running of the company. We're in the black, and the measures we've taken in the last eleven months have done wonders. Tightening our belt, letting redundant people go, retiring others was a brilliant idea on your part. Then the spas in the American hotels are doing record business, as are the hotels themselves. We're on a very big upswing, and shareholders know that.' Cecil sat back, and smiled at her warmly. 'You should be proud of what you've done, and also relieved to know that management at Dauphin aren't particularly interested in taking us over.'

'I am, and Francis made it very clear that a great deal of that takeover stuff is in her head. He told me he thought Marie Stewart was delusional.'

'That's more than likely. From what I understand, the uncles and her mother did a brainwashing job on her that genuinely rivals the Pavlov technique used on dogs.'

Elizabeth burst out laughing. Then taking a deep breath, she said, 'I need your advice about something else, Cecil. A company that I can buy . . . It's a chain of spas called Blissful Encounters, and it's owned by an American woman, Anka Palitz, who lives in New York. Anne Dunley told me about

Anka, and apparently she wants to sell the chain. Do you think I should buy it?'

'It depends on how good the spas are, how much she wants, and if you think they will enhance the spas you are about to open.'

'I think they probably will. They are on the high end, luxurious, very glamorous, I'm told.'

'I'd like more details,' Cecil said.

'I would, too. And once I have them, I hope we can have another discussion.' She looked at her watch. 'I've got a meeting with Sotheby's about the auction, so I must dash. Thanks, Cecil, thank you for everything.'

He walked her to the door of his office, and kissed her on the cheek. 'Walk, don't run,' he said with an affectionate glance. 'Things are going very well for us, Elizabeth. Very well indeed.'

'I know, thanks to you and Robin. We're a good team, aren't we? The Three Musketeers.'

'The triumvirate,' he replied.

'Thank you so much for seeing me today, Grace Rose,' Elizabeth said two hours later. 'I really do need to talk to you.'

'It's always my pleasure when you come over, Elizabeth, you know that. And especially when you want my advice. I like feeling useful. I don't have much to do these days, you know. As I keep telling you, I'm living on borrowed time.'

'Borrowed or not, I'm thankful you're still around. I don't know what I'd do without you.'

'You'd manage very well, there's no doubt in my mind about that. You're going to be fine . . . all of your life. But, of course, it's going to be an extreme life as it always has been. Never mind. You'll enjoy all of the challenges you'll meet. And you'll succeed.'

Elizabeth laughed, and took a sip of the sherry Grace Rose had insisted she pour for both of them. 'Down the hatch,' she said, after touching her glass to her great-aunt's. 'It's only four o'clock, Grace Rose, a bit early for a drink . . .' She let her voice trail off.

'Don't worry about the time, Elizabeth. It must be the cocktail hour somewhere in the world . . . Paris or even the Punjab. Anyway, my dear girl, a small glass of sherry is not going to get you drunk.' After taking a sip of the Amontillado, Grace Rose gave Elizabeth a questioning look, asked, 'What do you wish to speak to me about? Deravenels no doubt, since your love life is well taken care of by our lovely Robert.'

'Deravenels, yes. Actually, it's about my shares. I own fifty-five per cent and –'

'Which makes you the largest single shareholder. I am right about that, am I not?'

'You are. However, I would like to own more, to protect Deravenels against any takeover bid. I believe it's my duty to keep it safe.'

'A takeover would never succeed. The structure of the company is far too complex,' Grace Rose announced with genuine conviction, sure of herself on this matter. 'That has always been my understanding of it, explained to me long ago by my father, also by my great friend Amos Finnister. And by *your* father as well. Both my father and yours did change certain rules, modernized them.'

'Yes, I know, and it's the rules they made that protect it in many different ways.' Elizabeth paused, took a deep breath, and hurried on, 'I've come to ask you something, actually, Grace Rose, and I –'

'You want to buy my shares, don't you?'

Elizabeth was taken aback, and did not answer for a

moment. Then she said in a firm voice, 'Yes, I do. I realize you might want to leave them to your great-nephew, Patrick, but if you would at least consider it I would be very grateful.'

'No, I can't sell my shares to you because –'

'Please don't explain,' Elizabeth interrupted swiftly, cutting her off, not wanting to embarrass her great-aunt. 'I understand, really I do.'

'No, you don't understand at all, and please allow me to finish my sentence, Elizabeth. I can't sell them to you because I have already left them to you in my will.'

Elizabeth was stunned and she gaped at Grace Rose, momentarily flustered, unable to say a word.

Grace Rose began to laugh. 'For once I've rendered you speechless. That's unusual for you, my dear. You normally have a comment to make about most things.' Her eyes were twinkling; she was enjoying this moment. She knew she had just told Elizabeth she would receive the thing she most desired in this world – even more control of Deravenels. And she was thrilled she had made her great-niece happy.

Elizabeth finally spoke. 'I've never been more surprised in my life. You knocked the breath out of me, Grace Rose. I can hardly believe it. How wonderfully generous of you. Thank you, thank you so very much.' She jumped up, went over to her great-aunt and hugged her, then looking down at her, she laughed tremulously, and added, 'I still can't believe it . . .'

'You must believe it because it's true.'

Elizabeth went back to her chair, and sat back, trying to calm herself. She was flooded with many mixed emotions and close to tears, so touched was she by this most extraordinary gift.

Grace Rose sat studying her, loving this young woman whom she had known all of her life. She had attended Elizabeth's christening and watched her grow, often appalled and angered by the way she had been treated by Harry Turner . . . the child she had given her heart to so long ago, and whom she had loved as if that little girl had been her own.

Unexpectedly, Grace Rose experienced a marvellous sense of peace, of true fulfilment. She had forever tried to make amends for Harry Turner's despicable behaviour, and she had often succeeded but perhaps never more fully than she had today.

What a wonder Elizabeth had become . . . strong and brave and full of confidence.

Reaching out, Grace Rose took hold of Elizabeth's hand and squeezed it. 'Everything I have came from my father, Edward Deravenel, and it is only right that it should go back to a Deravenel. That is *you*, Elizabeth. *You* are the last of the line. And you are my heir.'

PART THREE

Dangerous Reversals

Be not afraid of sudden fear.

Proverbs 3:17

For he shall give his angels charge over thee, to keep thee safe in all thy ways. They shall bear thee up in their hands, lest thou dash thy foot against a stone.

Psalm 91

By night on my bed, I sought him whom my soul loveth: I sought him but I found him not.

The Song of Solomon 3:1

Dangerous Reversals

THIRTY-ONE

L *uck is running with me. And seemingly all the way.
At least, so far this year.*
*First and foremost, and of the greatest importance to
me, is my relationship with Robin Dunley. It has never been
better in my entire time with him, even going back to our
childhood. We are completely in step and in tune. And we
have never been more in love. I absolutely adore him, and
he feels the same. I know that very well. It is a meeting of
the minds; we think alike, speak alike, and, in fact, sometimes he takes the words right out of my mouth, or we say
something in unison. It is so uncanny, and so pronounced
some people think we have rehearsed beforehand. How silly
that is, yet I understand why they do think that.*

*He has my best interests at heart, just as his are fore-
most in my mind and heart. There are secret moments,
when I am alone, or he is sleeping and I am awake, that
I wonder what it would be like to have his child . . . a
small adorable Robin to love, to care for and cherish and*

watch growing up to become the man his father is . . .

There is no man like my dearest Robin, not in my estimation. He has the kindest heart, a most loving nature, and his thoughtfulness knows no bounds. And yet he is strong-willed, impetuous, sometimes temperamental and often bossy. A tough negotiator when it comes to business, he always says that when he's doing business, it's my business he's doing. All he wants is to make the best deals for me and to protect me in every way he can.

He makes me laugh, and occasionally he makes me cry. Only he can calm me down when I am angry, or upset, and I suppose, now that I think about it, I run the gamut of emotions with Robin. We are sexually attuned, have the same desires and needs and appetites, and being with him is sheer bliss.

He is the centre of my existence, just as I am the centre of his, and if ever there was a marriage made in heaven this is it. Because I do think of our relationship as a marriage. What else can one call it? We are partners in every way. No piece of paper do we need. He does not mention the legality of our union any more. Nor do I. He's as happy as I am, just the way it is.

I am happy on another level because of Grace Rose. Ever since she told me last September that I am her heir, I have been walking on clouds. She has left me the one thing I want most of all – additional shares in Deravenels.

It never occurred to me that she would do such a thing, because she has a great-nephew. Nor did I realize she owned ten per cent of Deravenel shares. That afternoon she explained everything to me. Her first shares were given to her by Edward Deravenel; these were boosted by shares from her special friend, Amos Finnister, who worked for Edward. He was the man who found Grace Rose in a cart in the East End when she was a child of four, and he had remained devoted to her all his life. After the death of Vicky and Stephen Forth, who brought her up, she inherited another two and a half per cent which created a grand total of ten per cent altogether.

Grace Rose went on to further explain that she had made various other bequests in her will, to charities and staff, and including paintings and jewellery to her great-nephew, Patrick. He was the grandson of Maisie Morran, Charlie's sister, who had married an Irish aristocrat when she was a star on Broadway. They had had one son who had died in his early forties, and Patrick was the only child, and sole heir to the title, the lands, and considerable money. In Grace Rose's opinion, Patrick had everything he could ever want or need, but she had left him the two Post-Impressionist paintings he had always admired, along with a few pieces of Cartier jewellery for his wife-to-be. 'The rest is yours, Elizabeth,' she had finished that day and had immediately changed the subject.

Many of our business ventures have come to a happy conclusion, and this has made Cecil, Robin and myself feel a degree of satisfaction that our considerable efforts have proved successful. I should include Ambrose here, because it is Robin's brother who has created our most beautiful resort. In Marbella. It was opened in March and we went to Spain for this important event. And even though I say so myself, success is stamped all over it. We know we have a winner.

Another thrill was the opening of my spas in April . . . in London. Paris and New York. I have Ambrose's wife Anne Dunley to thank for that. She is in charge in London and Paris; Anka Palitz in New York. Because of Anne, who helped with the negotiations, Anka runs our spas across America. Six of them used to be hers. We bought her company in December, with the understanding that she would remain

307

with Elizabeth Turner Spas for five years. She agreed and sold us her spas, and now she is my American partner.

At the beginning of May I met with a Russian, Alexander Maslenikoff. He was one of five people interested in buying the house in Chelsea. I knew he was a tough cookie, but he seemed the most likely candidate to pay what I wanted, and so I persisted with him. I won in the end. I asked for eighty million pounds; he offered fifty-five; I said thank you, but no thanks. And I walked away. I was confident that he wanted my beautiful house so badly he would increase his offer. He did. A day later he came back and said his final price was seventy million pounds sterling. Not a penny more, he added. I took it. Once we had agreed on the price, he was easy to do business with. After an immediate inspection by his surveyors and engineers, he signed on the dotted line, and handed me a cashier's cheque for seventy million. It cleared immediately. Now my beautiful house of bad memories is his and the money is mine . . . money to keep Deravenels safe, if needs be.

Robin keeps saying that I can't put a foot wrong, that 1998 is my year. Let's hope that he's right, let's hope that Lady Luck keeps running with me . . .

It was Tuesday May twenty-sixth, and tonight would be the first of the Sotheby's auctions . . . The Impressionist and Post-Impressionist paintings of the Deravenel–Turner Collections were going on the block. Robin had gone to fetch Grace Rose, and Elizabeth knew she must finish dressing. She was wearing a purple silk cocktail dress by Chanel and the gold medallion which had belonged to Edward Deravenel which she had inherited. As she stared at herself in the mirrored closet door in her dressing room, she realized how wonderful it looked against the purple silk.

As she turned around, the sculpture which Robin had given her for Christmas caught her eye and as always it brought a smile to her face. It was placed on a table against a back wall, where it was shown off to perfection, and it depicted a bed split down the middle diagonally. One half of the bed was made of bright-red silk roses, the other was composed of nails, nail heads down, sharp tips pointing up.

It was by the sculptor and painter Edwina Sandys, Winston Churchill's granddaughter, and a friend of Robin's. Most appropriately, it was called *The Marriage Bed*, and it appealed to Elizabeth's sense of humour just as much as it had to Robin's when he had first seen it.

'Here they are, Elizabeth,' Blanche Parrell said, hurrying into the dressing room. 'They were in the shoe closet in the bedroom. The evening bag must be in here though.'

'Oh, thanks, Blanche dear, and yes it is. I just saw it a moment ago.' After stepping into the high-heeled silk pumps, dyed purple to match the dress, Elizabeth went on, 'What time is Thomas picking you up?'

'He'll be here in a few minutes, with Kat. He went to fetch her first. I told him to wait downstairs in the car. You don't have time to be socializing right now.' Stepping away, Blanche now eyed Elizabeth appraisingly.

'Do I pass muster?' Elizabeth asked, smiling at this warm and loving Welshwoman who had been part of her life since her childhood. 'Obviously not. Why are you frowning, Blanche?'

'Earrings,' Blanche answered. 'That's what you need. Those gold hoops set with diamonds. I'll go and get them. Back in a jiffy.'

Elizabeth found the purple silk evening bag by Prada, put in a lipstick, tissues, then went to take out the purple silk stole which matched the dress. When Blanche returned with the hoop earrings she took them from her and put them on and said, 'I'm ready, and so are you, I see. You look lovely, Blanche, I've always liked you in navy blue.'

Blanche beamed at her. 'Thank you. I bet you're excited, aren't you? Tonight's the big night. On tenterhooks too, I suppose?'

'You're correct, Blanche, I'm excited, nervous, apprehensive and shaking inside, actually.'

'Well, if it helps you, you look as cool as the proverbial cucumber. No sign of nerves, or any other emotion for that matter.' Blanche laughed. 'You always were an actress, even when you were little. I often used to say to Thomas, "Let's not forget she's an actress, and she's a good one." You could have been on the stage, you know.'

They laughed together like the conspirators they'd always been as they went out of the dressing room, and Elizabeth suddenly said, 'Certain people think Sotheby's won't get the high prices tonight, and that some of the paintings might not even sell. The art business suffered at the beginning of the 1990s. There was a bit of a chill in the air because of the recession. Which everyone had predicted, of course. However, Cecil Williams believes that it's levelled off and the art market is now back to normal. He's very confident the prices are going to go high tonight.'

'Cecil knows what he's talking about,' Blanche remarked. 'But then you know that without me having to tell you.'

The intercom buzzed and Elizabeth went to answer it.

Robert said, 'I'm here, darling, with Grace Rose. And Thomas has just arrived to pick up Blanche.'

'We'll be right down,' she answered.

THIRTY-TWO

From the moment they arrived at Sotheby's New Bond Street galleries Robert knew the evening was going to be unique.

It was in the air. A buzz, a sense of excitement, the undercurrent of anticipation mingled with tension, a feeling that the auction which would soon commence would be the art event of the season. For one thing, it was an *evening* auction, and word had gone out that it would be plastered with the rich and famous, and also elegance personified.

And indeed it was. The crowd milling around were the *crème de la crème* of London society, all the women dressed in cocktail attire, the men in their best Savile Row numbers.

Within a few seconds Robert spotted many people he knew... friends, business acquaintances and colleagues. Most of the top brass from Deravenel had already arrived, and he raised a hand in greeting to Charles Broakes and Sidney Payne and their wives. He saw John Norfell talking to Jenny Broadbent, one of the top women tycoons in the

City, and an art-collector of some renown, and out of the corner of his eye he caught sight of Mark Lott and Alexander Dawson.

Elizabeth had seen them, too, and she whispered, 'Enemies as well as friends have gathered to see what happens to my famous art collection. And those two in particular want me to fall flat on my face.'

Robert smiled at her lovingly, and there was a great deal of confidence in his voice when he said, 'It's going to be your evening, Elizabeth, you'll see. I told you the other day, this is your year, and Lady Luck is walking with you all the way.'

She simply nodded, made no comment, but her dark eyes were full of sparkle and anticipation.

Turning to Grace Rose, who was holding onto his arm, Robert said, 'And you're going to be the *star* of the show, Grace Rose. You look spectacular and your sapphire earrings are . . . mind-boggling.'

'Thank you, Robert, you certainly know how to make an old lady feel special. But I do believe it is Elizabeth who'll be *the star* of this *show*, for undoubtedly it *is* going to be . . . quite a show.'

He laughed, and so did Elizabeth, who suddenly experienced a rush of pride in her great-aunt. Tall, slender, and straight-backed, with her shimmering silver hair and perfect make-up, she was indeed a knockout, and also the most regal woman present.

All eyes were on the three of them as they made their way to the room where the auction was to be held. As they moved along slowly, making their way through the crowds of people, Grace Rose suddenly announced, 'I think this lot are here to buy, Elizabeth. I can smell it in the air. *Money*. And there are art-dealers I recognize from Paris as well as here. They'll buy, mark my words.'

'I hope so,' Elizabeth murmured, glancing around, waving

312

to her cousins, Frank Knowles and Henry Carray, and spotting her great-uncle Howard, looking for all the world like the patriarch that he was.

'I know the global recession played havoc with the art market a few years ago, Grace Rose,' Robert said, 'but you told me months ago that it has gradually swung back up. It has, hasn't it?'

'Yes. Prices have been much higher lately, and especially so when the art is really good. That's the important thing, and I personally believe the paintings Jane Shaw collected, and those she found for Edward, are of the finest calibre. Don't forget another very important thing, Robert. Impressionist and Post-Impressionist paintings are always in demand. I have no worries, none at all. There may be a lot of socialites here for the fun of it, but I guarantee there are many serious buyers as well.'

When they entered the large gallery where the auction was going to be held, they were given catalogues and numbered paddles, and were directed to a section of the gallery where seats had been reserved for Elizabeth and her guests.

A moment later, Marcus Johnson was heading their way, looking purposeful, his handsome face full of smiles, his entire being filled with energy and enthusiasm. This kind of evening, one on which he had worked diligently behind the scenes, was just up his alley.

After greeting the three of them, he ushered them to their seats, made sure they were comfortably settled, then leaned closer to Elizabeth. He said, 'I've got to go and take care of the press now. Everything's set for Annabel's later. I'll meet you there, after the auction.' He gave her a huge smile. 'And we'll celebrate.'

Elizabeth, who was unexpectedly beginning to feel nervous, even apprehensive, could only nod.

As Marcus disappeared, she looked towards the door,

watched more and more people streaming in, only half listened to Robert who was talking to Grace Rose sitting between them.

She tried to take tight control of herself, feeling suddenly queasy. Nerves, she told herself, it's only nerves. Suddenly she spotted Blanche and her brother Thomas, Kat Ashe with her husband John, and right behind them her beloved Dunleys . . . Ambrose and Anne, Merry and her husband Henry, and in their wake Cecil, Francis and Nicholas with their wives. The others all stood back to let Cecil, Francis and Nicholas sit in the chairs next to Elizabeth.

Staring into her face, noting its extreme paleness, Cecil Williams said quietly, 'Don't be nervous, Elizabeth, everything's going to be all right.'

'Once the auction starts and gets rolling I'll be able to relax,' she murmured, squeezing his hand. She made a small grimace. 'Getting rid of all this family . . . *stuff*. Well, it's quite a responsibility, isn't it?' She lifted her eyes to the ceiling. 'I bet they're all looking down at me – angrily.'

Cecil chuckled. 'It is a responsibility, yes. But your decision was right, don't fret about that,' he answered. 'And as you keep saying, you're doing it for Deravenels – should we ever need the money.'

Grace Rose said to her, 'You know that the auctioneer controls the change in the amount of the increments, don't you? In other words, the price rises in increments at his will. Or drops down if he wants it to.'

'Yes, Alistair Gaines of Sotheby's explained that to me,' Elizabeth responded. Shifting slightly in her chair, she looked at Robert, who turned, smiled. 'It's very warm in here,' she murmured, 'and terribly noisy, overwhelming.'

He nodded. 'But the room is full now, and they'll be closing the doors any minute. Then the noise will stop. And the fun will begin.'

Elizabeth wondered why she had accepted the numbered paddle; after all, she wasn't going to bid. She was selling. She smiled to herself. It was a nuisance having to hold it, and she put it down on the floor, then stared at the thick catalogue on her lap. Printed across the front cover it said: *The Deravenel–Turner Collections. Fine Impressionist and Post-Impressionist Paintings.*

As she continued to look at it she was unexpectedly filled with a great sense of pride in her family and she completely relaxed. All the tension fled. She glanced up as the lights went off and then immediately came back on again. And there was the auctioneer standing at the podium. After bidding them all good evening, he spoke eloquently about the collection, and then gave details of the first painting to go on the block.

Elizabeth had known from the beginning which it would be . . . her favourite Claude Monet. She sat straighter in her seat, watching and listening attentively as the auction finally began.

Looking out into the gallery filled to overflowing with socialites, avid art-enthusiasts, potential big buyers and art-dealers from all over the world, the auctioneer now pointed to the Monet on an easel to his right. 'And there it is, a fine example of high Impressionism. Monet's *The Small Branch of the Seine at Argenteuil.* I will take bids.'

To the auctioneer's delight a paddle immediately went up, and he exclaimed enthusiastically, 'I'll take the opening bid to my left. One million pounds.'

Within a split second the auctioneer's eyes shifted, settled on the centre of the room. 'One million two hundred and fifty thousand pounds from the centre front.'

Elizabeth was clutching her hands together, looking straight ahead, her throat dry, tight with emotion. The auctioneer was going up in increments of two hundred and fifty thousand pounds, and she now knew how right she had been to think that this particular Monet was one of the best paintings in Jane Shaw's extraordinary collection.

After the first bid, and then the second, the price was rising rapidly. So rapidly, in fact, people appeared to be startled. Within the next twelve minutes the price escalated furiously and the auctioneer's hammer came down as the price hit nine million pounds.

Elizabeth was momentarily thunderstruck. Reaching across Grace Rose, she clutched Robert's outstretched hand, her face radiant. 'I can't believe it!' she exclaimed in a low, tremulous voice. 'You were right, Robin.'

His eyes were brilliant, sparkling with the same excitement she was experiencing, and he said, 'I told you it was going to be a huge success. Congratulations, darling.'

The excitement the two of them were feeling was running high throughout the entire gallery. There was enormous enthusiasm rippling through the room, and the bidding for the other paintings was brisk and lively. Elizabeth had put twelve paintings up for sale, and they were indeed selling. She could hardly contain herself, and she was trembling inside.

At one moment Grace Rose took hold of her hand, and murmured, 'Fantastic, Elizabeth! My dear, you're having a most stupendous auction!' Her voice became shaky and tears glistened in her faded blue eyes, as she added, 'Jane Shaw had wonderful taste, and all I can say is that we're all the luckier because of it.'

By the end of two hours the entire collection had been sold: her favourite Pissarro, with its red rooftops, the snow scene by Guillaumin with winter trees filled with red leaves, the two other Monets, a Manet, a Van Gogh, two Sisleys, a Rouault, and two paintings by another of her favourites, Henri Matisse. All had gone in a couple of hours and she had made millions of pounds. A sense of enormous relief flowed through her. No matter what happened, she was now certain she could keep Deravenels safe.

As the auction came to an end Robert jumped up, helped Grace Rose to her feet and then took hold of Elizabeth, held her tightly in his arms. He kissed her cheek, and whispered against her neck, 'You've done it, Elizabeth. And you're going to be the talk of the town.'

Leaning away from him, laughing with him, she said in that pithy tone of hers he knew so well, 'So what's new about that?'

Cecil, Francis and Nicholas were surrounding her, offering their congratulations, and Cecil showed her his notebook before he slipped it into his pocket. She knew he had been taking his notes as usual, and smiled. The Dunleys were there a split second later, and Blanche, Kat and John hovered on the fringes with Thomas; she managed to get to everyone, to chat for a moment, to thank them all for coming and for their support.

Suddenly Marcus Johnson was hurrying towards her, escorting a man and a woman to her side. Sliding through the crush of her special friends with the greatest of ease, he said, 'Elizabeth, could you have a few words with Phoebe Jones from the *Daily Mail* and Angus Todd from *The Times*, please?'

'Of course, it's my pleasure,' she answered and moved with Marcus and the two journalists to a corner of the room.

'How do you feel, Miss Turner?' Phoebe Jones asked. 'Excited, I'm sure.'

Elizabeth nodded. 'I think *that* might be the understatement of the year, Miss Jones. I'm ecstatic. There's no other word to use.'

'Did you know that a Monet entitled *The Railroad Bridge at Argenteuil*, considered to be another prime example of high Impressionism, was sold by Christie's here in London in 1988 for twelve point six million dollars?' Angus Todd asked. 'It was a record.'

'No, I didn't. As you know, my painting went tonight for nine million pounds, which is approximately thirteen point five million dollars, so I'm obviously thrilled I've topped the other one sold ten years ago.'

The two journalists went on asking her questions, but eventually Marcus stepped in, apologized to them, explained that he must now bring the interview to an end.

Marcus and Robert escorted her and Grace Rose out of the crowded gallery, through the auction house and into New Bond Street. Once Robert, Grace Rose and she were in the car, Marcus said he would see them later, and closed the door. Finally Elizabeth let out a long sigh as the car pulled away, and then began to smile. And she smiled all the way to Annabel's in Berkeley Square where she was giving a celebration dinner party for her closest friends.

THIRTY-THREE

Cecil Williams laughed when he walked into Elizabeth's office and saw her studying columns of figures in a black notebook. 'Well, well, well,' he said as he strode towards her desk. 'I see you've finally taken my advice and resorted to making notes that won't get lost.'

Lifting her head, Elizabeth gave him a big smile, nodding. 'Robin bought me this wonderful notebook – it's called a Moleskine. A lot of renowned writers and artists have used them over the years, including Ernest Hemingway, Henri Matisse, Vincent Van Gogh and Bruce Chatwin. I have everything about the four auctions written in here, so we can confer easily and whenever you wish. Let's go over the figures now, shall we?'

Seating himself opposite her, he pulled out his own notebook, opened it and stared at the first page. Then looking across at her, he explained, 'This is a new notebook I started just for the Sotheby auctions. Anyway, as I said to you the other day, you've done extremely well. My grand total comes to one hundred and twenty-three million pounds. My God, as I say that out loud I must certainly say that you've done *fantastically* well.'

'I know. And if we add the price of the Chelsea house, which I sold to Alexander Maslenikoff for seventy million, I've made one hundred and ninety-three million pounds altogether. *Gross*, of course, that's without taxes and the usual deductions.'

'I've done all those calculations for you, and we can discuss them when Martine has a print-out for you later today. In the meantime, I must say that the auction which surprised me the most last week was the second night . . . the jewellery. It all went for staggering prices, Elizabeth. More than I expected.'

'That's what Nicholas said to me, but when Robin and I started to look inside those many boxes stored in the vault at Ravenscar, we both realized that we'd fallen into a gold-mine. Or shouldn't I perhaps say diamond-mine?' She shook her head wonderingly. 'Think about some of those fabulous items that went on the block . . . twenty-two diamond tiaras to begin with, and the diamond necklace that came from the Royal Jewels of France . . . that extraordinary necklace made specifically for Empress Eugénie. That particular necklace and the tiaras went for millions and millions of pounds. And there were so many valuable rings from some of the greatest jewellers of the world – at least five fetched over a million each.' Glancing at her notebook she reminded him, 'Twenty-six million pounds for the Deravenel–Turner jewels and eighty-two million pounds for the art, that ain't bad, is it?'

Cecil nodded in agreement. 'Everything went at top prices. Just amazing, to me. Nine million pounds for all of the antique silver, gold plate, Georgian pieces by the great master silversmiths and goldsmiths, and the china, plus six million for the antique rugs, wall tapestries, English Georgian and fine French Furniture, and hundreds of other *objets d'art*. I must say, Elizabeth, I agree wholeheartedly with Grace Rose. There hasn't been an auction like this for many years, perhaps *ever*. Calling it the Deravenel–Turner Collections was inspired on your part, because those names helped to sell everything, in my opinion.'

'And also very clever publicity on the part of Sotheby's,' she remarked.

'Let's not forget that brilliant publicist you hired, Marcus Johnson,' Cecil exclaimed. 'In my opinion, he's a past master when it comes to spin. He brought in the right crowd, created something of a furore, drummed up real interest and excitement.'

'And I guess our family has always been linked to *scandal*, as well as money and power.' Elizabeth's mouth twitched and she couldn't help grinning as she added mischievously. 'And *I've* been touched with scandal, too, you know. Don't forget I did my part. And scandal is always *in*.'

Cecil gave her a small smile, said quietly, 'You know I never pry into your private affairs, but what *is* happening in regard to Robert's divorce?'

'I don't know, and I certainly don't care. However, he is going to Gloucestershire next week to see Amy. He delayed his trip because apparently she hasn't been well.'

'I see.'

'Don't expect me to rush into marriage, Cecil. You know full well I have no interest in it . . . and that's nothing to do with my wonderful Robin . . . I just don't want to marry anyone.'

Deep down, Cecil Williams knew she would never change her mind. Others thought she would, but instinctively he knew differently. She was unusually obstinate, always had been and for as long as he had known her. But there was that nagging question of an heir . . . Who *would* succeed her if something happened to her? He had no idea; he was acutely aware that now was not the right moment to bring this matter up. Instead, changing the subject, he flicked over a few pages in his notebook, announced, 'You owe the bank a lot, Elizabeth. The money you borrowed to open the first of the Elizabeth Turner Spas, then the second loan you took in order to purchase the Anka Palitz spas in America. I think you should pay the bank off as soon as possible, and save the money you're paying in interest. Those loans are very expensive.'

'I was just making those calculations when you came in.' Dropping her eyes, she looked at the second page in her Moleskine, and told him, 'I borrowed seventy million pounds from the bank, Cecil. Ten million to start the spas here, then the fifty million pounds it took to buy Anka's spas. The last ten million I put into my own company . . . I needed it as operating money for the spas here and in Paris. But yes, now I can get rid of the loan, retire it at once. I'll still have plenty of money left to put away just in case Deravenels ever needs it.'

'I have some thoughts about that. I think you should invest it carefully. No-risk investments would be the best, the safest. You simply can't have all that money not invested. It has to be earning more money for you.'

'I know, and I was –' She stopped and looked at the door at the sound of a knock. 'Come in,' she called as it opened.

Francis Walsington strode in and closed the door behind him, stood leaning against it for a split second.

'What's wrong?' she asked, instantly noting the gloomy look on his face. She knew him well, could read him like a book. Even though Francis was able to keep a poker face with everyone else, he seemed unable to do so with her.

'Sorry to interrupt, but I thought you both ought to know that another tanker has blown up. The second in three months,' he said, walking across the room.

'Oh, my God!' Elizabeth cried.

'Not ours,' Francis hastened to add, wanting to reassure her. 'But it's still cause for concern, in my opinion. I don't like it . . . I hope we're not seeing a pattern develop here. The tanker was one of Crestoil's out of New Jersey, and it blew up off the coast of Bali.'

'Have a lot of people been injured?' Cecil asked swiftly.

'Crew, of course, but there's been a really nasty oil spill, and Bali is a tourist haven, as you both well know. A lot of young people head there in the summer and from all over the world. Ecological problems are possible.'

'Do you think it's a terrorist operation?' Elizabeth stared hard at Francis. 'I wouldn't be surprised if it was. I'm always worried about terrorist attacks and sabotage these days, especially after the Spanish explosion last year. In fact, lately I've begun to wonder if we should sell Deravco Oil.'

'It's a good money-earner,' Cecil reminded her, knowing as he said it that she didn't need to be reminded of anything. 'A cash-cow most of the time.'

'I know. But I feel this constant threat hovering over us . . . at least in my head.' Sitting back in her chair, she continued, 'Was it Spencer Thomas who passed on the information?'

'No, actually it wasn't,' Francis replied. 'I happened to turn on the television set in my office a few minutes ago and caught a news flash on CNN. I gave Spencer a buzz right away, but he's seemingly away on vacation. He'll be back next Monday.'

'Maybe we should talk to *him* about selling?' Elizabeth said making it sound like a question. 'What do you think?'

'In order to sell we have to have a buyer,' Cecil pointed out. 'But we can certainly have a meeting with Spencer, and I trust his judgement implicitly. Let's hear what he has to say about the oil business in general. He usually has tons of information at his fingertips, and especially about OPEC.'

'Good idea,' Francis agreed. 'In the meantime, I'll gather as much information as I can about this latest rotten explosion. And I'll have Vance Codrill focus on taking extra security measures in our tankers, although to be honest I'm not so sure there is much else we *can* do.'

'I know you're always on top of things.' Elizabeth smiled at him, and then at Cecil. 'Tell you what, I'm going to break my rule about not having lunch . . . let's go to the Caprice. My treat. To celebrate the grand success of the auctions.'

'Good God!' Francis exclaimed, grinning at her, and strode over to the window, looked out. 'No bloody wonder it's raining!'

'Is it really?' she asked, making a face.

'No,' he answered, laughter in his eyes. 'Where is Robert? Will he join us?'

'I'm sure he will. He'll be back soon. He went to do a small chore for my aunt, Grace Rose.' She glanced at her watch. 'It's now eleven. Shall we head for the Caprice around twelve-thirty?'

Cecil, who had been even more astounded by her invitation than Francis, stood up. 'I'll have Martine book a table for four,' he murmured as he left her office with Francis.

Alone again, Elizabeth sat making notations in the Moleskine. Then she added up a list of numbers, and came to the conclusion that she could easily give a million pounds to charity this year. Perhaps even more.

Opening her desk drawer, she took out a sheet of paper Merry had prepared for her and read it slowly. It was a list of charities her assistant had thought she would be interested in, and as usual Robin's sister had read her mind very well.

Staring at the list, she put a tick against the National Society for Prevention of Cruelty to Children. If there was one thing she couldn't stomach it was cruelty to children. And cruelty to animals. She saw that Merry had included the Royal Society for Prevention of Cruelty to Animals, and she put a tick against this one as well.

Whenever she thought of a defenceless child or animal being deliberately hurt Elizabeth cringed, and she did so now, pushing away her dire thoughts. These two good causes would benefit from the sale of the possessions she had inherited, an incredible number of possessions and most of them no longer viable in this day and age.

She was happy she had auctioned them off; certainly the money she had made was much more useful in a variety of ways. And some of it she would give away. Oddly enough, no one had ever thought to tell her it was right to give back, to give to others less privileged than she. She had come to that conclusion by herself when she was much younger. She had wanted to be of help to a deserving charity for a long time and now she could be, and she would.

Her mind swung to the Deravenels and the Turners who had gone before her, and in a sudden impulse she jumped up, left her office and hurried down the corridor to the board room. Opening the heavy mahogany doors, she went inside, turned on the lights.

What a wonderfully handsome room it was, with its rich, mellow antiques, glittering crystal chandeliers hanging from the ceiling above the board-room table, and the magnificent oil paintings on the walls.

They're *all* my ancestors, she thought, as she walked slowly down one side of the room, not really understanding who *they* all were until she read their names engraved on the small metal plates attached to the ornate gilt frames.

Moving to the other side of the room, she came to three

faces she knew well: her grandfather Henry Turner, the first Turner to run Deravenels, her father Harry Turner, the second Turner to take the reins of the company, and her half-sister. After studying them for a moment, she moved on, came to a stop when she stood in front of the most extraordinary portrait of her great-grandfather, Edward Deravenel.

'God, he was gorgeous. Very dishy!' she said out loud, and then quickly glanced around, relieved to see that she *had* closed the door behind her. And it was true; he was the most handsome of men, and the life-size portrait of him was masterful. I look like him, she thought, I really do.

Stepping back, she gazed at those three imposing paintings of her father, her grandfather and her great-grandfather, and she couldn't help wondering what they would think of her latest venture . . . selling off their possessions, so blithely, as if she didn't care about their things. She did; but she had no use for them. Making sure Deravenels would always have a war chest had motivated her. Surely they would understand *that*. And she had succeeded in a most powerful way; they would admire her achievement, wouldn't they? She smiled to herself. They had been dyed-in-the-wool businessmen, and what she was doing was to simply follow in *their* footsteps. And that was the truth of it. *She* was managing director now and fully intended to be the best there had ever been.

Moving even farther back, scanning the three paintings from a distance, she exclaimed aloud, 'None of you is angry with me, I know you're not. I'm one of you. I'm cut from the same cloth even though I *am* a woman.' Elizabeth began to laugh. If anyone heard her they would think she was a mad woman, talking to portraits of three dead men.

THIRTY-FOUR

'So, to cut to the chase,' Nicholas Throckman finished, 'I'm pleased with the way things have turned out at the Paris office. The staff is smaller, but it's extremely efficient. We've got a good crew now.'

'I know Sidney Payne has been very effective in his efforts to find the right people, and actually we've never had anyone quite as good with personnel as he is.' Elizabeth sat back in the chair, smiling at Nicholas. 'As for you, old friend, I don't know what we'd do without you.'

Robert came striding into her office from his own and took the chair next to Nicholas. 'We were sorry you couldn't come to our birthday dinner, Nicholas.'

'I was, too, but you know I had to be in Paris.' He threw Robert an intent look, then his eyes went to Elizabeth. 'There's a certain amount of –' He paused when the door opened and Francis Walsington walked in with Cecil Williams.

'Sorry we're late, but we had to finish up with Charles Broakes and Norfell,' Cecil said, then gestured to the seating arrangement. 'Maybe we'd be better sitting over there.'

Standing up, crossing the room, Elizabeth asked, 'Is everything all right between those two? No more problems and disagreements, I hope.'

'They're fine,' Cecil reassured her, sitting down next to her on the sofa. 'Now that the manor houses at some of the vineyards have become really successful as small boutique hotels, and their spas are in the black, they're at ease with each other, more or less. But there's always been a bit of an undercurrent there, you know. I think Charles isn't much of a fan when it comes to John Norfell.'

'I doubt that *he* has any fans,' Robert muttered as he joined them, followed by Francis and Nicholas.

'I'm afraid we interrupted you mid-sentence when we came in, Nicholas,' Cecil said. 'Sorry about that.'

'It's all right, and I'm glad you and Francis are here. I was about to tell Elizabeth and Robert that there is a certain amount of gossip in Paris about François de Burgh. There are rumours that his health is not at all good.'

'What's wrong with him?' Elizabeth asked, her curiosity aroused.

'I've heard that he has a virulent type of leukaemia, and that his mother is frantic with worry,' Nicholas explained. 'And so is Marie de Burgh apparently.'

'Well, yes, she would be,' Francis interjected. 'If he kicks the bucket she's going to be out in the cold. His mother will take over Dauphin and groom one of the other sons to be the new head of the company. Catherine de Burgh is a pretty smart woman, and she has been involved in the running of the conglomerate for years. Henri de Burgh relied on her heavily when he was alive, and her son does, too.'

'If François de Burgh does die, and Marie Stewart is no longer with the conglomerate, which she won't be, does that mean she will go to Scotland to run Scottish Heritage?'

Elizabeth asked, her mind racing as usual. 'Aside from the fact that it *is* her company, she is consumed with overweening ambition and loves power.'

'That is exactly what she would do, I'm certain.' Francis exchanged a knowing look with Elizabeth. 'Then she would *really* be breathing down our necks.'

'Why is it that we pay so much attention to this woman?' Nicholas asked, a hint of sudden irritability in his voice. 'She's of no consequence to us, and we all know that. So let's not whip up a big dose of paranoia here.'

At this moment the phone on Robert's desk began to ring and he jumped up, went into his adjoining office to answer it.

'None of us is being paranoid,' Cecil said, addressing Nicholas. 'And in many ways you are correct. She can't actually *do* anything. But she can certainly make herself a bloody nuisance –'

Cecil instantly stopped talking when Robert appeared in the doorway, saw at once that he looked stunned.

From the peculiar expression on Robert's face Elizabeth knew something serious had happened to cause his obvious distress. 'What is it, Robin?' she asked anxiously, jumping up, hurrying across the floor. 'What's wrong?' she probed.

'Amy's dead,' he replied in a low voice. 'There's been an accident.'

'What kind of accident?' she cried, her voice rising, and as she spoke she took hold of his arm.

'She apparently fell down a flight of stairs. She broke her neck.' He shook his head, as if he couldn't quite comprehend this.

A horrified expression settled on Elizabeth's face; she drew him over to the sofa, made him sit down, realized he was not only shaken up but probably in shock.

She glanced at the other men, who were aghast and as

startled as she was, and said to Francis, 'I think there's a bottle of brandy in the credenza in Robin's office. Could you pour a glass for him, please?'

'Right away.' Francis pushed himself to his feet and hurried out.

'Who phoned you?' Cecil leaned towards Robert. 'Was it the police?'

'No, it was Anthony Forrest,' Robert answered, now managing to pull himself together, sitting up straighter, focusing on Cecil. 'You've met him. He's an old associate of mine, takes care of personal business for me. Actually, he also handles financial matters with Amy for me. He lives in Cirencester also.'

'So the Gloucestershire police got in touch with him, is that it?' Cecil asked swiftly, frowning. Worry had already settled over him.

'No, they didn't, at least they hadn't when he spoke to me. But I'm sure they will, and they'll no doubt be phoning me any minute.' Robert took several deep breaths to steady himself, and explained, 'It was Amy's housekeeper, Connie Mellor, who rang Anthony after she'd called the ambulance service and the police. She came back from the market around two o'clock this afternoon and found . . . Amy's body.' Robert turned to Elizabeth. 'I just can't believe this.'

'Neither can I,' she answered in a sombre voice.

Francis brought the glass of brandy to Robert, who thanked him, and gulped some of it down, then glanced at his watch. 'It's five-thirty. I'd better phone Connie. And also Anthony, let him know I'm coming to Cirencester tonight.'

Elizabeth said swiftly, 'I think Ambrose ought to go with you.' She crossed her office, picked up the phone and spoke to Merry, told her to find Ambrose, explained that she needed to see them both urgently, that there was an unexpected problem.

Then she sat down at her desk, her face paler than ever, and troubled. She fully understood why Amy's death was incomprehensible to Robert. It was to her; she was just as shocked and taken by surprise as he was. Well aware that Robert had seen Amy in August, Elizabeth also knew that he had recently spoken to her several times on the phone about the divorce, and matters pertaining to it.

Dropping her eyes, Elizabeth stared at the small desk calendar in front of her. It was Tuesday September the eighth, just one day after their joint birthday, which they had celebrated with a hundred friends and family at a big splashy party this past weekend.

She sat back in the chair, saying nothing. Nor did any of the men in the room. Everyone was quiet, lost momentarily in their own thoughts.

A moment later the door flew open and Ambrose and Merry hurried into her office; both looked concerned. Taking charge of the situation at once, Elizabeth stood up behind her desk, said, 'I'm afraid we've had rather upsetting news. Robin has just heard from Anthony Forrest in Cirencester . . . Amy has died in a dreadful accident. She fell down a flight of stairs at her home.'

Merry gasped, stood staring at Elizabeth as if she couldn't believe her words.

'Oh, my God!' Ambrose moved forward at once, hurried over to Robert, sat down next to him, grasping his arm. Their sister Merry followed suit, looking as stunned as her brother Ambrose.

'I must leave for Circencester as soon as possible,' Robert explained to Ambrose. 'Will you come with me?'

'You know I will. I wouldn't let you make a trip like that alone, for God's sake!'

When the phone began to ring on Elizabeth's desk she immediately picked it up. 'Elizabeth Turner here.'

'Good afternoon, Miss Turner. This is Inspector Colin Lawson of the Gloucestershire Police. I'm trying to reach Mr Robert Dunley.'

'He's still here at the office, Inspector Lawson. I'll get him for you. Just a moment please.' She pressed the hold button and stepped away from her desk. 'It's an inspector from the Gloucestershire police,' she said to Robert. 'Lawson,' she added, repeating his name.

Picking up the receiver, Robert said, 'Good afternoon, Inspector Lawson. I was expecting to hear from you, or rather someone from the police in Cirencester. I have learned from my associate Anthony Forrest, just a few minutes ago, that my wife met with a tragic and fatal accident earlier today. He gave me the details, said she fell down the stairs at her home.'

'That is correct, Mr Dunley,' the inspector answered. 'We do need to speak to you, sir. We have a number of questions we need answering.'

'My brother and I are about to leave for Circencester. We're going to drive down. Would you like us to come directly to the police station? Or do you wish to meet us at Mr Forrest's house?'

'The latter will be fine, Mr Dunley. We have to talk to Mr Forrest anyway, and we can do the two interviews at the same time.'

'That sounds practical, Inspector. If I might ask, where is my wife's body at this moment? Is it at the hospital or at the morgue?'

Robert caught the hesitation on the inspector's part before he answered. Lawson cleared his throat, finally said, 'I believe Mrs Dunley's body went to the medical examiner . . . to be autopsied. But I will have the proper information for you by the time you arrive.'

'Thank you, Inspector Lawson. We should be there in about three hours, depending on the traffic.'

After saying goodbye and hanging up, Robert stared at the others, and explained, 'The police inspector has a number of questions for me, and for Anthony.' He frowned, and addressed Francis. 'When I asked him where Amy's body was he seemed to hesitate, was evasive. Don't you think that's odd?'

'Not really,' Francis responded. 'He probably didn't know where Amy's body actually was at this precise moment. It was most likely taken to the local hospital by the ambulance crew and then went to the medical examiner's office for autopsy. It might still be in transit even. I don't read anything sinister into what he said, Robert, honestly I don't.'

'Why would the inspector want to talk to *you*?' Merry turned to her brother. 'I mean, how can *you* throw any light on the accident? You were here at the office all day.'

Robert shrugged, and then reassured her, 'It's just routine, I'm sure, Merry. After all, I am still her husband, her next of kin.'

Francis said, 'Robert's correct, it is routine, Merry. The police go right to the spouse of the deceased, most especially if that person has died in an accident, one that could be questionable.'

'Why do you use that word?' Elizabeth stared at Francis. 'What's questionable about Amy's fall?'

'A lot of things in the minds of the police, I can assure you of that, Elizabeth. How did she fall *exactly*? Was she alone in the house at the time? Could she have been pushed? Might there have been an unwanted intruder? What was the state of her mind? Was it an accident *really*? Could it have been murder? Or suicide? Was she depressed about anything? Was she ill mentally? Or physically? Was she on any medication? Did she take drugs? Was she a drinker? I can offer you plenty of questions the police will come up with,' he finished flatly.

Everyone remained silent. All had been struck by Francis Walsington's words, and they sat digesting them, analysing them.

It was Elizabeth who spoke first. She gave Francis a long, knowing look, the kind of conspiratorial look they often exchanged, and murmured, 'Perhaps you should go with Robert and Ambrose, be present at the meeting with this Inspector Lawson at Anthony's house tonight.'

'I don't think that would be wise,' Francis answered immediately, shaking his head vehemently.

'But why not?'

'Because it could smack of . . . paranoia, my being protective of Robert, something like that. I'm head of security at Deravenels, and also a lawyer, please don't forget those things. I assure you the police won't, and –'

'But he hasn't done anything!' Elizabeth's voice had risen the way it did when she became alarmed or upset. 'And you know it.'

'But the police don't know that. And yes, Robert was here at the office today, and we've all been with him since your birthday party on Saturday and the lunch on Sunday. But that doesn't mean he is innocent as far as the police are concerned. He's still a suspect . . . *if* they think there's been foul play of some kind. And why is he a suspect? Because he's the husband. I just explained about spouses being under a microscope in a questionable death.'

'*You* perceive this as a questionable death, Francis?'

'I don't, Elizabeth, but the police will.'

'I could have hired someone to commit a murder, Elizabeth,' Robert remarked, going over to her, wanting to calm her.

'Oh, don't be so daft!' she cried. 'Nobody would think that.'

'They just might,' he answered. And he was right.

THIRTY-FIVE

Alicia Forrest, Anthony's wife, met them at the door of Gosling's End, the Queen Anne house that had been in her husband's family for several centuries.

'You got here sooner than we expected,' she murmured softly after she had greeted them warmly and hugged them both. They were very old family friends, and close.

'The traffic was light,' Robert explained. 'Thanks for having us for the night, Alicia. You're very kind to put us up like this on such short notice.'

'Don't be so silly, darling. As if we'd let you stay in a hotel. Come on, Anthony's waiting in the library with the inspector and . . . a sidekick.' Turning to Ambrose, she asked, 'How's Anne?'

'She's well, Alicia, and she sends her love. Now, what's this chap like, the inspector, I mean?'

'Seems rather nice, actually, low-key, well spoken, polite. Probably Eton or Harrow, in my opinion, for what it's worth. He's a gentleman, that's obvious.'

'One of the new breed of cops, I've no doubt,' Ambrose volunteered.

'Perhaps,' Alicia said, and a moment later opened the door to the panelled library, saying as she did, 'Here are Robert and Ambrose, sooner than we expected, Anthony.'

Robert and Anthony had been close friends for many years and greeted each other warmly with a big bear hug, and then Anthony shook hands with Ambrose. 'Nice to see you again,' Anthony said to Robert's older brother. 'Sorry it's not under happier circumstances, old chap. Now, come and meet Inspector Lawson and Sergeant Fuller of the Gloucestershire police.'

Once everyone had shaken hands they sat down, and the inspector addressed Robert. 'It's my understanding that you and your late wife were separated, Mr Dunley. That's correct, isn't it?'

'It is. For five years, a little more, actually.'

'And was it an amicable separation?'

'Yes, Inspector, it was. We'd married young and we'd grown apart –' Robert cut himself off abruptly, suddenly remembering Francis's advice: don't volunteer anything; only tell them what they need to know; just answer the questions and that's all. Please keep your trap shut the rest of the time had been Francis's last admonition to him.

'You work at Deravenels as the Chief Operating Officer. That is your position isn't it?'

Robert inclined his head, studying Colin Lawson, whom he figured to be in his early forties. Nice looking, well spoken, and just as Alicia had said, he was a gentleman.

'And you've held this position for how long, Mr Dunley?'

'Since 1996, Inspector Lawson.'

'That is when Miss Turner took over the company, isn't it?'

'Yes, it is.'

'But you have worked for the company for many years, haven't you?'

'Off and on, at the London office and abroad.'

'In fact, you are following in the footsteps of your father and grandfather, aren't you?'

'That's perfectly true, yes.'

'And so you've known Miss Turner for a long time, have you not?'

Robert understood where the inspector was leading him, and he decided that he would have to ignore Francis's advice on this particular matter. His relationship with Elizabeth was a well-known fact, documented by many magazines and newspapers and for quite some time now. Leaning back in the chair, feeling perfectly relaxed, Robert now volunteered, 'Elizabeth and I have known each other since we were eight years old, Inspector Lawson. We were childhood friends, and also when we were growing up. So the answer is, yes, I have known her for a very long time.'

'When did you last see your late wife, Mr Dunley?' Lawson gave Robert a long stare.

'It was in August. On the sixth, I believe. I suggested that I drive down to discuss our divorce, and Amy agreed.'

'I understand. As you just said, your separation had been amicable, so therefore your divorce was going to be amicable, too? Am I correct in thinking this?'

'Yes, you are. It was friendly on every level.'

'And so you came to a satisfactory agreement with Mrs Dunley? There were no problems?'

'No, Inspector, there were no problems at all regarding the divorce. My wife and I had agreed to it, and we were working with Mr Forrest regarding a settlement as well as alimony.'

'And you never quarrelled about the divorce or the settlement?' the policeman probed, albeit gently.

'Certainly not. And if you've heard otherwise it's not true.' Robert glanced at Anthony. 'I think you can bear me out on that point, can't you?'

Anthony nodded and said emphatically, 'Mr Dunley is telling you the truth, Inspector Lawson. There was no disharmony between the Dunleys about their divorce, none at all. Nor was there any during their long separation. I knew Mrs Dunley well, as did my wife, and she was absolutely content with her way of life in the country, here in Cirencester. I think everyone who knew her will bear me out on that. And anyone who might suggest otherwise would be . . . *lying*.'

'Thank you, Mr Forrest, for clarifying that again.'

Robert said, 'Inspector Lawson, when Mr Forrest rang me this afternoon he said that Mrs Dunley broke her neck when she fell. That is correct, isn't it?'

'Yes, it is, sir. There were other injuries. She had a deep cut on her head and bruises on her body.'

'Would those injuries be due to her falling down the stairs? Which is my understanding of the way she died. By falling.'

'They might be, yes,' the inspector agreed.

'When we spoke on the phone earlier, you said you would tell me where my late wife's body is when we met here this evening.'

'I did indeed, and her body is at the mortuary, Mr Dunley, with the medical examiner. You can view her body tomorrow.'

'I wish to do that. I'm making the assumption there will be an inquest,' Robert now said, giving the policeman a hard penetrating stare. 'I was wondering when it would take place?'

'I'm not quite sure of that at the moment, Mr Dunley. But within the week. That would be normal given the circumstances and providing all the evidence has been pulled together.'

'I understand. And will it be held here in Cirencester?'

'There is no Coroner's Court in Cirencester. It will have to be held in Cheltenham, Mr Dunley. Now, just a couple of other questions. When is the last time you were in contact with your wife? Did you see her again after August the sixth?'

'No, I didn't. But we did speak on the phone. Several times in the last few weeks. I don't have the exact dates in my head.'

'In August or September?'

'I spoke to Amy in late August, and the first or second day of September.'

'And there were still no problems between you? All was harmonious.' Lawson sat back, studying him.

'Yes, Inspector Lawson, it was.' Robert frowned, seemed puzzled. 'Are you suggesting otherwise? Or is someone else suggesting that there were problems between us regarding the divorce or the money?'

'No, no, Mr Dunley, no one is suggesting anything of the sort.' Colin Lawson stood up, and so did Sergeant Fuller who had been silent the entire time.

'Do you think that Mrs Dunley might have been despondent about the divorce?' the sergeant now asked.

Robert was not only startled to hear him speak, but also taken aback by the question. 'No, I'm sure she wasn't,' he managed to say. '*Why?*'

'It suddenly occurred to me that she might have thrown herself down the stairs, not fallen at all. That it was suicide and not an accident.'

'She wasn't despondent at all!' Alicia Forrest exclaimed, infuriated by this sudden suggestion, walking closer to the group of men. 'I knew her extremely well, and she was perfectly normal.'

'I understand, Mrs Forrest,' Sergeant Fuller said.

The two police officers thanked them and finally took

their leave, after Inspector Lawson had told Robert he would be in touch about the inquest.

Alicia showed them out and went to the kitchen to check on supper.

Anthony walked over to the drinks table once they were alone, saying as he did, 'What we all need is a bloody stiff drink! What would you like, Robert, Ambrose?'

'A glass of white wine, please, Anthony,' Robert responded and walked over to join his friend.

Ambrose said, 'I'll have the same,' and followed in his brother's wake, saying in a truly puzzled tone, 'What the hell was all that about anyway?'

As he poured the Chablis into three large crystal goblets, Anthony answered him. 'It was a bit of a fishing trip, in my opinion. On the other hand, I think that Connie Mellor might have said something about Amy not being a happy woman. I'm not absolutely certain of that, mind you. But she made an odd remark to *me*, weeks ago now, regarding the divorce, and she just might have said something similar to Lawson. She's always been a bit of a busybody. I know he was over at the house earlier today, and spoke to Connie.'

'What was the remark she made to you, Anthony?' Robert took the glass of wine from him, and held his friend's gaze.

'Connie's remark to me was that she didn't think Amy was happy about divorcing you, that she enjoyed being Mrs Robert Dunley and that she'd only agreed because you'd pressured her. Connie said Amy told her she wanted to please you, because she still loved you even though you didn't love her.'

'What utter bloody codswallop that is!' Robert exclaimed angrily, his face flushing. 'First of all, I never pressured

Amy ever, and secondly, she didn't want to please me at all. What Amy wanted was money. She told me she had every intention of buying a flat either in Paris, the south of France, or somewhere *fun*. That was the way she put it. Furthermore, she didn't *still love me*, as Connie claimed she'd said.'

'I believe you, Robert, *honestly* I do. I told Connie at the time that she was barking up the wrong tree. But, you know, she may well have repeated those words to Lawson. Cheers.' He clinked his glass to Robert's, as did Ambrose.

The three men ambled over to the sofa and chairs clustered around a coffee table, and sat down. There was a short silence between them, as they sipped their glasses of white wine, and relaxed.

Suddenly Robert exclaimed, 'I couldn't believe it when Fuller finally spoke out. And I am absolutely *positive* that Amy did not throw herself down the stairs. She wasn't the suicidal type.'

Ambrose, who had been reflective for the last few minutes now said, 'You're forgetting something, Robert. Amy and her love of high-heeled shoes, her Manolo Blahniks and Jimmy Choos in particular. *She fell down those stairs.* It was an accident, I'm as positive as you.'

'The press is going to have a field day with this,' Cecil said, staring across the dinner table at Francis, and then turning to Elizabeth seated next to him on the banquette. 'And you both know it. You'd better prepare yourself for it, Elizabeth, steel yourself.'

'They'll certainly create a few sensational headlines,' Elizabeth agreed. 'I can just see them now . . . and they'll trash Robin, and me as well. It's going to be another scandal.

But there's nothing much we can do about it. We just have to grin and bear it. And rise above it.'

Francis took a sip of champagne, and looked from Cecil to Elizabeth. 'If the police make any suggestion at all that Amy Robson Dunley's death was somehow suspicious, then there will be headlines. Damaging headlines. But fortunately we're surrounded by lawyers.'

Neither Elizabeth nor Cecil said anything. Like Francis, they sat silently savouring their champagne. Elizabeth focused on the wall opposite. It was filled with beautiful dog pictures, many of them old, all of different shapes and sizes. Mark Birley, the owner of Mark's Club in Charles Street where they were dining, had been an avid collector for years. And the watercolours and oils of all kinds of dogs were a unique feature of the club that everyone loved.

Tearing her eyes away from the wall of paintings, Elizabeth focused her gaze on Francis. 'You can't possibly think that someone, i.e. the police, will try and pin Amy's death on Robin, do you?'

'They can't do that if there's no evidence of foul play, and I'm sure there isn't. Try not to worry, Elizabeth. In a few days all of this will blow over.'

'I hope so.' She pursed her lips. 'Somebody in the press might try to insinuate that Robin had Amy killed so that he could marry me. But, of course, the two of *you* know how little their divorce mattered, because I don't want to get married.'

'No one can write anything like that,' Cecil assured her. 'There are such things as libel laws in this country, you know. And Francis is right, not only are the two of us lawyers, but we are indeed swamped with them at Deravenels. Just keep a low profile, and don't go rushing down to Cirencester. Promise me that, Elizabeth.'

'I promise. Anyway, Robin doesn't want me around at the

342

moment. He thinks it's better we don't see each other for the time being.'

'A wise man,' Cecil said, and silently thanked God that he was.

THIRTY-SIX

*R*obin had nothing to do with Amy Robson Dunley's death in any way whatsoever, and neither did I. We are not murderers nor instigators of murder, but there are those who are envious of us and jealous, and out to get us both, who put about nasty and untrue stories, muttered with a knowing certainty behind our backs.

Chinese whispers, how I hate them. And they have been rampant ever since Amy's unexpected and tragic death became public knowledge. She died on the eighth: it was in the newspapers on the ninth, and they have not stopped printing stories ever since. But the press are careful not to libel us; the stories are all built on speculation and vague, and Francis says they won't stop until the matter is finally put to rest. That will be after the inquest. It is to be held at the Coroner's Court in Cheltenham this coming Monday, and I can't wait for it to be over and done with. It was supposed to be this Friday, but got moved to Monday the twenty-first because of some scheduling problem to do with the court. I am not worried. I have no reason to be. There are only two possible verdicts. Accidental death, sometimes called death by misadventure, or suicide. Robin insists Amy would not take her own life, and certainly not by throwing herself down a flight of stairs. Others insist the same thing, say she was in good health and good spirits. And I must believe Alicia Forrest and her husband Anthony. Both of them are squeaky clean, renowned for their good character and respected for their honesty. No one would ever doubt them because of their extraordinary reputation.

Alicia told me herself that she was positive Amy was not ill with any fatal disease, and that she was happy and carefree two days before her death. I am not worried about Robin. He has done nothing wrong, and the police have not brought any charges. As we all know, there is no evidence of any wrongdoing by anybody.

But I miss my dearest love, my dearest friend. And I know he misses me. We speak on the phone several times a day, and that helps, but I am lonely and a little lost without his loving presence, his jokes and his laughter, his caring nature. He is miles away in Kent, staying at Stonehurst Farm, at Grace Rose's suggestion. And here I am at my beloved Ravenscar. Cecil and Francis both thought we should do separate disappearing acts to escape the pestering of the press. And so we did. We put the whole of England between us. 'Nothing by half measures, that's you,' Robin said to me when I told him where I was going and why, explaining that I didn't want to be too near him in case I broke my word and rushed to see him. I had promised Cecil Williams I would play it cool, and I am doing that.

I still haven't changed my mind about marriage. I aim to have my freedom . . . my tune is the same . . . I've been singing it for years. Amy's sudden death changes nothing for me. Robin is now free to marry. I am not. And why is that? I've *sometimes asked myself that over the last few days. The answer is simple . . . I don't wish to take that step.*

It's Thursday the seventeenth today, I see from my engagement book, only a few days now until the inquest. And when it is over Robin will join me here in Yorkshire. Merry wanted to come with me to keep me company, but I prefer to be alone. Also, as I explained to her, I need her to remain in London, manning my office. Robin has a companion with him at Stonehurst Farm, his cousin Thomas Blunte. Thomas is a trusted relative and has spent most of his life looking after the Dunleys in some way or other, and in the most caring way. A good man whom Robin trusts and also enjoys being with. I am pleased he has company.

There have been more stories in the newspapers today, not really damaging but irritating. I'll be relieved when all this dies down. I marvel sometimes that such a grand edifice has been built on nothing but uninformed gossip . . .

Elizabeth walked along the beach below the cliffs, enjoying the fresh air. It was one of those extraordinary September days; the sky was brilliantly blue and unstained, the sun warm, the air balmy . . . an Indian summer day, the kind she had always loved. A rare kind of day for Yorkshire. All too often on this coastline the sun fled and dark clouds blew in to mar the sky, and the sharp wind off the North Sea cooled the air.

That had not happened this afternoon, and Elizabeth walked on, enjoying the beauty of the empty beach, the sense of freedom she experienced here on her land.

At one moment, she lifted her head and looked up at the brilliant sky, shading her eyes with her hand. The kittiwakes who lived in their nests on the sides of the cliffs wheeled and turned against the clear blue vaulted backdrop, their cries shrill on the air. Those beautiful birds had been here for centuries, just as her ancestors had. For over eight hundred years Deravenels had lived at Ravenscar. Before that beautiful Elizabethan manor house had been built there had been another house . . . All that remained of that one now was the ruined stronghold standing above her on the edge of the cliffs. She could see it in the distance, and instantly thought then of all those Deravenels who had gone before, and for whom she had always had a certain partiality. She had been attracted to them for as long as she could remember.

She and Grace Rose were the last of the Deravenel line. Suddenly her thoughts went to Richard Deravenel, and all that she had learned about him from Grace Rose. He had been blamed for a crime . . . the disappearance of his two little nephews, and their possible deaths. Yet Grace Rose believed in his innocence to this very day. Another mystery that no one could ever possibly solve.

And Amy's death would always be a mystery to some, whatever the verdict of the Coroner's Court next week. There were people who thrived on the theory of conspiracy . . . it was like manna to them. Who murdered Marilyn Monroe? Assassinated John F. Kennedy? Murdered Princess Diana? *Whodidit?whodidit?whodidit?* She could hear those frantic voices in her head, screaming the words, non-stop, and then the constant *why?why?why?* Amy would become another cult figure, wouldn't she? No matter what the coroner decided, there would always be a hint of suspicion about Robert Dunley and his lover, Elizabeth Deravenel Turner. She sighed under her breath, knowing there was nothing she could ever do about that . . . She was a Deravenel and scandal and rumour dogged them.

Francis Walsington sat with Cecil Williams in a booth at Wilton's, their favourite fish restaurant in Jermyn Street. As he slid his small fork under the fat Colchester oyster he said softly, 'I really do think I must go down to Cheltenham, Cecil. As an observer. And Robert just might need me.'

Cecil, who had been reluctant to agree about this matter, unexpectedly caved in. 'All right, go then, keep an eye out for Robert. Frankly, I can't imagine any other verdict than accidental death though, can you?'

'No, I can't. But then one never knows when life's going to throw you a googly.' This was said in a dour voice and Francis grimaced.

Cecil burst out laughing. 'You've been reading too many tabloid newspapers, me lad. Full of bloody awful stuff these days, scandals galore, and it's bad news in general in the others.'

'That's what newspapers are for, Cecil, to bring us all *bad* news. But listen to this. Nicholas just told me an hour ago that he saw John Norfell in Paris the other day.'

Cecil glanced at his old friend and colleague, his expression one of total puzzlement. He frowned. 'So what? Norfell has a right to go anywhere he wants.'

'Of course he does, but Nicholas saw him coming out of the Dauphin building just off the Champs-Élysées. How about that?'

'Did he now.' Cecil's thoughtful grey-blue eyes narrowed slightly. 'Why would our John be visiting Dauphin? To see Catherine de Burgh? Or her daughter-in-law, Marie de Burgh? That gives one food for thought, doesn't it?'

Francis said, 'Is he perhaps staking his claim . . . on Marie? Going shopping for the future? You know he was in Mary Turner's pocket.'

'I've never been really sure about that. And the kilt isn't his type.'

'Neither was Mary Turner, but I long harboured the suspicion that he wanted to slide in there, and would have done so if she hadn't married the Spanish gigolo.' Francis finally slipped the oyster in his mouth, relishing it.

'Robert has never stopped warning us that Norfell bears watching, and he's rarely wrong about those things. He has an instinct for sniffing out double-dealing and treachery.' Cecil also ate one of his oysters, and then looked off into the distance before adding worriedly, 'Norfell is very ambitious, no question of that. And if François de Burgh dies, and the kilt comes trotting over to the highlands, Norfell might get a few ideas –'

'About Scottish Heritage,' Francis finished, cutting across him.

'You'd better keep an eye on him,' Cecil suggested.

'A tail would be more efficient.'

'Do what you think is best, Francis. I don't need to know your methods . . . In fact, the less I know the better. Just do it soon.'

'Consider it done,' Francis answered and finished his plate of oysters.

THIRTY-SEVEN

On Monday morning, Robert Dunley, accompanied by Anthony and Alicia Forrest and Francis Walsington, stood outside the Coroner's Court in Cheltenham.

'It's good of you to come, Francis,' Robert said, and then introduced his friends who had just arrived. After they had all shaken hands, Robert went on, 'Anthony and Alicia both knew Amy for a number of years, and as you're aware, Anthony looks after some of my financial affairs. So he was frequently in contact with Amy. That's why he's here to give evidence to the Coroner, along with Alicia.'

'I understand,' Francis said, and then glanced at a tall, dark-haired woman heading in their direction. 'Is this someone you know? Whatever, she's about to descend on us.'

Robert followed the direction of his gaze. 'It's Connie Mellor, the housekeeper.'

'Is it really? She's a lot younger than I expected and quite a looker, isn't she?' Francis turned to Anthony. 'This is the woman who you thought might have been gossiping, isn't it? Tittle-tattling to the police?'

'It is,' Anthony said, and then had no option but to greet her as she came to a sudden standstill next to them.

'Good morning,' he said, and introduced Francis Walsington.

After she had said hello to everyone in return, Connie Mellor took a step away from them. 'I was told to be here at nine-thirty and I don't want to be late. If you'll excuse me.' Without another word she hurried away.

Francis watched her go, frowning. 'A bit abrupt, I'd say.'

Robert gave him a keen look. 'She may be feeling guilty, *if* she did do some gossiping. Anyway, she's right about one thing, we were told to be here for nine-thirty. So let's go.'

The four of them trooped across the pavement to the door of the Coroner's Court and went inside. They were immediately greeted by a tall, well-built man, who had apparently been waiting for them. 'Good morning, Mr Dunley,' he said, obviously recognizing Robert. 'I'm Michael Anderson, the Coroner's Officer.'

After greeting him, shaking his hand, Robert said, 'This is Mr and Mrs Anthony Forrest, old friends of mine, who are witnesses, and a colleague and friend, Francis Walsington.'

Pleasantries were exchanged, and Mr Anderson guided them through a small lobby, down several corridors and into a large room, rather like a concert hall, which was filled with chairs lined up in rows. At the far end of the room, in front of the chairs, was the Coroner's bench on a raised platform. Nearby was a witness box.

Mr Anderson guided them to the front row of chairs, and explained, 'Please sit here, and make yourselves comfortable. There will be other witnesses arriving momentarily, but as you can see there is plenty of space for everyone.

And Mr Dunley, those seats over there are for the press.'

'Oh, I hadn't realized the press would be here,' Robert answered, looking surprised.

'The inquest, any inquest, is open to the press and the public, Mr Dunley. Now, do you have any questions?'

'I don't think so.'

Mr Anderson smiled, nodded, and said, 'I've a few things to attend to, but I'll be back in a moment or two.'

Francis leaned into Robert and murmured, 'Don't worry about the press, or anything else, for that matter. This is going to be a smooth hearing. And incidentally, an inquest is held in order to establish who the deceased is, and how that person died, and when. It's not about why they died.'

'I understand.' Robert glanced around as he heard voices, and saw that the courtroom was suddenly filling up with people. He spotted Inspector Lawson and Sergeant Fuller, as well as Amy's GP, Dr Norman Allerton. Connie Mellor sat alone in one of the rows; the rest of the people he didn't know, but assumed they were also witnesses.

Suddenly the inquest began, taking Robert by surprise. He heard Mr Anderson saying, 'Everyone please rise,' and as they all did so a distinguished-looking man entered, went straight to the raised platform and sat behind the bench. Robert realized that this was the Coroner, Dr David Wentworth.

The Coroner began to speak, explained that they were present to look into the death of a woman who had fallen down a flight of stairs, and died of a broken neck. He then glanced over at the Coroner's Officer and instructed him to start the proceedings. Once Mr Anderson had taken the oath, sworn to tell the truth, given the name and address of the deceased, and manner of her death, he stepped down.

The Coroner spoke for a few moments about the forthcoming procedure, and in the process lost Robert for a moment or two . . . His thoughts drifted, settled on Amy and the ghastly way she had died. It need never have happened . . . one of those stupid accidents in the home. A feeling of sadness overwhelmed him . . . only twenty-six, and she was dead, just like that, in the blink of an eye. Such a silly accident, avoidable, really. But she had always rushed around, hectic and energized, for as long as he had known her. Ambrose had reminded him of this last week at her funeral . . . a simple affair at the church she liked in Cirencester. Anne had come with Ambrose, as well as Amy's half brother Jack, her only living relative other than him. A small sad funeral. Her passing had been a tragic affair . . .

The sound of a door banging brought Robert out of his reverie, and he sat up straighter. A second later he was startled even more when the Coroner called the first witness. He had expected to give his evidence before anyone else, but, in fact, the Coroner had called Connie Mellor to the witness stand.

After taking the oath, swearing to tell the truth, she gave her name and address, and, when asked, said that she had been employed as housekeeper for Mrs Amy Dunley for the past four years.

Robert suddenly realized what a kind face and voice Dr Wentworth had. Now he was asking the housekeeper if it was she who had discovered the body of the deceased.

'It was, sir.'

'Would you please be good enough to give us the full details of that discovery, and tell the court what happened that day.'

'I will, sir. Well, it was like this. After I'd served Mrs Dunley lunch I went shopping. In Cirencester. I was only gone about an hour, and I returned home to Thyme Lodge at two o'clock. After I'd put the groceries away, I went looking for Mrs Dunley. To discuss dinner. The menu, I mean. She usually worked in her office in the afternoons, an upstairs office, and so I went through to the front hall, to go upstairs. And there she was, lying at the bottom of the stairs. It was a real shock. She was all twisted up, skewed, sort of. I ran to her, Dr Wentworth, I was ever so afraid . . . I knew she'd hurt herself badly. And when I knelt down, I realized . . .' Pausing, Connie Mellor cleared her throat several times, and her voice was suddenly trembling as she went on, 'Well, I knew she was dead from her eyes. I didn't even have to check her pulse.'

'And after this, Mrs Mellor? What did you do next?' the Coroner asked quietly.

'I went to the phone and called the ambulance and the police. And they came ever so quickly. Together. It was one of the paramedics who asked me if I'd touched the body, and I said no, I hadn't, I knew better than to do that, I told him.'

'You formally identified Mrs Dunley at this time, and gave the police the information you have just given to this court?'

'I did, sir. It was another of the paramedics that told me Mrs Dunley had broken her neck. After a while, the ambulance men took her body away, and then Inspector Lawson talked to me. A little later I rang up Mr Forrest to tell him what had happened, and he said he would get in touch with Mr Dunley at once.'

'Thank you, Mrs Mellor. Now I would like to ask you about Mrs Dunley's state of mind that day, her mood in general. Was she unhappy? Sad, or despondent about anything? Or perhaps depressed?'

'Not that day, she wasn't, she was all right, sir. She was in a good mood. In fact, she told me she might be going away for a while, abroad, she said, perhaps to Paris, and she asked me if I minded being alone in the house. I told her I didn't. But there were days when she was ... well ... how shall I put it? A little out of sorts with herself. It was because of the divorce.'

'Bloody hell, why has she said that?' Anthony hissed to Alicia, and she shushed him softly, took hold of his hand, trying to calm him down.

'Did she tell you that in those exact words, Mrs Mellor?' the Coroner now asked, focusing his attention on the house-keeper intently.

'No, not exactly, sir, but I knew that was the reason.'

'I think that perhaps I might have to categorize that statement as an assumption on your part, don't you think?' The Coroner gave Connie Mellor another piercing look through very keen, bright blue eyes. 'A speculation perhaps?'

Connie Mellor appeared chastened. 'I suppose so,' she agreed, somewhat reluctantly.

'Did Mrs Dunley ever tell you explicitly that she was upset about the impending divorce? Or angry?'

'No, she didn't.'

'Thank you, Mrs Mellor. You may now step down.'

As Robert heard his name called he jumped up at once, and hurried over to the witness box. He swore on oath to tell the truth, the whole truth and nothing but the truth, etcetera, and then waited for the Coroner to question him.

'I see from your earlier statement to the police that you were separated from your wife, Amy Robson Dunley, the deceased, but that it was an amicable separation,' Dr Wentworth said, looking across at Robert with obvious interest. 'It is also the court's understanding that you were working on the financial arrangements of the divorce. Is that correct, Mr Dunley?'

'It is, Dr Wentworth. My wife and I remained good friends, and it was a mutual decision that we divorce; nor were there any problems about the financial settlement. I had already given her Thyme Lodge, just after we finally separated.'

'When did you last see the deceased?' the Coroner asked.

'On August the sixth. At Thyme Lodge. I drove down from London to discuss various matters pertaining to the divorce,' Robert said.

'And you did not see her after that date?'

'I did not, Dr Wentworth. However, I did speak to her on the phone, both in late August and early September. She also told me, as she apparently told Mrs Mellor, that she might be planning to spend some time in Paris.'

'Did you ever see her despondent or depressed, Mr Dunley?'

'No, I didn't. That was not her nature, not by a long shot, and she was in no way upset because we were divorcing. So I'm convinced that Amy fell, that her death was an accident. I'm certain she didn't throw herself down the stairs.'

The Coroner looked momentarily startled by Robert's comments but made no mention of them. He said, 'Did you have any reason to believe that the deceased might have been suffering from any physical or mental malady?'

'No. To the best of my knowledge she was in good health,' Robert answered crisply.

'Thank you, Mr Dunley, you may go back to your seat.'

The third witness was Dr Norman Allerton, Amy's physician, and after taking the oath, he was asked by the Coroner if Amy Robson Dunley had been his patient.

'Yes, she was, except that she was rarely sick with anything serious. All I ever treated her for was a cold, the 'flu, such things as that. Minor ailments.'

'When did you last examine the deceased?' Dr Wentworth now inquired.

'At the end of June.'

'Was she suffering from some kind of sudden complaint, Dr Allerton?'

'No, she was not. She came in to see me because it was time for her annual check-up.'

'And you found she was in good health?'

'She was in *perfect* health.'

'What was her frame of mind the last time you saw her?'

'Totally normal. The late Mrs Dunley was not suffering from anything. She was in good mental and physical condition.'

'Thank you, Dr Allerton, you may return to your seat.'

And so it went . . . witnesses were called and asked the same questions. More or less. Robert listened attentively, as did his friends, finding the proceedings amicable and somewhat informal, and ultimately repetitive and boring.

Suddenly, one of the paramedics, Arthur Tarlaton, was called to the witness box, and was asked by the Coroner to describe the deceased's injuries.

'When I entered the hall of Thyme Lodge, the house where the deceased lived, I saw that Mrs Dunley's body looked twisted where it lay at the bottom of the stairs. I thought it more than likely she had tried to break her fall. I examined her immediately, and noted that she had broken her neck. There was also a gash on the back of her head, where she had hit it on the hall floor, or perhaps on the edge of the stairs as she had tumbled down them. There was blood on the marble floor in the foyer, and later DNA tests proved that it was Mrs Dunley's blood on that floor.'

'Mr Tarlaton, in your opinion, did the deceased die from a fall down a staircase? Or could something else have caused her death? Or somebody? Such as an intruder?'

'I doubt it. After examining the deceased at the scene of the accident, I was certain she had fallen down those stairs, very steep stairs by the way, and that she died because she broke her neck.'

357

'So you do not think the gash on her head caused her death, or contributed to it?'

'No, sir, I do not.'

'Thank you, Mr Tarlaton.'

'Mrs Alicia Forrest, please take the witness stand.'

Relieved to have been summoned at long last to give her evidence, Alicia virtually ran to the witness box, and was sworn in.

Dr Wentworth, who knew her by reputation only, said, 'It is my understanding that you were a close friend of the deceased.'

'Yes, I was, Dr Wentworth, and I concur with everything her doctor, Norman Allerton, has just said. Amy Dunley was a happy, warm and outgoing young woman who would no more commit suicide than the Queen of England would. Furthermore, there were no problems between her and her husband. They both wanted the divorce, and it was common knowledge that they had remained very good friends. Neither were they at odds about money.'

'Thank you, Mrs Forrest, you may leave the witness box,' Dr Wentworth announced, understanding who and what he was dealing with. An opinionated, educated woman of enormous confidence who might prove hard to control on the stand.

The Coroner now called Anthony Forrest, who repeated everything Robert, his wife, and Dr Allerton had said. It was the same story, told in a different way, but, nevertheless, it *was* the same story.

Inspector Lawson now replaced Anthony Forrest on the stand, when he was called to come up by the Coroner. 'Please tell us what happened the afternoon you went to Thyme Lodge, in answer to a call from Mrs Connie Mellor, the deceased's housekeeper, Inspector Lawson.'

Lawson's testimony gelled exactly with the information

358

given by the paramedic, Arthur Tarlaton.

'As Mr Tarlaton informed you, Dr Wentworth, the deceased's body was twisted in the most peculiar way, and I agree that she might have reached over to grab the bannister, and in so doing propelled herself down the stairs with more force,' the inspector explained. 'I was informed by Mr Tarlaton that her neck was broken and he also pointed out the wound on the back of her head. Later the medical examiner informed me that the deceased had died from the break in a vertebrae at the top of her spine. Toxicology reports showed that there were no drugs, barbiturates or alcohol in her blood.'

'Thank you, Inspector Lawson. I see from your report that there were no signs of forced entry at Thyme Lodge, and that Mrs Mellor found nothing untoward anywhere in the interior of the house. Is that correct?'

'Yes, it is, sir. I'm positive there was no unwanted intruder. I doubt there was foul play.'

'Do you have anything to add, Inspector Lawson?'

'No, I do not, Dr Wentworth. Other than that the deceased was wearing very high-heeled shoes. And it occurred to me much later, only two days ago actually, that perhaps they had contributed to the late Mrs Dunley's fall. Especially if she was in a hurry.'

Alicia Forrest sat bolt upright in her chair, and made such a fuss and commotion, waving her arm and trying to speak out, that the Coroner's Officer immediately came over to her. 'What is it, Mrs Forrest? Is there a problem?' he asked worriedly, endeavouring to quieten her.

'No, Mr Anderson, but I would like to be recalled to the witness stand. If that is permissible? I have something extremely important to add to my original testimony.'

'Well, I'm not sure . . .'

'Ah, Mr Anderson, is there a problem over there?' the

Coroner asked, craning his neck to see what was going on.

'Not really, sir,' Mr Anderson answered and then hurried over to the bench. 'It's Mrs Forrest. She says she has something to add.'

'Oh, dear, I was afraid of that. All right, have her come back to the witness stand then.'

A moment later, Inspector Lawson had stepped down and Alicia Forrest was on the witness stand in his place. Looking directly at the Coroner, she said quietly, in a much more subdued voice, 'Dr Wentworth, I would just like to add something. It is in reference to Inspector Lawson's comment about the high-heeled shoes the deceased was wearing at the time of her fall. Mrs Dunley *always* wore *very* high heels, and she was forever running, rushing, moving rapidly wherever she went. And I frequently warned her about that, and about those steep stairs at Thyme Lodge. You see, I myself almost had an accident on them last year. I too was wearing very high-heeled shoes – and I was in a hurry and I practically went head first down the staircase. I broke my fall because I was near the bannister and grabbed on to it. But I did sprain my ankle. It was the shoes that caused me to fall, those heels can be perilous, Dr Wentworth.'

'I see. Well, thank you for this additional piece of information, Mrs Forrest. I do believe you have thrown a little more light on the situation, as did Inspector Lawson. You may return to your chair.'

Robert squeezed Alicia's hand when she came and sat down next to him, and Francis and Anthony both beamed at her.

And then they sat and waited as the Coroner examined his notes and looked at various reports. He then started his summing up, and by the end of twenty minutes he finally finished. He announced, 'With the evidence that was brought to me earlier, and from what I have heard in this courtroom today, I am convinced that this death was accidental, caused by misadventure.'

Outside in the street, Robert's friends waited for him as he went off alone. After punching in a number on his mobile, he waited until he heard her voice. He said, 'It's all right. Everything's all right, darling. The Coroner just brought in a verdict of death by misadventure . . . in other words, it was an accident.'

'Oh, Robin, thank God,' Elizabeth whispered through her tears.

'Stay where you are. I'll see you soon.'

THIRTY-EIGHT

'This would suit *you*, Miss Turner,' the sales assistant said. 'If you don't mind me saying so, madam, I've always liked you in red.'

Elizabeth smiled at her. 'Why thank you, Clarice, I must say I do, too. Is it a pashmina?' As she spoke she examined the long shawl on the hanger – vivid scarlet, each end beautifully embroidered with bugle beads and lace, a truly sumptuous item.

'No, it's not, it's cashmere and silk, but it *was* made in India.' Clarice found the label and nodded, showed it to Elizabeth. 'By a very good house. It's hand-embroidered.'

'I probably will take this for myself, but I did actually come to do some Christmas shopping,' Elizabeth explained. 'Let me look at some of the others, please. If you have a navy, a black and a lovely blue, those colours would work for three of my friends.'

'They're over there, Miss Turner.' Clarice guided her to another area on the floor. Elizabeth liked shopping here at

Fortnum and Mason. The merchandise was of high quality, they had unusual, rather stylish things, and the store was always relatively tranquil. She could shop quickly, be certain of fast personal service, and be back at the office in record time.

'This is a rather special one,' Clarice said, bringing out a purple shawl, also beautifully embroidered with beads and ribbons, 'and look at this green one. It's quite a unique green, wouldn't you say?'

'They're spectacular!' Elizabeth exclaimed, thinking of Grace Rose as she touched the purple, and then of Anne Dunley, who she knew would look wonderful in the apple green. 'I'll definitely take these two, and the red one. For myself, Clarice, at your suggestion. And if you could come up with a black and a navy, then I'll have had a great morning of Christmas shopping.'

'I know I have those particular colours. Give me a moment, madam. And by the way, we have some very special gloves in from Paris, if you'd like to take a look. They're over there on display in the glass case.'

'I will look at them, and thank you, Clarice. With a little luck I might be able to do all my shopping in your department.'

The sales assistant smiled and hurried away, explaining she would return as fast as she could. 'Because I know you're always in a hurry, Miss Turner.'

'I'm not so pressed today,' Elizabeth replied, and at the sound of her mobile ringing she rummaged around in her handbag, finally pulled it out. Walking towards a window, she said, 'Hello?'

'Elizabeth?'

'Yes. Is that you, Francis?'

'It is. I tried to reach you at the office. Merry said you were out. Where are you at this moment?'

'I'm at Fortnum's.'

Francis Walsington began to laugh.

'What's so funny?'

'Nothing, it just so happens I need to talk to you about something, and guess what? I'm only a stone's throw away, at my tailor in Savile Row.'

'Do you need to speak to me urgently?'

'No, privately. Listen, Elizabeth, let's meet at the Ritz, we're both so close to it. Say in half an hour?'

'What do you want to talk to me about, Francis?'

'Not on the phone, Elizabeth, especially a mobile. Will you meet me at the Ritz for a drink?'

'Yes, I'll be there, Francis. 'Bye.' Clicking off the mobile, she dropped it in her handbag, intrigued. She couldn't help wondering what special titbit of information Francis had to offer this morning. But it must be important for him to track her down.

Walking back to the glove case, she stared at the selection, hoping to find a pair of purple ones to go with the shawl. The two together would make a perfect gift for Grace Rose.

When Clarice returned with the navy and black shawls which were from the same fashion house in India, she took both. After choosing several pairs of gloves, and matching them up to the shawls, she said, 'I think that's it, Clarice. For today, anyway.'

'Very good, Miss Turner. Shall I have everything gift-wrapped? I'll mark each package on the bottom, so you know the colours of the shawls, and the same with the gloves.'

'Thanks, Clarice. You can charge them and have them sent to my flat, please, if you would. I'm afraid I have to rush now.'

'No problem, Miss Turner, they'll be sent by messenger later today.'

Francis stood in the lobby of the Ritz Hotel, and hurried forward to meet Elizabeth as she walked in at exactly twelve noon. After kissing her on the cheek, he took her arm and escorted her into the promenade area, saying, 'Let's have a drink here, shall we?'

'It's fine. Actually, I like this promenade, or whatever it's called: it has a lovely Edwardian feel to it. Anyway, what do you have to tell me?'

'Once we've planted ourselves down and ordered, I'll fill you in. All right?'

'I'm very intrigued, Francis. It's not like you to be so secretive. You usually can't wait to give me bad news, which I assume this is.'

'I didn't want to talk on the phone, that's all. Oh, look, there's a nice table near that potted palm, let's go and sit over there.'

Within seconds a waiter arrived to take their order. Francis chose a glass of champagne, and so did Elizabeth, surprising him.

The waiter departed, and now that they were alone she leaned forward, and looked him right in the eye. 'Okay, shoot. I want to know what this is all about.'

Francis glanced at his watch, and said, 'It's exactly five minutes past twelve. At approximately ten minutes to eleven this morning I got a phone call from Paris. François de Burgh died half an hour earlier.'

For a moment she gaped at him, startled by his announcement, and then exclaimed, 'You certainly found out *très rapide*, didn't you? Do you have somebody embedded at Dauphin, for heaven's sake?'

'You know very well I can't tell you anything like that,

Elizabeth. The less you know . . . all that stuff. But I do have extremely well-placed contacts in Paris, and I can assure you his death will be announced on French television any minute now.'

'Sad, really, he was so young.' Elizabeth took a breath, blew out air, and leaned back in the chair. 'His death worries you, Francis, doesn't it? That's what this is all about.'

'It does, because I've no doubt that the widow woman will be trekking over to this side of the English Channel . . . *ultimately*.'

'When do you think she'll come to Scotland?'

'Hard to say. There's no place for her with the de Burghs in Paris, not in the long run, anyway. I know Catherine, and, whilst she's a woman with great ambitions for her sons, I don't believe she's heartless. There's a certain humanity to her. There'll be a mourning period for them all, and she'll treat her daughter-in-law kindly. But in the end, the kilt will have to leave. Very simply, Catherine won't want her around.'

'Leave Dauphin, you mean? Not necessarily leave Paris? Or France?' Elizabeth gave Francis a questioning look.

'I suppose she could stay on in France, but why would she? With not one ounce of power, and nowhere to hang her bonnet, so to speak, where else would she go but to Edinburgh? After all, she does own Scottish Heritage. No doubt she'll want to take it over from her half-brother James, who's been running it since her mother died.'

'He's not going to like that, is he?' Elizabeth asserted.

'I'm not certain. After all, he did work with her mother, and made the best of things.'

'You believe Marie de Burgh is going to make trouble for me, don't you?' Elizabeth paused as the waiter arrived with two flutes of pink champagne, sat back in the chair.

A moment later Francis was lifting his glass to her. 'Here's to you, Lady Boss.'

'And to you, Francis. I don't know what I'd do without you.'

'Quite frankly, neither do I. And yes, she'll be vocal about you, and Deravenels, and –' He cut his sentence off, and fell silent, and she stared at him intently. Never anything but articulate and eloquent, he suddenly seemed to have been rendered speechless, was at a loss.

'She can't really do anything, Francis, can she? Everyone says she doesn't have a claim on Deravenels.'

He shook his head. 'She does have a claim through her grandmother, and if you are no longer alive then she *is* the legitimate heir.'

'But what about my Greyson cousins? Surely they have a strong claim, too.'

'They do. And your brother Edward certainly believed they did, but actually Marie Stewart de Burgh takes precedence over them. Because her grandmother Margaret Turner Stewart was the elder sister of Harry, whilst Mary Turner Brandt was your father's younger sister, and her daughter Frances is the mother of those Greyson girls. So the kilt would win in the end ... *if* you were dead.'

'But there is my father's will!' Elizabeth pointed out. 'He added a codicil debarring a foreigner from inheriting Deravenels, and she is *not* English.'

'You know, Elizabeth, some people can be very wilful, stubborn and deaf to the truth, and she is certainly all of those things. She is avaricious, hungry for power, loaded with ego.' He sighed. 'Since the beginning of time people have killed to possess wealth and privilege.'

'Do you think she would have the gall to have me killed?' she asked him softly, knowing he would tell her what he believed to be the truth.

'I don't know that, and I don't want to speculate. But many a murder has been made to look like an accident. I've told you that many times before. And you know it anyway, your family's been *dogged* by murder.'

'This is about having a bodyguard, isn't it?'

'You're damned right it is.'

Leaning forward, she reached out, put a hand on his arm. 'Look, I believe everything you say, Francis, and I trust you implicitly, and I know how much you worry. But . . . well, she is my *cousin* –'

'She's your enemy!' he exclaimed in a low but vehement voice, 'and don't you ever forget that, Elizabeth Deravenel Turner. And you know full well that blood is *not* thicker than water, surely your own family's history must prove that to you. I want you to have a bodyguard, and I want you to have one who is the best. Not some driver who we hope can protect you if an incident occurs. I want a bodyguard sitting *next* to the chauffeur, not driving the bloody car. I want a –' He broke off and looked at her intently. 'Can I tell you one of my little show-business stories?'

She nodded. 'Of course. But what does it have to do with a bodyguard?'

'You'll understand in a minute. I have an old friend who works in Hollywood at one of the studios. And one day, a few years ago now, some of the top executives were asked to interview a young actor out of New York, an actor who a well-known agent thought had great potential, who he believed could be a big star. The agent was hoping the executives would see what he saw, and sign him for an upcoming film. A big film. But they didn't quite know how to typecast him . . . was he the leading-man type? Or the romantic comedy type? Or would he be better as a character actor? They didn't quite know what to do with him. Very simply, they couldn't put him into a slot. And neither could my friend. However, he trusted the judgement of an executive, a woman who headed the promotion and publicity department, and he set up a meeting between the actor and her. The idea was that perhaps she would be able to . . . cast the young actor, give them some ideas about how to use him. After half an hour with him she hurried out of her office, rushed to see my friend, her boss, and said, "I don't know what kind of role he is right for, or what movie he's right for. I don't know if he can even act. All I know is that he's one dangerous fucker. Sign him immediately." And they did. And that's what I want for you as a bodyguard. *A dangerous fucker*. Someone who will stop at nothing to protect you any way he can. A man who's tough, organized, lethal, and *dangerous*, who scares people off, and who's not afraid to pull a gun if he has to.'

'I don't like guns,' Elizabeth muttered.

Francis stared at her, and then he began to laugh. 'You'll have to get used to a bodyguard carrying a gun. Will you do that for *me*? Please.'

'Yes.'

'You haven't asked me who the actor was.'

'I'd prefer to know if he became a big star, as big as the agent thought he could be.'

'He did indeed.'

'So what's his name?'

'Bruce Willis.'

'In that case, I'll have a bodyguard,' she replied and grinned. But her voice was serious, when she said, 'I know it's a dangerous world we live in today, and that I'm vulnerable because of who I am, and not just because of someone like Marie de Burgh, who wants to sit where I'm sitting and actually believes she's more entitled to the seat than me.' Elizabeth swallowed some of her champagne, and finished,

'I'm not stupid, Francis, you should know that by now. I understand that I'm a target.'

'Look how beautiful this dining room is,' Francis said twenty minutes later, glancing around the Ritz restaurant. 'Aren't you glad you agreed to have lunch with me, Elizabeth? Just to enjoy this quite extraordinary place. And the food's not bad either,' he finished, smiling at her. Apart from admiring her tremendously, Francis Walsington cared about Elizabeth Turner, had a need to protect her at all times. He was devoted and concerned about her and her safety.

'I'm always happy to be with you, Francis, you know you're one of my favourites. And the room *is* lovely. So is the view of Green Park. Oh, look, it's snowing. Maybe we'll have a white Christmas this year.'

He followed her glance, looked out of the window, saw that it was a snow storm, in fact. 'Where are you and Robert going for Christmas?' he asked, eyeing her. 'Not abroad?'

'No, don't worry about that. Actually we're going to Stonehurst Farm with Grace Rose. We promised her ages ago, and well –' Elizabeth paused, shook her head. 'She's old, and Robin and I decided we must go and stay with her this year. Who knows how long she'll live? Such a great age, ninety-eight, isn't it?'

'It is, and it'll do you good to have a rest in the country for a few days. You're a genuine workaholic, Elizabeth.'

'But I enjoy it, you know that, Francis, and we do have some fun as well, Robin and I.'

'I'm glad you're going out and about again, not hiding behind closed doors. You've nothing to be ashamed of, and the two of you haven't done anything wrong. You should have a good time together.'

'But there are still those ghastly Chinese whispers, and I suppose there always will be. Some people want to believe we're responsible for Amy's death.'

'It doesn't matter, and the people that count don't blame you and Robert, honestly they don't. Besides which, scandals have been known to float around the best of families, not to mention your own.' He began to laugh. 'And that doesn't matter.'

She joined in his laughter, and then said, 'Once Marie de Burgh dries her tears, I bet you John Norfell goes sniffing around her, don't you?'

'He has already, but then Cecil must've told you that.'

'He mentioned it in passing. If John Norfell did get involved with her, as he might now that she's a widow, can we get rid of him? Can he be dismissed?'

'Only if the board of directors can prove some kind of wrongdoing against Deravenels on his part, Elizabeth.'

'Well, we shall have to wait and see, won't we?'

'Indeed we will, no alternative . . .' He let his sentence drift, smiled at her across the table as the waiter arrived with their first course. 'I'm glad to see a plate of food in front of you for once. You never seem to eat.'

'Oh, I do, I do.' She picked up her spoon, tasted the tomato soup, said quietly, 'And go ahead and find the right body-guard for me, Francis. You're right as usual. I should have proper protection.'

'I can't believe we're actually standing here in Number Ten Downing Street,' Elizabeth whispered to Robert later that evening. 'And I was thrilled to meet Tony Blair and Cherie, weren't you?'

'As thrilled as you, darling. They're charm personified,

the two of them.' Robert gave her a fond smile. 'And I'm happy to see that, despite all of *your* success, you're not a bit jaded.' Taking hold of her arm, he led her down the long reception room upstairs in the Prime Minister's official residence, where an early Christmas party was being given.

Elizabeth, glancing around, exclaimed, 'Gosh, there are so many celebrities here tonight . . . film stars, famous writers, television and media bigwigs. And pop stars. Oh look, Robin: isn't that Sting with his wife?'

He followed her gaze, nodded. 'It is, and I just spotted David Hockney, one of my favourite painters, who's talking to Emma Thompson and Alan Bennett. And over there, near the Christmas tree, is Jenny Seagrove, one of my favourite actresses.'

'She's just gorgeous, isn't she? And who's the man she's with?'

'I'm sure it's her partner, Bill Kenwright, the theatrical impresario. Come to think of it, there's someone here from every area of the arts and culture. And plenty of sports stars as well, Elizabeth.

'I'm so glad we came, I wouldn't have missed this fabulous party for the world.'

A waiter came up to them carrying a tray of drinks and they both took a flute of champagne. They touched glasses, and Robert said, 'Here's to Cool Britannia, as the Prime Minister calls it.' His face became a little more serious, as he added, 'There really has been something of a seismic change in British society since New Labour came into power, and the Blairs arrived in Downing Street. The whole country's been reinvigorated. I for one feel as if anything is possible . . . that we can rule the world.'

'I thought *we* did,' Elizabeth shot back, and then added in a serious voice, 'But going back to your last comment,

Robin, I think everyone feels it. I know I do. It's . . . well . . . it's a new order of things.'

'Yes, I agree,' Robert answered, and took hold of Elizabeth's arm, propelled her across the room. 'Let's go and talk to Jenny Seagrove.'

THIRTY-NINE

*M*illennium. *Suddenly it was here, upon us, and the year two thousand began with a big bang. At least for Deravenels. I gave a huge party and invited the entire staff, and what's more they all came, every single one of them. I held it in the ballroom of the Dorchester Hotel . . . cocktails, dinner and dancing. I spared no expense and it was a great big bunfight of a party that everyone enjoyed. And I did, too. I loved every minute of it.*

To be truthful, it wasn't given only to celebrate the arrival of the millennium and the new year, but rather to celebrate Deravenels, which I had pulled into the twenty-first century. Kicking and screaming maybe, but nevertheless I did it. However, I did not do it alone. I had the best help in the world. And so I should have said that Cecil, Robin and I did it together. The Three Musketeers. Cecil usually corrects me, saying with a wry smile, 'The triumvirate,' and I smile back, because I appreciate his scholarly attitude and the way he applies it to most things in life. And backing us up were

Francis Walsington, Nicholas Throckman and Ambrose Dunley. Good men all, and we run this vast conglomerate as a team. And together we have made it as great as it ever was under the leadership of Edward Deravenel, and later that of Harry Turner, my father. My half-sister pulled it down; we have managed to raise it up, make it even bigger than ever it was. And the miraculous thing is that my team and I have actually done this in four years. I took over in 1996 and now it's October of 2000. The City boys admire us; I admire us . . . I'm proud of us.

Deravenels is once again extremely solid. We've built it on steel girders. Every division is in the black. The hotels are flourishing; so are the vineyards and the manor-house boutique hotels; my spas are considered some of the most luxurious and beautiful in the world, and have won numerous awards for the healthy and effective treatments they provide. And because of the success of the Marbella Resort we have started a new division, and are creating similar resorts in some of the great beauty spots of the world.

Ambrose is the mover and shaker behind this new enterprise. He proved himself so clever, efficient and innovative when he was in charge of the Marbella Project it seemed only right that he should head up the new division. Robin's brother is a marvel. But then so are all of the men and women who make up my winning team.

Well, we did have some trouble last year with John Norfell, who fell under the spell of Marie de Burgh when she came to live in Scotland in 1999. She had had no choice. Francis told me that her mother-in-law had been tough with her in the end, and had forced her to leave Dauphin, and Paris.

Seemingly she has a way with men, but John Norfell learned, much to his chagrin, that she is a user, and was manipulating him for her own ends. It didn't take him long to realize that she had no intention of sleeping with him, let

375

alone marrying him. That blew away any ideas he might
have had about running Scottish Heritage with her.

Norfell admits he never became her lover and claims that
when he understood she was devious, and dubious in certain
areas, he swiftly fled south to England. All of this information came directly to me from Francis, who advised us, the
triumvirate, to turn a blind eye to his escapades. He pointed
out that no real damage had been done. We agreed to do
that, with the understanding that Cecil and Robin would
meet with Norfell to read him the riot act, and caution him
to behave himself.

It was Robin who told me that John had admitted to him
that Marie de Burgh was most alluring, and as John put it,
'a delicious bit of crumpet'. On hearing that, I told Robin
I felt like vomiting. What a demeaning way to describe a
woman. It certainly gave me a new perspective on John
Norfell. Warned by Cecil and Robin that he would be thrown
out of Deravenels if there were any more transgressions,
Norfell has toed the line for the past year. I watch him
closely.

I sometimes think of her, this strange cousin of mine who
wants to be me, who would like to take all that is mine,
longs to be in my place at Deravenels. What cheek, such
utter gall. And she is forever wanting something . . . asking
me to meet her, begging to come and stay with me, demanding
to be made my heir in my will. That would be signing my
own death warrant.

I couldn't believe it when she actually sent me a photograph of herself. I looked at that picture and acknowledged
her beauty, but I knew that in no way did it indicate the
true potency of her so-called overwhelming sex appeal. Only
Nicholas Throckman has had the nerve to explain that to
me. He told me recently that Marie de Burgh, without saying
a word, manages to make a man think she could be his. He

376

added that she is a woman of beauty and grace, a potential heartbreaker.

Be sure of one thing, I will not let her break my heart. That's why I plan to keep her at arm's length. I consigned the photograph to the fire, and have turned deaf ears to her pleas for a meeting. Francis holds me steady on all of this. He is not a fan of hers, and says she is desperately seeking a husband, and he predicts that she'll come to a bad end. Unlike a lot of men, Francis Walsington has his eyes wide open when it comes to women, and he's familiar with all of their many wiles. I discovered that his dislike of Marie Stewart de Burgh runs deep. He knows her half-brother, son of her father and his long-time mistress, born before James Stewart married her mother. He is twelve years older than Marie, also called James after his father; although illegitimate, he has been involved in the running of Scottish Heritage since he was old enough to hold a job. Francis likes him, believes he is capable and straight talking. But he has wondered aloud about the feasibility of a partnership in business between these two 'half-siblings', as he calls them.

But, all in all, the year 2000 has been good. So far, at any rate. Deravenels is running smoothly. Francis is now more content since he hired his idea of the perfect bodyguard, a really strong, tough man who totally fulfils Francis's requirements. Certainly Gary Hinton fits the bill for me, because he is quiet, mannerly, and 'still' . . . I cannot stand being with anyone who is a physical and mental fidget, and he is not. He is calm, focused and alert. He makes me feel safe, and I am certain he will keep me safe.

Robin also likes Gary Hinton and recognizes his superior skill, and so he is more relaxed about my safety as well. Everything is good between us, and we've managed at last to banish the shadow Amy's unexpected and tragic death cast over our lives. Thankfully, most of the gossiping has stopped, and the press have found other more interesting stories to cover. Occasionally Robin reminds me teasingly that we are notorious.

Robin and I are in New York. We have come to spend a few weeks at the Manhattan office of Deravenels, and I also have meetings set up with Anka Palitz about the spas . . . The only problem is that I left London with the most ghastly cold and I wish I could shake it off . . .

Elizabeth couldn't stop coughing, and sat down in a chair, covering her mouth with her hand. A moment later Robert came striding into the bedroom, a look of alarm on his handsome face.

'Are you all right?' he asked, worry suddenly echoing in his voice. 'You sound terrible, Elizabeth.'

'I don't know what happened,' she managed finally in a low voice. 'The coughing came over me all of a sudden. But it does that and then goes away. I'm all right, Robin, really I am.'

'Do you think you have bronchitis?'

'No, I'm sure I don't.' She stood up, straightening the skirt of her red wool dress and walked over to the wardrobe, took out the matching coat. 'We're running late, you know. We're meeting Anka at La Grenouille in half an hour.' She gave him the brightest smile she could muster, wanting to reassure him.

'If you're up to going then come on, darling, I'm ready.' Picking up her coat, he helped her on with it, and walked with her to the door. 'Gary's waiting for us downstairs.'

Anka Palitz, blonde, pretty and very chic, was already at the restaurant, and she smiled warmly as Elizabeth and Robin were shown to the table by Charles, the owner of La Grenouille.

'It's lovely to see you both,' she said as Elizabeth slid onto the banquette next to her and Robert took the chair at the opposite side of the table.

'Sorry we're late, we misjudged the traffic,' Elizabeth explained.

'There's no problem. What would you like to drink? Champagne, wine, or a soft drink?'

'Thank you, water is fine, Anka. I really can't drink alcohol at lunchtime, it makes me sleepy.'

'Me, too. Robert, what about you?'

'Just water, the same as Elizabeth,' Robert answered.

Anka motioned to the waiter, gave the order, and Robert stared at Elizabeth, realizing that she now looked suddenly positively ill. Her face, was whiter than ever and her eyes were slightly glazed. He decided she had a fever.

He was staring at her so hard, Elizabeth said, 'I'm fine, Robin.' She always knew what he was thinking, and his expression left nothing to the imagination.

Anka turned and glanced at her, noticed at once her ghastly pallor. 'Are you sure? Don't you feel well?'

'Oh, it's just a stupid cold I brought with me from London. I'm fine. By the way, this is for you.' Elizabeth reached into her large handbag and took out a manila envelope. 'This is the whole programme I've mapped out for the American spas. You can study it and tell me what you think. No hurry at all, but I would like your input whilst we're in New York. And what I also need to know is whether you want to remain with the spas, after I've sold them to Deravenels. Nothing will change, you know, it's just a paper transaction, and obviously you'll still be working with me.'

'I understand that, and I'm pretty certain I will stay, Elizabeth, but I would like to look everything over, and we can talk later in the week, have another lunch or dinner, whichever you prefer.'

'Of course, and it's –' Elizabeth stopped speaking as a fit of coughing overtook her. Pressing her napkin to her mouth, she coughed until she was red in the face. Finally she managed to control the cough, and took a deep breath. As she did she winced, brought a hand to her chest.

'What is it?' Robert asked, concerned by her obvious discomfort.

Elizabeth said, 'It really hurts when I take a deep breath.' Weakly, she leaned back against the banquette. 'I feel dizzy, Robin.'

'I think we ought to get you to a doctor,' Robin exclaimed in a worried voice, and fixed his gaze on Anka, raising a brow.

'I agree, and we'd better leave here at once,' Anka announced briskly, instantly in charge. 'I have an excellent doctor, Robert, and I feel sure he would see Elizabeth immediately. Let me go and call his office. I know Charles will let me use the phone.'

'All right, and I'll come with you. I have to phone Gary, the car's parked somewhere near here.' He stood up, helped Anka out from the banquette, and stared at Elizabeth. 'I won't be a moment, darling.'

'I'm fine, I'm not going to die on you, Robin.'

Dr Andrew Smolenski, having been told by Anka Palitz on the phone that Elizabeth Turner was obviously very ill, understood that this was an emergency. The moment they arrived at his office he saw them at once. Even as Anka was making the introductions Elizabeth started to cough, and Dr Smolenski was instantly alarmed.

Once she had calmed herself, he said, 'How long have you had this cough, Miss Turner?'

'Since last week . . .' She stopped, shaking her head, passed a hand over her face. 'Sorry, I feel a bit lethargic.'

Robin cut in, swiftly explained, 'We arrived in New York last Friday, the twentieth, Dr Smolenski. Elizabeth had a really bad cold when we left London. But the cough only developed once we were here, over the weekend actually.'

'I understand.' The doctor made a few notations on a pad, and then addressed Elizabeth again. 'When you take a deep breath do you have a pain in your chest?'

Elizabeth nodded.

'Do you have sputum?' Are you spitting anything up?'

'This morning, rather early, but not much.'

Rising, he walked around his desk. 'I must examine you, Miss Turner. Please come in here.' As he spoke he opened the door to an examination room, adding, 'Please take off your coat and dress. My nurse will come in to help you.'

Elizabeth got up, walked across the floor, and Dr Smolenski ushered her inside, leaving her alone. Then the nurse entered from another door, smiled and said, 'It's just a routine examination, Miss Turner, don't worry. Put on this robe when you've undressed.'

A moment or two later the doctor came in and began his examination. He took her temperature, felt her pulse, listening to her chest through his stethoscope, and checked her blood oxygen level. When he had finished, he nodded and said, 'Please get dressed, Miss Turner, and come back to my office.' Once he had left, the nurse returned to help her put on her clothes.

When she went into his private office, the doctor was talking to Anka and Robin, his face serious. 'Ah, there you are, Miss Turner,' he said. 'You have a temperature of 101.2 and a thready, rather rapid pulse. You also have an elevated respiratory rate, and a blood oxygen level of eighty-four per cent. I believe your lungs are not taking in enough oxygen. Mr Dunley just asked me if you had bronchitis, and I told him you don't. However, I believe you *do* have pneumonia, and I want you to go to the emergency room at the hospital immediately. For more tests.'

'Oh,' she said, staring at him, looking startled.

'I'll make all the arrangements,' the doctor announced in a firm voice, one which forbade argument.

Elizabeth underwent a number of tests in the emergency room of New York Cornell Hospital. A diagnosis was arrived at fairly quickly after a chest x-ray and routine blood work had been done. She had pneumonia and the symptoms were severe.

Dr Melanie Roland, the doctor who had been assigned to do the tests, came into the small examination room where Elizabeth sat with Robert and Anka to explain the situation. 'We want to admit you to the hospital at once, for twenty-four hours,' the doctor explained. 'You'll be in a non-ICU bed, and we'll start you on some antibiotics while we await the results of the cultures we've taken.'

'I don't want to stay in the hospital, not even overnight,' Elizabeth protested, glancing at Robert.

'It would be the wisest thing for you to do, Miss Turner,' Dr Roland told her. 'Your symptoms are quite severe. You *do* have pneumonia, you know.'

Robert went to Elizabeth, put his arm around her. 'It's just for one night,' he murmured soothingly. 'I'll go to the hotel and get a few things you'll need, and come back to be with you.' He glanced at Dr Roland. 'I can stay with her for a few hours or so, can't I?'

Dr Roland had been about to refuse this request, but instead she nodded, gave him a warm smile. 'Of course, Mr Dunley.'

'And you *can* arrange for a private room for Miss Turner, can't you, Doctor?' he asked.

'I'll attend to it immediately.'

Anka said, 'I'll stay with you until Robert returns, Elizabeth.'

'Thank you, Anka, I'd be grateful for that.'

The following morning Robert went back to the hospital to discover that Elizabeth had been moved from the private room. She was now in the ICU, with tubes in her and was on mechanical ventilation. 'What on earth has happened?' he asked Dr Roland, who had taken him into the ICU to see Elizabeth, but only for a moment.

The doctor led him back into the corridor. Once they were outside, she said, 'She's sedated and it's best she is.' Then she sat down with him on a nearby bench, and explained, 'During the night she became very feverish, her oxygen requirements went up, and so far she's shown no response at all to the antibiotics.'

Robert, gripped by anxiety, nevertheless managed to stay calm. He asked, 'What about the cultures you took? What have they told you?'

'I'm still awaiting those results, Mr Dunley. In the meantime, I've put Miss Turner on different antibiotics, hoping we'll get some better results. But I have to inform you that this *is* a most critical stage.'

'But why? What's happened?'

'I think the pneumonia has really grabbed her, and the medicine hasn't worked. So far. We're hoping the new anti-biotics will do the trick. I'm sure they will,' she reassured him, aware of his enormous concern.

Robert rubbed a hand over his face, and took a deep breath. 'People can die from pneumonia . . . Elizabeth's not going to die, is she?'

'As I just told you, Mr Dunley, this *is* a critical stage, but we're going to do our best to pull Miss Turner through. And once we have the results of the cultures, we will certainly know more.'

'Shall I stay here, wait until she wakes up?' he asked, sounding desperate.

'I honestly don't think you should. She may be out of it for hours. In fact, I'm hoping she will be.'

'I understand,' he said. 'And thank you, Dr Roland.'

FORTY

Over the next several days Elizabeth's situation remained critical and tenuous, and Robert was frantic with worry and totally at a loss. He longed to do something to help her but there was nothing he *could* do. He was not a doctor, and he was smart enough to understand she was in the best of hands. Dr Smolenski was on the case, and kept him informed of her progress, and he had great trust in Melanie Roland. He had known from the moment he met her in the ER that she was a dedicated doctor.

He went to the hospital twice every day and looked in on Elizabeth, then crept away. He knew that all he could do was wait. And pray. He prayed a lot. And he spoke a lot to London. Cecil was as devastated and anxiety-ridden as he was, and was on the verge of getting on the next plane to New York. 'Wait another day, until the cultures come back,' Robert had insisted. But when they finally did come back and he heard the results he was filled with dismay. Dr Roland told him that Elizabeth was positive for one of the rarest forms of pneumonia, and one which had a high death rate.

'Oh, my God, no! Can't you save her?'

'Yes, we can,' Melanie Roland reassured him. But she wasn't sure that they could.

Elizabeth lay in the ICU, her eyes closed, face impassive.

Robert stared down at her, loving her so much, unable to do one single thing for her. He turned away from the bed and left, a prayer on his lips. She had to live. She must. What would he do without her?

I am dying. I feel sure of that. I don't want to die. I'm only twenty-nine years old. I would like to live a little longer. For Robin's sake. Oh, my God! ROBIN. What will happen to him if I die? He needs me. So I must live. But what if I don't? I must fight this deadly disease. But if I should die he will be vulnerable. I can't leave him like that, so terribly exposed. I must protect him. How can I do that? I must ensure that he has a solid place at Deravenels. The best position. Yes, position and wealth. That's what I have to ensure he has. I need Cecil Williams here. He has to come. I need Cecil, and witnesses, and lawyers. I need to add a codicil to my will.

A day later Cecil Williams arrived in New York. 'I do wish you had let me come before this,' Cecil said, staring hard at Robert across the breakfast table in the restaurant of the Carlyle. 'I've been worried to death about Elizabeth, and I still am.'

'I know you were. *And are.* But there's nothing either of us can do. It's up to the doctors, not us.'

'How is she *really*, Robert?' Cecil's light grey eyes were troubled.

'A little better. She's finally been transferred to another unit, she's no longer in the ICU, and she's being weaned off the mechanical ventilator, but she's not out of the woods yet.'

'Why not?' Cecil asked, his voice turning more sombre than ever.

'There's always the possibility of a relapse at this stage. But let's not dwell on that. Let's hope she gets better, not worse.'

Cecil placed his napkin on the table, and pushed back his chair. 'I'm ready to go to the hospital, if you are.'

'Then let's go. She'll be thrilled to see you, Cecil,' Robert said, leaving the restaurant with his friend and colleague.

It was pleasant weather, even though it was November; they walked to the end of the street and managed to hail a cab on Madison Avenue. Robert gave the driver the address of New York Cornell Hospital, sat back on the seat, and said, 'She's lost weight, and she's paler than ever, so don't be shocked when you see her.'

'I won't, I promise,' Cecil said, but he was when he finally saw her. Elizabeth was gaunt, for one thing, and her face was the whitest he had ever seen it.

He hurried over to the bed, bent down and kissed her cheek, and she took his hand and squeezed it, and the smile reflected in her dark eyes instantly cheered him up. 'I came as soon as Robert would let me. He's been very difficult.'

Moving the oxygen mask she was wearing, Elizabeth said, 'I know. And he was right. I was out of it for a bit. You would have been bored silly, waiting around.'

Robert joined them, gave Elizabeth a kiss, and pulled over

387

a chair for Cecil, went to fetch another one for himself.

Cecil talked to her for a while, mostly about Deravenels, filling her in about a variety of things, and she listened attentively, nodding from time to time.

Watching her keenly, attuned as usual to her every mood, Robert soon noticed that she was beginning to tire. Touching her arm he said, 'I think we'd better go, let you rest now. We'll come back and see you again later today.'

Elizabeth nodded, then pulled the mask away. 'I have to speak to Cecil, Robin. Could you give us a moment?'

'No problem,' he answered, and kissed her again. If he was surprised he did not show it. He simply strode out of the room, giving her the privacy she obviously needed.

'What is it, Elizabeth?' Cecil asked, leaning closer. 'Is there something important you need to say?'

She nodded, and took off the mask. 'If anything happens to me, if I don't recover, I want Robert Dunley to be made managing director of Deravenels in my place. Promise me you'll see to it.'

'But I can't, Elizabeth! As much as I want to please you. Don't forget, you would have to have the rules of the company changed in order for that to happen. You see, he's not a Deravenel, and only a Deravenel can be managing director.'

'Then let's change the rules.' She quickly put the mask back on her face, suddenly needing the oxygen.

'There would have to be a board meeting for that.'

'Then let's think of another title. Administrator maybe, like Edward Selmere was for young Edward.' She slipped the mask in place again, and leaned forward, grasping Cecil's arm. After a moment, she moved the mask and said, 'I want him to head the company if I die. We must do it now, Cecil. Please. Because I might die, you know.'

'I'll do what I can,' he promised, and then gently made her lean back against the pillows, adjusted the oxygen mask for her, and went to fetch Robert so they could say goodbye, let her rest.

Much to everyone's relief and delight, Elizabeth Turner came out of the hospital exactly three weeks after being placed in the ICU. She looked thinner than ever, frail, even debilitated, but she had recovered from the rare type of pneumonia which had been a brutal assault on her system and had almost killed her.

'But here I am, alive and well,' she exclaimed, settling on the sofa in the sitting room of their suite at the Carlyle. 'And thank you for being there for me.' She smiled up at Robert, and at Anka Palitz, then patted the seat next to her. 'Come and sit here, Cecil,' she said, her affection for him echoing in her voice. 'I'm so happy you're here. Now, shall we order afternoon tea? That's what *I* feel like anyway.'

The others agreed, and Robert went to order afternoon tea for four; Anka excused herself, going in search of her handbag, wanting to retrieve the documents she had brought back for Elizabeth. Cecil drew closer to her, and said, 'I didn't want to go to the lawyers Deravenels use, Elizabeth. So I've arranged for a separate law firm to represent you, regarding Robert being named Administrator, if that becomes necessary.' He spoke in a confident tone, using this moment they were alone to fill her in. 'You must give me a date for a meeting with them.'

Elizabeth looked suddenly thoughtful, stared off into the distance, and then she answered softly, 'I think I prefer to change the rules of the company, Cecil, so that Robin could become managing director if I die. When I get my strength back, and we return to London, I'll call a special board meeting. I'm sure there won't be a problem, the board will do what I want.'

Cecil was not so sure she was right about this, but nodded his acquiescence.

Although Robert Dunley had finally relaxed, filled with relief that Elizabeth had made such a good recovery, he was, nevertheless, vigilant about her health and well-being. He had been so frightened, terrified really, by her brush with death he insisted that she slow down.

Once Dr Smolenski said she could travel, they had flown to California to spend Thanksgiving with friends. He had wanted her to recuperate in the warm weather and in a relaxed environment. And even when they returned to London in time for Christmas, he was a hard taskmaster. He created a schedule and she had had no alternative but to stick to it . . . After all, they did live together and he monitored her all the time. He insisted she keep more normal hours at Deravenels, made sure she ate properly, and forced her to take weekends off.

The regime worked eventually, and as 2001 drew to a close she was finally coming into her own again. It had taken her a whole year, but she was suddenly full of her old vitality and energy.

'I'm back to being Elizabeth,' she said to Robert one morning in December of 2001, going into his office adjoining hers. 'The old Elizabeth, I mean.' She hovered in the doorway, smiling at him, her expression flirtatious.

Standing up, he went over to her, and took her in his arms. 'And you look . . . just fabulous,' he said, and kissed her on the mouth lightly. 'I have something for you.' He continued walking back to his desk. 'It's what I call a pre-Christmas present.'

Intrigued, a look of surprise on her face, Elizabeth followed him over to the desk, and took the jewel case he offered. When she opened it she let out a small gasp. 'Oh, Robin, they're beautiful!' She was staring at a pair of emerald-cut emerald earrings, perfectly square with four small diamonds set along the bottom of each earring. 'Thank you, thank you so much.' Stepping closer, she hugged him, then kissed him on his cheek.

'They're for being a good trouper and following orders,' he teased, laughing. And she laughed with him. She loved him so much. He was the centre of her life . . . her entire life, just as she knew she was the centre of his.

PART FOUR

Scuttling the Enemy

'Look for a long time at what pleases you, and longer still at what pains you . . .'

Colette

'Yea though I walk through the valley of the shadow of death, I will fear no evil: for thou art with me; thy rod and thy staff they comfort me. Thou preparest a table before me in the presence of mine enemies: thou anointest my head with oil; my cup runneth over. Surely goodness and mercy shall follow me all the days of my life: and I will dwell in the house of the Lord forever.'

The Bible: Psalm 23

FORTY-ONE

Robert and his brother Ambrose stood in the middle of the newly erected barn in one of the larger fields at Waverley Court in Kent. An indoor riding ring had been completed during the past week, and they were studying it from every angle.

'They've done a damn good job, Robert,' Ambrose said, continuing to eye the ring critically. 'And it's going to be marvellous for you in winter, especially in the bad weather. You can practise your dressage in total comfort. I notice the builders put central heating around the sides of the barn.'

'Good thing, too. It can get very cold down here, and there's frequently a bitter wind blowing off the sea across Romney Marsh. The other barn which I had them build earlier this year turned out to be very cold in the bad weather. I'm going to have central heating installed in that one, too.'

Taking his brother's arm, Robert walked around the ring one more time, and then they strolled outside.

It was a lovely Saturday morning in early September of

2002. A bright blue sky was dotted with cotton-wool clouds and the sunshine was golden, and warm. Robert glanced up at the sky. 'There's nowhere quite as beautiful as England when the weather's good, is there?'

'Damn right,' Ambrose agreed, and stared at Robert, frowning. Then he continued, 'You've never told me what it's like to be a landowner, the squire, in a sense, of this fantastic property.'

Robert laughed. 'It's wonderful, why wouldn't it be? And frankly I haven't recovered from my surprise, if you want the truth. I was astonished when Elizabeth gave me Waverley Court. You see, she has always loved this house so much herself.'

'I know that, and I was surprised for the same reason as you.'

'It wasn't like giving it to a stranger,' Robert remarked. 'And she's here every weekend with me. The truth is, she's going to inherit Stonehurst Farm when Grace Rose goes, and she's asked Elizabeth not to sell it. Or give it to anyone. She wants it to stay in the family.'

'And obviously Elizabeth agreed?'

'She did, Ambrose. How could she not? Grace Rose has made her the heir, left her virtually everything, her entire estate, in fact.'

'I understand. Waverley Court must be expensive to run, isn't it?' Ambrose ventured, glancing at his brother as they walked in the direction of the rose garden which Robert was creating and building.

'It's not too bad. We don't have a big staff, only Toby and Myrtle, and some daily cleaning help when we're here. Toby grooms the horses, and generally keeps the property in good shape, but I do have a gardener now. Anyway, Elizabeth made a trust fund for the upkeep of Waverley Court, on the lines of the one which Edward Deravenel put in place for

Ravenscar. Also, she has created a trust for me personally, which gives me an income.'

Ambrose was delighted by this news, and exclaimed, 'I'm glad Elizabeth has looked after you properly, Robert. You work like a bloody fiend at Deravenels, and are devoted to the company. And to Elizabeth. And after all, your relationship *is* a marriage . . . without the benefit of a piece of paper.'

Robert said quietly, 'I believe it to be that, yes, and don't think I haven't wanted to make it legal, because I have. Elizabeth won't. So I don't push her any more. It's better to leave it alone, and I'm quite happy with the status quo. It's not that she doesn't want to marry *me*. She just doesn't want to marry anybody, and she's stubborn about it.'

Ambrose was silent for a moment, and although he knew better than to intrude on his brother's private life, he couldn't stop himself from saying, 'But don't you want children?'

Robert remained silent, and walked on, hurrying now. Ambrose kept up with him and after a moment he said, 'Sorry. I didn't mean to pry.'

'I know.' Robert sighed. 'I *would* like children, but she's more important to me than anything else, she's always been my priority. We ought to have children, though, because of her need for an heir, but she turns a deaf ear to that. We're both only thirty-one, so there's still time, Ambrose. Can you believe it, Elizabeth and I have been living together for six years now? *Tempus fugit*, eh?'

'Yes, time does indeed fly,' Ambrose agreed. 'And where is Elizabeth this morning?'

'With Grace Rose. She went to see her at Stonehurst Farm where she's been living all summer. She's actually one hundred and two years old, but you'd never guess it. She looks wonderful and she has all her marbles. By the way, you *are* staying for the weekend, aren't you? I didn't see a suitcase.'

'Toby took it off me the moment I arrived earlier. And as my wife is in New York on business, of course I'm here for the weekend. I brought a very *large* suitcase.'

'Then by now it's up in your room and unpacked! Myrtle is very efficient. And incidentally, in case you didn't know, Elizabeth has been very generous to Cecil Williams. She created a trust fund for him, gave him land she owned so he could build a house, and bought him a Bentley. Which I couldn't believe he wanted, he's so laid-back and low-key.' Robert put his hand on his brother's shoulder. 'I'm not the only one she's rewarded.'

'I know that. She's created a pension fund for me, and also for Francis and Nicholas . . . she's been generous to all of us and to a fault.' By now they had arrived at the sunken garden, and Ambrose was surprised at the progress Robert had made. 'This is gorgeous! And what beautiful roses!' he exclaimed.

'The last of the late bloomers,' Robert explained. 'And it *is* a unique garden, actually. I was rummaging around in the attics here and found an old book on gardens. I fell in love with one of them, and have copied it here. This is pure Elizabethan, a Tudor rose garden from the 1560s. All it needs now are the finishing touches.'

Later, over a light lunch outside on the terrace, Robert suddenly said, 'What's happening with Mark Lott and Alexander Dawson, do you know?'

Ambrose put his fork down and frowned, shook his head. 'What do you mean?'

'Francis told me they've been up to Scotland on numerous occasions, and not always together. Is there a plot being hatched between them and the kilt, do you think?'

398

'Doesn't Francis *know*?' Ambrose gave his brother a quizzical look. 'After all, plots and intrigue are his business.'

'No, he doesn't, strangely enough, just implies trouble is brewing. He says everything is quiet in Edinburgh, although he did remark that he wondered if this was the lull before the storm.'

'What did he mean by *that*?' Ambrose asked, sounding genuinely puzzled now.

'I don't know, but probably he's thinking about the kilt. He did say that Marie de Burgh is working alongside her half-brother James, at Scottish Heritage. And that it's not always tranquil between them, seemingly. Lots of fighting. She's still single, and Francis did tell me she is more desperate than ever to grab herself a husband.'

'She couldn't possibly be interested in either Lott or Dawson, could she? They're dummies, in my opinion!' Ambrose asserted.

'Don't be too sure of that,' Robert cautioned. 'They're a couple of double-dealing buggers.' He shrugged. 'Well, she no doubt has her hands full with business right now.'

'There's one good thing – she hasn't been screaming and shouting about Deravenels lately. And Norfell seems to be keeping his hands out of the cookie jar. He's stayed away from her, I believe.'

'If he does go near her, he'll be hung, drawn and quartered!' Robert couldn't help chuckling when he added, 'Cecil and I put the bloody fear of God into him. We threatened to . . . well . . . emasculate him is the polite way to put it.'

In all the years she had been coming to Stonehurst Farm, Elizabeth had never seen it looking quite so beautiful. Although it was September the gardens were extraordinary, filled with glorious flowers and exotic plants, flowering shrubs, bushes and the most magnificent trees. It was a typical English garden, the kind Elizabeth loved, and over the years Grace Rose had turned it into something quite spectacular.

Inside the house everything sparkled and shone and gleamed. Sunlight bounced off the mellow antique furniture, the polished wood floors, and the many large mirrors, and all the rooms were light-filled and beautiful. There were many silver and crystal bowls of roses scattered around on tables and chests, and these late-summer blooms filled the rooms with their sweet scent. And other delicious fragrances hung on the air ... mouth-watering smells emanated from the kitchen ... apples cooking, bread baking ... fresh herbs and mint being chopped ... all mingled together ... and now, wafting in on the warm air, came the tantalizing smell of cheese being cooked.

Turning to her great-aunt, Elizabeth exclaimed, 'Grace Rose, you spoil me! I have a feeling it's cheese soufflé for lunch. *My favourite!*'

'And mine, too. And yes, that *is* what we're having.'

'Before I forget, I want you to know I did take your advice about charities, and in the end I went with *your* favourite, Parents and Abducted Children Together. I gave them a donation, and I'll continue to do so, it's such a good cause.'

'I've given to PACT since it was started two years ago,' Grace Rose said, and then paused, suddenly scrutinizing Elizabeth. She announced, 'You've looked awfully pinched and drawn this past year. You *are* feeling all right, aren't you?'

'I'm in very good health. I've never felt better,' Elizabeth was swift to reassure her great-aunt, knowing how she worried about her.

'Sometimes you seem ... *so preoccupied.*' Grace Rose emphasized the last word. 'And I know it's not Deravenels or Robin that you are worried about. But I do think you *are* worried.'

'To be honest, I'm very frequently concerned about Marie Stewart de Burgh. I get suspicious when she's quiet, and it is totally *silent* up there in Scotland. Francis worries about that, too.'

Grace Rose was disconcerted to hear this. '*Why?*'

'Like me, he thinks her silence is odd. On the other hand, one must remember that he can't stand her. He's constantly said she'll come to a sticky end, and I keep pointing out that he can't possibly know that since he's not an oracle.'

'But I do trust him, Elizabeth. He's a rather brilliant man, and he knows what he's doing. He can also make clever judgements, realistic ones, about people. Take note of what he says. Remember, it could be gut instinct telling him things. I've always put great store in that.'

'So have I.' Elizabeth shifted in the chair. 'What is it you wanted to give me?'

'This key,' Grace Rose replied, showing it to her. 'It's for the big black suitcase in the closet in my bedroom. The suitcase is full of papers, and many are valuable family documents which belonged to Edward Deravenel. In a sense, they are the history of the Deravenels, and, to some extent, the Turners as well. I thought you should be the custodian of them after I'm gone.' Noticing Elizabeth's anxious look, Grace Rose was swift to add, 'Let's just say I take great pride in our family history . . .' Her voice trailed off, and she handed her the key.

'I understand,' Elizabeth said, putting the key safely in her handbag. 'And I can't wait to read them. You know how much I've been intrigued by the Deravenels all my life.'

At this moment Maddie, the housekeeper, appeared in the doorway and told them lunch was ready. Elizabeth helped Grace Rose up out of the chair, and together they walked to the dining room.

Once they were seated, Maddie served them the cheese soufflés right from the oven, piping hot, all puffed up and brown on top in their individual white dishes.

'They look perfect,' Grace Rose exclaimed. 'My compliments to the chef.'

'That's me, Mrs Morran,' Maddie answered with a laugh.

Grace Rose smiled, and winked at her.

After lunch the two of them sat on the long, covered terrace overlooking the lawns surrounded by giant oak trees and sycamores which Stonehurst Farm was so renowned for. All of them were hundreds of years old and breathtaking in their dark green beauty.

They sipped passion fruit tea and talked about the Deravenel family, which had always been Grace Rose's favourite subject. To Elizabeth she seemed preoccupied by the past, what had gone before, and more than ever. She mostly lived in the past these days, drifting along with her memories.

There was a moment or two of silence between them, and then Grace Rose suddenly said in a very clear, light voice, 'You will be fine, my dearest Elizabeth. Whatever happens to you in your life, you will always come out on top . . . you'll be the winner every time.'

Elizabeth leaned into her and squeezed her hand, so soft yet dry, like old paper. 'I know I will, Aunt Grace Rose . . . because I'm a Deravenel just like you.'

The old woman smiled at her, and her face was full of love. And they sat together holding hands until Grace Rose finally roused herself. 'I want to go inside. It's getting too warm for me out here. Although I do enjoy seeing the garden. It's very beautiful, isn't it?'

'It's lovely,' Elizabeth responded, and helped her to her feet.

'It's Vicky's garden really. My mother originally created it, you know . . .' Grace Rose swayed slightly and clung to Elizabeth. In a worried voice, she said, 'I don't think I can make it inside.'

'Sit down again.' Elizabeth managed to settle Grace Rose in the chair, then stepped away, intending to fetch Maddie.

'Don't leave me, Elizabeth,' Grace Rose said in a whispery voice.

Immediately, Elizabeth sat down next to her and took her hand. 'Don't you feel well?'

Grace Rose smiled at her. It was the most radiant of smiles and the faded blue eyes somehow looked brighter, bluer all of a sudden. 'I never felt better, my dear,' Grace Rose murmured and closed her eyes.

After a moment she spoke again. 'They're all here with me . . . oh, my darling Charlie . . . there you are . . . with Bess . . . Father . . . wait for me . . . I'm coming to you . . . Charlie . . . wait, I'm running to your arms . . .'

'Grace Rose! Grace Rose!' Elizabeth exclaimed, leaning over her. Her great aunt was so very still, did not respond, and Elizabeth knew then that she was dead. She kissed her cheek, the tears trickling down her face, splashing onto the old wrinkled skin. Brushing her eyes with one hand, Elizabeth choked back the tears, and against her great-aunt's face she said softly, 'They came for you at last. All those whom you loved so much through your long life. And you have gone with them. How happy you must be now . . . God speed, Grace Rose. God speed.'

FORTY-TWO

'She gave birth on Saturday night,' Francis Walsington said, looking from Elizabeth to Robert. 'It's a boy . . . to be called James, after his grandfather James Stewart. And one day Scottish Heritage will be his.'

'So she beat me to it. She has produced an heir,' Elizabeth said at last. Settling back in the chair, she went on, 'Well, some good it will do her. She borrowed trouble when she married Henry Darlay, and we've known that right from the beginning. And even though he is a relative of mine, through his mother who's my cousin, this doesn't bring her any closer to Deravenels.' She glanced at Cecil, and finished, 'Let's not forget that *other* clause in Father's will.'

Cecil stared back at her, his eyes narrowing slightly. 'However much she insists she has no knowledge of that clause, it doesn't matter. The clause *is* in your father's will, you're correct, Elizabeth, and it is absolutely clear and it's legal. Harry Turner debarred not only foreigners from inheriting Deravenels, but his sister Margaret's line as well. And we know he did that because he loved his younger sister better, was closer to her. Anyway she was married to his childhood friend Charles Brandt, who was actually Harry's best friend all of his life.'

'That is why my brother also favoured their descendants, our Greyson cousins, as do I, I've told you that all along,' Elizabeth said.

'I've never not understood that,' Cecil replied crisply. 'But in any event, Marie Stewart de Burgh cannot challenge you.'

'Cecil's correct,' Francis interjected. 'And the kilt has never done anything but spout a lot of codswallop. Truly, there is no reason for you to worry. Anyway, she's got her hands full at the moment, between Henry Darlay and a new baby, wouldn't you say?'

Elizabeth couldn't help laughing at Francis's expression. It was gleeful. 'And I actually do own sixty-five per cent of the shares. Don't let's forget *that* fact.'

'I'm surprised she carried that child to full term,' Robert said, glancing at Francis. 'A lot of women would have miscarried if they'd seen their personal assistant murdered in the street before their eyes. My blood runs cold thinking about that horrendous incident.'

'I agree,' Elizabeth exclaimed, but then she usually did agree with Robert; they were so attuned in their thoughts. 'Imagine, David del Renzio got mugged in front of her, stabbed to death. And his briefcase grabbed. I wonder what they imagined was in it?'

'Money, more than likely . . . and the police never caught anybody,' Francis pointed out. 'Although Nicholas has his own ideas about that murder.'

'Who's taking my name in vain?' Nicholas Throckman asked, coming into Elizabeth's office and closing the door behind him. 'No doubt it's something to do with up yonder beyond the border. I suspect you've heard already that there's a new heir to Scottish Heritage. As if anybody would want to inherit that company –'

'Not doing too well, is it?' Francis cut in, moving along the sofa so that Nicholas could join them. 'It's hardly worthy of the name *conglomerate*.'

'Just before Marie Stewart married Darlay her half-brother was complaining to me that her knowledge of business was nil and the ideas she wanted to introduce were witless,' Robert told them. 'He was not happy with her interference, and he even confided that he needed to borrow money for the company.' Robert grimaced. 'He wanted me to recommend a bank.'

'You should have offered to lend it to him,' Cecil murmured, a small amused smile playing around his mouth. 'Eventually we would have had them by the short hairs, and we could have probably taken them over,' he finished drily.

Robert laughed, as did Francis and Nicholas, although Cecil was poker-faced.

Elizabeth exclaimed, 'I wouldn't have permitted *that*! And I wouldn't touch Scottish Heritage with a barge pole. In fact, they couldn't even *give* it to me.' Turning to Nicholas, she said, 'What about the murder? What did you hear?'

'Rumours, a lot of them, about a jealous husband. But I'm sure Francis knows more than I do.'

'Not much. It happened in March, over two months ago now, and the police haven't come up with a thing. Naturally Darlay has been under suspicion. But there's no evidence to show he was in any way involved. Two masked men grabbed David del Renzio, stabbed him, snatched his briefcase and ran like hell. They'd disappeared in an instant. And Marie Stewart was standing there all alone on a street in Edinburgh, her personal assistant bleeding to death at her feet. And she was pregnant to boot.'

Nicholas nodded. 'I've heard stories ... gossip ... those

Chinese whispers we loathe, and the one story which keeps going the rounds is that Darlay was virulently jealous of David del Renzio, misguidedly believed he was Marie Stewart's lover, and hired assassins to do his dirty work. But you must remember Darlay is no longer popular, he's turned out to be an arrogant young pup who likes his wine and his women, and can't get enough. Marie Stewart wishes she'd remained the de Burgh widow. Apparently she regrets ever marrying Darlay, so I've been told.'

'The toy boy,' Elizabeth muttered. 'Younger than her.'

'And somewhat depraved, as I understand it,' Robert volunteered. 'Drugs, and all that.'

'You reap what you sow,' Cecil said. 'Darlay will come a cropper before we can say Jack Robinson. In the meantime, I have a meeting in a few minutes. If you'll excuse me, Elizabeth, gentlemen.' He left for his own office.

Elizabeth now said to Nicholas, 'I suppose what you were saying is that *if* Darlay is involved in del Renzio's murder he's probably going to get away with it. Get away with murder.'

'Indeed. However, as I've said before, we must not dwell on our highland lassie. She's no threat to you or this company, Elizabeth. Take my word for it. Today is Monday, June the twenty-first in the year two thousand and four, and you're going to be thirty-three in September, and I guarantee you'll grow old in that chair. You'll still be sitting in it when you're sixty, mark my words.'

'Oh, Nicholas, you do make me laugh,' Elizabeth declared. 'There's just nobody like you.'

There is nobody like Nicholas, that's absolutely true. And there is no one like my dearest Robin, the love of my life. I

407

was upset last night when we went home, because I hate violence. And David del Renzio's murder had haunted me all that day. I kept asking myself, and then Robin later, what Marie Stewart had done to make her young husband so suspicious of her. I had no real answer to that, and neither did Robin. Except that he did eventually explain that some men are naturally jealous and suspicious of their wives, for no reason. And he also reminded me that my oddball cousin Henry Darlay had a reputation for being spoiled, arrogant and dim-witted. That he was extraordinarily good-looking attested to the bit of Turner blood he had in him, Robin also said, teasing me. But Darlay was good-looking and ambitious. And I agreed with Robin in the end that his suspicions were ridiculous in that his wife was so heavily pregnant. How horribly vindictive of Darlay to set assassins on del Renzio when the man was actually with Marie Stewart in the street. How easily she could have lost the baby.

A baby. Last night, after we had made love, Robin asked me if I'd ever wanted a baby. I suppose I sort of fudged the answer the best I could because I didn't want to hurt his feelings, and if I'd said 'no' I would have done just that. Instead, I answered his question with a question. 'Haven't you always wanted a child?' I said, and he admitted he had often thought about it, but added he wasn't particularly concerned if he didn't become a father.

He's not here. He went to Paris this morning with Nicholas Throckman to check on Deravenels, and hopefully hire a new manager for our head office in France. He'll be gone for a few days. And I shall look at more of the Deravenel papers and documents which Grace Rose left in my care. I can't believe she's been dead almost two years. I miss her.

As for Marie Stewart, I must put her out of my thoughts. I felt a degree of sympathy for her yesterday, when we were discussing del Renzio's murder and the circumstance of it, *but I think I have to set that aside. Francis reminded me that she is my enemy. And her own worst enemy, perhaps. Francis Walsington has always predicted she would come to a bad end, and Grace Rose had enormous faith in his ability and many talents. Well, we shall see. I know I've not heard the end of Marie Stewart just yet . . .*

'I think we might have to ask Norfell to step down,' Cecil Williams said to Elizabeth, his voice low. He did not relish this discussion because it involved Robert Dunley, and he'd been putting it off for days.

'Why? Has he been dabbling in Scottish matters?' she asked and then chortled. 'Hardly possible, Cecil, since madame up yonder is solely interested in her new infant.'

'No, nothing to do with Scotland, Elizabeth,' Cecil responded, and took a sip of wine, preparing himself.

The two of them were having supper at Mark's Club in Mayfair. Cecil had invited her to dine with him because Robert was still in Paris with Nicholas, and he believed this was a good time to talk to her privately.

'If it's not about the kilt, then what *is* it about? What has Norfell done for you to think he has to go?' Elizabeth asked, her curiosity fully aroused.

'I shall be blunt, and tell you straight, and without any fancy folderol. Norfell is not your friend.'

'That's not surprising since he's another five-times removed relative of mine,' she retorted with a wry smile. 'They all seem to want to get at me somehow. But go on, Cecil, tell me more.'

'He's not your friend because he's Robert's enemy, I'm convinced of that.'

She stared at him, a mixture of sudden annoyance and

astonishment crossing her face, and exclaimed, 'And Robin has always said he bears watching! So he was right about Norfell, wasn't he?'

'Indeed he was. It's jealousy, basically. I don't mean romantic jealousy, but envy of Robert's success at Deravenels. He's done a lot of backstabbing, so I've been told, and he would truly enjoy seeing Robert take a stumble. To fall out of favour with you.'

'The latter is not likely or even possible, and you know it. If you want to give Norfell the sack, go ahead. But let's not forget he's been doing wonders with the hotel division. Isn't there a way to render him powerless whilst still employing him?'

Relieved that she was taking this so well and not flying into a rage, as she often did, Cecil allowed himself to laugh with her. 'The only way to do that would be to send him off to some far-flung spot. Like the South Seas. Pity we don't have a project for him, he enjoys these jaunts.'

Elizabeth stared at Cecil alertly, then gave him a radiant smile. 'You've just jogged my mind. I've long wanted to open a place in Fiji, that area anyway, a hotel and a spa combined. They've become extremely popular, and Anka Palitz has been after me to create a really luxurious club. Why don't we send John Norfell to Fiji? Or wherever we decide, to scout locations, etcetera, etcetera.'

'You're serious, aren't you?' Cecil sat back, nodding to himself.

'I am indeed. But I would like to discuss it with Robin first.'

'Will you tell him the reason why?'

'Certainly. He should know, shouldn't he? In fact, if we, the triumvirate, agree that it's a good idea to keep Norfell and to send him away –' she laughed with sudden gaiety, and went on, '– to Fiji or Bali, or wherever, then let's have

Robert send him.' When Cecil was silent, she said, 'No? Yes? What?'

'I think it's a brilliant idea, and it would be most diplomatic if Robert was the one to tell him.'

'Then that's settled.' She stabbed her fork into a shrimp, and then looked Cecil right in the eye. 'I bet it was Charles Broakes who shopped Norfell, wasn't it? They're not so close, you know, even though they'd like us to think that. I believe Charlie loathes him, actually.'

'No, it wasn't Charlie Broakes.'

'Come on, who was it, Cecil?'

'Mark Lott.'

Elizabeth gaped at him, totally taken aback. 'Bloody hell!' she exclaimed, using one of Francis's favourite expressions. 'I would never have guessed it. And why do you think Mark Lott carried tales out of school?'

'No idea,' Cecil replied succinctly. 'But I'm glad he did.'

FORTY-THREE

Francis Walsington sat in total silence, listening attentively to the man he was lunching with, his face unreadable, without expression, despite his growing alarm.

'And that's it, all of it,' Giles Frayne finished at last, and took a long swallow of water.

'All I can say is it's a hell of a yarn you've just told me, Giles, hardly believable.'

'I was shocked when it all started to fall together. Aren't you?' Giles threw Francis a questioning look and sat back on the banquette waiting for his reaction.

'Shocked, and dismayed. Now, let's order. You must be starving. And thanks for flying down from Scotland. I appreciate it.'

'I believe it was wiser, Francis. What the eye doesn't see, the heart doesn't grieve over, as my old mum used to say.'

Francis half smiled, and hailed a waiter, who came over at once with the menus. The two men were lunching at The Ivy, sitting at the far end of the restaurant in a quiet corner where they were unobserved, and could talk privately and without being overheard.

'I can never resist the haddock here,' Francis muttered almost to himself, his mind racing, trying to fit this puzzle together. It was a bit of a conundrum.

Giles said, 'I think I'll join you – fried haddock and chips sound good, and I'll start with oysters.'

'So will I.' Francis beckoned to the waiter, who came, took their order, and handed Francis the wine list.

'Would you like a glass of wine, Giles?' Francis asked.

'I won't, thanks.'

'Neither will I.' Looking at the waiter, handing back the wine list, Francis said, 'Thanks very much, we'll stay with the water.'

Leaning forward across the table, Francis addressed Giles in a low voice. 'You were right, by the way: we can't be seen in Edinburgh together, that would give the game away. And whilst we could have spoken on the phone, I prefer to meet person-to-person. Under the circumstances. I also wanted to give you this.' Francis reached into the inside pocket of his jacket, and took out an envelope, handed it to Giles.

'Thank you,' Giles said, putting it in his trouser pocket.

'Events have moved rather more rapidly than I expected,' Francis continued. 'In fact, I would say they've moved with the speed of lightning. I'm going to have to do some fancy footwork, to say the least, to control this situation and avert a disaster.'

'Yes, you will, I agree. In the meantime, what do you want me to do?'

'Bloody hell, Giles, you've got to stay in place! Embedded in there! I need to know exactly what's happening, and all the time. You're the best undercover operative I've ever had.' Francis sat back, giving him an appraising look. 'Nobody suspects you, do they?'

'Not on your life. I'm cool. Don't worry.'

Giles Frayne, who at thirty was a few years younger than Francis Walsington, happened to be a good actor and a brilliant dissembler. That he was highly intelligent and had had plenty of business experience added to his value; he was at the top of Francis's list when it came to important and sensitive jobs such as this, and had been for a number of years.

'I suppose it's hard to anticipate what their next move will be, isn't it?' Francis leaned back in the chair, rubbed his mouth, frowning. 'Bloody impossible,' he muttered, answering his own question.

'I hate to second guess anyone, don't you?' Giles seemed at a loss. 'Anything can happen. At any moment. They're unpredictable.'

'You're going back tonight, aren't you?'

'I am. As we agreed. You need me where I'm supposed to be . . . tomorrow morning.'

Francis nodded. 'Today's the fourth of April. Let's meet again on Saturday, the ninth. Is that okay?'

'Yes, it's fine. I'll bring my wife and daughter up to London for the weekend . . . a good cover, and they'll enjoy it.'

'How will you handle a meeting with me?'

'No problem. Let's get together for a drink early on Saturday evening. Can you manage that?'

'I certainly can, Giles. Six o'clock at the Ritz Hotel. Ah, here's our lunch.'

Later that afternoon, back in his office at Deravenels, Francis Walsington sat down at his desk and began to ponder everything Giles had told him.

He was appalled by the events which Giles had recounted in such precise detail, and wondered what they would mean in relation to Elizabeth. How would they affect her? How could he intervene? Could he guide her to safety if indeed she needed that? Deep down he *knew*. Trouble, he thought. There's trouble heading our way. I must find a way to avert it.

At six o'clock that evening Francis hurried to Elizabeth's office and knocked on the door before opening it.

'Hello, Francis!' Elizabeth exclaimed when she saw him hovering in the doorway. 'Don't stand there, come in.'

'I need to talk to you,' he said as he walked across to her desk.

As he sat down Elizabeth knew something was wrong. His eyes were troubled, his expression unusually gloomy. 'Francis, what is it? You look as if you're the bearer of bad news.'

'I am. Where's Robert? I think he should be here. And Cecil.'

'They're together in Cecil's office.' As she spoke she picked up the phone and keyed in Cecil's number. 'Francis is here in my office, Cecil,' she said when he answered. 'He has some news for us – apparently *bad* news.' After putting down the receiver, Elizabeth sat back, and said, 'You can never hide anything from *me*.'

He gave her a weak smile, and then laughed hollowly. 'I wasn't trying to hide it. I just don't know what to do about it, that's my problem.'

A moment later Robert and Cecil came into Elizabeth's office looking concerned, and Robert said, 'Let's sit over here, Francis, it's more comfortable.'

Cecil and Robert seated themselves on the sofa near the window, and Cecil asked, 'What's happened, Francis?'

Following Elizabeth across the room, Francis exclaimed, 'That damned bloody foolish woman! She's found herself another man, and he spells nothing but trouble for her. And perhaps for us. She's got to be out of her mind.'

'Marie Stewart!' Elizabeth exclaimed. 'You're talking about the kilt, aren't you?'

'I am.'

'You say she's got another man . . . but she's only just been widowed!' Elizabeth sounded shocked.

'I know . . . the whole world knows,' Francis replied. 'And obviously she doesn't give a damn what anyone thinks.'

'Who's the man?' Cecil asked.

'Jimmy Bothwith.'

'The Scottish tycoon?' Elizabeth asked, sounding incredulous.

'*He* thinks he's a big deal, but I can assure you he isn't,' Cecil exclaimed. 'And Francis is right, he's bad news. He's been in more shady deals than I care to think about. It's a miracle he's stayed out of jail.'

Robert stared at Francis. 'If I'm not mistaken, he's a married man, isn't he?'

'Do you think that matters to the kilt? She couldn't care less,' Francis answered.

'Darlay killed in an explosion in February. New man strolls onto the scene in April.' Elizabeth raised a brow. '*Correct?*'

'Oh, long before that, according to my sources,' Francis replied. 'The story is that they were having an affair before Darlay was killed, and that the explosion and fire at the country house was not an accident at all. People say it was a very well-planned bit of work.'

'Arson?' Elizabeth whispered. 'Or a bomb?'

'That's the general idea,' Francis said. 'The talk is that they wanted to be rid of Henry Darlay as soon as possible, in order to indulge in their romantic dalliance without any interference.'

'*They*?' Elizabeth gave Francis a sharp glance. 'Do people speak of her *complicity*? Do they think she was involved in her husband's murder – if he was, in fact, murdered?'

'Some people do, yes.'

Elizabeth shuddered but made no comment.

Robert said, 'So Marie Stewart de Burgh Darlay is onto her third husband? Is that what you're telling us, Francis?'

'I don't know if she'll marry Bothwith, but she's with him in every meaning of that word, and has been for a while apparently. The thing is, she's fighting with her half-brother, as we all know, and it looks as if she's about to push him out and bring Jimmy Bothwith into Scottish Heritage.'

'But that doesn't affect us in any way,' Elizabeth pointed out, looking perplexed.

'True. However, I have it on good authority that Bothwith has been swaggering all over Edinburgh, telling anyone who'll listen that he is going to make sure Marie Stewart gets what's hers. And that is your job at Deravenels. He's going to replace you with her.'

'That can't happen!' Robert asserted.

'I know *that*. We all know it, but once again it's the harassment factor being brought into play. Jimmy Bothwith might be of dubious character, but he's not stupid. In fact, he's rather clever in certain ways. So he knows very well that giving interviews, talking it up to the press in general is only going to irritate the hell out of *us*. Nuisance value, and all that shit.' Francis shook his head. '*Ego*. That is Jimmy Bothwith's fatal flaw. He's always comparing himself to Jimmy Goldsmith and Jimmy Hanson, two of the greatest tycoons ever invented, who ruled the world in the seventies and eighties –'

'He might have the same first name as them, but that's

all he has,' Cecil remarked pithily, cutting in. 'He's a fool.'

'Marie Stewart has tried to harass us in the past, and in the end it came to nothing. So it'll be just the same this time, won't it? If she and Bothwith attempt to do that, I mean.' Elizabeth looked at Francis, and then at Cecil and Robert sitting on the sofa.

'The answer is yes,' Francis answered, and went on swiftly, 'Where do we stand on the deal with Norseco Oil?'

'The contracts came in about two weeks ago, and we've been going over them with a fine toothcomb,' Robert said. 'Why do you ask?'

'I was told today that Jimmy Bothwith owns a company called Belvedere Holdings, and another one by the name of Castleton Capital. And these two companies are heavily invested in Norseco Oil. *Very heavily.*'

There was total silence in the room.

Finally Robert broke the silence when he said slowly, in a thoughtful voice, 'Norseco has a lot of shareholders, and I can't say that those names ring a bell. But we can quickly find out from Spencer Thomas.'

'I think we should do that,' Cecil exclaimed, then looked at his watch. 'Though I doubt that Spencer's still here at this hour. In fact, I believe he went to his daughter's school play this afternoon: he mentioned it in passing.'

'If Belvedere Holdings and Castleton Capital *do* own a big block of shares in Norseco, then that means we're about to buy a company that's partially owned by Jimmy Bothwith,' Elizabeth said. 'And we'll have the kilt on our backs. Let's not forget that big shareholders inevitably want a seat on the board.'

'You've got it,' Francis said, and stood up. He paced the floor for a moment or two, and continued, 'I'm going to double check a few things, and then let's have a meeting on Thursday. I'll have all my ducks in a row by that time, but I do need a couple of days.'

'Morning or afternoon, which do you prefer, Francis?' Elizabeth stood up as she spoke, walked over to her desk, checked her engagement book. 'I'm free all day, and I'm sure Cecil and Robert will fit in with us.'

'Let's make it late afternoon,' Francis answered. 'I need as much time as possible.'

'Can I ask you something?' Robert ventured quietly, giving Francis a cautious glance.

'Go ahead.'

'Are you absolutely positive about those two companies?'

'The source was good. I've no reason to doubt the accuracy of what I've told you.'

'We could ask Jake Sorrenson, the chairman of the North Sea Consolidated Oil Company. He knows who owns shares in his company.'

'Of course he does,' Francis agreed. 'And if he doesn't have it in his head, he can look up the list of shareholders. The problem is, Sorrenson doesn't know *who* owns Belvedere Holdings and Castleton Capital. And neither do I. My source assured me Bothwith is the owner, but that he has straw men fronting for him. He's a devious sod.'

'Who is your source?' Elizabeth asked.

Francis looked at her and smiled. 'Even if you were the Queen of England I couldn't tell you that, and you know it, Elizabeth.'

'It's Francis.'

'Is everything all right? You sound awfully strained,' Elizabeth said, her grip on the receiver tightening.

'There are no problems, but I want to cancel the meeting for this afternoon.'

'*Oh*. Why?'

'Because we don't need to have it. However, I would like to come to your office now. I only need ten minutes of your time.'

'That's fine. I'm working on my charity donations at the moment, but that's nothing pressing.'

Three minutes later Francis Walsington walked into Elizabeth Turner's office and sat down opposite her. 'I'm now going to tell you what you have to do. So please listen carefully.'

And she did.

FORTY-FOUR

'And I thought this year was going to be peaceful!' Elizabeth said, reaching out, clasping Robert's hand resting on the table. 'But it looks as if 2005 is going to be as hectic as all the others.'

Robert brought her hand to his lips and kissed it. 'What was it Grace Rose said to you . . . that your life was always going to be *extreme*.'

'I miss her, you know. She was a marvellous sounding board for me.'

'And now you only have me. And Cecil . . . blokes who don't understand women!'

'Oh, the two of you understand all right, and so does Francis. I really felt sorry for him on Monday, he seemed at his wits' end, don't you think?'

'I think he was really pissed off about the kilt. Let's face it, she's being pretty callous, flaunting Bothwith and Darlay hardly cold in his grave. He died in February, and this is April. By God, she's a swift one. Fairly takes my breath away.'

'I don't understand the police. Haven't they done a proper investigation?'

'I'm sure they have, darling. But if a crime's not solved in the first forty-eight hours it usually isn't . . .' He beckoned a waiter, and ordered two more glasses of pink champagne, then continued. 'That seems to be the rule of thumb these days, so I'm told.'

'I wish this new problem hadn't come up. We need it like holes in our heads. By the way, I've changed the meeting with Spencer Thomas, made it next week. He was a bit startled, and actually rather anxious, but I stonewalled him like Francis told me to, and just re-set it.'

'That's fine. Have you told Cecil?'

'No, I will tomorrow. In the meantime, when are we going to Paris again?'

'After we've dealt with our current problem.'

'That sounds like very soon then,' she murmured, smiling at him, and inclined her head as a couple walked past their table at Harry's Bar, another of their favourite Mayfair restaurants.

'Who was that?' Robert asked. 'I didn't recognize them.'

'No, you haven't met them, and she's the person I know, not her husband. I just met her, in fact. She has a beauty line that I'm hoping to buy . . . the company, I mean. For the spas.'

The champagne arrived, and they touched glasses, and then Elizabeth said, 'I do make you happy, don't I, Robin Dunley?'

'Yes, you do, my darling girl. Do you realize we've been together for nine years now?'

'As grown-ups, you mean. If I remember correctly, you first kissed me when I was eight years old, under that big oak at Waverley Court.'

'No, you kissed me first, you little minx!'

'It was you who made the first move, Robin Dunley.'

'No, no, I did not. You were rather a fresh little thing, as I recall. All over me like chickenpox, you were.'

They laughed together then, for the first time in several days. Elizabeth drew closer and murmured, 'Can you imagine . . . the kilt said all those nasty things about me years ago. Castigated me for having a scandalous affair with a married man. And now she's doing exactly the same thing with James Bothwith.'

'Francis was always right about her . . . he detected something strange in her, the first time he met her in Paris when she was married to François de Burgh.'

'Do you think she was involved . . . in Darlay's death, I mean?'

'It's hard to know, but to be truthful I'm a bit dubious about that accusation by the gossips.' He stared at her. 'After all, let's not forget that there were those who pointed a finger at me, said that I murdered my wife. And you know I didn't, so maybe Marie Stewart is innocent of that particular crime, too.'

Elizabeth walked along the corridor to the boardroom at Deravenels, her face unreadable as she opened the door and went inside.

Cecil was sitting at the table with Robert, and Spencer Thomas, the head of Deravco, their oil company. The three men stopped talking as she entered and stood up; Spencer hurried to greet her in the doorway. After kissing her on the cheek, he led her into the room.

Elizabeth sat down and placed the folders she was carrying on the table, and said, 'Sorry to keep you waiting. I was delayed by a phone call from New York.'

'No problems,' Spencer responded, beaming at her. 'Imagine, you'll soon be the proud owner of Norseco Oil, one of the biggest oil companies in Europe. *Congratulations!*'

'Oh, no, no, not so fast, Spencer! I'm superstitious, I'm afraid, and I don't congratulate myself until a deal is signed, sealed and delivered.' She patted the pile of folders in front of her. 'And I've been going through everything again. All these are documents pertaining to Norseco, and there are a number of things that have come up.'

Spencer's face fell. '*Oh.* But last week you were gung-ho. Is there something wrong?'

'I wouldn't use that word.' She shook her head. 'Not *wrong*, Spencer, but maybe not *right*. For us that is, for Deravenels.'

Spencer Thomas, in his early fifties, was a boyish-looking man whose unlined face, blue eyes and blond hair belied his age. A Texan, genial and outgoing, he was a long-time veteran of the oil business and had been at Deravenels for eighteen years. Elizabeth liked him, and she trusted him, but not quite enough to share her secrets with him. Always wary, cautious, even cagey, she now dissembled.

'I'm sorry, Spencer, but I'm afraid Deravenels will have to pass. We can't go forward here.'

He frowned, appeared totally bewildered. 'What do you mean? I don't understand.' He was almost stammering in his confusion.

'I'll put it in the simplest terms. We are not going to buy Norseco Oil,' Elizabeth announced, her voice neutral.

Spencer sat back in his chair, so startled he had lost all power of speech. Eventually he asked in a voice suddenly scratchy, even hoarse, 'But why ever not? It was a great deal, you said so yourself.'

'A lot of reasons. The company's not right for us. It's basically too big, and I've suddenly grown worried again about terrorist attacks. Also, I've had word, a very *confidential communication*, from a government terrorist expert who says that various extremist groups are planning new attacks on tankers. Most especially British and US tankers. They will be major attacks. Several well-known groups want to create ecological disasters, quite aside from damaging the oil business in general – disasters costing us billions, by the way. I've been advised by an unimpeachable source to cancel this deal. And that is what I'm doing. *Now*.'

'Good God! This is terrible. What am I going to tell Jake Sorrenson?'

'Exactly what *I've* told *you*, Spencer. Because it's the truth. And naturally I shall write a letter to Sorrenson, apologizing.'

It was a warm day in May when Francis Walsington walked into Elizabeth's office, closed the door behind him, and said, 'She's married him.'

'I'm not surprised,' Elizabeth responded in the same neutral tone Francis had used. 'You always said she wasn't very bright.'

'Apparently not. She keeps compounding mistake after mistake. Anyway, they tied the knot this morning, and no doubt there will be repercussions. She's ousted her brother, who's up in arms about everything, and Jimmy Bothwith rules the roost.'

Elizabeth grinned at him. 'Cock of the muck heap, eh?'

'That's one way of putting it. But she's made a lot of enemies, Elizabeth, and that's understandable. She's from a notable family in Scotland . . . and she eventually comes back from France, manages to create havoc. Widowed, she's soon married to her second husband, who dies in a weird explosion. Or fire – you name it, it's mysterious to say the least.

425

He's hardly been put to rest when she's seen gallivanting around with a local, so-called tycoon, who gets an instant and questionable divorce and marries her. *Today*. Before she even gets married to Jimmy Bothwith she installs him in the ancient family business, getting rid of her brother in the process, who's actually been cast aside without a second glance.'

'While she's busy making mayhem in Edinburgh she's leaving me alone,' Elizabeth felt compelled to point out.

'I always said she'd come to a sticky end, and she will,' Francis remarked, ignoring her comment. 'There's no doubt about that. I understand Jimmy's been interfering in Scottish Heritage for months now, and there's been a lot of double-dealing. Some very questionable deals have been made, and I've even been informed that some of them may well be considered criminal acts. Those two could easily be prosecuted.'

Elizabeth sat up straighter in her chair and leaned across her desk. 'What are you getting at?'

'I have a lot of information on her, on them, and what they've been doing with Scottish Heritage.'

'How did you manage to get *that*? From her half-brother?'

'You've asked me such questions for years, and I keep telling you I cannot talk about my methods. I'm your head of security, and I will not permit you to *know* anything. That way you can never be blamed. Or take responsibility for anything I do. Understood?'

'Yes. You don't have to say another word. But I'm not stupid by any means. The kind of information you usually get has to come from inside the company. And if her brother's not your source then obviously you have somebody embedded who's doing your bidding, and that's perfectly all right by me.' Elizabeth took a sip of water, and finished, 'How do you like them apples?'

'They're very good for cooking,' Francis said, and finally chuckled.

'I just need to know one thing,' Elizabeth began, and took a deep breath. 'What are you going to do with the information you have on Jimmy Bothwith?'

'I'm not sure, but I do believe I have to report it. I had a drink with a friend of mine who's with the Fraud Squad. He used to be an inspector with Scotland Yard, then moved on to handle white-collar crime. He told me this afternoon that I must speak to his equivalent with the Scottish police. That it is my duty to do so. Nobody can withhold that kind of information.'

'Are you going to do that, Francis?'

'What choice do I have?'

'What will happen to Jimmy Bothwith?'

'I suppose he will be arrested, sent to trial. Finally. He's always been two steps ahead of the sheriff.'

'And Marie Stewart?'

'The same. She's been hand-in-glove with him all along, and she's possibly an accessory to murder. But certainly she's been his partner in business . . . in her family business, which they've ruined, brought to its knees in the last few months. *Ransacked* is the word most often used.'

'So they'll be prosecuted and sent to jail? Is that what you're saying?'

'I'm afraid it is.' He stared at her. 'Why do you look like that?'

'Like what?'

'As if you're suddenly feeling sorry for her . . . stricken. And don't start saying she's your cousin. She's your enemy, Elizabeth.'

'I don't feel sorry for her,' Elizabeth protested.

'I'm glad to hear it. She deserves what she's going to get.'

One morning towards the end of June, Robert bent over Elizabeth and touched her shoulder gently. 'Wake up,' he said against her ear. 'Darling, wake up.'

Elizabeth roused herself immediately, and looked up at him, saw the face she loved the most in this world. 'Robin, what is it? Oh, heavens, have I overslept?'

'No, but I have some news for you. From Francis. He just called on my mobile.'

'At this hour?'

'It's eight o'clock, and it's Saturday.'

'I must have been dead on my feet last night.' She struggled up into a sitting position, and threw her legs out of bed. 'Oh, we're at Stonehurst. I'd forgotten we drove down last night.'

'Come on, darling, let's have coffee.'

'What did Francis have to say? Bad news, no doubt.'

Together they went downstairs, but he didn't answer her. With his arm around her they went into the breakfast room; Robert poured two mugs of coffee and carried them over to the table.

After taking a good swallow he volunteered, 'Francis phoned because he wanted us to know that Marie Stewart has just been arrested by the Edinburgh police. She's in jail, pending her trial for fraud. There are other charges which Francis says he'll tell us later.'

Elizabeth shivered, despite the warmth in the breakfast room, and goose flesh speckled her arms. Somebody walked over my grave, she thought, and began to shudder.

'Are you all right?' Robert asked in concern.

'Yes. What about Bothwith? He's been arrested with her, hasn't he?'

'No. Francis told me he fled some days ago. To Denmark of all places.'

'Why Denmark? How weird.' Elizabeth leaned back in

her chair, lost in thought, her eyes staring off into the distance. Unexpectedly she felt a tightening in her chest and a strange aching sadness flowed through her. Tears came into her eyes, and she found a tissue in the pocket of her robe, wiped her eyes.

'What is it? What's wrong?' Robert asked, his concern spiralling. He noticed that her face was the colour of bleached bone.

'I felt terribly sad . . . How awful to be left alone like that . . . how can she bear it, Robin? I don't think I could.'

Wanting to change the subject he said, 'Come on, let's go out onto the terrace. It's a beautiful morning.' As he spoke he picked up their mugs of coffee, and walked out to the terrace.

Elizabeth followed him slowly, understanding how lucky she was to be with this most extraordinary man.

They stood together, looked out at the glorious gardens created so long ago by loving, caring hands. At one moment Elizabeth turned to Robert, touched his cheek. 'I love you . . . and I thank you for this life you have given me.'

He looked deeply into her face, the face he had loved since childhood, and put his arm around her. 'To love you is all I could ever need in this world . . . and to be loved by you is all I could ever want,' he said.

EPILOGUE

Woman of the Year

'. . . so he shall never know how I love him; and that, not because he's handsome, Nelly, but because he's more myself than I am. Whatever our souls are made of, his and mine are the same . . .'

Emily Brontë: Wuthering Heights

'My face in thine eye, thine in mine appears.
And true plain hearts do in the faces rest,
Where can we find two better hemispheres.
Without sharp North, without declining West.

John Donne

'Tis time this heart should be unmoved,
Since others it hath ceased to move;
Yet though I cannot be beloved,
Still let me love!'

George Gordon, Lord Byron

EPILOGUE

When Elizabeth walked into her office at Deravenels, she automatically looked at the door leading into Robert's, but it was closed, not for the first time lately. Frowning to herself, she went over to her desk and sat down behind it.

She had been at the hairdressers for several hours, because tonight was a big night for her... She was to receive the Woman of the Year Award from the International Association of Business Executives, and it was considered something of a big deal by everyone.

Pulling her engagement book towards her, she opened it and looked down at the page. It was the nineteenth of May in 2006, and she was in her thirty-fifth year. My God, I'll be thirty-five in September, and so will Robert. I can hardly believe it, she thought.

May the nineteenth... last year at this time Marie Stewart had been up to her crazy tricks with Jimmy Bothwith, and the towering edifice of her supposedly grand life had come tumbling down like the proverbial house of cards. Elizabeth sighed to herself, thinking of that misguided woman, one so foolish and impulsive she had been led by her heart and not her head. For there were those in Scotland who now said that the marriage to Henry Darlay had not been good, and that Marie Stewart had fallen head over heels in love with Jimmy Bothwith. 'Who deserted her and left her in the lurch in her time of trouble,' Elizabeth muttered out loud.

What a bastard he was to do that, and after he had manipulated her, gained control of Scottish Heritage, pillaged her company, committed bank fraud in her name, and made dubious deals with dubious men, most of them with criminal minds . . . like him. He had been her final downfall.

And so now Marie Stewart de Burgh Darlay Bothwith languished in one of the new open prisons for white-collar crimes where conditions were not as arduous as most other standard jails were. And her little boy was being brought up by relatives, one of her illegitimate half-siblings.

'If you're not careful, that kid will end up being your heir one day,' Francis had warned her at the time of the kilt's staggering downfall, giving her one of his odd looks. She had not answered him.

Elizabeth was grateful to Francis because he had saved her from making a terrible business mistake. Through his own not always legal means, he had averted catastrophe for her. How ever he had come across his knowledge about Belvedere and Castleton she did not care, but those companies *had* been owned by Jimmy Bothwith through others. If she had gone ahead and bought Norseco Oil he and Marie Stewart, by then his wife, would have insisted on being on the board, would have had a big say in the running of the oil company.

Bothwith had owned so many shares he was almost at the same level as the chairman, Jake Sorrenson, the founder. Also

434

jailed by now for mismanagement, misappropriation of company funds, tax fraud, bank fraud, and other criminal misdeeds. And she would have been stuck with the mess if she had gone ahead and taken over Norseco.

A narrow escape, she said to herself. I just missed a bullet, thanks to Francis Walsington . . . Her devoted colleague and friend had only had *her* welfare at heart. She was convinced deep inside herself that more than likely he had managed to set Marie Stewart up, trap her. But she did not care if he had, or how he had done it.

Staring at the page in her engagement book, she made a note that she had to leave early for the cocktail reception before the award dinner. Then she closed the book. Now she must work on her speech for tonight, that was imperative.

Picking up her pen, pulling a pad towards her, she soon discovered she could not concentrate. Robin was on her mind. Pushing back her chair, she got up, opened the door to his office and looked in. He was not there. Not only that, the lights were out. This was unusual. He generally left them on.

Elizabeth sighed. She had run out early this morning, gone to have her hair done. It was long now, and took some time to set and dry. Robin had been in the shower and she had left him a note. She had hardly spoken to him today; where was he?

She went back to her desk, and fell down into her thoughts.

Robin hasn't been the same for a long time now. As I sit here thinking about him I realize he has been . . . quieter, more passive, accepting of things . . . not so argumentative with me when he disagreed with me. He just let it go. I think, as I look back, that it began last year at this time . . .

when we were all so consumed with Mary Stewart and her shenanigans. I have a horrible feeling that he identified with her in one thing . . . the strange and questionable death of Darlay. His wife had died in odd circumstances, too, and her demise had been questioned, at least the cause of it had. And some people blamed him; as others had blamed Marie for Darlay's death. Snap.

But Robin Dunley and Marie Stewart are as different as chalk and cheese. She is wilful, and careless in her dealings with others: my darling Robin is thoughtful, considerate and caring, and he never makes rash decisions. Not any more.

It's funny, thinking about it, but he doesn't do a lot these days. Not so much riding, or exercise, and his hours practising dressage in the indoor ring have lessened. Why? Is he tired? Or not well? Neither. I know that. He may not be twenty any more and at the height of his physical power and strength, but he is only thirty-five, or he will be in a few months. He's slowed down . . . he's not so interested in certain things . . . I sense a . . . disappointment in him.

I wonder if it's something to do with Deravenels? Perhaps I should tell him to start a new division, head it up, like his brother heads up our Resorts Division. But Robin has so much power, masses of it. He runs the company with me and Cecil. No, it can't be that, it can't be work. But something is wrong . . . he's been out of sorts for a long time . . . almost a whole year . . . My gut instinct tells me that . . .

The ringing phone brought her upright in the chair, and she automatically reached for it. 'Hello?'

'It's me,' Robert said.

'Where are you?' Elizabeth asked, relieved to hear his voice.

'I had some things to do, and decided today was the best time to run around doing them.'

'What things?'

'My tailor. Needed a haircut, the usual . . .'

'What time are you coming in?'

'I'm not sure, darling. Maybe I won't. You know how long my tailor takes, and I've two suits to fit. Also, it's a short day in a sense. I'll have to get back to the flat by four-thirty to change. And you will, too, Elizabeth.'

'Yes, I know.'

'All right then. I'll see you later at the flat, darling,' he said and hung up.

She stared at the receiver in her hand, frowning at it, puzzled.

Elizabeth stood in front of the mirror in her dressing room, studying herself for a moment. She was wearing a deep purple silk Valentino gown, cut straight in the skirt that fell to the floor in soft folds. It had a plain, round neckline and long sleeves, and with it she wore purple high-heeled silk shoes.

Satisfied with the gown, she put on Edward Deravenel's magnificent gold chain and medallion, added gold-and-diamond hoop earrings and a gold bracelet. Then she picked up a purple silk evening bag and went into the living room, seeking Robert's approval as usual.

Robert was standing near the fireplace, drinking a glass of water, and he put it down, came towards her as she appeared in the doorway.

'You look absolutely beautiful, Elizabeth! Ravishing.'

'So do you,' she replied. 'A new dinner jacket, I see. It fits you perfectly. You're just impeccable, too gorgeous.'

'I picked it up this afternoon,' he murmured and reached

437

into his pocket. 'I also picked up something for you.'

'You did?'

'I did indeed.' He kissed her on the cheek, opened the small leather box in his hand and took out a ring. 'Here, this is for you,' he said and, smiling, he reached for her left hand, slipped the ring on her third finger. 'There! How do you like that?'

Elizabeth gasped when she saw the large solitaire diamond, forty carats at least, glittering on her finger. 'Robin! Darling! It's just magnificent. Thank you, oh thank you so much. I never expected anything like this.' She threw her arms around his neck and hugged him.

He grinned at her wickedly. 'And now we're engaged. *Finally*.'

Elizabeth, caught unawares, pushed down her astonishment and exclaimed, 'I see we are. How about that!'

Everyone stared at them as they walked through the lobby of the Savoy Hotel. The beautiful redhead, so striking in purple, and the incredibly handsome man in the impeccably tailored Savile Row dinner jacket, tall and dark and exuding panache.

They had the same effect on everyone else as they entered the reception room where cocktails were being served. Heads turned as they strolled through the room saying hello to friends and greeting associates. Colleagues from Deravenels were out in full force; Cecil had bought six tables seating ten people each. Elizabeth moved through the crowd, talking to many of them . . . Francis, Cecil, Nicholas and Ambrose, who were happy, and congratulated her warmly. She spotted Spencer Thomas, and went to have a word with him, and tried not to miss anyone out.

Champagne flowed and canapés were served, and the cocktail hour flew by. It seemed to Elizabeth that they had only just arrived when they were being called into the ballroom for the award ceremony and dinner.

Harvey Edwards, President of the International Association of Business Executives, stood on the stage at one end of the ballroom. 'And so,' he said, 'we come to the presentation of our Award for Business Excellence. This year we are honouring a very special woman, a unique woman in the world of business . . . a woman whom we all recognize for her enormous ability, her brilliance, her vision and her leadership. One of the few women to shatter the glass ceiling. Ladies and gentlemen, it is my great honour to present to you Miss Elizabeth Deravenel Turner, managing director of the oldest conglomerate in the world . . . Deravenels.'

The applause was thunderous.

Elizabeth's heart thudded as she walked up to the stage, and she shivered as she mounted the steps. She had written her speech that morning and decided not to bring it at the last minute, knowing it would be much more personal and meaningful if she spoke extemporaneously.

Harvey Edwards greeted her warmly, kissed her cheek, and presented her with the award. This was an elegant crystal obelisk, engraved with her name and an inscription.

Elizabeth thanked him, placed the obelisk on the podium and brought the microphone closer. Once she had thanked the association for honouring her and everyone for coming, she began her speech.

At first she talked about her father, the late Harry Turner, who had been one of the world's great magnates; she touched on her grandfather, Henry Turner, who had held the company steady in bad times, and said loving words about her great-grandfather, Edward Deravenel, the man who had done so much to make Deravenels one of the greatest companies in the early part of the twentieth century. And then she moved on, spoke with fervour about the importance of women in business, and all of the contributions they had made and were making in the world of business in the new millennium.

She was eloquent, articulate, and funny, frequently making the audience roar with laughter, which pleased her. And then all of a sudden she had said all she wanted and needed to say . . . except for thanking certain colleagues at Deravenels, mentioned some of them by name.

And finally, pausing for a moment, she began in a very clear and vibrant voice, 'And now I must thank Robert Dunley, my partner in life as well as in business.' Seeking him out, her eyes focused on him steadily. 'Robin, without you by my side I would not have achieved anything. You are the one who showed me the way . . . Showed me how to be Elizabeth Deravenel Turner. And I thank you for that from the bottom of my heart.'

She knew there was something wrong the moment they got home. He walked into the living room and stood by the fireplace, his face rigid, and she realized he was full of tension, taut, pent-up. And perhaps angry? But why?

'What's wrong, Robin?' she asked swiftly, following him into the room.

He did not answer at first. He simply stared at her, frowning. At last he said, 'Why did you call me your partner? Why not your fiancé, since that is what I am as of tonight?'

'I didn't think . . . I'd written those words this morning . . . they'd stayed in my mind. I'm sorry, really I am.'

'And there's something else, Elizabeth, something I don't understand. You changed the ring. What I mean is that you took it off your left hand and put it on your right hand. Does that mean we are no longer engaged? Brief, wasn't it, my magic moment?'

'Robin, please, listen to me! I was nervous about the evening, and giving the speech. I put the ring on my right hand because I didn't want to explain anything to anyone. Not tonight when I was facing that huge audience. I just wanted to get through the evening.'

'I suppose that's why you called me your partner, so you didn't have to . . . *explain me away!*'

He sounded angry, but also hurt.

She took a step forward, wanting to hold him, touch him, make him feel better. She was also slightly perplexed. She had never seen him behave like this.

'Don't come any closer,' he warned in a tight voice, glaring.

'Robin, I'm so very sorry if I've hurt you, demeaned you in any way. You must believe me. I love you. I would never do anything –'

'Oh, to hell with it! And to hell with you!' he cried, his voice rising. 'I don't know why I put up with this, I really don't.' His voice broke, and she saw sudden tears glistening on his dark lashes. 'I'm leaving. For good.'

Before she could say a word, he had rushed across the room and gone out through the front door.

Elizabeth stood staring at the door, shaking her head, for a moment not understanding. He had said he was leaving. *For good.* Oh, my God, he had left her!

Within seconds she was out of the flat and in the lift, going down to the street level. Wrenching open the front door into the street, she half-ran, half-stumbled down the outside steps. She could see him in the distance, hailing a cab.

'Robin! Robin!' she shouted and began to run faster. He paid no attention to her, just kept waving his arm, trying to flag down a taxi.

'Robin! Robin! Wait for me, please. Wait for me. Robin Dunley, stop! Don't go.' She hitched up her dress with both hands and ran after him, screaming his name at the top of her voice. Oh, God, *no*, she thought, when she saw a taxi coming to a standstill. His hand was on the door. He was going to leave.

'Robin, wait! Wait for me. *Please!*'

He finally turned around, one foot on the taxi's step.

'I wouldn't say no to that, Guv,' the cabbie said, leaning out of his window. 'Go on, go to her. I bet you won't regret it, Guv.'

Robert stepped back, banged the door and turned around, watched as Elizabeth came rushing towards him, her hair flying out behind her. As she fell against him he caught hold of her tightly. She was out of breath, panting hard, tears streaming down her face. So frantic and distressed was she, he realized she wasn't even able to speak.

Holding her upright with one arm, he pulled out the silk handkerchief in the top pocket of his jacket and wiped the tears from her cheeks.

'You'll have to take me home,' she mumbled against his chest. 'I've no door key.'

'I wouldn't leave you out in the street like this,' he answered curtly. 'I'll get you into the flat, and then I'm leaving.'

Once they were back in the living room, Elizabeth leaned against the front door, said in a raspy voice, 'You can leave if you wish. I don't suppose I can stop you. Just tell me what I've done.'

A deep sigh rippled through him and he closed his eyes for a moment, then went and leaned against the mantelpiece. 'I told you a few minutes ago.'

'I'm so sorry, so very sorry,' she began and tears filled her eyes again. 'Can't you understand my anxiety about this award thing, and forgive me, or excuse me . . . ?' She left her sentence unfinished.

'I'm just so bloody tired,' he said, and so softly she hardly heard him. 'I've had it up to here. *And I'm fed up.* We've been together for almost ten years, living together as man and wife, and now I think we should make it legal. And what about a child? You really ought to have an heir, you know. However, I need to say this . . . I want you to marry me, Elizabeth.'

'You know . . . you know how reluctant . . .'

'Oh, yes, I know all about that . . . your reluctance. What it boils down to is that you can't marry me because you're married to Deravenels. You love your business more than you love me,' he yelled accusingly.

'That's not true!' she cried, shouting back at him. 'I do love *you*. I always have. You're the only man I've ever had, the only man I've ever wanted.'

'I've heard all this before. And now I have to go.' He began to walk towards the foyer.

She rushed after him, grabbed his arm, pulled him around so that he was facing her. 'I love you so much . . . please give me another chance . . . I'll try to overcome it . . . that fear I have of marriage. Just help me . . . let's be engaged for a bit, and I'll try very hard –'

'You just can't forget your father, and the way he treated your mother and all his other wives. He's ruined you for marriage, I know that only too well, Elizabeth.'

She began to weep, clung to him and finally he brought her into his arms, held her close, stroking her hair.

After a moment she took a step backward, pulled the silk handkerchief out of his top pocket and dried her eyes. Swallowing, she said, 'I've never loved anyone else the way

I love you. We've been together for twenty-seven years actually, since we were little. Most people don't have marriages that last so long.'

Robert stared at her, saw the tangled mess of her hair, the tear-stained face, the smudged eye make-up, and he understood it all then. He could never abandon her; they were twin souls, as one.

Reaching out for her, he brought her closer to him, held her by the shoulders, looking deeply into those dark, mysterious eyes. 'I cannot leave you. How could I? I'm your creature, just as you are mine. I belong to you, and you belong to me, and I can never love another woman . . .'

'And I will never love another man,' she whispered. 'Please don't leave me, Robin. I'll die without you.'

When he was silent, she begged, 'Please don't leave me.'

Touching her cheek gently, he nodded. 'I promise you I will always be by your side . . . until the day I die.'

And he was.

BIBLIOGRAPHY

Edwardian London by Felix Barker (Laurence King Publishing)

The Sons of Adam by Harry Bingham (HarperCollins)

Eminent Edwardians by Piers Brendon (Pimlico)

Henry VII by S.B. Chrimes (Eyre Methuen)

Victorian and Edwardian Décor: From the Gothic Revival to Art Nouveau by Jeremy Cooper (Abbeville Press)

Great Harry: The Extravagant Life of Henry VIII by Carolly Erickson (Summit Books)

Mary Queen of Scots by Antonia Fraser (Weidenfeld & Nicolson)

The Lives of the Kings and Queens of England by Antonia Fraser (Weidenfeld Nicolson)

Born to Rule: Five Reigning Consorts, Granddaughters of Queen Victoria by Julia Gelardi (St. Martin's Press)

Elizabeth & Leicester by Sarah Gristwood (Bantam Press)

The Edwardians by Roy Hattersley (St. Martin's Press)

Churchill: A Biography by Roy Jenkins (Pan Books)

Richard the Third by Paul Murray Kendall (W.W. Norton)

The Wars of the Roses by J.R. Lander (Sutton Publishing)

Queens of England by Norah Lofts (Doubleday)

Gloriana. The Years of Elizabeth I by Mary Luke (Coward, McCann & Geohegan Inc)

The Wars of the Roses by Robin Neillands (Cassell)

Victorian and Edwardian Fashion from La Mode Illustrée by Joanne Olian (Dover Publications)

The Edwardian Garden by David Ottewill (Yale University Press)

The Edwardians by J.B. Priestley (Sphere)

Seductress: Women Who Ravished the World and Their Lost Art of Love by Elizabeth Stevens Prioleau (Penguin Books)

Symptoms by Isadore Rosenfeld (Bantum)

Edward IV by Charles Ross (Methuen)

Six Wives: The Queens of Henry VIII by David Starkey (HarperCollins)

Elizabeth: The Struggle for the Throne by David Starkey (HarperCollins)

Consuelo and Alva: Love and Power in the Gilded Age by Amanda Mackenzie Stuart (HarperCollins)

The Daughter of Time by Josephine Tey (Arrow Books)

Tycoon: The Life of James Goldsmith by Geoffrey Wansell (Grafton Books)

The Princes in the Tower by Alison Weir (Pimlico)

The Wars of the Roses by Alison Weir (Ballantine)

The Uncrowned Kings of England: The Black Legend of the Dudleys by Derek Wilson (Constable and Robinson)

Warwick the Kingmaker (W.W. Norton)

Author's Note

Being Elizabeth starts in 1996 and ends in 2006. It tells the story of Elizabeth Turner, a young woman of twenty-five, who inherits Deravenels, an ancient family-owned conglomerate, which she must bring back to its former glory and successfully launch into the 21st century.

Elizabeth Turner, as she is written in this book, is my own creation. However, she is inspired by, and based in part, on Elizabeth Tudor – in my opinion England's greatest monarch.

In essence, what I have done is tell a contemporary story about a very modern woman set in today's world, and yet it is one that exactly parallels Elizabeth Tudor's life during the first ten years of her reign. Many of the things which happened to the Tudor Queen in this period happen to Elizabeth Turner. But obviously I had to adapt and slightly alter certain historical events in order to make them work in the modern world we live in today.

The historical facts are these: On November 17th, 1558, when Elizabeth ascended to the throne at twenty-five, she had two staunch and trusted allies by her side. They were her loyal childhood friend, Lord Robert Dudley, whom she would eventually elevate to the peerage as the Earl of Leicester, and William Cecil, formerly the surveyor of her lands. Cecil she made her secretary of state and Robert Dudley became Master of the Horse. Both men would serve her loyally and be by her side for the rest of their lives. Cecil was also elevated to the peerage by the Queen, at a later date, and became Lord Burghley.

For the next thirty years, until Dudley's death in 1588, Elizabeth, Dudley, Cecil and Francis Walsingham, head of the Queen's Intelligence Service, ran England together. And they ran it like a business. Elizabeth trusted and relied on these three men, but it was Robert Dudley who was the most important person in her life. He was not only her earliest friend from her troubled childhood but when she took the throne he became her adviser, councillor, confidante, bodyguard, escort, commander of her army, and of course, her Master of the Horse. He cherished this post, which was one of enormous power, and held it almost until the day of his death.

Dudley was her most intimate companion in all things, as well as work, and was rarely far from her sight. They were partners in life as well as in business. Historical documents prove that the entire court and government knew that he was the only one with any influence over her, because he truly understood her better than anyone else. Only Dudley could make her see reason in a crisis; induce her to change her mind when this was necessary; persuade her to take a different course when disaster loomed.

Were they lovers?

Most of their contemporaries believed they were; certainly they were not shy of displaying their great affection for each other in public. To me it beggars belief to think that they were not sexually involved, and they surely loved each other. But there is no real proof either way, and this question will always remain unanswered. I personally think there was far too much passion between them for it to go unconsummated.

And think on this: When he died she locked herself in her suite of rooms to grieve for him alone, and would not come out for days. She only did so when her councillors broke down the doors, in order to make sure she was all right. She wasn't, of course, and she was never quite the same woman ever again. For the rest of her life, Elizabeth Tudor kept the last words she had received from Robert Dudley in a casket next to her bed. On the document she had written: 'His last letter'.

I do not need any further proof to understand that this was the only man with whom she had ever really been in love, and loved until the day she herself died.

In my modern, fictional story about Elizabeth Turner and her childhood friend who I renamed Robert Dunley, these two main protagonists are indeed lovers. For them not to be would seem peculiar in today's world, to say the least.

Why did Elizabeth Tudor never marry Robert Dudley, the Earl of Leicester? He was the man she trusted and loved, and upon whom she heaped so many great honors and much wealth.

It was not for want of his asking. He did propose, and many times, and he was extremely frustrated when she said no.

When they were both eight years-old she told him she would never marry, and seemingly she knew her own mind as a child. Every other suitor was also turned down over the years, all of them royal by birth who would have been important political allies for England in a troubled Europe constantly at war.

Most historians have accepted that there are a number of reasons why Elizabeth avoided marriage, reasons with which I concur. She did not want to share her hard-won throne and the power it brought her with any man; her father's terrible record as a husband (six wives) had turned her off marriage, which she believed did not work. She had the overwhelming need to be in control of any situation and, most especially, her own destiny.

I know that many writers who have also written about Elizabeth Tudor have come to the same conclusion as I did when I finished my research. And it is this... England's great Tudor Queen was a brilliant, independent, highly-intelligent and hard-working woman, who was driven and ambitious. And a woman before her time, perhaps?

For those readers who wish to know more about the relationship between Elizabeth Tudor and Robert Dudley, Earl of Leicester, please turn to the bibliography on page 445. Listed are the books I used for my research.

BREAKING THE RULES

Look out for a new standalone novel continuing the Harte series, publishing September 2009

When those you love are threatened, there's nothing you won't do to protect them… you'll even resort to Breaking the Rules.

Following a terrifying encounter in the quiet English countryside, a young woman flees to New York in search of a new life. Adopting the initial M as her name, she embarks on a journey that will lead her to the catwalks of Paris, where she becomes the muse and star model to France's iconic designer Jean-Louis Tremont.

When M meets charming and handsome actor Larry Vaughan in New York they fall instantly in love and marry. Soon they become the most desired couple on the international scene, appearing on the front cover of every celebrity magazine, adored by millions. With a successful career and a happy marriage, M believes she has truly put the demons of her past behind her.

But M's fortunes are about to take another dramatic turn. A series of bizarre events turn out not to be accidents at all, but assaults on M and her family. She vows to stop at nothing to keep them safe. But the dark figure from M's past, a psychopath with deadly intent, has also made a vow: to shatter M's world forever.

From New York to the chic fashion capitals of London and Paris, to the exotic locations of Istanbul and Hong Kong, Breaking the Rules is a gripping story of courage and revenge, love and passion, treachery and triumph.

If you enjoyed *Being Elizabeth*, why not try the other two novels in the Ravenscar Trilogy...

THE RAVENSCAR DYNASTY

1904; Cecily Deravenel breaks the news to her 18-year-old son Edward of the death of his father and brother. Devastated, Edward determines to battle his cousin Henry for control of the Deravenel business empire.

Handsome Edward loves women, especially older women. Beautiful Lily Overton, cool society beauty Elizabeth Wyland, and married woman Jane Shaw all dominate and influence him, but will his womanising be his downfall?

The Deravenel family's fortunes rise under Edward's glamorous leadership. But his position at the head of Deravenels is fatally rocked when betrayal comes from within, Soon catastrophe threatens to destroy all he has strived for since his father's murder...

HEIRS OF RAVENSCAR

As the First World War draws to a close, all seems golden for young Edward Deravenel, charismatic head of the family empire and master of Ravenscar.

Yet beneath the surface lies discord. Elizabeth Deravenel, his beautiful wife, is jealous and her lies and gossip damage the family name. Worse still is Edward's brother George. His reckless behaviour and treachery lead to blackmail and betrayal.

The fortunes of the house of Deravenel begin to suffer. It is up to Edward's daughter Bess, and her son Harry to secure the Ravenscar inheritance – whatever it takes...

EMMA'S SECRET

Paula O'Neill, granddaughter of Emma Harte and guardian of her vast business empire, believes all that Emma left to the family is secure. However, beneath the surface tension is mounting and sibling rivalry brewing. Into this volatile mix walks Evan Hughes, a young American fashion designer. Her grandmother's dying wish was that Evan find Emma Harte. But Emma has been dead for thirty years...

UNEXPECTED BLESSINGS

Evan Hughes is trying to integrate into the powerful Harte family. Tessa Longden, Evan's cousin, is battling her husband for custody of their daughter, Adele. When Adele suddenly goes missing, Tessa seeks her sister Linnet O'Neill's help. Linnet O'Neill is the natural heir to her mother, Paula, but her glittering future at the helm of the vast Harte empire means many sacrifices. When Evan discovers letters from Emma Harte to her grandmother, the story is swept back to the 1950s. But it is the revelations in Emma's letters to her grandmother that give Evan a new perspective and help to set her free from her own past.

JUST REWARDS

Linnet O'Neill finds herself following in the footsteps of the original woman of substance as she battles to save what Emma Harte created, and to bring the Harte empire into the twenty-first century. Meanwhile, Emma's American great-granddaughter Evan faces her own headache. Her adopted sister Angharad is making trouble in the family, latching on to Jonathan Ainsley – deadly enemy of the Hartes – and so putting them all in danger. And when grief and heartbreak strike the family, all of Emma's great-granddaughters are tested to the limit as the extraordinary story of the Harte family takes another astonishing turn...

This year, we are celebrating the 30th anniversary of Barbara's classic novel,

A Woman of Substance

To find out more about our exciting plans, please log onto www.barbarataylorbradford.co.uk

What's next?

Tell us the name of an author you love

| Barbara Taylor Bradford | Go ▶ |

and we'll find your next great book.